THE BUZZ @ CHICKY-PIE'S CAFÉ

IRIS CARIGNAN

Copyright © 2023 by Iris Carignan

All rights reserved.

Published in partnership with Jessica Suggs Marketing, LLC. Chandler, AZ 85248

No part of this book may be reproduced in any form or by any electronic or mechanical means, including information storage and retrieval systems, without written permission from the author, except for the use of brief quotations in a book review.

This novel is a work of fiction. The author drew inspiration from real-world individuals and businesses, but any parallels to actual individuals or entities are unintentional and should not be construed as accurate representations of their real-world counterparts. The story unfolds in real and fictional cities; however, the characters, events, and settings are entirely fictional and subject to the author's creative license.

All Scripture quotations, unless otherwise indicated, are taken from the Holy Bible, New International Version®, NIV®. Copyright ©1973, 1978, 1984, 2011 by Biblica, Inc.™ Used by permission of Zondervan. All rights reserved worldwide. www.zondervan.comThe "NIV" and "New International Version" are trademarks registered in the United States Patent and Trademark Office by Biblica, Inc.™

ISBN 979-8-9893227-0-1 (trade paperback)

ISBN 979-8-9893227-1-8 (ebook)

Cover Design by Jessica Appel

Cover Illustration by Iris Carignan

Layout Design by Jessica Suggs

PRAISE FOR THE BUZZ @ CHICKY-PIE'S CAFE

"*The Buzz @ Chicky-Pie's Café* is a compelling novel of drama and suspense. As a child, Elise is adopted, but her hopes of a happy life quickly dissolve as she becomes a victim of human trafficking, abused by her adoptive parents for domestic servitude and worse.

Carignan tackles this tough subject with sensitivity, giving light to an all too important issue that threatens many today. She creates a highly sympathetic character in Elise, the novel's strong protagonist. Readers will cheer on Elise as she uses her wiles and faith to escape the very real threat of immigrant domestic abuse.

The question of where is God during difficult times resonates and carries throughout this powerful novel."

- Mia Walshaw, Author

"Carignan has done a brilliant job telling the story of so many of the broken and abused in our world. *The Buzz @ Chicky-Pie's Café* will hold your attention and draw you into the world of Elise. Through her story, you will learn much about love and hope!"

- Sam Gallucci, CEO and Founder of The Kingdom Centers

"In *The Buzz @Chicky-Pie's Café*, Iris Carignan takes us into the dark reality of human trafficking right next door and does it through the eyes of characters we'd like to have as friends and share a peach pie with. The story shows God's power to deliver, and it challenged me to do more to fight this terrible blight on our world."

- Rich Bullock, Author perilousfiction.com

"*The Buzz @ Chicky-Pie's Café* by Iris Carignan is an evocatively written tale, showcasing Carignan's vivid and engaging writing style. The characters undergo poignant development—none more so than Elise. Readers will become deeply invested in Elise's journey.

Carignan's powerful grasp of words connects us with Elise's suffering at the hands of evil people and deepens one's compassion for all who endure similar pain. Amidst the tale's shadows of despair and brokenness, Carignan beautifully weaves a testament to the unparalleled hope and healing found in our God. A must-read for those seeking a story of redemption and resilience."

- Shawn Thornton, Senior Pastor, Calvary Community Church, Westlake Village, CA

"*The Buzz @ Chicky-Pie's Café* by Iris Carignan hooked me from the first page. I began rooting for Elise to escape and to find healing from the trauma of her stolen youth. This is a heartwarming story of healing that can occur when we find community and purpose."

- Yvonne Noblitt, Director of Development, Gabriel's House, a program of The Kingdom Center

ALSO BY IRIS CARIGNAN

Fresh Eyes: Seeing God in the Unexpected

Moriah's Wings

To my husband for his loving support and to all of those who have been hurt by abuse and trafficking, as well as the many faithful servants at Gabriel's House and Forever Found who minister to them, I dedicate this book.

ONE

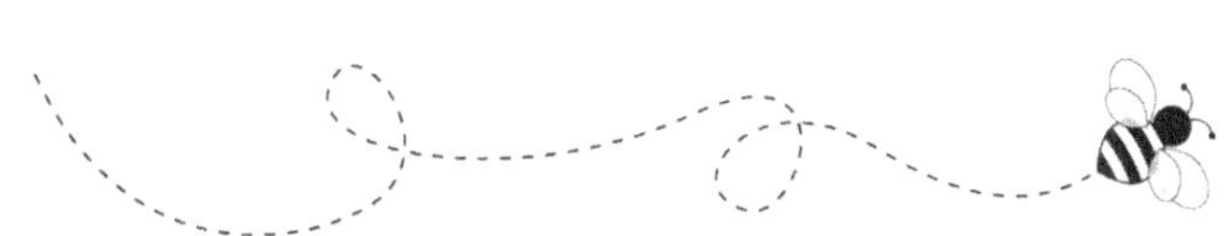

It were in 1965 when my mama, Millie, first opened my place. She noticed we had potential ta be a different kine a cafe an' saw that things could be somethin' special round heah. She hepped that special spirit ta grow more by given me 'couragement and knockin' down some a' my old walls of trouble and bias. She also gave me pretty new colors that made me fill good 'bout myself. She even painted my door bright yellow. She say it's a happy color.

That was in the beginin'. But that ain't all they is ta know 'bout things at Chicky-Pie's. So, keep on comin' by and see if you fine some good folks and some good food too—food for the soul.

2007, Elise

Shivers swept up and down my arms, yet a hot blanket of fear weighed heavy on me. I thrust it aside. Whispers outside my room faded like a vaporous mist as I slowly opened the door. I peered down an empty hallway, looking for something or someone—I wasn't sure what. Darkness enveloped me, and the air hung stale, suffocating. I inhaled frantically—a foul metallic taste lingered in my mouth. Shadowy figures flickered by as I ventured out of my room. Heart racing, I stumbled towards an exit door and jiggled the doorknob.

LOCKED!

Gasping for air, I turned with dizzying speed as a guttural sound escaped my throat. A parked car sat empty outside the window to my left. The front passenger door was wide open in invitation.

I have to get out! To my right, another hallway appeared, and a door left ajar at its end. I lunged forward. Peering out, a second car waited, engine running, no driver in sight. I stopped mid-step, breath catching in my throat. It was the perfect opportunity for escape. Too perfect. A clock began ticking. *I've got to get out of here.* Tick. Tick. Tick. A swarm of bees swooped in through an open window. Buzz, **Buzz**, **Buzz**—I jolted awake.

Gasping for real this time, I took a moment for my heart and breath to steady. Buzz, **Buzz**, **Buzz!** The blaring noise repeated. I slammed the top of my alarm clock; deafening silence replaced the angry hum. My face and neck were moist with perspiration, and my body felt cold and clammy. I tried to rise, but my head fell heavily onto my pillow. My heart was still racing, my mind grasping for reality, and my eyes begging for more rest. The dream dredged up frantic emotions I'd tried to stuff deep within. A trail of lingering questions pleaded for answers, demanding resolution. "It's up to me," I said out loud as if my audible command would make a difference.

"God, please help me," I whispered desperately to the ceiling. A deep impression marked my spirit—a premonition. *I have to get out now! But how?* Discouragement settled in. "God, are you even real?" If He was, I imagined Him a stern old man looking down from the sky, watching us flail about in misery. That's how God felt to me anyway. So maybe my ideas about God are distorted mirages skewed by my experiences and not based on truth. I let out a deep sigh.

Finally getting up, I poked my cold feet into slippers and

pulled a robe over my chilly goose-bumped body. Making my way to the bathroom, a heaviness clung tightly to each step. The whapping noise of my slippers hitting the heels of my feet amplified on the wood floor—sounds reminiscent of the abuse I'd taken over the years. All the slapping and whapping and whoring a child could unwillingly submit to without dying.

Was it my imagination, or was the dream a warning? Whatever it meant, I would have to find a way out alone. I had no one. How would I ever escape without help? I took another steadying breath and thought, *Okay, God, I'll take a chance. If you're there, I need you.*

I stood at the sink, reality staring back from the mirror. A stranger's face who, at the ripe old age of eighteen, bore the wearied signs of abuse and heartache. What had begun as a promising home of hope became a nightmare. Deep wounds were embedded in my spirit. I hadn't realized how deep until the dream shattered my protective shell.

Stepping into the shower, I let the hot water wash over me, wishing it could wash away the feeling of dread. Hoping to freshen my outlook, I thought about the kids. *I have a lot to do today. Can't be cranky; it'll just trigger Jane's temper.* I mentally prepared myself for the day. *Gotta get Bobby to school on time … and keep Bea from dawdling too much.* Imagining Bea and her sweet, cheerful personality brought a wide smile to my face, brightening my spirit. Her hugs are the best and only love I've ever known.

I'm probably just tired. Yeah, that's all it is. Can't wait to get started on Bea's costume. Hmmm. Maybe I can use some of the costume fabric to make something else, too. My mind drifted, imagining ways the extra material might help in my escape plan that was starting to form. Encouraging myself was something I'd done most of my life, and creative projects always seemed to help. I toweled off and dried my hair. A quick ponytail would have to do for today—no time for primping. Nodding at my reflection in the mirror, I decided the peroxide highlights on my dull brown hair looked pretty cool against my olive skin. A smile emerged.

Down the hall, I knocked on Bobby's door. "You up yet, Bobby?" Hearing a groan, I slowly opened the door, attempting to maintain his privacy. "Come on, kiddo gotta get going, or you'll be late again." He pulled his covers higher; a muffled grumble blurred through the sheets.

"I'm making pancakes, so better get up now, or you won't have time to eat." That ought to get him moving.

In Bea's room, I walked in without hesitation. She pulled a glittery purple sweater over a green mesh tutu and orange tights. "Good morning, sweetie. Oh, I like that sweater you chose. Don't forget, it's arts and crafts day, and you might get your pretty skirt and sweater messy with paint. How about we save them for another day?" She glanced down at her brightly colored outfit, considering my words. "Why don't you wear the dress I made you? You can bring your apron to wear over it. If it gets stained, I can make you another one."

"Okay, Mommy." Bea smiled and started changing clothes immediately. It touched me deeply. Not that she willingly changed out of the mismatched outfit—but because she called me mommy. Jane had frequently admonished Bea for that.

"*I'm* your mother, not Elise!" Jane constantly crowed but to no avail. I always feigned disapproval while Jane was present, but when she left the room, I'd kiss Bea on the cheek or hug her. Positive reinforcement seemed to work well, and the relished title remained mine. I couldn't help longing for Bea's affection; no one else gave me any.

Trotting quickly down the stairs, I dashed into the kitchen to start breakfast and make the kids' lunches. Hearing Skippy whimper in the mudroom, I realized no one had let him out yet. "Good morning, little buddy." Skippy wagged his tail, putting his paw on my leg as if in thanks. "There you go, boy." I opened the back door and left it ajar so he could get back in. A slice of my dream flashed before my eyes. Once again, I saw the two doors beckoning me. I envied Skippy and his few moments of freedom.

Back in the kitchen, Jack sauntered in, an overwhelming scent of cologne preceding his entrance. His rumpled, half-tucked shirt and disheveled appearance screamed sloppiness. How could such a slob keep a respectable job as an insurance agent? It made no sense.

"Do I smell bacon and pancakes?" He drooled at the thick smell hanging in the air.

Jane came in as I drizzled the last bit of batter onto the griddle. She immediately shot me a disapproving glare. "You made pancakes *again*? Did you forget what I told you last time?" The sizzling heat of her anger was hotter than the griddle. "Jack sure doesn't need the calories, and I'm trying to find my waistline again." Her bitter tone pierced any cheerfulness I had mustered. Oddly, my inner response surprised me. *I should be used to this by now.*

"Sorry, Jane. Just thought the kids would like something besides yogurt today. I can fix you something different if you want," I offered, quickly moving away from her.

"I'm going to eat the pancakes," Jack informed us. "You eat what you want, Jane."

"Well, they do smell tempting. Maybe just this once." Jane's anger seemed dispelled for now. It probably wouldn't last.

The kids scarfed down breakfast as I took my usual place at the counter, plate in hand. Jack piled on a second helping, and I caught Jane licking her syrup-covered fingers. I'd never understand how a woman of forty-five could look more like sixty. Jane went to her hairdresser weekly and got her nails done nearly as often, but she had no sense of style. Her permanent scowl and clothing two sizes too small weren't doing her any favors. *She probably has that common condition called denial.* I smirked inwardly.

"I have to go into town today. Looks like another shipment may come in this morning. So, probably won't be home until seven," Jack informed his wife, making it clear to me with a glance that dinner needed to be kept warm until he got home.

"How about honey habanero chicken?" I suggested.

"Yeah. That'd be great! I love your chicken." Jack perked up, but Jane gave me another dirty look. She knew her culinary skills were sorely lacking but hated any praise I got. Quickly changing the subject, I handed both kids a packed lunch. "Okay, kiddos, grab your jackets, and let's get going, or you'll be late."

"Get some more yogurt on your way home," Jane ordered. "Oh! And pick up my dry cleaning, too." She gave Jack a look and nodded.

He searched his wallet, pulled out a fifty, and asked, "Will that be enough?"

"Should be plenty. I'll bring you the change." I hoped he'd offer to let me keep the change, but I didn't count on it.

"I'm sure you'll give me what's due, Elise." His furtive smile said what I already knew—he expected a return on his investment. I cringed and quickly turned away. *God, I have to get out of here.*

Hustling the kids into the car, I took a deep breath and tore out of the driveway, barely giving them time to buckle their seatbelts. The twenty-five-minute round trip to their private school was a welcomed reprieve from the turmoil in the house. I was grateful for a few moments to myself.

After dropping the kids off, I drove to the market, rushed in for the yogurt, then stopped at the dry cleaners for Jane's pickup. My favorite fabric shop was next door. Checking my watch, I figured I had just enough time to make a quick stop. Slowing my pace, I leisurely gazed at the beautiful fabric patterns and colors, imagining what I could make with them. An idea sprang into my head when I noticed the black and yellow fabric I used to make Bea's costume. The bumblebee costume was nearly done, but the extra material could play well into the escape plan forming in my mind. Plus, Jane didn't know how to sew, so she wouldn't question the amount of fabric I bought.

Bringing the bolt to the cutting counter, I was glad to see my favorite clerk. "Hi, Betty. Just a yard, please." Always enjoying our chats, I sometimes stopped by the store just to see her friendly smile. I even brought her some brownies last Halloween. "How's everything with you?"

"Elise, good to see you." She smiled. "Got another project, I see." She rolled the bolt out to measure and cut.

"Yeah, just finishing the costume for Bea. It's coming along but needed a little more yardage." It was a fib but made for easy conversation.

Betty measured and then began cutting the fabric, a silver cross swaying at the end of her necklace with eye-catching sparkle as she snipped away. "How's that sweet little girl?" she asked, unaware of my difficult situation. Most neighbors assumed I was Bea and Bobby's big sister; others thought I was their nanny. Either way, it was clear I was their primary care-taker. No one suspected the abuse.

"She's still cute as a button, and I know she'll be the hit of her class play." Being grateful for regular social interaction made me wonder if I would ever have a normal life. As she cut and folded the fabric, Betty's pocket began ringing. "Oops! Forgot to put it on silent." She pulled out her cell phone and punched it off. "Sorry! Cell phones—a little like men, can't live with 'em, can't live without 'em."

"Hah!" I perked up at her words. "You know, I was thinking of getting a cell phone, but not sure I can afford it. They don't pay me much, you know?" I shrugged—another fib. I didn't get paid at all. "But a cell phone sure would come in handy."

Betty's expression softened as she looked up. "You know what? I've been considering getting a new one with all the latest features. But my current phone still works fine. So, I've been trying to justify trading up before my plan expires. How about you take it?"

"Oh, Betty, I couldn't do that. Besides, Jack and Jane wouldn't be happy with me getting cell service."

Betty lit up with excitement. "No worries, you can use the rest of my plan until you get your own. It gives you time to sort it out with your parents. It only has a few months left, and I'm thinking of changing carriers anyway."

Giddy with anticipation, I gave her a grateful smile. "Are you sure? I could pay you for the phone or pull something together to pay the monthly service fees."

"Oh, no need to. We pre-paid the plan ages ago." She waved the thought away. "And anyway, I'd love to help you out! How about helping me with a sewing project and baking your delicious brownies, and we'll call it even?" Betty's generosity and smile were like the sun, warming my heart.

"Well, that would be amazing!" Barely able to contain my joy, my smile took over for me. "And I love any excuse to make brownies." I was thrilled. A cell phone would offer freedom I'd never had before. And the timing couldn't be better.

"Perfect. I'll dig out the instruction manual and get all the plan info together. Let's meet later this week, and I can give you everything. Can I get your phone number? I'll give you a call once I've found everything." Betty pulled a small pad of paper out.

"Uh, sure, but better call between one and two in the afternoon; that's when it's easiest for me to talk." *Jane usually takes her nap then.*

Betty ripped another piece of paper off the pad. "Here's mine, just in case you need to call me."

"Thanks. Where do you want to work on that sewing project? I have a pretty good machine we could use, and I don't always have access to the car." *Hopefully, Jack won't come home looking to have me.* He'd been an ever-present fear lately. But as much as I liked Betty, I couldn't tell her that.

"I'd be glad to come to your house if that's easier for you, Elise. What are some days that work for you?"

"Well, Friday afternoon between two and four could work.

That's when Jane plays bridge, and the kids have after-school activities."

"Perfect!"

Humming a tune as I left the fabric shop, my head buzzed with ideas, and my enthusiasm grew. Then, exiting the store, I noticed a crumpled receipt with a twenty-dollar bill peeking out. *Hmm, Maybe God is up there after all.*

FEELING LIGHTER than I had in a while, I sang along with the radio as detour signs took me a different route home. A peculiar sight made me pump on the brakes as I turned down an unfamiliar street. I saw Jack standing in the parking lot of an abandoned outlet mall, chatting with a police officer. At the rear of a big rig stood a man who looked a lot like Jim, our neighbor. A chill ran down my spine as I spotted the unkempt driver in the truck's cab.

What in the world was Jack up to? I kept moving, not wanting Jack to recognize the car. I remembered his mentioning "a shipment coming in." It had seemed an odd comment, but I'd brushed it off as none of my business. It didn't dawn on me, until now, just how out of place it was, especially for an insurance agent. And what was Jim doing there? He's always been friendly to me. A little *too* friendly.

Approaching the intersection, the light changed to yellow. I could've sailed right through, but what I saw baffled me. Checking my rearview mirror to ensure I was out of Jack's purview, I stopped. A disheveled girl about sixteen hunched out the back of the truck. Then another girl, around thirteen, got out. Her blue dress was covered with reddish dirt stains, her black hair a matted mess. Just beyond the truck, five or six other girls huddled under the covered entrance of an empty store.

The light turned green. The pit of my stomach roiled at realizing the crime I'd just witnessed. Whatever it was, Jack was involved. *I've gotta do something.* Slowly pulling out of the intersection, I looked at the big rig's license plate through the rearview mirror and recited the number repeatedly. Then, at the next turn, I pulled over and wrote it on the only paper I had—the one Betty put her number on. The rest of the drive was a blur. I hated Jack. Had good reason to. But I never imagined he'd be capable of this.

Snippets of memories arose as if shaken loose from the depths of my heart. A beat-up old car. A hot, dusty ride that seemed to last forever. Mama screamed at me to get out of the car. A sign in the background, Warning – International Border. A grungy-looking man forced me into a truck.

It was a puzzle with most of the pieces still scattered, waiting to be fit together. So many pieces were still missing, but one held my heart captive—Did Mama sell me?

TWO

Afta Mama Millie get my place fix'd up good, she learnt how to cook. Now, I don't jes mean cookin' ta fill yo stomach. No. I means food that brings comfort. Food that soothes and heals from inside your soul to the outside of yo smile. An' that's cause Mama had the kine a food in her own soul that comes when a person meets the master chef—God. An' Mama sure got Him. It showed in Mama's eyes, her smile, and all a way down to her happy feet.

Mama tole me back then that makin' a business successful, takes lots a workers an everbody has ta work tagetha with the same heart. Jes like worker bees in a hive. It's kinda like comin' to the Lawd. The Bible say, "I planted, Apollos watered, but God gave the increase...For we are God's fellow workers."

※

AS I PULLED into our driveway, I noticed Ruben, the Burrows' landscape gardener. A thought occurred to me: He's *a nice guy. Probably someone I can trust.* Yet before I could call him over, Jane came out and stomped over to me, her hands on her hips and smoldering anger contorting her face.

"Where the hell have you been?" she hollered at me, with

ears that reflected her red-hot anger and poked out of her mousey gray-brown hair like parentheses.

"Oh, hi," I replied nonchalantly, shutting the car door and walking past her into the kitchen. Moving to the fridge, I started putting away the groceries. "I had to get more fabric for Bea's costume. Yesterday, I realized I didn't have enough." I began making excuses. "Here's the receipt. They raised the price per yard, and I needed some thread and notions, too." I handed Jane a five-dollar bill and some coins (less than it should've been). Using the receipt I'd found on the sidewalk, it looked like I'd spent more than I had. In my heart, I knew I was stealing, but I told myself it was necessary. *Besides, they don't pay me anything for everything I do here.*

Jane examined the receipt, creasing her brow in thought. I could tell she was trying to do the math in her head to no avail. After a moment, she relaxed her stance, seeming to buy my lies.

Over the past few years, I'd been able to store away a little cash, mostly from change after one errand or another. Jane wasn't sharp at figuring out how much difference she should get back. Over time, I had accrued a whopping $450. Adding the $20 from today's found treasure would give a nice boost to my escape fund. *It's just a few bucks,* I absolved myself.

"All right," Jane finally said. "But you'd better get to work mopping this kitchen. It's filthy, and we have company coming tomorrow night. Get this place sparkling clean, or you'll be paying in more ways than usual. I'm meeting a friend at ten, so you'll need to walk the dog too." She stormed out. Shoulders relaxing, I uncoiled in relief. I'd likely escaped a blow only because Jane needed me to have the strength to clean the house. I was grateful despite the reasons.

After dusting, vacuuming, and mopping, I took a break and got Skippy, who was sequestered in the mudroom again. "Gonna walk the dog now," I announced. It was a surprisingly breezy day, so I grabbed my jacket. Skippy danced excitedly, making it hard to clip on his leash. Finally successful, we made our way into the fresh air and momentary freedom. As he trotted happily alongside, I breathed in the beauty of the day.

Green Street was a manicured neighborhood of lush botanic succulents and high-end homes. Despite my weariness, I enjoyed walking outdoors, especially in cooler February weather. It was a peaceful retreat. Trees swayed, and birds sang as if serenading their creator. It gave me a glimpse of hope. Of a greater good. Sometimes, a neighbor would walk by and stop for a quick chat. Others waved as they passed in their cars. It was another world for me each time, even if for just a few moments.

As I turned a corner, I caught the glint of something shiny alongside a neighbor's driveway. Bending over to examine it revealed a yellow and black California license plate. Odd, since we live in Phoenix. Hidden under some nearby weeds were two more plates—a white Texas plate and one from New Mexico. Unwanted, I wondered why they'd been discarded here instead of thrown in a trash can.

Strange!

I started leaving all three plates, but something nudged me to keep one. Taking the California plate and concealing it under my jacket, Skippy tugged me on, only to stop again and dig his heels in. Then, pulling me behind a bush, he went nuts sniffing one area between the Burrows' and Jim's property. "Okay, Skippy. That's enough." Seeing coyote droppings, I yanked him onward.

Skippy did his business closer to home, and I noticed Jane's car wasn't in the driveway. *Must've left for her meeting.* Entering through the side door, I heard the phone ringing and hurried to answer it.

"Hello, Elise? Is this a good time?"

"Hi, Betty. Yeah, perfect. Are we still on for Friday?" Betty's cheerful voice was just the medicine my slumping spirit needed.

"Yes. I found the manual and chargers for the cell phone and can give them to you when we meet. My son, Sean, said letting you have my old phone should work out fine."

"Great!" I checked the wall calendar. *Jack's meeting in Sedona is still marked for Friday, Jane's hair appointment is at eleven, and her bridge game is at two o'clock.* Can you come a little earlier—say noon?"

"Sure can."

"Why don't I make lunch, and we can have brownies for dessert?"

"Sounds divine. I'll be there with bells on, fabric in tow, and notions galore. Tell me how to get to your house," Betty chirped.

Giving her directions, I asked Betty to give me a quick phone call before she came over. But I didn't want to take any chances. I couldn't believe I was going to have a friend around. I couldn't remember even having a friend before.

"Can't wait!" I said before hanging up the phone. I glanced at the clock; it was almost one o'clock. Feeling revived, I decided to work on the final details of Bea's costume. I finished the costume using the extra material I'd purchased, making its skirt extra wide. After cutting off the excess, I made a gathering stitch on the top and bottom of the skirt and attached a small foam pillow to the inside to form a bulge for the bumblebee body. Then, I fashioned a set of two small curtains with the extra fabric.

The whirring needle of the sewing machine jigged up and down, and memories whizzed by furiously, transporting me to another time. Once again, I was ten. I could see Nancy, the Burrows' previous nanny. Her skinny legs dangled beneath the red skirt she wore almost daily as she flitted through the house doing her abundance of chores. How had she managed to stay so strong? A flash of memory washed over me, a vague recollection of Jane hitting her with a broom for having missed a spot of crumbs. Jack hovered over her at the sewing machine when Jane was out, whispering in her ear as she tried to pull away.

The searing pain of losing her overcame me as I remembered the stress of taking on all her previous responsibilities. My thoughts landed on that day when Bobby had been incredibly fussy. He'd been carrying on for hours, and I was worn out.

Jane handed me another sewing project, berating me for the

clumsy job I'd done on the last project and threatening to take the buckle to me if I didn't do better. Taking hold of the fabric, I threw it against a wall, then ran to the back porch, bawling my eyes out. Jane chased me and grabbed my arm, nearly wrenching it out of its socket. She slapped me so hard I saw stars. "I'll give you something to cry about!" Her angry scream still echoed in my ears; the pain was so real it felt like it had happened just today.

I winced and slowed down the sewing machine to finish off a corner in the fabric.

Our sudden move to Phoenix three weeks later hadn't brought relief. Instead, the abuses just elevated in frequency and degree. Jane used Nancy's departure as an excuse for leaving Austin and adding all her chores onto my plate. *Why hire help when you have free labor?* The loss of Nancy had me crying for weeks after. *Why did she have to go away?* Having experienced firsthand Jane's beatings and unwanted advances from Jack, I knew Nancy was better off away from the Burrows' house. But at the time, my young heart mourned the loss of my friend and protector.

Skippy's pathetic whine pulled me from the memory as he trotted into the sewing room with soulful eyes and a dog toy in his mouth. Patting him on the head, I sighed. Then, loosening my shoulders, I cleaned up the notions and scraps. *No sense in reliving the past; there's a lot I have to do before time to pick up the kids.*

I rushed upstairs, made the beds, straightened up the kids' rooms, and scrubbed their bathroom. I then moved to Jane and Jack's bathroom. As I scoured Jane's sink, I reached up to close the medicine cabinet, peeking inside first. Alongside the usual Pepto Bismol, cold medicine, and laxatives, there was a prescription bottle of white Zolpidem tablets—Jane's preferred sleeping pills.

Hearing a car's engine entering the driveway, I peered out the window. It was Jane. *Must have been a short meeting. Better not let her catch me snooping.* I quickly shut the cabinet door and grabbed my cleaning supplies.

⚱

Friday

The morning was quickly slipping away. *Betty will be here soon, and I still need to start lunch.* Then, opening the fridge, I froze at the sound of a car driving in—Jack's car. *What's he doing here? He's supposed to be on a business trip.*

The kitchen door slammed, and the phone rang. Suspecting it was Betty, I ran to the den to answer it. "Hi. Yes, it is. Oh, yes, but I'm sorry, Mr. Burrows is home for a rest. Would next week work for you?" No doubt Betty thought my responses were strange, but I couldn't let Jack overhear and realize it was someone calling for me—a friend. "Okay, thanks. Bye." I quickly hung up before my disappointment turned into tears.

With Jane at her hair appointment, her bridge game afterward, and the kids at school, Jack coming home now meant only one thing—he wanted me. *God, help me get through this. I can't bear it anymore.*

I tried to avoid Jack, quietly moving towards the front door but heard his footsteps approaching from behind. My time was up. I swirled around, hoping to catch him off guard. "Hi. What happened to your business trip?"

"Canceled." That was all he said. Walking straight towards me, he put his enormous hands around my waist. Forcefully pulling me to his boulder-sized body, he kissed and fondled me. From past carexperiences, I knew he would get violent if I resisted. At least I was on the birth control pill now. Jack had ensured that after I'd given birth to his baby.

I tried to keep my mind distracted the whole time he assaulted me. I tried to disconnect from what was happening. But vivid images came to mind—torturous recollections. I relived the shame of my pregnancy and the pain of childbirth. The agonizing memory of my baby's death pierced me the instant Jack reached climax.

I cried out. He chuckled, thinking my scream was from satisfaction. As he climbed off me, I lay silent, tears streaming down my cheeks, and my resolve to leave strengthened.

Later that night

The dinner party was in full swing. Guests included one of Jack's policeman buddies, his wife, and another couple. The men were friends Jack usually met at the local bar. Naturally, I was expected to make and serve all the food as if I were their servant. *Oh, that's right, I am their servant.* I sighed inwardly.

Jack introduced the cop as Patrol Officer Manuel Ruiz. "You can call me Manny," he said, firmly shaking the other guy's hand. He was dressed neatly, his light brown crew cut standard for a police officer. But, not in his uniform, it was hard to say if he was the same cop I'd seen with Jack by the big rig. He may have dressed nicely and acted friendly, but the air around him hung heavy. There was something not quite right about this man.

Manny didn't speak to me during the evening, but at one point, his piercing stare spoke volumes about his attitude. Did he know something about Jack's abuse of me? Or was it simply loathing and disrespect for lower-class servant types like me?

For most of the evening, I avoided the party whenever possible but found some of the conversation interesting. I noted how curious and attentive Jack and Jane seemed about current real estate in other areas of Arizona. *Wonder if they're considering another move.* Our last move was so quick that I barely had time to pack. They even left the family cat behind.

THREE

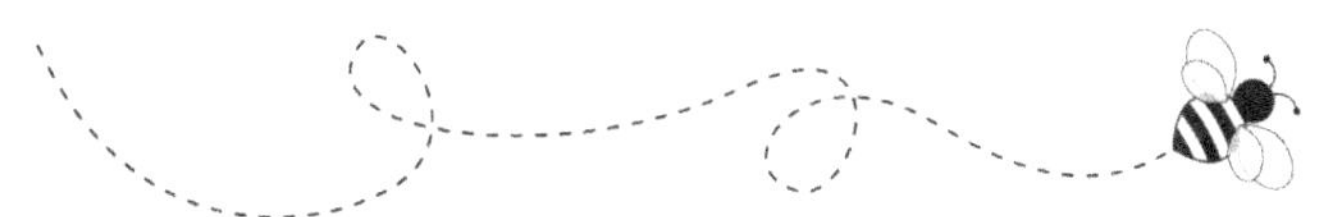

I t wadn't long afta Mama Millie learnt ta cook real good, that she started inviten' her friends ta come by an visit me. She was a wise woman, my mama. But I think the most fun part was how she done it. She cooked so much food it smelt like a potbelly full of good eaten and people jes started followin' the wonderful 'roma, right to my front door. Pretty soon folks was comin' heah ever' day and linen-up at my door to buy her food. So, she nailed a sign above my door that say Millie's Diner. Then Mama got down on her knees right by that door, an' she pray to her Lawd. She axed Him to guide her and hep her with all the cookin' and the business. That was way back in 1963.

It's a good thing she done that, cause even though folks start comin' heah ta eat, sometimes they'd bring they troubles too. An yeahs later when Mama Millie pass, an her granddaughter Mell take ova an change the name ta Chick-Pie's Café,' folks still bring they worries in.

Mama Millie use a tell me lots of things about honeybees. She say that comin' to the Lawd is a little like bee's work. Bees don't do they's work cause they wanna earn something. No, they do it cause the good Lawd put it in them ta do it. An when we ask Him ta come in our hearts, he puts his Spirit in us. Then we do works that we is designed ta do in the first place. So it goes in that order, not ta other way round.

Saturday

Looking at her number on the paper, I dialed Betty's cell phone: "Hi, this is Elise. Do you have a minute?" Then, whispering, I glanced around to ensure no one could hear.

"Elise! Are you all right? You sound upset."

"Yeah, I'm fine, but I need to make this quick. I'm sorry for not being able to work with you on your project yesterday. I hope I wasn't rude on the phone. I mean, it's just that when Jack comes home unexpectedly, he can get sort of mean. It, well, it makes me a little nervous. I never know how he might act when he's, uh, tired."

"Don't worry about it. I understand. I get a little grumpy when I'm tired, too. You want to try and set up another day?" Betty was amazingly gracious. For a second, I thought about telling her—but I'll never be able to tell anyone about what Jack does to me.

"Would Tuesday work for you?"

"Yes, Tuesday's good," Betty confirmed. "Do you still want me to come over there?"

"Well, I was wondering if maybe I could go over to your place instead," I asked shyly. I couldn't run the risk of another delay. "About ten in the morning, if that's okay."

"Sure. I live about two miles from the store. Do you know where the Canyon housing tract is?"

"Yeah, I go right past there on my way to and from the kids' school every day."

I was relieved to hear it was along my usual route so I could make an excuse to buy groceries and fabric. That would give me a couple of hours. It wouldn't leave much time to visit Betty, but it shouldn't raise any alarms with Jane either.

"I'll just pick up the kids from school on my way home from your place, so that should work well," I told her.

"Okay, great! I'll look forward to it. Why don't you let me make lunch for us, and you bring the brownies?"

"Oh, that would be awesome. But I don't want to be a bother. I could pick something up on my way over?" I offered but hoped not to have to explain those purchases to Jane.

"No bother at all. See you next Tuesday!"

I said goodbye, thanking Betty for her understanding and flexibility, then sighed with relief. Sure hope it works out this time.

Tuesday Morning

Still warm, I scooped up the brownies and placed a few on a small plate before inserting two in a baggie for the kids. Stacking the rest on a disposable plate and then covering it with foil, I started out the door when Jane stopped me short. "What the hell… are you doing with those brownies?"

"Oh, thought I told you." Being quick with an excuse, I sidestepped Jane's nasty mood. "Bea's teacher asked if I could bring a snack to share. They have the play rehearsal, so I made these for the kids. I left a few for you and Jack." Pointing to the small plate of brownies, I felt proud for thinking on my feet, even if it was another lie.

Quickly avoiding more inquiry, I hollered, "Come on, kids. We need to leave for school now." I dashed out anxiously, avoiding Jane's weighty glare.

Jane came out as we loaded into the car but not to say goodbye. "Don't you need money for groceries?" She sounded suspicious.

"Uh, Jack gave me some already. See you after I pick up the kids from school. Oh! I might drop into the fabric shop. They had some blue cotton material that would look beautiful with

Bea's eyes. I saw it the last time I was there and think it's on sale now." I blabbed on with confidence as if it was all true.

"Okay," Jane said, now speechless.

I continued to layer on more excuses and lies. "I'll probably get a bite to eat and hang around till time to pick them up. No sense going all the way home only to turn around and go back a few minutes later. It'll just waste gas." *Boy, am I getting clever!*

I cringed inwardly, remembering why Jack had given me $100, far more than his usual silencing bribe. Jane knew something was going on but was probably in denial. Maybe she thought Jack had told her the truth when he said he wasn't interested in me any longer.

Jane turned to go back into the house. Putting the car in reverse, I started to pull out, then saw her stop short and turn around—her steely stare slapping me nearly as hard as an actual hit, its message a sharp blow. Realization of why Jack had given me money filled her eyes with rage.

I better get moving! I thought as I swiftly pulled into the street. Heading out of the driveway, a movement next door caught my eye. On Jim's side yard was the girl I'd seen in the empty parking lot days earlier. The one with black hair and a blue dress that was now void of stains. She looked up briefly, her eyes full of sadness, rimmed with dark circles. I wondered if she was replacing their other nanny, Alejandra, whom I hadn't seen in several weeks. No doubt, they'll keep tight reins on her, too.

HOLDING the brownies in one hand, I knocked on Betty's door.

"Hi Elise, come on in. I'm so glad you could come today." Her smile, as bright as her magenta dress, was even more striking than her glossy black hair.

"Thanks. Me too." Still standing in the entryway, I drank in the beauty of Betty's home. The room felt light and airy, with artistic touches everywhere you looked. Escorting me on a brief tour, she flitted in and out of every room like a butterfly, happily revisiting her favorite flowers. As we entered the sewing room, its cheerful curtains, shreds of multi-colored fabric, and squiggly pieces of thread lay scattered with abandon, speaking of her love for sewing.

"So, what are we making?" I asked.

"Oh, that's right! I haven't told you yet. I need to make a costume for myself. I'm in our church play next month and want to look authentic. I'm good at sewing curtains and things of that sort, but not so much when it comes to clothes. You're always making such cute outfits for Bea and yourself; I thought you could help me."

"Sure. Should be fun."

After nearly two hours, Betty leaned back, expelling a long breath. "Oh, goodness, I must be getting old. Can't seem to work very long before getting tired these days. Why don't we take a little break? Would you like something to drink?" She got up and headed towards the kitchen.

"Cold water would be great. Thanks." I continued sewing. Knowing nothing about biblical attire except what I'd seen in The Ten Commandments movie, I hoped my ideas would make the costume look authentic and attractive.

Betty returned to the sewing room, holding two glasses of water. She set them down on the table, reached into her pocket, and pulled something out. "Almost forgot. Here's your phone." Timidly grasping this key to freedom, my eyes widened with awe.

"Oh, Betty, this is so wonderful. You have no idea how much this means to me. Can you show me how to use it? I've never had one."

"Really? It's very easy." Betty gave me a quick tutorial and explained that she would let me use the rest of her contract at no cost. "It will run out in about two months anyway. Here's a charger too. You'll need to make sure it's charged every night. Otherwise, it won't be much good the next day."

"Thank you so much, Betty. You are a lifesaver." I meant it. Literally.

"Why don't we have our lunch now?" she happily suggested.

Watching someone else prepare and serve the meal felt weird, even if it was just salad and bread. I had to keep reminding myself that I was not a servant in Betty's house. "Can I set the table?"

"Relax. You're my guest." She smiled at me.

So, I sat and tried to enjoy the rare opportunity while the aroma of baking bread filled my senses. Then, filling the awkward silence, I asked, "Betty, I was wondering. How long have you been married to Joe?"

"Twenty-two years now. We met at a friend's party, and it was love at first sight," she reminisced. "Oh my! We had our hands full in those early days! Joe and I went to vastly different churches. We were about the same age as you are now, and we didn't know how to connect spiritually. Merging two sets of lives, traditions, and experiences sure isn't easy! Especially when you don't have faith in God as your common ground." She darted over to the oven, checked on the loaf of bread, set a timer, and then dashed back to finish the salad.

"It wasn't long before we were knee-deep in serious discussions about faith. I was brought up in a Bible-believing church, but the church he went to was more focused on rituals and rules than a relationship with God."

She tossed the dressing into the salad and continued. "I didn't have any big issues with what I'd learned growing up, but I wanted to be sure that my beliefs were truly my own and not just a hand-me-down faith. As we both started to study and learn more about Jesus, it raised many deeper questions for Joe about his denomination."

"Are you sure I can't help you with the lunch or something?" I was starting to get a little antsy. Not sure if it was all the talk about God or because she was waiting on me, but I felt awkward.

"Oh, I'm sure!" She tossed some pre-cooked sliced chicken, feta cheese, and dried cranberries into the salad. "Well, his questions didn't go away, so Joe made an appointment with his minister. After sharing all that was troubling him, the minister said to him, 'Well, you do have problems, don't you?'" (She embellished with a husky voice) "'Go home and get your head on straight. When you figure it out, come back and see me.'"

"Whoa! That's terrible. Did he really say that? I mean, aren't pastors supposed to answer our questions?" I was stunned.

Betty brought our plated salads over and placed them on the table. She poured more water into my glass and put a basket of warm bread in the center of the table.

"That looks amazing!" My mouth watered at the sight of the fresh homemade bread.

"Thank you, and you're right. They *are* supposed to help with our questions about faith. But when he got home that day, Joe told me he knew his church didn't have the answers he needed. All the questions he'd had about that church's doctrine and beliefs, God had answered him directly. So he never went back to that church again."

"Wow! That's amazing." I reached for a slice of the heavenly-smelling bread and patted some butter on top. Still warm, the butter quickly spread its creaminess across its top.

"How about you? Do you go to church with your family?" Betty took a bite of bread and asked.

"No, I've never been to church. Maybe one day." I shrugged. Gulping water, I decided to take a chance. "Honestly, I *think* God might be real, but I… I just don't understand why He allows so much suffering." My tone was dubious, "My life, well, let's just say it hasn't been easy. I mean…" My voice drifted as tears welled in my eyes. I looked away as I tried to rein in my emotions.

Betty put her hand on mine, saying, "Oh, Elise. God is our heavenly Father, and He loves us. He loves YOU. Sometimes, it's hard to feel His love or presence when we're in pain. But, like a good father, He wants to give us gifts, not because we do anything to earn them, but because He loves us so much. Someday, you may have children of your own, and you'll understand that concept even better."

I nodded and looked down at my lap.

Too bad I hardly knew my father. I didn't even know what a good father looked like. And besides, God couldn't possibly love me. I lie and steal. And why would God love someone who let her adoptive father have sex with her? My body started tensing up, and I think she could tell.

Betty got up and asked, "Ready for some brownies? I know I am."

"Oh, yeah!" I was glad for a break from all the religious talk.

"How about a glass of milk with all this chocolate?"

"That would be great." I smiled.

While pouring my milk, she asked the very thing I hoped she wouldn't. "Do you have a loving father, Elise?"

"I haven't seen my father since I was five." I paused, considering. "My memories of him are dim; one or two come to me sometimes. I remember holding his hand when I was little—but that's it. Maybe he was a good dad, but I don't know. He left me." I looked away, trying to hide the sadness creeping in.

"Oh, Elise, I'm sorry. I didn't mean to pry. I can't even imagine how that must feel." She seemed sincere, yet continued picking at my wounds. "What about your mother? She must've taught you how to sew because you're very good at it. Is she still in your life?"

"I haven't seen her since I was six." I was starting to get angry now. "She gave me away. The nanny I had when I was little taught me how to sew."

"She must've been a great nanny."

"Yes, she was. Her name was Nancy. Although she was eighteen, and I was only seven, she was like a sister to me." I continued, "Jane wasn't the mothering type—and that's putting it mildly. Nancy's thick, tongue-clucking Vietnamese accent sometimes made it hard for me to understand her, but her kindness always spoke volumes. When I was nine and Bobby was two, Jane must've decided Nancy wasn't needed anymore."

"Was she fired?"

"Don't know." I shrugged. "One day, she just wasn't there anymore. I never had a chance to say goodbye. But her parting gift was the love of sewing. Of course, Jane was happy about my new skill. She had me making baby blankets and clothes for Bobby when I was ten."

"Wow, sounds like you were given a lot of responsibility when she left." Worry cut a crease in Betty's forehead.

"I didn't mind at first, but at ten, it was a lot to handle, I guess." I shrugged.

"Elise, I am so sorry. It sounds like you had a tough childhood. Is there anything I can do to help you?"

"No thanks, Betty. You've already helped more than you know." My anger crumbled. "I can't thank you enough for the phone." I fumbled momentarily, then blurted, "I probably won't be around much longer. I can't tell you about everything, but let's just say I need to get away from that house. Soon. Before it's too late."

Getting up, I glanced at the clock. "Oh, no! It's almost one o'clock. I've got to go, or I'll be late."

"Okay." Betty stood and put her hand on my shoulder. "Can I just say a prayer for you before you leave?"

"Uh, okay." Tears welled in my eyes. "I'm scared." I looked up, and Betty's wide-open heart spurred me on. "I don't know for sure what I'm going to do. You've been so kind, and I appreciate everything you've done for me. Just having a friend to talk to is, well, something I've never had."

"Of course. Let's pray, Elise." I followed her lead and bowed my head, too.

"Lord God, I come to you in love and praise," Betty began. "I'm asking that you hear our prayer today. Lord, I ask that you reveal yourself to my friend Elise and show her your love. And heavenly Father, please keep Elise safe. Watch over her in the coming weeks and months as she faces difficult decisions. Help her to experience you as a loving father and bring her mother to a place of conviction and faith. Amen." Seeing my tears, Betty gave me a warm hug.

"Thank you, Betty. I will always remember your friendship and help." I turned to leave. "I'll try to call you soon, but please don't think bad of me if you don't hear from me for a while."

"Hold on a sec." Betty dashed into her front room and returned with a Bible. "Here, I want you to have this."

"Oh, Betty, I can't take your Bible. I don't deserve anything so nice."

"Remember what I told you about gifts? You don't earn them; if you did, they wouldn't be gifts. This is a gift from me. I am blessed to know you, Elise, and I will continue to pray for you for a long time, whether or not I hear from you again." She added, "Besides, I have another Bible." She winked. "Promise me you'll read it."

"I will. Goodbye, Betty." I waved.

"Goodbye, my friend." She waved back.

A tear slipped down my cheek as I realized I'd probably never see her again.

⚜

RUSHING INTO THE GROCERY STORE, I threw items in the shopping cart. Thankfully, I had a list handy, so I wouldn't forget anything important. At the meat department, I grabbed a couple of good steaks that were marked down and chicken. *That ought-a keep Jack happy for the week.* I got some milk for the kids and yogurt for Jane, then rushed to the cash register. On my way there, I picked up a jar of peanut butter. "Oh," I said out loud. "Better get some bread." Grabbing a loaf, I went to the shortest checkout line.

The cash I had from Jack covered everything with $41.50

change left over—another gift. I glanced at my watch. *A quarter past two. Gotta get the kiddos now.*

Bobby and Bea were waiting out front of the school. After they were buckled in, I handed each of them a brownie. Seeing their faces light up made me realize how much I liked making them happy and giving them gifts.

"Oh boy!" Bobby said, taking a big bite.

"Thank you, Mommy, these are so yummy." Brownie crumbs tumbled onto Bea's dress.

"You're welcome," I said, remembering Betty's words about God giving us gifts without us having to earn his love. *That, I told myself, was what I was doing for Bea and Bobby—giving them a gift because I loved them.*

"Did you have a good day?" I asked.

"Yeah. I guess." Bobby shrugged.

"Uh-huh. It was fun! We painted, and we rehearsed the play," Bea bubbled out.

For the remaining drive home, I listened to Bea's sweet chatter and offered God a little "Thank you" for my time with Betty.

※

AFTER DINNER, Jane sat on the back patio with a glass of wine. Jack had a late meeting to attend and jumped in the shower. Both otherwise engaged, I took the opportunity to sneak into his room and look at his computer. He'd been on it minutes before, so, luckily, I didn't have to enter a password to get in. Instead, I jiggled the mouse, and as the screen turned on, I was assaulted with graphic sexual images, many including children. Wincing, I quickly clicked off the site and opened a new browser window. Then, searching train routes, times, and costs, I purchased a one-way ticket to Flagstaff.

"Oh no! I need a credit card." *Now what?* I paced around the room trying to figure out what to do and nearly tripped over

Jack's pants on the floor. Picking them up, his wallet fell out of his pocket. Without a second thought, I pulled out one of his credit cards. *No time for ethics. I need to escape, and this might be my only opportunity.* After entering the number, I sent the ticket order to the printer, biting my lip nervously as I waited. It came through just as Jack turned the shower off. Returning to the computer, I clicked off the site, put the laptop in sleep mode, and closed it. Grabbing the printed ticket, I dashed out, closing the door carefully. I could hear the bathroom door open and Jack's damp feet slapping against the wood floor seconds after I shut the door.

Whew! That was a close one. Running to my room, I hid the ticket in my backpack on the top shelf of my closet. I still had a lot to do, but I'd taken the first step. No going back now.

FOUR

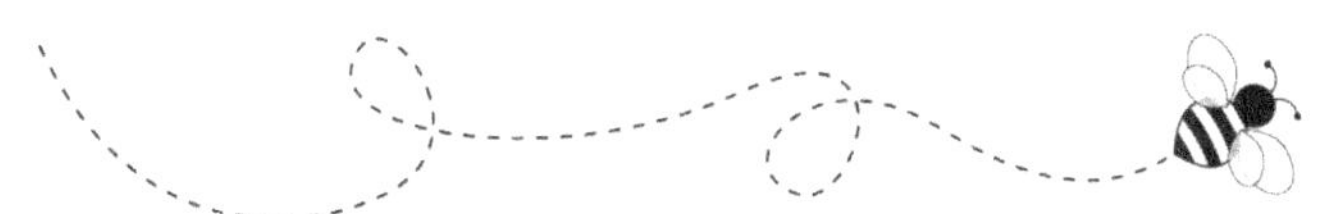

Mama Millie kept own learnin' more good recipes, like delicious pies. An' Mama's heart grew bigger from heppin' folks. Her belly growed a lot too, from all the good eaten.

My daddy, Millie's husband, was a white man an he come heah to work in the bankin' business. He say California got lots ta offer folks of any color. An even though I call her Mama, she didn't give birth ta me the usual way like you folks might be thinkn'. No! An if you is thinkin' I has a particular race or color, well, you'd be wrong. No. I'm a whole rainbow of colors that folks see when the Lawd's light shine through.

I'm kinda like the feelin' you gets when you in a church an hear a touchin' gospel song or maybe more like the spirit in the home of a loving, happy family. A spirit that lives on fer generations ta come. I am the spirit of Chicky-Pie's Café. An the Good Book promises that "where two or three are gathered together in My name," the Lawd will be there too.

Two Weeks Later

My alarm hadn't gone off. It didn't need to. I'd barely slept all night. Today was the day I'd been waiting for. I'd tossed and turned all night, drilling the steps of my plan into memory. While it was doubtful anyone was on to me, anxious shivers rose inside, prickling my sweat-soaked skin. My heart raced, its pulse screaming at a feverish pitch inside my ears.

This is it. No turning back.

Attempting to calm my heartbeat, I took a few deep breaths. *Okay, Ruben and the landscape crew should be here about two o'clock. He's probably on his way to his first job of the day now.* I took out my new cell phone and quickly texted him. I hoped it wouldn't be too early for him to respond. "Buenos dias' mi amigo. Are we all set for today?"

His response came back immediately. "Si. No problema!"

"Muchas gracias! See you pronto," I texted back.

Let's see, Bobby has early release from school today, so I pick both him and Bea up at noon. They'll need lunch, so I'll make a few extra sandwiches for myself at the same time. I might even bake some brownies as my parting gift. Wouldn't hurt to sweeten Jack and Jane up a bit.

After lunch, I'll suggest we play some baseball. Bobby will love that. I'll play umpire. My backpack is already mostly packed. If I put it on backward, it'll be a great substitute for a catcher's vest. Plus, then it shouldn't set off any suspicions. Hopefully, Ruben will step in as promised. Oh! I can't forget to wear the green baseball cap.

After a quick shower and blow-dry, I slipped into my jeans, a white T-shirt, and tennis shoes. My hands shook so hard it took three tries to clasp my necklace. Touching the locket, my attachment to it was as delicate and precarious as the chain it hung from. I glanced in the mirror and noticed a package of feminine pads sitting behind me on top of the toilet. Stuffing the whole pack inside my backpack, I spread their bulk out evenly. Perfect!

Just the right padding this umpire needs. Hopefully, it will be enough protection against a fastball.

Reaching under the bathroom sink, I grabbed the two black plastic garbage bags I'd shoved in the vanity a few days ago. Hidden behind them was a small, pre-addressed package containing critical evidence. Taking the package and sacks to my room, I doubled one inside the other. Pausing briefly, I gingerly placed the package inside the bag. Hiding it between layers of clothes, I added a few pairs of slacks, blouses, two dresses that I'd made, a sweater, and a jacket. I put my hair dryer, brush, comb, and essential toiletries in a smaller plastic bag and then added that to the larger garbage bag. Glancing at the row of shoes lined up at the bottom of my closet, I tossed in one dressy pair and my favorite sandals. The tennis shoes I was wearing would have to do with everything else.

Gathering the top corners of the bag together, I wrapped a twist-tie to close it securely. Then, with a stroke of brilliance, *if I do say so myself*, I trotted back to the bathroom and grabbed a bright yellow scrunchie. Wrapping it tightly around the top of the twist tie made the perfect marker to distinguish it from the other black bags Ruben would be handling. *Don't want to grab the wrong bag and wind up with yard clippings.* Stuffing the bag behind some winter clothes in the back of my closet, I nodded. Out of sight but easily accessible if I needed to add anything throughout the day.

Taking a deep breath, I looked at my image in the full-length mirror on my bedroom door. "You can do this!" It would be the first of many pep talks I'd give myself.

"ELISE. Get your butt down here and make the kids their breakfast!" Jane's voice bristled with anger. "It's nearly seven thirty, and you're gonna make them late if you don't get your lazy ass moving."

"Coming, Jane!" I dashed down the stairs.

Jane stood blocking the kitchen doorway, feet planted, hands on her hips, and beady black eyes glaring.

WHAPP!

I felt the stinging blow of Jane's hand across my cheek. Stumbling, I caught myself against the doorjamb. Bobby smirked as I entered the kitchen, flushed with pain. He'd begun to act more like his father lately. I cringed.

Little Bea skipped in a few minutes later, unaware of the incident. I gave her a morning hug, receiving comfort as her arms wrapped around my waist.

"Would you guys like some pancakes and bacon?" I managed.

"Yeah!" they both chimed in unison, not realizing it would be the last breakfast I'd make for them.

I smiled at Bea, "You can even have some real honey on your pancakes." With that thought, I grabbed a couple of restaurant packets of honey from Jane's stolen stash, put a few on the table, and put the others in my pocket. Next, I took out a bag of frozen peas and held it to my throbbing cheek while stirring the pancake batter with my other hand. *Sure hope this one doesn't turn black like all the rest. That's the last thing I need while trying to look normal today.*

"Did you finish making Bea's costume for the school play? You better get it done today, or you know what's coming," Jane hollered another blistering order down the hall, spoiling any chance to enjoy my breakfast.

"Yes, ma'am, it's nearly finished. I'll have it done in no time." I'd almost forgotten about it. Thankfully, this gave me the perfect cover to work with that extra material.

Making clothes for Bea had been a bright spot in my time with the Burrows. And doing a costume for her was extra special. Tears came to my eyes, realizing that I wouldn't be there to watch her dance across the stage with precious honeybee cuteness.

Stuffing a final bite of pancake in my mouth, I hurriedly stuck the dishes in the dishwasher, barely scraping off the scraps or rinsing first.

"Now, you two scoot to your rooms and dress for school. I've got to get your lunches ready." Bobby dashed down the hall. "Wear a *clean* pair of jeans today, and don't forget to brush your teeth!" I called after him.

Bea sidled up next to me. "Can I wear the blue dress you made and my new shoes?"

"Sure, honey. That would be perfect." I gulped as she ran to the stairs. The hardest thing I'd do today is say goodbye to Bea.

Jack strolled into the kitchen just as the kids ran out. They paid no attention to their father, and he none to them. "Good morning, Elise," he said with a sly look that made me cringe. He could make a simple greeting sound dirty without trying.

"Good morning." My tone was rife with disdain. He was oblivious to it.

Bending backward slightly, his hands grasping his lower back, Jack looked at me and groaned. "Boy, is my back sore this morning. Guess I need another massage." Then, hollering down the hall, he asked, "Jane, you have bridge club today. Right?"

"Yeah," she replied.

Turning back to me, he rubbed his hand up and down my arm. "So-o-o?"

I said nothing as I slid away from his grip and the overpowering scent of his aftershave. Instead, I busied myself preparing school lunches. He repulsed me to the core, but a growing sense of strength and power rose from somewhere within. A feeling that he no longer had the same fearful hold on me. How I longed to say that to his face.

Yet, in an instant, my courage took a nosedive back into insecurity. I may look older and more mature than eighteen, but inside, I still felt like the twelve-year-old whom Jack had molested. My hands trembled again.

AFTER DROPPING the kids off at school, I took a quick detour. Dashing into a home store, I bought a pair of simple curtain rods that could be attached easily to a van's window and some concealer makeup for the bruise blossoming on my cheek. The rods should work well for the curtains I finished the other day. Walking towards the checkout, I found a cute plastic headband for the antennae on Bea's costume. Then I spotted some large magnetic flowers perfect for colorfully disguising Ruben's van.

Pulling into the driveway, I saw Jack's car was gone. He shouldn't get home till after four o'clock. *So glad I didn't have to give him his usual goodbye today.* I shivered at the disgusting thought of his hands on my body and his tongue in my mouth. Thoughts of Jack's ravishing suddenly washed over my spirit and nearly crushed my tenuous courage. Once again, my body and soul felt the burden of having a baby—Jack's baby.

Yet somehow, a wave of strength swelled within me. Emboldened with fury, I gathered my wits and dashed into the house. Glancing at the clock showed only three hours left. The countdown was on.

Taking the headband for Bea's costume, I stopped in Jack's office on my way to the sewing room. Digging through his desk, I found the perfect parts for the bumblebee antennae—the inner springs of Jack's executive ballpoint pens. Back in the sewing room, I stacked them over a couple of black pipe cleaners and attached them to the headband. A fuzzy ball at their ends made them the cutest bouncy antennae.

It'll be a fitting parting gift for Jack. I almost wish I could be here to see his face when he realizes I used his prized pens for a honeybee costume.

"I'm going to my hair appointment now and then my bridge game." Jane poked her head into the sewing room. "Don't forget to pick up the kids from school early today," she barked on her way out. "I'll be home at five, and you'd better have dinner ready this time." *Slam!*

"Don't worry. Everything will be perfect!" I hollered back, then added under my breath, "Witch! Yes, this time, it truly *will* be perfect. This time, I'll be gone."

AFTER JANE LEFT, I took Bea's costume and hung it on the sewing room doorknob so she'd see it when she got home. Then I went back to my room and looked around the sparse furnishings. On my dresser was Bea's old baby brush, and next to it, a tattered teddy bear from when I was little. Both held wisps of hair and spoke of memories nearly lost. I put them both in the black bag, took the recent photo of Bea from my nightstand, and put it in my back jeans pocket. *There, a little piece of sunshine to keep me company.*

I stood a moment in silence, racking my brain. Had I forgotten anything important? What-ifs rattled in my head. *What if I get caught? What if things could get better here? What if it's even worse out on my own?*

I took out my small shoulder-strap purse, found my train ticket, unfolded it, and examined it again to be sure I had my schedule straight. *The train departs at five o'clock.* Sighing, I put the ticket back in my purse. Only a few hours to go. Good thing Jane doesn't know how to use a computer. And even if Jack thinks to check his credit card statement for a train ticket purchase, it'll be too late by the time he does.

In the kitchen, I prepared sandwiches for the kids. Carefully placing a few sandwiches and snacks in a ziplock, I put them inside a shoe box to keep them from getting squished. Running back to my room, I put the box in the now-bulging garbage bag. I started to re-tie it but stood back and quickly surveyed the room once more.

"Something's missing." I opened the bottom dresser drawer

and stared at the few clothes left inside. A sliver of metal poking from under a pair of shorts caught my eye. It was the black and yellow California license plate I'd found while walking Skippy. Something had nudged me that day to keep it. Now, I felt pressed to bring it with me. Picking it up and grabbing my pillow off the bed and a shawl, I tossed them in the bag and re-wound the twist-tie, adding the yellow scrunchie again.

Back in the kitchen, I preheated the oven and took out the box of brownie mix and a bowl. With super speed, I mixed the ingredients, spooned the batter into an 8 x 13 pan, and then shoved it in the oven. After setting the timer, I dashed back to the bedroom and made my bed, folding and plumping an old pair of sweatpants in the empty pillow spot. The Bible that Betty had given me caught my attention next. *Haven't read it yet, but I promised.* Quickly stuffing it into my backpack, I grabbed the green baseball cap, touched my back pocket to ensure my cell phone was still there, and headed back out of the bedroom.

"My charger!" Turning on my heels, I dashed into my bathroom and found it in the top drawer of the vanity. *Better keep it handy.*

Taking a firm grip on the overstuffed makeshift luggage, I lifted, then half dragged the bag down the stairs and out the back door, laying it against the side of the house close to where Ruben would park. Then, returning to the mudroom, I hung the backpack and hat together on a coat hook.

Heading inside, the sound of a car door slamming startled me. Turning to see who it was, I gasped. Jack!

As if my day wasn't already stressed to the max, Jack's early arrival amped it up to a whole new level. I felt pushed over the edge beyond my breaking point. *What am I gonna do?*

It finally registered when I looked at my watch for the third time in fifteen seconds. *I only have thirty minutes before time to pick up the kids. Okay, gotta think quick. I've got to stall Jack somehow.* An idea flitted through my mind. *It's a long shot, but maybe...*

The oven timer began chiming. I grabbed two potholders,

threw open the oven door, and nearly dropped the brownie pan as I pulled it out. Plunking it down on the kitchen counter triggered another ingenious idea. *Think I'll sprinkle some powdered sugar on top, along with a bit of insurance. "Heh!" Maybe stress helps me think better.*

Sprinting upstairs to Jane's bathroom, I flung open the medicine cabinet, my heart racing. A quick scan of its contents revealed just the right prescription for this emergency—white sleeping pills. The label read: *Take one tablet before bedtime to aid in sleep.* Dumping three tablets into the palm of my hand, I stuck them in my front right pocket and returned the prescription bottle to its place on the shelf.

Stepping as quickly and quietly as possible, I descended the stairs without incident. Darting back into the kitchen, I cut three brownies and scooped them onto a small plate. Then, I smashed the sleeping pills onto a napkin using a kitchen mallet. Folding the napkin, I used it as a spout to sprinkle most of the white powder on top of the three brownies I'd set aside. After pouring a glass of milk, I dumped the rest of the powder into the milk and stirred. Grabbing the box of powdered sugar, I sprinkled the real sugar directly from the box on top of the medicated brownies.

The remaining brownies in the pan got a white blanket of unadulterated real sugar and were left to cool a bit longer.

I scrambled up to my room with a brownie plate in one hand and a glass of milk in the other. Just as my feet touched the top of the stairs, *Bang!* Jack slammed the garage door and came into the house.

"Yap, yap, yap!" Skippy barked at the unexpected intruder.

"Shut up, you stupid mutt," Jack yelled, "or I'll turn you into tacos." Yelling riled Skippy into a more hostile bark. You'd think he'd learn not to antagonize Skippy, especially after last month's dog bite. I couldn't help laughing at the image of Jack's ankle torn in a jagged wound that bled profusely. He had limped around for a few weeks, his pride taken down a few notches.

Even better, it kept him away from me. I guess dogs are a good judge of character.

Placing the brownies and milk on the table next to my bed, I quickly scurried into the bathroom and turned on the shower. Leaving the shower running, I went to my dresser and took out the only sexy lingerie I owned—purchased by Jack. Even looking at the lacy item made me feel sick to my stomach. Baiting him was risky, but the novel idea of tainted brownies gave me a sense of empowerment I'd never known. I was desperate, and nothing was gonna get in the way of my escape plan. Laying the lingerie on the bed, I quickly scribbled a note.

Jack,

Have to pick up the kids in a few.

Help yourself to the brownies. I hear chocolate is a good aphrodisiac.

Elsie

I propped the note between the glass of milk and plate of brownies. *He has to eat these brownies.*

"Aie-e, aie-e!" A squeal from downstairs rang out, and I knew Skippy had probably felt the blow of Jack's boot.

I raced back to the bathroom and locked the door, my ear pressed against it, listening. A few minutes later, I heard my bedroom door open and Jack walking around the room. The footsteps stopped. He must have found the negligee and note.

Clomping footfalls came near the bathroom door. My heart was beating so hard I thought it might burst. Surely, he won't break down the door. *Hope he doesn't know where I hid the key.* Forcing a happy tune, I put my head behind the shower curtain and began singing the only song that came to me. "Raindrops keep falling on my head…." Then, tiptoeing back to the door, the shower still blasting, I listened intently. The bed creaked, and something scraped the table. He must be eating the brownies. Good!

The bed creaked again, and I heard his big feet hit the floor and start walking. The diminishing sound of his footsteps followed. *He's going downstairs.* The room grew quiet again. I relaxed some but kept the shower running. After a minute, I slowly opened the bathroom door and peeked out to see if the coast was clear. Scanning the room, I noted that all the brownies were gone from the plate. Only a few crumbs were left, some of them on the bed.

A few more minutes passed, and once again, the stairs creaked. The sound of heavy lumbering footfalls ascending the staircase could mean only one thing—Jack was ready. Never thought I'd be so grateful for creaky floors and stairs.

More footfalls clunked around my bedroom with increasing heaviness. The bed creaked again. A thud on the floor, then another thud followed. *What the heck? Oh—shoes! Must have been his shoes. He's getting undressed*, I determined, as the bed creaked a few more times.

Just stay put a little longer, I told myself. The clock on the bathroom vanity indicated it was nearly time to pick up the kids. *Oh Lord, if you're real, help me, please. I can't go out there and risk him getting near me now.*

A few more minutes ticked slowly by. All sounds on the other side of the bathroom door had gone silent. Then—a sound of snuffling, blubbering snorts followed by a long, gravelly hum penetrated the door. Seconds later, the same sound, only more like a growling bear this time.

It could mean only one thing—Jack is snoring. I sighed with victorious relief.

I turned off the shower, then wiped the bath towel on the wet floor, making it appear used. Then, clutching my purse and gently opening the bathroom door, I carefully peeked into the room. Sure enough, he was sleeping. He was fully nude and flat on his back, with his legs splayed out, his fat stomach protruding upward, and his private parts partially covered by the negligee. The lacey bra was across his face, but it didn't stop his gaping mouth from snoring away. On impulse, I took out my cell and snapped a couple of quick ones.

Devilish thoughts of what I'd do with the pictures flashed

through my mind. Hmm. I could post them to social media with this title: "Looks like the ego has landed." I cracked a small smile, tiptoed down the stairs as quietly and quickly as possible, grabbed the car keys, and sprinted for the car.

Turning on the ignition, I sighed deeply. "Whew! That was a close one. With any luck, he'll still be out when I get back." *Please, Lord!*

AFTER PICKING up Bea from the pre-K line, I drove to the front of the school to pick up Bobby. Bea was buzzing with excitement about the school play. "Mommy, did you get my costume done yet?"

"Yes, honey. You're going to be the cutest little bee ever." A lump was forming in my throat. "Are you excited?"

"Yes! Can I put it on when we get home?" Bea pleaded.

"Maybe for a few minutes to make sure it fits." I couldn't help myself. I wanted to at least see how Bea would look in the costume.

Bobby noticed Jack's car in the driveway as we approached the house and squealed in glee. "Daddy's home!"

"Yes, your dad came home a little early today. I don't think he's feeling well. He's taking a nap, so you guys need to be quiet. You know how grumpy he'll be if you wake him." Glancing at Bobby in the rearview mirror, I saw his smile turn upside down. "Made you guys some sandwiches and brownies," I tried reviving it, "...and I thought we'd play a little ball this afternoon."

"Really? That's great!" Bobby perked up. I wasn't sure which he was happiest about—the sandwiches, brownies, or playing baseball.

"Yes, but remember you have to be very quiet. No brownies if you wake him!"

The kids clamored into the kitchen as I put out the plates of food. I stood admiring my handiwork. The white sugar-powdered top made the brownies look extra tasty. *Think I'll do the same thing next time I make brownies, but without the secret ingredient, of course. Guess you might say Jack's brownies are to die for.* I grinned mischievously.

"Eat your snack, and I'll be back in a few minutes. Remember—sh-h-h!" I said, holding a finger to my lips. Grabbing a brownie, I savored its chocolaty richness as I dashed down the hall—a few powdery white crumbs scattered to the floor. I ignored them.

Let them be a sweet reminder of all I've done for this family.

As the kids gobbled their sandwiches, I walked to the bottom of the stairs, straining to hear any sounds indicating Jack was awake. Muffled sounds of snoring filtered through the upper hallway—he was still asleep. *Thank God!* I dashed into the mudroom and took my purse off the coat hook. Putting the car keys in the what-not plate as I passed, I scooted out the back door to the side of the house where the black bag was still lying. Quickly removing the scrunchie, I placed my purse into the bag, then re-closed it.

Re-entering the house, I stuck my foot backward, catching the door so it wouldn't slam. Bobby and Bea were putting their dishes in the sink as I walked into the kitchen. "Can we go out and play now?" Bobby asked.

"Yes, but go put your baseball uniform on first. You have practice later tonight. Bea, do you want to try your costume on now?"

"Yes. Yes!" She danced with excitement.

"Okay, it's hanging in the sewing room, so let's go in there to try it on."

Bobby started to run, and I quickly stuck my arm out, stopping him. "Uh-uh-uh! Walk quietly, Bobby. Remember, quietly."

"Oh yeah. Sorry." He tiptoed out. I watched him ascend the stairs, listening again for any signs of the waking monster. *Sure am glad I shut my bedroom door.* Hopefully, he doesn't realize the snoring is coming from my room. He may be a bit of a brat, but I wouldn't want him to know what his father does to me. Thankfully, there were no sounds of my bedroom door opening. *Thank God for squeaky doors!*

"Bea, come on, honey, let's try on that costume." As I walked her to the sewing room, the rumbling sound of a lawn mower indicated that Ruben and his crew had arrived. I glanced out the window and confirmed that the white van had been backed into the driveway.

As Bobby returned in his baseball uniform, I suggested, "Bobby, why don't you go outside and warm up while I help Bea with her costume? I'll be out in a few minutes." He nodded and ran out the door, flipping his baseball in the air as he ran.

Helping Bea put her costume on, I placed the antenna head-band on her curly blond hair and then stood back to admire her. She was the cutest little bee I could have imagined. The costume fit perfectly, and the wings I'd borrowed from last year's angel costume worked well as bee wings. Not to mention the priceless antennae on her head.

"You look like the sweetest little bee I've ever seen," I said as I hugged her. "I know you'll be a big star in the play." I beamed at her with pride. Taking my cell phone out, I snapped a quick pic.

"Can I keep it on? Please? Please?" she pleaded.

"Okay, but just for a few minutes. It's almost time for your nap." And with that, Bea twirled around and admired herself in the hallway mirror several more times.

"Let's go out and show your brother." Quickly leading her outside before Bea's excitement turned into loud squeals of joy. *Don't want to wake the sleeping dragon.*

"Bobby, doesn't your sister look cute in her bee costume?"

He swung at a baseball, hitting it square on. Skippy took off after it and brought it back to Bobby. He grabbed the ball out of the dog's mouth and then turned to look. "Oh, yeah. You look cute." It was a rare moment of praise from Bobby, and Bea swelled with pride in response.

Knowing Bobby would want to call the shots, I commented, "Hey, how 'bout I bat first today?"

"No, I want to be at bat," Bobby insisted.

"Then I'll be the umpire," I suggested.

His face fell. "But who will be our pitcher?" Bobby asked. "I could wake up Daddy and see if he wants to play." My heart ached for this boy, desperate to spend time with his father—a father who, sadly, didn't seem capable of truly loving anyone, not even his children.

"I will be pitcher if you want." Ruben approached, offering in the nick of time (and according to plan).

"Oh, Ruben, that would be great. Bobby's dad isn't feeling well today and won't want to play," I said, acting as if Ruben's offer was unexpected. Bobby looked unsure.

"I am glad to do," Ruben encouraged, "but you let Elise help me after. I used to play baseball a lot as a kid. I even played on my high school team as pitcher."

"Okay. Sure." Bobby shrugged.

"That's great!" I chimed in. "You guys finish warming up while I put Bea down for her nap."

"All right." He tossed a ball in the air and took a swing at it.

🐝

SAVORING ONE LAST LOOK, I hugged Bea, then helped her out of her costume. Tucking her in was something I treasured. It was when she'd share her sweet, childish stories with me that her imagination took flight. Knowing this would be the last time I saw her for a while, maybe even forever, my heart sped up, and tears welled in my eyes.

"Honey," I said as I looked into her wide eyes. "I want you to know that I love you very, very much. And I will always love you."

"I love you too, Mommy," her sweet voice crooned.

"I have to go away for a little while, but someday I'll come back. Remember, you're my little Bumble Bea. And remember all the times we had fun painting pictures. Okay?" A lump formed in my throat, and my eyes brimmed with tears. I somehow managed to keep them at bay as I kissed Bea's cheek and hugged her tightly.

"Just a minute." Bea got back out of bed and went to the bulletin board above her little desk. Reaching up, she took the pushpin out of a picture and took it down. It was a watercolor of a bumblebee hovering over a flower that I'd helped her paint.

"Here, this is for you. It's my favorite, and I want you to have it forever." Hesitantly taking it from her pudgy little fingers, I nearly broke down. Tears slid down my cheeks.

"Oh, sweetheart. This is so beautiful. I will treasure it forever. Thank you, my little Bumble Bea." I hugged her again, not wanting to let go. "I promise never to forget you. Remember to keep watching for me. I promise I'll come back."

"Can you sing me the roses and bows song? Please," Bea pleaded.

"Okay, but just one verse. I have to get back outside, or your brother's gonna be mad."

After blowing my nose and clearing my throat, I started singing the lullaby. "Roses and bows, butterflies and toads, these are the things that a baby sees. Soft whispered breeze and kisses on the knees tell of the love that they know. Bend down to see what the angels see. Soft teddy bears and music for their ears. God blesses all the babies with these things. So, don't miss the joy that a baby brings."

Cradling Bea's sweet face, I brushed away two stray curls hiding her beautiful eyes. Crystal blue eyes that were gathering puddles for a coming storm. She knew something was changing. I could see it in her look. "I love you, Mommy," she sputtered through tears that streamed down her rosy, warm cheeks.

And that's all it took. Finally, the dam broke, and my tears burst from their captivity.

Spreading her arms wide, we hugged tightly again. Then, tucking her blankets around her, I waited, humming softly until she drifted asleep. Then, rising from her bedside, I composed myself, grabbed more tissues, and bolted to the mudroom before I could change my mind.

Pausing momentarily, I stood staring at the green baseball cap hanging on its hook. Aside from being the same color Ruben and his crew wore, its green color seemed to signal me to go. As if it was telling me it was time to move forward and not look back. *Am I making a big mistake? What if something happens to Bea when I'm gone? Surely, Jack won't touch her. She's still so little—and he didn't rape me until I was 12. I'll come back before then.*

Emotions raced through my body, setting my nerves on high alert. I squeezed my fists together, willing the tears to stop and the fear in my heart to recede. Another thick snore rumbled from the bedroom above, giving me courage.

No. If I stay, it will get worse. I can sense it coming. It could be the death of me.

Before I could change my mind, I grabbed the hat and slung it onto my head.

FIVE

Back on the front lawn, Bobby had just hit the ball over Ruben's head. "Wow! Did you see that one, Elise?" Ruben proudly announced.

"Sure did. That was amazing!" I praised Bobby. "I see you have a new bat. Must be a good one."

"Yeah! Dad got it for me last week. Here!" he said, glowing with pride as he tossed me the catcher's glove.

Tucking my ponytail inside my green cap, I thought, *Probably should have devised a catcher's mask, too.* Strapping the backpack on my chest, I was proud of how well it served a double purpose. The black quilted material lent a look similar to a real umpire's vest and should weather the days ahead.

Ruben wound up and pitched to Bobby. It was a ball. The next pitch landed right in the strike zone. "Ste-e-rike!" I yelled in my best umpire voice. Bobby gave me a dirty look. *I swear his dark brown eyes are as piercing as his mother's.*

Another pitch came, and *whap!* Up the ball went, a high fly into left field. Bobby ran around the makeshift bases and slid into home with a flourish. Ruben chased after the ball but took his time on the play, allowing Bobby to score easily. With the thrill of the hit and flushed from running, Bobby's chest puffed out as we cheered for his home run. After a few more pitches to Bobby, I took my turn at bat. Not being the best ball player, I hoped Ruben might give me a little help—no such luck. I was out one, two, three strikes in a row. Bobby went to home plate to bat again.

The game proceeded for about ten minutes. Except for a tiny hit, I was behind three to one. Finally, Ruben put his hands up in a cross pattern to indicate a break was needed.

"O-O-Okay is time I work now. It was fun. You a good ball player, Bobby. Who know, maybe sometime the Diamondbacks or Dodger scouts, they will call you." Bobby beamed at Ruben's praise.

"Elise, can you help with bags now?" Ruben waved me over to his van.

Stopping short, I pivoted back around and ran back to Bobby. Giving him an unexpected shoulder hug, I said, "You did well today, Bobby. I hope you'll continue to pursue baseball, as Ruben said." I snapped a quick pic of him, then added, "I won't be gone forever. Be good till I come back."

I was pretty sure Bobby thought I meant I'd be back to the game in a few minutes, but I could see in his eyes that my tone caught his curiosity. I hoped he would think back on it later and realize it was my way of encouraging him after I was gone. Really gone. As I walked towards Ruben, he turned and hollered, his expression revealing he was processing my farewell. "Maybe Dad will sign me up at the batting cage since he never has time to practice with me." I gave him a small smile, "I hope so, Bobby."

The ball game was short, but the adrenaline it provided was a welcome relief from the day's stress. As I walked towards Ruben's van, my heart picked up speed. I turned my cap around and undid the backpack "umpire's vest." At the van, Ruben and I went to the other side so Bobby couldn't see us. He handed me the keys and repeated the directions to the organic waste dump, where I'd take the extra yard trimmings.

Opening the van's back doors, he commented, "They already put some bags in. You only need to put two more. Be careful, mi amiga. I pray for you."

"Ruben, thank you so much for your help. Don't worry, I'll get the bags to the dump and will park the van at the train station by four-thirty." Glancing at my watch, I continued, "I should be able to dump the weeds and get to the station in plenty of time." Looking him in the eye, I asked, "Ruben, can you keep an eye on the kids until I return? I don't know how long I'll be gone… and… well, I want to make sure they're safe."

"Jes, I will." He nodded.

"Did you leave the bag of decorations in the back for me as we talked about?"

He nodded again and handed me a fluorescent vest, marking me as one of his crew. I gave him a quick hug and darted over to my pre-packed bag. I glanced towards the window as I neared the kitchen and backside of the house.

Jack stood looking out.

Keeping my head down, I slinked the rest of the way past the window and grabbed the end of my bag. Dragging it as quickly as possible, I hoisted it into the van without incident. Glancing over my shoulder, I caught sight of Jack again. Standing at the front door now, coffee cup in hand, wearing his robe and slippers, his big mouth yawning.

"Yap, yap, yap!" Skippy came to my rescue, barking a mean threat at Jack's heels, distracting him.

I scrambled to get the remaining bags Ruben's crew had set aside. Lugging them into the van, I kept my head down low, using the bill of the cap to hide my face. *Please, Lord, if you're real, help me get away safely.*

The bags were heavier than I expected, but somehow, I managed to lift and toss all three into the van. Slamming the back doors closed, I ran to the cab and jumped in. Fumbling nervously for the keys in my pocket, I started to panic. "Where the H… did they go? I'm sure I put them in my pocket." Digging deeper, I groaned. Then, searching my left pocket, I exclaimed, "Ahh! Thank God!" I attempted to put the key in the ignition, but my hand shook violently so the key wouldn't hit its mark. Grabbing hold of my right hand with my left, I tried twice until finally getting the key in. Cranking the ignition, the starter made a winding ruh-ruh-ruh noise and then went silent. Glancing toward the house, perspiration gathered on my brow as I tried again.

There he was—Jack, now fully dressed, walking out of the house right towards me.

"Oh Lord. Please!" I cried out. *Ruh, ruh, ruh* and again, *ruh-ruh-ruh*. Then—Ruh-*mm*. "Finally!"

Jerking the van quickly into drive, I hit the gas and nearly spun out but eased back off the pedal. Fortunately, a leaf blower began its loud rumble simultaneously, offering decent cover for my screeching tires. As I pulled onto the street, I saw Bobby talking to Jack. From his wide arm movements, I could tell he was reliving his home run from earlier. Fortunately, he blocked Jack's view of me. Jack craned his neck around the moment I passed by, following the van with his eyes. I turned away, hoping he didn't get a good look. I gunned the engine when the house was out of view and took off for the waste dump.

"Okay, go three miles north of the housing development, turn right at Rancho Lane, and take the dirt road about two miles farther." I rehearsed Ruben's instructions out loud. Just as he said, Rancho Lane was on the right. Before turning, I spotted a carwash on the left side of the road next to an auto body shop and hardware store.

The green waste site was situated off a dirt road in a remote area. Panicking as the clock ticked closer to four-thirty, I pulled in quickly and parked behind several sycamore trees and large shrubs. Jumping out, I left the engine running. Throwing open the back doors, I unloaded all the bags of yard trimmings, tossing them on the mound but only partially spilling their contents out. Thankfully, unloading was easier than loading the truck. Reaching into my bag, I took out my purse and kept the hat and vest on until I got farther down the road.

Just as I finished, a police car raced up the street, passing the dump in a flash of lights. *Better get outta here now.* I jumped back in the van and gunned it. Slowing as I reached the cross street, I pulled into the carwash. I ran the van through, getting all the layers of dirt washed off. I was astonished at the difference as it came out the other end. "Wow, Old Blanco really is white."

Then, driving the short distance to the backside of the hardware store, I parked behind a rusted dumpster. At the back of the van, I looked closely at the license plate before opening the back door. Taking out the sack containing the colorful magnetic decorations I'd given Ruben and frantically rummaging through my bag, I found the California license plate and went to work disguising the van.

Wheee whooo wheee whoo! My head jerked up as the racing cop car sped back down the hill, lights flashing. Catching my breath, I took the new rods and hung the yellow and black curtains in the back windows. They didn't look half-bad. When I put on the magnetic flowers, I stood back. *There's no way anyone would think this was the same van.*

Even though I hadn't broken any laws, I knew Jack would send his cronies, maybe even the police, after me as soon as he knew what I was up to. *Does he suspect anything? Could he have already called the police?* A shiver of fear wound through me. *If Jack suspected it was me who raced out of his driveway, he would use any means he could to stop me.* He had a lot of connections with unsavory people and a few "on-the-take" cops in town.

Hands shaking, I struggled to remove the plate holder and the license plate. *Ugh! I thought this would be the easy part!* Rummaging through Ruben's toolbox at the back of the truck, I found a Phillips screwdriver. "Ah ha! That's what I need!" I put the old black and yellow California plate on but left Ruben's plate cover off. It promoted a Christian Spanish-speaking radio station. I placed it and Ruben's plate into the back of the van, partly under my bag. "Good, that should keep them out of sight."

Glancing at my watch, I saw it was already four forty-five. "Ugh! I'm late!" I groaned. I hadn't factored in the carwash or the challenge of changing the plates. *Just a few minutes left to catch the train to Flagstaff.*

FINDING a place to park at the train station took forever. As I finally pulled into a space and turned off the ignition, I released the breath I'd been holding. Jumping out of the cab, I raced to the back of the van. With a snap, the curtains came down, rod and all. I circled the van, removing the floral décor before returning Ruben's license plate to its rightful place. Tossing the curtains, vest, and green cap in my bag, I locked the van and stashed the key under the back tire.

Positioning my backpack on my back, I grabbed my purse and threw the black bag over my shoulder. *Bet I make quite a picture. Probably look like a Goth Santa or a homeless person. Oh, wait.* I stumbled at the thought. *I am homeless.* Running as fast as the heavy bag would allow me, I dashed into the station. It was busy, people milling all around. Scanning the marquee over and over, I couldn't find my route. *Where is it?*

Nervously glancing around the platform, my breathing heavy, I weaved in and out of travelers towards the ticket booth window. Showing my ticket, I mustered up some calm and asked, "Sir, can you tell me where I should wait to take the next train to Flagstaff?"

"I'm sorry, Miss, but that train has already left the station. The schedule was changed the day before yesterday. It left at four-thirty instead of five. You should have received a notice."

"Oh no! Is there another one leaving for Flagstaff soon?" I asked, my panic rising.

Tipping his head down, he glanced over the rim of his glasses and gave me a quick once-over. By the look on his face, he'd guessed that getting on a train quickly was more important to me than my destination. "Not till tomorrow," he said, "but there's one leaving for Riverview shortly if that'll do."

"Where's that?" I asked as I fought back tears.

"It's a small town in California, south of San Juan Capistrano. Been there a few times myself, and it's quite nice. By train, it's gonna take you about thirteen hours ta get there."

"When does that one leave?" I asked anxiously.

"Well, let's see. It'll be leavin' in about fifteen minutes. The train comes in right over there." He pointed to the platform just behind me. "Track number five."

I closed my eyes and prayed silently. *God, what should I do?* Flagstaff had seemed so right. Now, this. Looking towards the depot entrance, I saw a familiar figure walking towards the ticket booth. He turned his head slightly to the side, almost looking my way.

It was Jack.

"I'll take the ticket to Riverview. One way, please." I handed him the money, realizing it was costing me twenty extra dollars, but it was my only choice now.

The man smiled and handed me a ticket. "Hope it goes well for you in Riverview."

"Thanks." As I turned to leave, cramping pain seized my stomach. *Great! Just what I need—my period is starting.* "Oh, can you tell me where the nearest restroom is?"

"Right over there," he said, pointing. Stuffing the ticket in my purse, I dashed towards it. At least the bathroom offered a good hiding place. On my way there, I could go behind the ticket booth, staying out of Jack's sight.

Stopping short in my tracks, a coin-operated slot sign declared fifty-cent entry. "What?! I thought they got rid of pay toilets a long time ago." Rummaging through my purse, I found the loose change I'd stolen from the what-not dish at home. After taking care of business, I stood at the sink washing my hands.

The mirror above it revealed my latest blow—a bluish-black bruise forming on my right cheek.

"Oh S...t! No wonder the ticket guy gave me a funny look. I bet he knew I was a run-away." I took out the cover-up foundation and rubbed it a little on the spot. It didn't help much. "Guess it's better than nothing," I murmured, quickly changing into grey sweats and a hoodie. Pulling the hood over my head, I carefully exited the restroom, peeking out cautiously. I spotted Jack walking towards the van. He tilted his head as if trying to see if anyone was inside. A truck pulled up on the other side of the van, and someone stepped out—Ruben.

As he grabbed the key and jumped into the driver's seat, Ruben quickly waved to the guy who'd dropped him off. Jack stepped up his pace when Ruben looked up and spotted me. I wasn't sure if he'd seen Jack, so I motioned wildly for him to get going. Ahora! Now! (I mouthed silently, then pointed to Jack). With a swift nod, he slammed the van door. Thankfully, Old Blanco started up pronto. Jack was now only a few car lengths away. My heart raced as I watched Ruben roar out of the parking space and towards the highway.

Jack stood frozen, a bewildered look on his face. He scratched his head, then shrugged and turned back towards the station.

I ducked back behind the ticket booth, out of sight. The sound of a horn made me jump, and a rush of hot wind blew through the station. The loud rumbling of train cars along the track muffled the noise of people gathering their belongings. As passengers stepped out, I nudged toward the queue, awaiting entry. Cautiously looking around, I didn't see Jack anywhere. My heart hammered in my chest, and my sweating palms made it hard to hold onto my black garbage bag. The yellow scrunchie kept sliding off, so I shook my hair loose, threw my hair into a messy bun, and then put my hoodie back up.

I made my way into the middle of the crowd as the final passengers exited the train. Sweat dripped down my back, the Arizona heat stifling. Families and business commuters surrounded me. A cranky child let out a frustrated whine just to my left. I watched as the boy's mom gave him a bag of goldfish crackers to keep him quiet. Finally, a speaker overhead announced that the train to San Diego, Riverview, and San Juan Capistrano would leave in five minutes.

"All aboard!" a conductor called, and the swirl of bodies around me started slowly moving, the surge pushing me forward. Wedged between two large men, a line started forming, and others quickly fell behind us. I could hear the little boy crunching his crackers and chattering happily. As the line moved forward, we passed into a roped queue, placing our luggage on a moving belt for security scanning. A security guard scanned everyone's tickets and let them enter the coach. *Come on, come on!* I glanced behind me again and saw Jack at the ticket booth. He wasn't looking my way, but I began to shake. *Hurry!* I pushed myself forward, lugging my bag onto the security belt and handing my ticket to the guard. I heard someone call my name as I stepped onto the train.

"Elise! Wait!"

THE TRAIN'S door slid to a smooth and solid close behind me. I whipped my head around and saw Jack through the small window on the door. He attempted to jump the fence behind the security barrier when two security guards stopped him. Manners aside, I squeezed and pushed my way around passengers filling the aisle. Once at the back of the coach, I plopped down in an unclaimed bench seat. Staring ahead in dazed shock, my chest heaved up and down. I attempted to stop my hands from shaking by clasping them between my legs.

A few minutes later, my breath finally evened out, and I lifted my black bag onto the bench, discouraging anyone from sitting next to me. *W-A-A-A. W-A-A-A,* the train's wailing horn, announced its departure, and soon, we were moving farther and farther away. Away from Jack. Away from Jane. The tightness across my chest slowly eased. I stared out the window blindly, watching the landscape blur. When the fog in my mind finally lifted, I reached into my bag and pulled out my shawl and pillow. Wrapping myself in the shawl, I collapsed lengthwise onto the pillow. The train picked up speed, and the whirring noise of the engine lulled me into a trance-like sleep.

IT SEEMED ONLY moments later when I awoke to the gurgling emptiness of hunger. Disoriented, I looked out the window at the rush of trees and foliage blurring past. I glanced across the aisle where a pleasant-looking woman sat knitting.

"Excuse me, ma'am, can you tell me where we are now?"

"We just crossed through Orange County, almost in San Diego County now." She smiled.

"Thanks." Glancing at my watch, I saw it was eight in the morning. My backpack was still on my back. Tugging it off, I found the baggie of sandwiches and brownies. Devouring my morning feast, I gulped some water from the complimentary bottle the train attendant had left. Then, pulling my jeans from my bag, I found my way to the restroom to change.

SIX

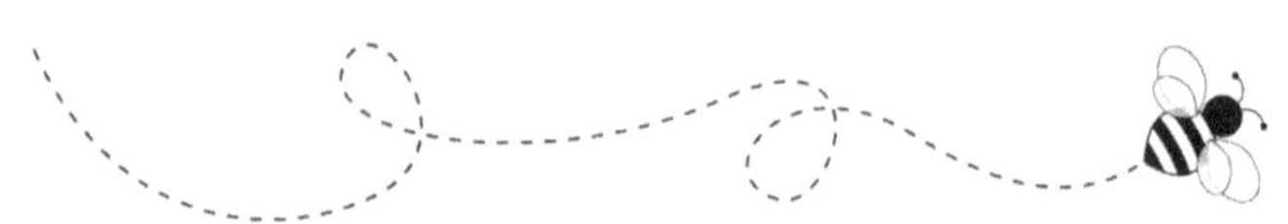

*I*n 1968 Daddy close-up the Colony Bank and say he wanna do *somethin' different. He kept the buildin' and with the money he got from the banking business they make the big buildin' behind the café into a hotel. They still call it the Colony but took off the part that say Bank. An afta that, everbody begin ta call Mama the queen. She still run the diner an Daddy mostly run the hotel. One thing she say he has ta do is have some rooms for folks that are having bad troubles an need a little hep.*

Mama Millie's husband use a work on the railroad, befo' he become a banker. So, maybe tha's why she end up heah in a town with a train goin through it. There's somethin' romantic an mysterious bout trains. We neva knows what kine a troubles or blessins they may bring in or take out. An the folks that ride in all has hopes fer what they gone fine heah.

LURCHING FORWARD as the train came to a stop, I grabbed my bags and peered out the window. I had made it—Riverview, my new home. After exiting the train, I lugged my bags to a nearby bench, wondering what to do next. From where I stood, the town presented an eclectic combination of old-world charm and contemporary influences. *Guess I better check it out.* Hauling my heavy bag over my shoulder, I groaned and started walking down the street.

It didn't take long before I plopped down on another bench. I had barely managed to make it across the street before collapsing on it. "Well, this sure isn't gonna work." Grumbling at the heaviness of my load while catching my breath, I observed a lady pushing a shopping cart out of a small corner grocery store. She wheeled the cart to her car and unloaded her goods. As she pulled out of the parking space, I tried to push aside the idea rattling in my head. Desperate, I shoved aside all sense of pride and ran to the empty shopping cart. "I can't believe I'm doing this." I pushed it over to the bench and with a loud grunt, heaved my heavy bag into it. "Well, I guess it's official now. I'm homeless. But at least I've got wheels."

After wandering for most of the day, I gave up and parked my new wheels near the window of a coffee shop and went inside. The ache in my tired back and feet was nearly as agonizing as the discouragement starting to set in. Wedging my toe against the heels of my tennis shoes, I let them drop to the floor, hoping no one would notice. *Now what, God?* Relaxing some, I sipped on coffee and munched on a muffin as the coolness of the concrete floor rewarded my swollen bare feet. Then, glancing around the room, a bright yellow flyer caught my eye.

Walking to the bulletin board, I read: *Need a Safe Place to Stay? Try the Colony at 134 Amber Street. Call Mell at (760) 595-1345.* At the bottom of the flyer, it said, "'For I know the plans I have for you,' declares the Lord, 'plans to prosper you and not to harm you, plans to give you hope and a future.'"

A nudge deep in my soul gave me the strangest sense that I should trust this Mell. I started to enter the phone number in my cell, then noticed my phone only had 5% charge left, not enough to make a phone call. I ripped the flyer from the board and put it in my purse. Pulling my charger out, my eyes searched the room for an available outlet. Not spotting one, I slumped back into my chair and said a silent prayer. *Oh God, I feel lost. What do I do now?*

Stuffing my hand into my pocket, I reached for any remaining coins. *There's got to be a pay phone somewhere around here.* Instead of money, something gooey stuck to my fingers. Pulling my hand back out, I saw honey dripping from my fingers. "Uggh! The honey packets!" I'd forgotten all about them. "Well, it's not the sweet sight of money, but it does taste sweet." I licked at the amber drips to make the best of the mess. Grabbing a paper napkin, I began wiping furiously, to no avail. The napkin stuck to my fingers. I wet the napkin with some water from my bottle but still, no luck. Trying to rip the napkin off, I stared at the shredded remnants on my hand. *Somebody ought to bottle this stuff as glue*, I thought. *It works better than Elmer's.*

Everything I touched now stuck to me no matter how hard I scrubbed. "I hate sticky. I hate sticky!" I grunted in anger, stomping my feet. It was the last straw. The moment it hit me. *I don't have a clue where to go or what to do next.* I tried flinging my fingers so the napkin would fly away—*no such luck.* Weariness and long-held sadness welled up from deep inside. I put my head in my hands and wept softly.

Moments later, a gentle touch on my shoulder startled me and abruptly stopped my crying. Pulling my hands away from my face, stickiness now tugged at the fringes of my hair too. *Well, that's just great!* Looking up, the friendly face of a Black woman smiled at me, tenderness gleaming in her eyes.

"Looks like you're having a bad day," the woman said gently.

Wiping at my eyes with the back of my hand, I muttered through my tears, "Yes, I am."

"Is there anything I can do to help?" she asked.

Showing her my cell phone, crazy frustration started spewing from me. "I don't know what to do. I got honey on my hands and in my hair, my cell phone's dead, and I can't find anywhere to charge it. I had to get away. I don't know what to do. Where to go. I don't have a place to stay. I just feel so…." My breath shuddered as I stifled a sob. "So lost and alone." I sat silent. Drawing deep breaths, I tried to calm my nerves while picking at a stubborn piece of sticky napkin. Then, once again, my eyes lifted to the woman's kind eyes. "Can you help me find somewhere to charge my phone?"

"Sure can, but it seems ta me you might need someone to talk to right now." The woman pulled a chair out to sit. "Mind if I sit here?"

"Sure." I shrugged in defeat. "I mean, it's fine."

The woman gently reached across the table, offering me a small packet of moist hand wipes. "My name is Mell," she said.

Later that Evening

The haunting sound of a train's horn announced its approach cutting through the perfect stillness of the night. Like a hobo hitching a free ride, I wondered if it also announced my arrival. Letting everyone in Riverview know a terrible person had come into their town. It's funny how different the horn sounds when you're not riding inside the train.

I sat on the edge of the bed, pondering my journey so far. Every speed bump and winding turn from the start of my life, not just the days, weeks, or months before arriving here. I'd been abandoned, taken in, abused, and eventually, I'd run for my life. Even with the distance between myself and Phoenix, fear hounded me. Was this only a reprieve? Or was I safe for once?

I picked up the flyer beside me and thought about Mell's timely help. A streak of color found my heart. It begged to stay, yearning to paint a long overdue picture of hope. Mell had been a light on my path. She had helped me find a place to stay.

A half-hour later, there it was again—the horn. But this time, its quickly diminishing sound declared my troubles were departing. Who cares where or to whom they would visit next, as long as they were going away from me? Still, I felt torn. It was hard to accept that trouble was truly behind me. *Am I safe, God? Or is there another train wreck heading for me just around the bend?*

SEVEN

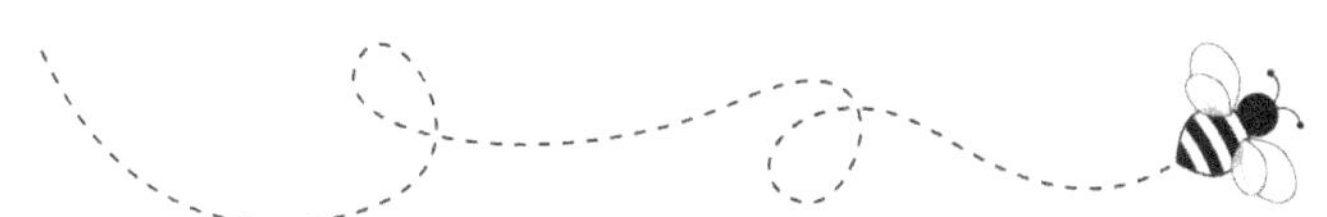

*N*ow *that Mama Mell is runnin' things round heah, I started learnin' even mo bout the good Lawd. She tell me that folks has ta obey what the Lawd has showed them ta do. Sometimes they has ta be brave and strong an step out in faith. An when they do it, God cen make things sweet again.*

It make me think bout what it say in the Bible bout that. In the book a Judges, it say this: "Out of the eater came something to eat. And out of the strong came something sweet … What is sweeter than honey? And what is stronger than a lion?"

The Next Day

I awoke begrudgingly to a mockingbird's repetitive song outside my window. *I don't want to get up yet.* Groaning and pulling the covers over my head to block the morning sunlight, I squeezed my tired eyes shut, my body begging for more rest. Nearly dozing off again, I mumbled, "Ugh! I gotta get up and make Bobby and Bea's breakfast…." I stopped short.

"Wait!" I hollered, bolting straight up out of bed. "I'm not there anymore." I triumphantly thrust my fisted hands to the sky. "I did it! I *really* did it." A feeling of unfettered freedom washed over me. I jumped up and whooped, declaring victory for myself.

Bouncing joyfully, I walked over to the window and cranked it open as I gazed at sleepy Riverview. The town was waking up, too. From my third-story window, a distant river glistened in the morning sun. A handful of people were strolling along the street below as if they had all the time in the world. Colorful storefronts poked in and out with an uneven greeting, vying for the walkers' attention as they passed. Dressing each street corner, ornate lampposts hung with lush flower baskets and shade trees added fresh green texture. Their leaves sparkled in reflection of the rising sun, handing off the breeze from one leaf to another, fresh and full of the town's eclectic scents. Finally, a street sign posted a name—Riverview Village Drive.

I'd landed in a Southern California town, but it felt like a new world, far removed from the desert landscape of Arizona.

A baby's laughter and creaky stroller wheels animated the street scene. Footfalls of a man briskly clicked by, his casual suit and briefcase swinging jauntily as he walked towards the lady and baby. "Good morning!" He nodded as he passed by. An older woman swished dirt away from a gift shop entrance. The sudden screeching of tables and chairs arranged in front of a nearby café rudely interrupted all serenity. Then, a fresh breeze wafted the pleasant aroma of cinnamon and sugar up to my window as if making sweet amends. My stomach growled in response. A busboy walked inside a cafe and then returned to the patio with an American flag. Placing it in a holder high above the door brought my eyes to the sign overhead. It read, "Good News Café."

Well, I guess I could go there for breakfast. Maybe then I'll feel up to figuring out what comes next. Just then, a ping indicated a text coming in. I reached for my phone. It was from Ruben.

"Got Old Blanco. Don't remember it ever being so clean.

Muchas gracias! All is clear aqui. Be safe. Hasta luego! Mi amiga. Ru."

Texting back a happy face emoji, I wrote, "Si! I saw you yesterday. You were great! Muchas' gracias, mi amigo. Sorry, I didn't get your plate cover back on. Ran out of time. Let's talk soon. E."

Shuffling into the ensuite, I splashed cold water on my face and brushed my teeth. When I stepped back into the bedroom, I saw the trash bag containing everything I owned lying on the floor. Looking around the room, I took inventory, hoping to see some new treasures. But except for my backpack, there wasn't much there. The room had a chest of drawers with a small microwave on its' top. A pen and notepad were on the bedside nightstand. To my delight, a coffee pot and coffee grounds peeked out from the other side of the microwave.

Pouring the coffee grounds into a filter and filling the reservoir with water, I tapped the button to start the coffee brewing. The scent was heavenly. Then, digging into my backpack, I found my leftover bagel and spread it with peanut butter. Gulping it down with a few swigs of water curbed my appetite, if only a little. My last meal was a PB&J sandwich and a few crackers with cheese. I noted some cheese remained and decided to save it for lunch. Then, opening the room closet, I saw a small fridge sitting inside. *Perfect.*

"Can't believe I found this place. Maybe God likes me after all." *At $40 a day, this place is a steal!* I mused.

"Buzz!" went the coffee pot, and I reached for a cup.

With the warm cup of joe, I sat at the mirrored dresser, pen poised to lay out a plan. But, instead, the events of yesterday and all the reasons that precipitated my move came flooding in on me. *Hopefully, Jack thought I was headed for Flagstaff—if he found evidence of the ticket on his computer.*

"My plan worked. I know it did. They'll never think of looking for me this far away. They're probably celebrating that

I'm gone—it saved them the mess of getting rid of me themselves."

"Wa-a-a!" a horn blast from an approaching train jarred me back to the present. Jolting up, I knocked the chair backward onto the floor. Coffee sloshed out of my cup, nearly hitting my sweatshirt. The solid steel chair, no doubt from some 50s café, crashed onto the wood floor with a loud bang. Wiping up the spilled coffee and righting the chair, I hoped I hadn't disturbed anyone.

"Well, guess it's time to unpack." Plunking down on the floor, I pulled the black bag towards me and leaned against the foot of the bed to begin. The first thing out of the bag was my paint box. I'd thrown it in last minute, imagining I'd have a chance to do a little art after things settled down. Setting it aside, I pulled out the clothes I'd brought and tossed them into one of the dresser drawers before hanging my few dresses in the narrow closet.

"Not much. But it's better than nothing." Somehow, talking to myself helped me feel less alone. *Hope that's not a bad sign, talking to myself.*

Next, I pulled out Bea's baby brush, pacifier, and a photo. It was a picture of Bea—big blue eyes, soft blond hair, and a smile that won everyone's heart the second she flashed it. Emotions tugged at my chest as I thought about the sweet girl I had to leave behind. Tears filled my eyes as I gazed at the snapshot. She was the one bright light I'd known since I was a little girl. The *only* shining light. My chest tightened. I hunched over, clutching her photo to my heart, and let the tears flow.

"I'm the one who raised Bea. I was the one who loved her— loved that she called me Mommy instead of her real mother, Jane. Jane didn't give a damn. Not about me, or Bea, or even Bobby." I had been more than glad to leave the horrors of that household, but leaving without Beatrice tore me apart.

A slightly crumpled paper caught my eye from inside the bag. Lifting and smoothing it out, I smiled at Bea's parting gift.

The picture of a bumblebee on a flower. "Oh, my Bumble Bea, will I ever see you again?" I held the painting up, admiring its childlike simplicity. It was better than any masterpiece hanging in a gallery. I swiped at the tears still trickling down my cheek as I stood to put the picture in a prominent place by the mirror.

As I shuffled past the bag, a pink teddy bear tumbled out, landing on my toes. Although a little tattered and worn, it was my only childhood memento. Picking it up, I cuddled it, hoping for some comfort. Looking into its little glass eyes, it stared back at me, triggering a terrible memory.

Some childhood memories never go away. They're like waxy crayons colored into our hearts, nearly impossible to erase or cover-up. This one had a bad habit of resurfacing as a brutal reminder of my abusive beginnings, but this time it was more complete. I saw myself as a little girl, cowering and trembling in the front seat of the family car. I could still hear my screams of fear, rejection, and betrayal. Trancelike, I relived the experience like it was yesterday.

The mere memory of the bumpy ride up to the Mexican border and the dust blowing in through the open window caused me to cough. Again, my body felt the acrid heat of the desert, and sweat dripped down my face. Once again, I felt my heart being torn to pieces as I was jerked out of the car and forced to go with a stranger.

Finally stopping in Laredo, my mother got out, slammed the car door, and came around to the passenger side. Even at six, I sensed something wasn't right. I sat crouched down in the front seat, tightly clutching my teddy bear and trembling with fear. My mother walked over to a stranger and began talking with him, excitedly waving her arms around. I didn't know what they were saying, but could sense it wasn't good. The man handed a wad of cash to my mother.

Cowering in a fit of fear that grew with every second, I waited. She returned to the car, yanked the door open, and shouted, "Get out now!" I could still see her angry red face. I was sobbing as she shouted senseless words in Spanglish and ordered me out of the car again. But confused, I stayed put, frozen in fear. Then, Mommy marched to the rear of the car, opened the trunk, and took out a bag. Stomping back to the open car door, she jerked my arm, lifted me, thrust me into the arms of the strange man, and handed him the bag.

The last memory of my mother was of her back as she ran to the car. Sounds of that day still thundered in my ears—the car door slamming shut, the roar of the car's engine blasting away. The wind swirling clouds of dust all around. Men shoving me into the back of a large truck amid other children crying. I swallowed my sobs just enough to open the bag my mother had packed. Inside, I found a handful of clothes, a book, and a photo of me. Clinging to my pink teddy bear that day, the realization hit me, knocking the air from my chest. Mommy planned to leave me all along.

Coming out of my daze, I considered the scene and the scattered items before me. In retrospect, the thought of her premeditation stung even more. Now, squeezing the bear unmercifully, I wanted to cry, to wail, but a sputter of tearful gasps was all that came. All the pain and trauma of those moments—Mommy driving away, Jack forcing himself on me, and the fear gripping me as I waited for the train doors to open—I wanted all the pent-up emotion to pour out of me like a flood held back for too many years. But the tears wouldn't come. I sat staring instead, my fingers subconsciously rubbing my locket. Oddly, I'd had an attachment to it for as long as I could remember, yet couldn't recall why.

After a long while, I got up from the floor, lay down on the bed, and gave in to more rest.

EIGHT

When I awoke, the ragged teddy bear was still tucked under my arm. Glancing at the clock, it was almost ten in the morning. I'd been out for two hours. Rising, I decided to fix myself another cup of coffee. After pouring half a cup, I filled it to the top with creamer hoping the milk would add at least a little nourishment. Lukewarm now, I stuck it in the microwave.

Sunshine streamed through the window with friendly invitation. Walking over, I let its warmth penetrate and soothe me. A flicker of hope kissed my heart briefly. The town was bustling now, and I glanced out the window noting an alteration shop named Alter Ego. It sat next to a beauty salon, Her-Mane's Hair. Then, as if in a contest for the cleverest name, a nail salon boasted a cartoonish sign—the Nail Chimp. A smile snuck up to my face. "Think I'm gonna like this place."

Drawing a long sip of coffee, I savored its flavor as two other signs flashed into my mind with rude interruption. Highway signs that had me, and a dozen other sweaty, bedraggled children, blinking at the sun's glare on them. After a long dark ride in a huge box truck, we had been shoved out and stood staring at the glinting sign that declared where we were headed next,

Highway 59, to LAREDO, TEXAS. The other said US BORDER CHECK SLOW YOUR SPEED.

Like a black hole in space, nothingness followed that memory marker with a long void. But creeping in after it was a frightening image of two strangers, a man and a woman, opening the door of a fancy house and smiling with large toothy grins—Mr. and Mrs. Burrows.

Even now, that horrifying picture made me flinch. Feeling lightheaded, my head jerked forward causing me to spill the remains of my coffee all over my shirt. I grabbed the heavy retro chair to steady myself.

"Guess I'd better get some real food in my stomach."

After a quick shower and change of clothes, I ventured out. Descending the stairs, I thought, *Seems like I saw a restaurant next door when I checked into the room last night.* At the bottom of the third flight, I stepped into the lobby. Mailboxes lined one wall, adjacent to a long desk housing multiple computers. No one was manning registration. A small sign at the check-in counter said: *Room inquiries only after 2 p.m.*

The night before, I had stood intimidated at the hotel door, weary, needy, and desperate. Now, as if viewing the underbelly of a puppy, tail-wagging on its back in submission, all sense of foreboding was gone. I swung the door open, letting daylight flood every part of me with a sense of emancipation. *I'm free!*

Outside, I leaned against the white wooden rails decorating the edge of the stoop and peered both ways down the street, then up to the top of the building. There, above the porch roof, was the sign I'd seen last night—Colony Hotel & Trust Residences. *Huh, such an odd name for a hotel, yet reassuring somehow.*

Walking to the south end of the building, a hexagon tower flared out of one corner and soared high above the three-storied main structure. Painted light blue with white trim, and laced with gingerbread-like flounces, the building's beautiful Victorian style intrigued my wanting soul. The face of the building boasted its era further with tall windows and decorative black and white awnings that hovered over them like ladies' skirts. A large yellow door and intricately covered entry beckoned my hungry heart up a stairway.

Gathering my wits, I walked towards the sunny yellow door inhaling the aroma of fried chicken and fresh pastry. Stopping on the stoop, I peered up at the glowing neon sign: Chicky-Pie's Café.

Entering, I saw a familiar face with a warm smile as wide as the sky. It was Mell.

NINE

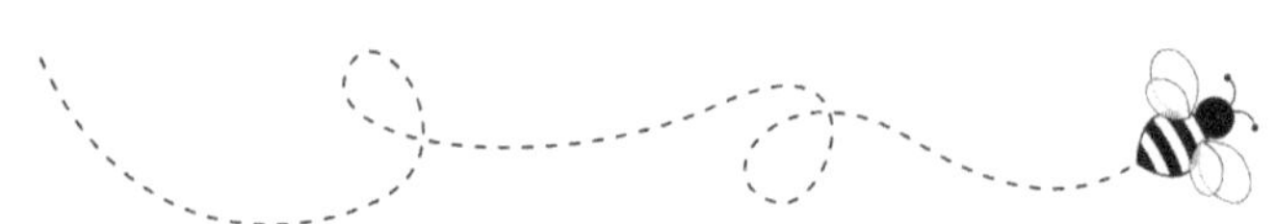

There are some folks that come in heah with they troubles, but they also has a chip on their shoulder. It seem like nothin' is eva good. They always see the glass half empty. Maybe it's 'cause they has too many sorrows and they jes cain't get past them. I dunno, but I heard someone say that "to carry a grudge is like being stung to death by one bee." I think the man that say that was name William H. Walton. He mus be a smart fella.

Still, I seen some a that kine come in heah all down and worried bout everthin', then leave with a smile own they face. When I see that, I knows they has been touched by the love heah.

Katie come in heah one time, lookin' pretty sad, an' actin' moody. But we learnt she had been through some trials that she couldn't seem to rise above. Then, things got even worse fer her.

⚜

January 2007, Phoenix, Arizona

Katie sat up slowly. Deliberately. It had been twenty-four hours since her procedure. *Surely, I should be feeling better by now.* The bedside light was still on. *Must have forgotten to turn it off,* she thought. Twisting carefully to the left, her arm outstretched, she tried to reach the book on her bedside table. As she lifted the novel she'd previously attempted to read, pain seared through her arm beginning at the armpit and finishing at her fingertips. "A-a-h-h!" she screamed.

The nurse had warned, "No heavy lifting." But reading "The Secret Life of Bees" hardly seemed to qualify.

A junior volunteer walked in, and Katie asked, "What time is it?" The young girl simply pointed to the large analog clock on the wall directly in front of her. For some reason, she hadn't noticed it before. "Guess I've been too preoccupied to notice much of anything. Eleven in the morning, Woo! That's gotta be a first for me. Don't think I've slept in that late since I was a teenager." The young woman smiled, concluded her work in the room, and left without a word.

At thirty-nine, Katie had lived through more than she ever thought possible. Now this, a lump in her left breast the size of a marble. They'd done a lumpectomy as prescribed, but she was told they may have to remove one or both of her breasts. While scared, she tried to keep a positive outlook, desperately hoping there wouldn't be a need for chemo or radiation. Still, fear kept knocking its ugly knuckles on the door of her emotions.

Lord, how could you let this happen after all I've been through? Her emotions were getting the best of her, but it was no wonder. The surgery had been more extensive than anyone had anticipated. Looking down at her breast, she realized they had removed a lot more than she thought they would. About a fourth of that breast was gone. Apparently, the bandages and hospital gown had hidden the damages pretty well. *No wonder I'm still in this hospital bed. It was just supposed to be an outpatient thing.*

"Oh, well, never had big boobs anyway." She tried to console herself with self-deprecating humor, but the reality of her situation grated at her already raw emotions, and she broke into deep sobs of loss. As tears came spilling out, memories flooded in.

Katie had married David when she was eighteen, and before she'd reached twenty-one, she was pregnant. Though unprepared for the onslaught of all that came with motherhood, her baby girl was the light of her life and David handled fatherhood like a champ. He even helped with the laundry and gave the baby walks in her stroller.

By the time their beautiful green-eyed little girl was one, David had gotten a promotion from clerk to store manager at the grocery store where he worked. Soon after, he'd been elected as foreman of the Retail Clerks Union which came with a small salary and helped supplement his primary income. Katie had thrown herself fully into motherhood and homemaking. She also found a part-time job as a tailor that helped them make ends meet. On the days she worked, her mother watched little Mary. Taking some of her tailoring work home with her made it possible to spend more time with her daughter.

Using her artistic flare, Katie enjoyed making their house feel like a home. When Mary turned two, her handmade birthday decorations had everyone raving. Reminiscing, she thought, *I drew and painted Cinderella characters and made a one-of-a-kind Cinderella gown for little Mary.* The mere thought of it brought a smile of pride to Katie's face.

After the party, friends started asking Katie to help with their kids' parties. Sometimes she earned a little extra money doing that too. But as lovely as those memories were, a torrent of tears unleashed with the memories that followed. She reached for the nearby tissue box as the pain cut deep. Mary was almost three when doctors discovered a tumor in one of Katie's kidneys. That was when everything started falling apart. The surgery had gone well and thankfully there was no cancer. The residual pain, however, continued and led to an addiction to prescription pain medication.

"Why, God? Why?" she cried out. "How could you let me get addicted? You knew my family history. You knew I'd need pain meds after the kidney surgery." The memories overwhelmed her and she quickly became a jumbled mess. Any sense of sequential order vanished with every painful recollection. Every hurtful event, every loss, ran together into one big, mashed ball of anger and pain.

Dave had tried to understand, but his patience ran out after nearly a year of dealing with the effects of her addiction. The drugs had taken their toll. She had gone from a beautiful honey-blond with bright green eyes, to a weathered, dim-eyed junkie. Though she tried to quit, each spiraling crash drove her back to the medication and drove him, and their daughter, further away. Life had become a living hell, and worse yet, little Mary was growing more and more fearful of her own mother. Storming out of the house, Mary in his arms and carrying their suitcases, Dave slammed the door on their marriage. The divorce papers arrived a week later further sealing its demise and all chance of reconciliation.

Alone in the hospital room, Katie ranted and shook her fist at God. "I cleaned up my act, Lord. I stayed straight for months, but that just wasn't good enough, was it? No, you let him take her away. You let him leave me."

Now, fourteen years later, the deep wounds still remained. She hadn't seen or heard from her daughter since the day David took her. During the divorce, the judge indicated he was planning to give her full custody of Mary. So David vanished and took Mary with him. Katie had put on a clean face of sobriety for the courts, but Dave wasn't buying it. He saw through her charade. The police put out an Amber Alert and promised to find them.

"They lied to me too. They broke their promise just like everyone else," she ranted, grabbing a wad of tissues from the box on her lap. A moment later her room door slowly creaked open and a nurse poked her head in. "Well, glad to see we're up now," the nurse chirped.

Katie blew her nose and hid her face under the covers. *How can she be so perky? Doesn't she know I'm in pain?*

"Are you all right?" Nurse Rose softened her tone with genuine concern.

"I'll be fine. Just hormones putting me in a spin," she mumbled before acquiescing, "but yes, some pain now too. Can I have something for it?" She sniffled and wiped her nose again.

"I'll see what we can do. How about some lunch first? Don't want to take any meds on an empty stomach now do we?" Rose suggested. Katie knew any pain medicine they prescribed wouldn't be very strong and certainly not addictive in nature.

"Guess I *am* a little hungry. What culinary delights does this place have to offer today?" she said a little sarcastically.

Rose picked up the printed menu lying on Katie's bedside table. "Looks like a club sandwich, chicken soup, and cottage cheese with fruit today. Oh, and mac n' cheese too."

"I'll have the mac n' cheese, please," she said politely, then added, "Could use a little comfort food right now, and some Dr. Pepper if they have it."

"Comin' right up. Let me get your vitals first."

Rose had come in to take Katie's vitals but sensing a more immediate need had tenderly addressed her patient's deeper issues. She knew the hospital didn't have Dr. Pepper but figured she would grab some at the nearest market while on her break.

⚜

KATIE SAVORED every bite of the mac n' cheese. *I haven't had mac n' cheese since I was little,* she mused. The unique taste of Dr. Pepper gave a bubbly tickle and energizing lift to boot. She asked the day nurse for help getting to the bathroom. The nurse obliged and then helped her snuggle back in bed for a nap. She hadn't thought to ask her to shut the blinds and her hospital room was still bright with sunshine. Her mind lit up with activity now, preventing any sleep she thought would come. *Could be the bright light, or maybe the caffeine in the Dr. Pepper.*

Whatever had her wide awake also conjured up a slew of memories—thankfully good ones this time.

Looking back, she remembered when she and David had gone for dinner at their favorite diner. They couldn't afford fancy restaurants, but always managed to find places with good eats and decent atmosphere on their date nights. She pictured his dark brown hair and year-round tan giving an alluring contrast to his bright blue eyes. *Even Matthew McConaughey isn't as gorgeous as David was.* And his quick wit always had her laughing.

"He often told me he liked my green eyes and smile." *Guess I was a bit flirtatious, too,* she thought. *And I think my Irish heritage was both a challenge and an attraction to him. My temper did cause a few fights, but our love was passionate and strong at least for the first few years.*

I really shouldn't blame Dave for leaving me. I was a real mess then and who knows what would have happened to Mary if I had taken custody. My mind was so screwed up, I might have actually harmed her. A tear escaped Katie's eyes as she thought of the awful possibility of hurting her little girl. Guilt threatened to overwhelm her again.

"But Lord," she prayed softly, "I've tried so hard, and stayed clean for many years now." *And I* know *Dave saw that I was clean that one time he came home. Guess I couldn't blame him for not bringing Mary then either. He needed to see if it was safe to have her near me. But I know he was convinced I was back to my old self by then. So why didn't he bring her after that?*

"Mary's been gone so many years now she probably doesn't even remember me. That is if she's still alive." *And now I might have cancer.* "Why hasn't the doctor come in to talk to me yet?"

Wiping away more tears, Katie did her best to compose herself and be positive.

NURSE ROSE RETURNED to Katie's room an hour later. "I'm done for the day. Just wanted to stop in and check on you once more before leaving."

"Thanks, Rose." Katie was lying on her good side with her back to the door, her voice weak and muffled. Rose had caught Katie just before she drifted off to sleep.

"Would you mind if I prayed for you?" Rose asked timidly.

Katie lifted her head craning around to face Rose. "I'd like that."

Coming around the bed to face her, Rose placed her hand gently on Katie's shoulder and prayed softly. "Heavenly Father, I ask you to hear my prayer for Katie. Your daughter is suffering and weary. Please put your hand of mercy and healing upon her. Let her know the depth of your love. And Lord, I pray you will hear her deepest desire and demonstrate your grace to Katie in a clear, evident way. In Jesus' name, I pray. Amen!"

Deeply touched, Katie was barely able to express herself. "Thank you. You have no idea how much that means to me."

"I'm glad to have the blessing of praying for you. Now try to get some rest." Rose drew the covers higher over Katie's arms and closed the room door quietly behind her as she left.

Closing her eyes, Katie tried to rest, but as her pain began throbbing again, she started wondering about her prognosis.

Minutes later, her room door opened. In walked her doctor.

TEN

W hen Elise come heah in 2007 ta get a new start, it were a lot like when Mell first come. Mell say Elise is like a delicate jar, an she needs a place to stay, so that the Lawd can hep her.

You may think I'm not so smart, 'cause I don't talk very elegant, and maybe you'd be right. But they is some things I do know. One thing I knows, is God's word is the truth. When Mama Mell say Elise is like a jar, I think she's talkin' 'bout a verse in the Bible where it say: "But we have this treasure in jars of clay to show that this all-surpassing power is from God and not from us. We are hard pressed on every side, but not crushed: perplexed, but not in despair; persecuted, but not abandoned; struck down, but not destroyed."

I also know a little 'bout bees, 'cause Mama talk about them so much. She say that in many countries, bees are kept in different kine a containers. Sometimes they is kept in baskets and sometimes in clay jars. I think Mama knows that Elise is like a jar, 'cause she's delicate and need hep from God. So you see, that is another thing Mama Mell an I knows about.

2007, Riverview, California, Elise

"Good morning, Elise! Welcome to Chicky-Pie's." Mell's bright smile greeted me.

"Good morning, Mell. What a surprise. I didn't expect to see you here."

"I hope you slept well. Sit wherever you want. I'll make sure you get served right away. You look a little peaked."

"Thank you. I'm hungry, that's for sure." I was grateful yet felt a mixture of shame and shyness after our previous night's conversation. As a busboy brought a menu and glass of water, I fumbled to count the few dollars in my pocket. I was famished, but really couldn't afford much. Barely two minutes later, a waitress came to take my order. "I'll have a glass of orange juice and scrambled eggs with toast." I mentally calculated the total, *$6.50 plus tax. I still have a few hundred dollars left, but who knows how long it'll be before I find work. Gotta stretch every penny.*

"Coming right up, dear," the waitress happily assured me. "Do you want some bacon or sausage with that?" She must have noticed my hesitancy, so she leaned closer and whispered, "Don't know if you know, but breakfast is on the house today. Mama Mell's orders."

"Really?" I said with surprise, "In that case, yes, I'll have sausage too." I don't think I've been so excited about a conglomeration of pork since I tried spam. My empty stomach grumbled in agreement.

Scarfing down every bite and guzzling the sweet orange juice, the waitress returned and this time I noticed her name— Josie. "Looks like you were pretty hungry. Can I get you anything else?" she asked cheerfully.

"Thanks, Josie. I'm pretty full. But I'm wondering, are you guys looking to hire some help?"

"Well, now, just so happens we are. Yesterday one of our busboys quit or was fired, I'm not sure which. Anyways, it was just as well, 'cause he wasn't worth a squat. You got any experience washing dishes, cleaning tables, and such?" Josie asked.

"Sure do! Who should I talk to?" I asked anxiously.

"Mama Mell. She's the owner. I think she's in the back right now, but I'll tell her you wanna talk. Might wanna praise her peach pie too." She winked at me. "She's pretty proud of all her pies, but peach is her favorite."

"But I haven't had any of her pie yet," I confessed.

"Coming right up!" She turned and left for the kitchen. Two minutes later Josie returned with a large slice of peach pie. "Here, ya go. It's two days old, but I'm sure it's still good. Oh, and this one's on me. Enjoy!"

All my shyness disappeared as I gobbled down every bite. It tasted like pure peach heaven. Josie refilled my coffee as I finished the last few bites. "Thank you so much. Wow, this was delicious! I didn't think I had any room left, but somehow I managed to find a corner. May I have some more cream?"

Even though I'd already eaten, and I'd never been in the habit of saying a blessing, I felt the overwhelming desire to pray. The joyful ambiance of the restaurant reminded me of Betty's house, and the generosity and warmth from Josie and Mell filled me with gratitude.

"Thank you, Lord," I whispered. "Thank you for bringing me to this beautiful place. I know it's been a long while since I've talked to you, but if you really do love me like Betty said, please help me get this job. Amen."

Lifting my head, I opened my eyes and spotted the carafe of cream sitting on the table. Josie must have set it down while I was praying. Well, that was it for me—not the cream, but the step of faith I'd just taken. Would I be rewarded?

As I sat sipping coffee and waiting for Mell, my thoughts wandered to the chaos I'd left behind. *They must be furious by now. Jane is probably frantic trying to figure out how to juggle the kids' school schedule and all her appointments. Bobby and Bea will be wondering where I am and if I'm coming back.*

"The play!" I slapped the side of my head. *It's tonight. Oh Lord, please help little Bea to do well. Let her know I'm thinking about her,* I prayed once more. Tears filled my eyes at the thought of Bea dancing in her bee costume. My heart ached for not being able to watch her perform. Covering my eyes with both hands, I tried to compose myself.

A tapping startled me. Opening my eyes, Mell was staring at me with a puzzled look. "Oh, hi. Sorry, I didn't notice you there." Quickly grabbing the napkin on my lap, I wiped my tears.

"The food wasn't that bad, was it?" Mell gently joked.

"Hah!" I spit out a laugh. "No, it was delicious. Especially the peach pie."

"Glad you enjoyed it," she smiled. "I heard you wanted to talk to me about a job. We need a bus person. Think you can handle that?"

"Uh, yes. I'm sure I can. I've been a nanny, cook, and house-keeper for the past ten years, so I've got plenty of experience handling messes and hungry appetites."

"Well, that sounds like the right qualifications to me," Mell said hesitantly.

"Having a reliable bus person and good waitresses are an important part of a successful business like yours," I continued, laying on some praise. "You must have an excellent cook as well. Don't think I've ever tasted peach pie that good anywhere."

"Make my own pies," Mell corrected with pride.

"Really? Wow, that's amazing." Then mustering some nerve, I pressed on. "About the job, I could help you as a bus person for a few months, but I'm hoping to get work as a waitress. I heard a girl at the Claim Jumper in San Diego will be going on maternity leave soon. So, I'm considering taking that position." It was a lie, but I hoped it didn't show on my face. *Sometimes, I have to fudge the truth,* I excused myself.

"You can waitress too?" Mell cast a doubting look my way.

I crumbled inside. I'd been lying so much lately that it was hard not to keep on doing it even though I knew it wasn't right. "Well," I humbly admitted, "I think I'd be able to. I haven't really waitressed before. But, if you give me a chance, I'm sure I could rise to your expectations. Been doing *that* all my life."

"All right then. Fill in for a few weeks as a bus person until we find someone else. After that, I'll train you to be a waitress. If you handle it all right, I'll hire you full-time. To start, I pay minimum wage, but the tips here are good. You can stay in the room at the Colony for half of what I'm charging now while you get on your feet. That is if you work hard and do well here at Chicky-Pie's. After three months, if you prove yourself as a worker worthy of your wages, I'll raise your salary to $10 an hour."

"That's great! I promise I'll do you proud. You'll see. Thank you so much." I was so happy I almost hugged her.

"Okay. Be here tomorrow morning at seven, and we'll get you started. I have an apron for you, but wear something clean and simple. Be sure to wear comfortable shoes, too," Mell instructed.

"Oh, sure. One more thing, can I have Sundays off?" The boldness of the request surprised me as it came out of my mouth, but the next thing astounded me even more. "So I can go to church."

"You go to church?" Mell inquired.

"Well," I hedged, "I thought I'd check it out. Do you know of a good one nearby?" I came back quickly, wondering what I was getting myself into. *Maybe I will give it a try.*

"Sure do. I attend the church down by the river. It's a little far to walk to, but I'm sure I can find someone to give you a ride."

"Great! Thank you so much." I stood up to leave. "See you at seven sharp."

IT FELT like walking on air as I strolled out of the café. The hearty meal, caffeine, and Mell's willingness to give me a job planted a seed of hope. Maybe things really were looking up for me. As I walked down the street, glancing in shop windows, Riverview took on a whole new light. I had a feeling it would be the perfect place for a new start.

After an hour or so, I returned to my room, taking the elevator this time. The key and knob took some jiggling before the door finally opened. The room was darker now as the sun moved behind the building. I flipped on the light, illuminating the scattered remnants of my life still lying on the floor. A colorful rug caught my attention. I hadn't noticed it earlier and couldn't remember ever seeing a rug quite like it. Rings of color wound their way in a pattern that formed an oval shape. Somehow, the rug seemed analogous to the disorganized items that lay before me. A riot of color without a semblance of order. It added warmth to the room, serving a purpose. *Maybe that's mostly what I need—to find purpose.* I sighed and shrugged my shoulders. I'll think about that later.

Feeling a little chilly, I walked to the closet and pulled on a sweater. I grabbed my backpack and started rummaging through it. Finding my journal brought a surprising sense of security. I'd unpacked my clothes that morning but hadn't touched the other items I'd brought. Flopping the black bag onto my bed, I sat down, leaning back on the cozy pillows. *Might as well get comfy this time,* I thought, knowing the bag's contents might stir up my emotions. They did.

Reaching into the sack, my hands felt the familiar shape of the brown paper-wrapped package I'd intended to drop at the post office. Holding it up to eye level I considered its contents. Contents that held promise and the heavy weight of hope. Contents that held secrets. Was I ready to finally uncover them?

I AWOKE the next morning feeling lighter than I had in a long time. After showering, I found an iron in the closet and proceeded to press the wrinkles out of my best dress—the aqua-blue one. I thought of Bea and how she might be wearing the matching dress I'd made her. I circled my arms around my waist in a sort of hug. It was a sad imitation of what a real hug from Bea would feel like, but imagining it brought comfort all the same. Somehow, standing on the precipice of a new job—a new life—gave me tremendous joy.

Practically skipping down the three flights of stairs, I got to the first floor faster than the elevator could. I couldn't wait to start my new job at Chicky-Pie's.

🐝

AFTER ONLY TWO WEEKS, Mell was able to fill the busboy position. On my first day as a waitress, she sat me down in the kitchen for orientation.

"In order for you to work here, you need ta understand everything about the beginning of Chicky-Pie's. And ta understand that, you need ta hear about Mama Millie an' Tamara. Not only was Millie my grandmother, she was the queen bee that started this place. Except, back then, she called it Millie's Diner," Mell began explaining. "My Grandmama was the bravest woman I ever knew an' if it hadn't been for her, I don't know what I would a done."

Something told me this was going to be a long orientation, so I got as comfortable as I could in the steel dining chair—reminiscent of an era long past.

"When she and my granddaddy came out here ta California, it wasn't easy. 'Course in the mid-sixties there was lots a turmoil 'round the country. Back then, people was tryin' to figure out how things is supposed ta work for us black folks—well," she sighed, "we still tryin' a figure that out. Mama Millie was married to a white man, an' it was hard for lots a people ta know what ta do with that. But they loved each other, and at least in California, things were gettin' better in those matters."

Mell searched my face with scrutinizing measure. Squirming under her gaze, I thought, *What's this got to do with waitressing?*

"Now, my grandmama not only had a big appetite, she had a big heart—especially for folks with troubles. Maybe that's why she loved me so much. It prolly' didn't hurt that I liked to cook, too. Then, there came a day when my troubles started swellin' up and overflowin' like a batch of bad stew with spoiled meat. That's when I came ta live with Mama Millie and learned to work in the restaurant."

Mell looked me in the eyes now. Shifting in my seat, I thought, *A batch of stew? What in the world is she talking about? Is she trying to make me feel sorry for her? Am I supposed to feel good about my own troubles because she's faced a few herself? Well, it better not be about that, or I'm outta here now.*

Glancing at her watch, a flicker of urgency flashed in Mell's eyes. "Let me skip ahead a little. A few years after I got here, God started showing me new things. I had a vision and took a road trip up a tall mountain. And when I made it to the top of the mountain and saw the expansive beauty of God's creation, it brought me a new perspective. It was a revelation of God's lovin' hand in my life, even during my trials. Ya' see, although hardship provoked my comin' to Riverview, it ended up strengthening my self-confidence and gave me faith. It changed me into the woman God intended me to be."

Mell turned her gaze toward the kitchen window; the morning sun brushed a golden glow on her coffee-colored complexion, lighting up her white smile with a sparkle. I gulped down my nerves and sat waiting. She finally started in again. "It was like peering out a big picture window," she pointed at the glistening river view, "and it gave me a broader perspective of things. I saw how God had used the people and events in the winding river of my life. How He even used the tough times to mold me into His good vessel."

I almost jumped up out of my seat. *What on earth does this have to do with training as a waitress? I must be stupid or just plain desperate to stay here listening to this.* Who did she think she was, trying to give me a lecture about God and trials? She has no idea what I've been through.

Mell continued, "That's when I realized the full potential of Chicky-Pie's and the Colony. They could be places of refuge and encouragement. Ya' see, when I came here, I was pregnant and alone. Bein' here with Mama Millie helped me see the best kind a food she offered wasn't the things printed on the menu. It was the good soul food of love, friendship, and hope. After I got back on my feet and my daughter grew up some, I got an education in the restaurant business."

Huh, she had a child, too.

"That's when I decided not to use my first name anymore. Instead of being called Tamara, from that day on, I started going by my middle name, Mell. The name Tamara was a constant reminder of my abusive childhood and the abuse I suffered at the hands of my husband. For a long time after leaving him, I would duck every time someone addressed me as Tamara."

I flinched with empathy. *Maybe she does know something about the things I've endured.* "How'd you get the money to buy this place?" I ventured, my interest sparked.

"My Grandmama Millie left it to me when she died. By that time, I had a pretty good feel for the business and had already started dreamin' up ideas for making it even better. And, if I do say so myself, I'd also built a pretty good reputation for my pies."

"I can't argue there," I chuckled. "That was the best peach pie I've ever had." I offered encouragement, my defensive armor slipping a bit.

"So, I went to work remodeling the place. New paint colors, tables, and booths, along with the jukebox, got things looking and feeling more invitin' around here. The final touch was to give the place a new name, just like I'd done for myself. So,

Chicky-Pie's was born, or reborn, you could say. It wasn't long before the place was fillin' up with customers again." Mell tilted her head contemplatively. "Ya know, knocking down real walls and changing things up was a piece of cake compared to tearing down the old walls around my wounded heart."

I looked down, trying to hide the pain and anger of my own wounds. It was unnerving how her words hit so close to home. Instead of yelling at me like I was used to, she smiled tenderly.

"Elise, I know you have a story to tell, too. No doubt you got some tough stuff baked into your soul, but I hope you will come to learn that you are safe here. An' any time you feel like sharing any of your own troubles with me, I'm here for you."

Once again, I sensed her caring heart. *Guess I might as well give this place a chance. I got nowhere else to go, anyway.* "Thanks, I appreciate that."

"Waitress work is hard, but I have a feeling you can handle it," Mell said with a twinkle in her eye.

"Well, it probably *is* hard work, but I gotta feeling it's like a spa retreat compared to what I came from." I returned the smile in her eyes.

As we started more hands-on training, I could tell she was right. Waitressing wasn't going to be easy. Even beyond learning the ins and outs of the kitchen and working in a restaurant, I knew it would take more than a few weeks on a job and a handful of warm smiles to scrape away the leftovers on the plate of my soul.

By the end of my first day as a waitress, Mell commented that I was a quick study, giving me a new kind of satisfaction. Josie carried on with my training when Mell went back to her duties in the kitchen. She was patient, more patient than I would have been! But it was Mell's empathetic words and our shared commonalities that encouraged me to stick it out. Even so, the fear of Jack and Jane searching for me had me constantly looking over my shoulder for weeks to come.

As for attending church, it wasn't the musty, dank place I'd imagined it to be. The lack of stained-glass windows and gaudy gold ornamentations made my prejudice stutter. The church by the river wasn't anything like I expected, so I kept my promise to go, but only sporadically. After all of the abuse I'd endured, it was hard to believe Jesus loved me, as the pastor frequently said. Cynical most of the time, I chose to believe some of what I heard. The rest, I figured, was up to God to show me.

⚽

2010, Phoenix, Arizona, Katie

The phone rang as Katie came in from the garage, her arms full of groceries. "Hello, yes, this is Katie. Hold on a minute." She put the two grocery bags on the kitchen counter and again picked up the phone. "Hi. It's good to hear from you, Detective. Have you found out anything about my daughter?"

His voice was serious. "Hello, Katie. I don't have news about your missing daughter, but I do have some about David." He paused, and Katie swallowed hard. *Was David out of prison now? Had he gone back to Mary?* She worked at a loose thread on her shirt sleeve.

"David was recently released from prison but, unfortunately, was killed just a few days later," the detective gently informed her. "It seems David was involved in a bar fight near the border. Two guys were taken in for manslaughter. I hate to bring such bad news, but I knew you'd want to know."

Katie was struck silent with shock. While she hadn't hoped for reconciliation with her former husband, news of his death hit harder than expected.

The detective continued, "Unfortunately, we still haven't uncovered your daughter's whereabouts. And his death will only make it harder to track her down now."

Thinking back to the last time she saw him, Katie remembered Dave's surprise visit three years after taking their daughter. He hadn't brought Mary with him, but at least it had given her some hope of seeing her daughter again. When the police got wind he was back in town, they dispatched quickly, slapped cuffs on him, and threw him in jail. Both Katie and the police begged him to reveal where Mary was, but he didn't divulge her location until they'd offered him a deal. It was only then that he'd finally told them where Mary was.

"I ran off with Mary for her own safety," David had explained to the police. "Katie was a junkie and would've hurt her, but the judge wasn't seeing it, so I had to take her. I love my daughter, and I swear I would never hurt her. She's safe. Living with my new wife in San Jose, Mexico." He gave them the location of his house in Mexico, but it took several months before the authorities finally found it. Once they did, there was no sign of Mary. The only evidence they'd found was a faded photo of her standing next to Dave and one of his union shirts hanging in the closet with his nametag pinned on it.

His new wife claimed David had taken Mary with him and hadn't returned for six months. Suspicions remained for the police, but whatever trail they might have followed had been cold by the time they'd found the house.

Shaking her from her reverie, the detective continued, "David served a six-year term for child abduction and failure to pay child support. He would have served longer if they hadn't removed the kidnapping charges. We think he went to his wife's house right after his release, but we can't be sure. Rumors are sketchy about what happened to him."

Katie choked back tears. *By now, Mary had been missing for eighteen years. So she would be twenty-one—assuming she was still alive.* "I'm never going to see her again, am I?" Katie whispered.

"I am so sorry," he repeated. "But I promise I will do everything possible to find her."

ELEVEN

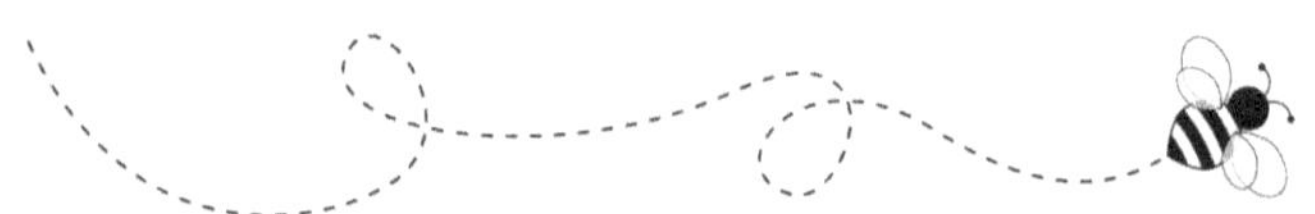

Now you gone read some mo 'bout what happen with my friend Elise. You'll see that she done good for a while afta comin' heah an makin new friends, but then something happen that bring new trouble to her heart.

They say that bees can sleep, but no one knows if they has dreams. I sure do know that Miss Elise has dreams, and sometime they is special kine that come from the Lawd.

2012 (Five Years Later), Elise

The Santa Ana winds were blowing every day now. Their dry, hot air stirred up anxiety for most folks in Southern California. Temperatures cooled some in the evening and early mornings, usually bringing a measure of calm, but not today. Not for me.

I lay still, mind wavering between consciousness and sleep. Burrowing deeper into my pillow, images flickered before my eyes. Traces of a dream lingered, as did the oppressive feeling of danger, fear, and an urgent need to escape. But from whom? Or what? I wasn't sure.

Tuning in to the sounds around me, I clung tightly to the vision, willing it to continue, longing for a resolution. A clock ticked nearby. It wasn't the first time I'd had this dream. No, it was the gift that kept on giving—a familiar taunt. The first dream had me fleeing to Riverview. The similarities were startling, and yet, this one left the impression it was *someone else* in danger this time. But who?

If I could fall back to sleep, maybe this time would be different. Or at least would answer some of my questions. Filled with a sense of foreboding, I ruminated, "It's been five years. The Burrows aren't part of my life any longer."

Pete stirred next to me, groaning, "Umm-hmm."

Assuming he was awake, I asked, "Why would it return now? It just doesn't make sense." He didn't answer.

Smokey, my grey and white kitten, leaped onto the bed and poked her cold nose against my cheek. She rubbed her soft whiskers down my neck with a consoling comfort. Then, with a cupped hand, I cuddled her furry cheeks and scratched her head.

"Good morning, you silly kitty," I cooed. The soothing purr from my feline friend was meant to encourage more petting. But my somber mood wasn't that easy to dispel. "I don't understand. Everything is going so well. I'm happier than I've ever been."

Wide awake now, I lifted up a prayer. "God, if you're listening, show me what this dream means. Please?" Staring at the ceiling fan, I imagined my words drifting up to it, whirling around, then flinging off without sticking to anything of purpose. *Do my prayers do the same thing?* I wondered.

Everything is so much better now. I've come a long way from the person I used to be. If somebody even thinks about hurting me, I deflect and move on. Thank God for Mell and Pete, *even if they do see through my emotional armor and continue to nag me into their way of dealing with things—faith.*

Thoughts of the past five years flashed through my mind. *I am so much happier now. I feel settled, safe, and sane. Why would God give me another dream about escaping?*

Yet, the dream *is* back, and there's no denying its pull on my emotions. The old sense of fear, unworthiness, and abandonment now clung like a wet blanket. Smothering. It brought back memories of the very real nightmare I once lived. *Maybe this one's just a bunch of symbolism and isn't another premonition.* Smokey jumped off the bed, sat, and cocked her head at me.

Glancing at the bedside clock, my tired eyes registered the time—six a.m.! "Ugh!" I groaned. *Way too early for a Saturday morning. Naturally! Since I don't have to be at work till eleven today.* Flinging the covers off, I jumped out of bed.

"Gonna get a little cardio in for the day," I informed my slumbering hubby. He didn't respond. Putting on a sports bra and squeezing my skinny legs into tight black and teal leggings, I pulled a matching tank top over my head. *At least it'll make up for the workout I missed on Wednesday.* I was determined to stay on a regular exercise schedule. Glancing in the mirror triggered self-imposed body shaming. "Maybe this time my belly fat will tighten up." I pulled back my long brown hair into a simple pony and proceeded to the home gym.

After some stretching, I hopped on the treadmill and hit the start button. Beginning with a slow jog, I clicked on the TV in front of me. Flipping through the channels couldn't shake the dream from my memory. *Well, maybe trying to decipher it will make my workout time sail by.* Ramping up the speed, I picked up my pace. "Okay, so what were the similarities between the two dreams?" I mumbled out loud. *I was in a house, and people there were trying to kill me. There was a clear sense of imminent danger.* "But I'm not in danger any longer. I just don't get it."

"*Meow.*" Smokey meandered into the gym, startling me back into reality. Rubbing her furry back against the doorjamb, she cried a little louder. "Me-e-ow!"

"It's too early for breakfast," I told her. Nothing would slow me from the physical and mental exercise I needed today. Clearly insulted, Smokey lifted her tail, stuck her nose in the air, twirled around, and sauntered away.

Okay, get focused. What was different about last night's dream? Hmmm, there were two kids—a boy and a girl. The boy was older than the girl and seemed bratty, while the little girl was sweet. "That fits the description of Bobby and Bea. But that's absurd! I haven't seen them in ages."

I continued turning over the dreams in my mind. *A strange woman walked towards me. Then, when she opened her mouth, syrup spilled out with a babbling sound, and then her mouth changed into scissors.* "This is so bizarre."

Could that represent Jane? She sure knew how to cut me down. There weren't many waking moments when she wasn't either screaming or hitting me.

After several minutes, I pushed pause on the treadmill to catch my breath. While my body rested, my mind continued on in decipher mode... *There was a man in the dream this time, but he looked more like an animal, some kind of rodent or weasel with huge, ugly brown teeth... Then, a dark cloud came at me, making a loud hum. Two large hands reached towards me. But... hmmm... well, it felt like it was me, but it wasn't me. Strange! That's different, too. What could that possibly mean?*

I hit start again, increasing the speed and the incline. Jogging briskly now, I held tight to the handrails, feeling the tension build between my shoulders.

"I've got to calm down and let this workout work!" I scolded myself.

A full minute passed before I slowed my pace again. This time, my mind drifted back to my very real past. I could see the house I'd once called home—and the people who had lived there. The ones represented in my dreams. Jack and Jane were supposed to fill a parental void, but instead, they became a living nightmare, warping any hope for a happy childhood.

The man in the dream, the weasel-like one, was undoubtedly Jack. He was good at burrowing into my heart. Digging deeper and deeper, preying on my young, fragile spirit while gnawing away at the roots of my happiness. *That was Jack, all right. He plundered my most precious childhood jewel—my innocence.*

Grabbing the remote, I turned the TV on again. I needed a distraction. The channel was pre-set to my favorite news program. "Nope, not in the mood for news." Changing the channel to a morning show, the host was saying, "I pray those of you watching today will come to realize the purpose and plans God has for your life."

Purpose and plans for my life? I've heard that before. Just glad to be somewhere else now.

Another 20 minutes passed, and I slowed my gait and stepped off the treadmill. Glancing at the wall mirror, I paused, turning sideways for a view. My turquoise eyes were the only feature I liked. People often complimented their bright contrast against my brown hair and olive-tan skin. They said I was "striking" and unusual for someone with a partially Hispanic heritage. *I might as well forget my mother and my home in Mexico.* They only make the hole inside me hurt more. Faded memories of my dad hinted he was Caucasian, but I couldn't remember him clearly, making my heart ache with loss. It was my twelfth birthday when Jane told me my daddy had died. She'd read it in the newspaper the day before and saved the news for my actual birthday. *Won't ever forget that gift—it was just sooo kind of her.* A bitter lump filled my throat.

Exercise usually lifted my spirits, but that dream, and all the bad memories it dredged up, had taken a toll. Walking out of the gym, I looked at the photos in our hallway. Pictures of Pete and our wedding, adorable baby photos of our daughter, and more recent snapshots of our sweet little family. I couldn't help but smile. Seeing those faces I held so dear lifted my spirit, bringing my attitude back to a more grateful focus.

What's that verse Pete's always telling me? "Whatever things are true, whatever things are noble ...ah...whatever things are... some-

thing… something." I only partially remembered. He always encourages me to find hope and comfort through faith.

"If it weren't for my faith and the Lord's help," he'd say, "I don't think I would have made it when my mother died."

I loved that Pete had a steady faith he could rely on. But believing in God the way he does wasn't that easy for me. It would take a giant leap, not a "simple step," as he calls it. Too many scars. Too much heartache. Forgive my mother and father's rejection? Forget the abuse that Jack and Jane did to me? Well, there's just no way.

Even so, I couldn't deny that Pete's faith made a difference. It's the only explanation for the joy and blessings I have in my life now.

I am so lucky to have him. Those beautiful brown eyes, his cleft chin, and broad shoulders. Who could resist? I loved him the first time I saw him. I just can't help wondering how long it'll be before he realizes who I am deep down inside. What I've done. It's enough to make any man leave me. While Pete knew bits and pieces of my past, I'd been hesitant to share all the gruesome details with him. The shame rested thick within me, even now. *But I must have done something right for God to let me have him and my sweet little Bella.*

Adding the cutest punctuation to my thoughts, Bella peeked her impish face around the doorjamb. "Good morning, sweetheart." Spreading my arms, I gave her a wide-open invitation for a morning hug. A stirring in the kitchen indicated Pete was up, too.

"How about some pancakes this morning?" he hollered down the hall.

"Sounds yummy!" I hollered back. *Diet?* I thought to myself, *What diet?*

Taking hold of Bella's hand, I willed myself to shake the feeling that this was another prophetic dream, one dragging me towards danger instead of out of it this time.

TWELVE

An now you gone learn 'bout otha friends who come heah needen' hep. One a them is Lily. Now I know ya'll think I talk funny but guess I'm not the only one. Seems there's lots a folks from the South that talk like I do. So when Miss Lily come into my home, I was happy ta heah somebody sound a little like I do. Course she more refine' than me, her words is like the smooth slow drip a honey comin' off her tongue. But remember what I tole ya'll 'bout some folks who is strong and still have times when they need hep? They's feelin' like they is old dry clay that's ready ta break? Well, I think that a little like my friend Lily. She knows the Lawd, but she been through a hard loss an it make her feel broken and scared. But mostly, she jes lonely. I think God gone give her clay jar something new ta fill it with purpose.

Elise

Life was getting stale, but I couldn't say why. Bella was a delight. I was happy and grateful for everything Mell and Pete had done for me, but I was restless.

Then Lily arrived.

Lily was a breath of fresh air that blew in from Georgia. She brought a new flavor of hospitality to Chicky-Pie's, filling a need we didn't know we had. It didn't matter that she, a woman of about sixty, was much older than me; we clicked right off the bat. Perhaps it was the way her words spread smooth like honey on a hot roll. Or, it could have been her high energy and creative flair reflected in the stylish way she dressed. Or, maybe her peaceful demeanor drew me to her as a friend. Whatever it was, Lily was a welcome change.

While things had never been fast-paced around here, her leisurely manner and prolonged Southern drawl invited us to slow down even more. To spend more time with each other and rediscover who we were deep down. Part of what made Lily so attractive was the fact that she was oblivious to the power she wielded over us. Likewise, I don't think she realized the power Chicky-Pie's Café had over her.

I guess you could say we needed each other. In culinary speak, Mell would say it was the perfect pairing of a sweet honey-dripping sauce on top of a crispy, well-seasoned entrée.

So, how about we let Lily tell her own story?

Lily

It was about two o'clock when I pulled into Riverview and parked next to a cute Victorian-style café. Stepping out of the car, the stifling heat slapped me in the face, nearly laying me out flat. Hot and hungry, I didn't waste time lookin' for a place ta eat. 'Sides, the tantalizing aroma of fried chicken drew me in with an irresistible lure before I even reached the yellow door of Chicky-Pie's Café.

"Afternoon! Sit anywhere you like." The radiant smile of a petite Black woman greeted me. The familiar warmth in her demeanor made me feel welcome. Her stylish dress and beautifully box-braided hair added a touch of class seldom seen in what otherwise looked like a casual café.

Choosing a booth, I asked the waitress, "What's your specialty?"

"Southern fried chicken," *Guess I shoulda known.* "…and pies to die for!" she added with a bright smile of her own.

A course! I thought. "Sounds good ta me. Haven't had fried chicken in a couple a yeahs." *Not since they took my gallbladder out,* I thought begrudgingly. "I really shouldn't, but why not? Probably gained a pound just inhaling the aroma, anyway." She chuckled in response.

"I'll have some ahhs tea too. Oh, and can ya hold the salad and give me some cooked vegetables instead?"

"Coming right up!"

Sinking my weary body into the soft leather of the booth, I let out a long sigh. Bein' alone, I felt a little guilty sitting at such a large table, but after my long drive, it sure felt good. *'Sides, the place isn't exactly buzzin' with customers.* Elevator music floated through the nearly empty room, failin' miserably at creatin' any ambiance.

I started goin' over everythin' I needed to do. *Let's see, the moving van should arrive in a couple of hours, and I'll need ta get to the house in time to meet them.* Even with everything on my mind, I was grateful for a safe trip and was happy to finally be here. *Just relax and veg out,* I told myself.

I tried, but it wasn't long before my ADHD kicked in, and I was distracted by the colorful things in view. My gaze shifted to a wall nearby. *Well, would you look at that? An original watercolor painting.*

Surveying the dinin' room with closer scrutiny, I noticed other details I'd missed on my way in. *The leather seating looks new, but the outdoor patio isn't being used.* Even though it'd been about six years since my last trip to Riverview, I remembered it well. The last time John and I were here, he was startin' to have trouble walking, especially along the sandy beach. Finding out he had Parkinson's was devastatin'. His image washed over me, and I willed myself not to cry. *Not gonna do it. Not now. Not here.*

Memories of my very first visit to Chicky-Pie's Café drifted in. *At least, I think it's the same place. Pretty sure it had a different name, though. That was the time I had that amazing encounter with a young woman.* "Gosh, that would have been at least twenty years ago. Where does the time go?"

As had started to happen more and more lately, I found myself whispering my thoughts out loud. People nearby probably thought I was crazy. *It helps my loneliness,* I countered. *Still, I better keep my thoughts where they belong—in my head. It's time to move on. Gotta look for a new adventure,* I reminded myself. *Besides, I don't want to be upset when April and Steve arrive.* "Ooooh!" I let out a little squeal. "I can't wait to see little Amy and Joey." *Grandchildren grow up faster than they ought.*

Moving was tough, but coming to such a small community scared me half out of my wits. Surely, the Lord had prompted it. I clung to the hope that He had some new purpose for me to fulfill here.

When John and I moved from Georgia to California, that was big, especially so soon after we married. Now, that *was exciting. This time's different. Course, anytime a Southerner moves ta California, it's an adventure. The culture shock alone is enough to make a good girl blush.*

Hmm, maybe God has a new love waitin' for me here. Guess I still look pretty good for an old lady. I do stay reasonably active. "'Course havin' some work done didn't hurt either." *Who am I kiddin'? Trying to outguess God? Who knows, maybe this quaint little town will be the inspiration for my next novel. Or, better yet, maybe I can make some friends. I sure would love to be of help to someone again. I miss feelin' needed. Life's felt so purposeless since John passed. An' movin' here by myself—oh, what was I thinkin'? Maybe I'm the one who needs help.*

Thud! A busboy plunked my iced tea down a little too vigorously. *You'd think he was tryin' to wake the dead!*

"Thank you," I startled. "Nothin' like a tall glass of ahhs tea ta quench your thirst." Before he could rush back to the kitchen, I continued, "Umm. I noticed your patio is closed. Hope ya'll don't mind me puttin' my little dog out there while I eat?" He pivoted back my way.

"Sure. Don't see why not." Then, swiveling on one heel, he tried to dash away again.

I called out, "Oh, could ya bring me some sweetener? And a lemon slice, too?" He briskly nodded and went to the kitchen. I craved real Southern-style sweet tea, but it was hard to come by in the past thirty-plus years. Hadn't had any since I married and left Atlanta. "Probably a good thing. Real sugar woulda just turn me diabetic," I muttered to myself.

As I sipped my newly sweetened tea, I was instantly transported back to my childhood. My mother would put a whole cup of sugar in the pitcher, then pour fresh hot tea over it, stirring to let the sweetness blend into a smooth melody of thirst-quenching heaven. The mental picture was so rich I could almost taste its unique sweetness.

I've always craved sweet things, not just tea and food. No, I crave all things lovely in life. *And why not?* I almost said out loud. *Why not go for what is good, pure, and sweet in everything?* Taking another swig of tea, a long sigh slid out at the pleasure of its cool refreshment. *Got ta be at least ninety-five degrees today.*

Glancing around the room, I noted the mix of folks in the café and wondered how many of them were lonely like me. How many of them also craved sweetness in their life? Sweet moments, sweet love, sweet peace, and sweet salvation. I figured that most everyone wanted those things at one point in their life. But, like me, there were probably lots of things that got in the way. *Life's got a way of slippin' in moments of disappointment and bitterness no matta how hard we try to steer clear a them.* But, after all these years, I've finally learned that some of my most cherished times came when using the talents and gifts God gave me. Just like sweet tea, I deduced, we sometimes need to stir up the gift within us so we can be infused with true sweetness.

"I can't believe John and I were married nearly forty years," I declared out loud to no one. A long, happy marriage and well-established friendships sure didn't make it easy to step away from it all. But it wasn't an impetuous move. It was a needed and thoughtful one. After he died, nothing seemed to matter anymore. My paintings sat along the walls of my studio un-hung and mostly unfinished. My students begged me to start art classes again, but I couldn't muster up the want to, to want to.

Besides, the large house and yard we'd owned for over twenty-five years needed far more care than I could give. My son and grandsons helped when they could, but they were all busy with their lives. I knew it wouldn't be long before the house would get run down and hard to sell. It was time to downsize. *Oh John, how I miss you.* I was the lucky one. John was loving, kind, full of faith and wisdom—and a fantastic handyman to boot! A tear trickled down my cheek. *Oh, there I go again. I gotta stop blubbering like a baby.* Thankfully, my thoughts and tears were interrupted as the waitress approached.

"Here you go." She set a hot plate of plump fried chicken with all the fixins' in front of my wide eyes.

"Thank you. That was fast!" This time, I noted her name —Elise.

"You're very welcome. Enjoy!" With a bright smile, she continued, "Is that your cute little dog out on the patio?"

"Yes, her name is Chiquita. Hope it's okay."

"Of course. I'll bring her a dish of water." She darted off.

"You're so kind. Thank you," I called after her.

Eyes closed, I bent over my plate and whispered a prayer of thanksgiving for my safe arrival. "Lord, please show me why you brought me here."

The scent wafting from my plate was divine. Diving in, I took a bite of the crispy chicken, savoring its perfect balance of crunchiness, juiciness, and flavor. *Mmm...just like Mom's home cookin'.*

"Everything good?" Elise caught me with my mouth full, my

hands holding a drumstick, poised for another bite. *Of course, she asked when my mouth was full. Must be part of their training.* So, I gave her a silent thumbs-up and mumbled, "Mm-hm."

As I continued eating, memories of that first visit to Chicky-Pie's entered my mind more clearly. John and I had found the town by mistake. My mind wandered down memory lane as I gobbled three pieces of chicken, most of the potatoes, and vegetables in record time. Waving my napkin 'cross my mouth, I sighed again. "Boy, that was good." Embarrassed by my audible exclamations, I glanced around, wondering if anyone had heard me. If they did, it wasn't obvious. Then, as if she'd been spying on me, the waitress showed up right by my side.

"Did you enjoy your meal?" Elise asked.

"Yes. Delicious!" That was a close call. *She almost caught me licking my fingers!* Seeing I finally had her attention, I started waxing on about memories.

"You know, I remember the first time I came ta Chicky-Pie's. Being an artist and very visual, I can still picture it today, even though it had to be nearly twenty-five years ago. My husband and I were on our way down ta San Diego for our anniversary. It was late, and we were both famished. We'd gotten off the 5 freeway in hopes of finding a restaurant." I continued, "We took a couple a wrong turns and got lost. 'Course we didn't have a GPS back then." I grinned.

"A fork in the road forced us to make a quick decision, and a wrong turn led us into Riverview. Ya know, there were only two restaurants in the whole town back then. I decided this one looked the best, so that's where we went!"

"Heh!" Elise chuckled. "How about some pie now?"

"I really shouldn't. But, uh… what kind do you have?"

"Today we have apple, peach, and lemon meringue. Peach is Mama Mell's specialty, but I like the lemon meringue too."

"Oh my, those all sound wonderful. Can ya give me a minute ta think while my stomach settles?" I asked, hand on my tummy.

"Sure," Elise said before bouncing away. As she did, an old

song filled the air; its upbeat, cheerful tune brought the past flashing forward. Ironically, the song was "Apple, Peaches, Pumpkin Pie." *Couldn't be any more apropos than that.* Then, another familiar song began. It was louder than the canned music and had a few of us patrons bouncing. We all joined in for the chorus, "Sweet Caroline, bah, bah, bah, Good times never seemed so good…" Warmth enveloped me. It had been one of our favorite songs. The part about *hands, touching hands,* always made me think of John's gentle touch. Oh! How I loved holding his hand.

Must be a sign, I told myself with a smile and nod as I spotted the jukebox at the other end of the dining room. *Wonder how I missed that? Guess someone must have dropped some coins in.*

"So? What will it be? Peach or lemon meringue?" Pulling me from my reverie, Elise walked up a few minutes later.

"Lemon meringue, please. It's my favorite. But I'll be sure to try the peach sometime. I plan on comin' in here a lot. I'm movin' in today," I told her, hoping she'd stay and chat a little longer.

"Really? That's wonderful. Where are you from?"

"Well," I began, "originally, I'm from the South. But that was a long time ago. We lived in Atlanta for the first few years of our marriage, then moved to California after my husband got a job at a big construction company. We lived in Northern California for about ten years before moving to Ventura." Then, realizing I was giving way too much information to a stranger, I felt my cheeks blush and stopped short. *She's just being nice, prolly doesn't really care to hear all this history.*

"Well, that explains the accent." She smiled.

"Oh, guess you might say I've been cross-pollinated!"

"I've always loved a Southern accent. It's so warm and friendly. Do you ever go back to Atlanta?" Elise asked cheerfully.

"Oh, no. I haven't been to the South in a long while."

"That's too bad. Well, let me go get your pie. Want some coffee, too?"

"No thanks, I'll stick with ahhs tea. Too hot for coffee today."

Remembering little Chiquita out on the patio, I pulled some chicken off my leftover drumstick, wrapped it in my napkin, and took it out to her. The patio gate squeaked open onto the small terrace. Lush greenery in big round pots made the space more inviting. Upon seeing me, Chiquita's tail wagged with such excitement it ricocheted through her whole body.

"Sit." I pointed in command. Chiquita's excited little bottom went down to the ground for two seconds, then sprang back up. I placed the chicken in front of her, to my furry friend's delight. "Okay, sweetie. Here ya go." I couldn't help spoiling her. Bending down, I gave her a loving pat on the head, noticing the ceramic bowl of water within perfect reach of Chiquita's leash.

Back inside, Elise arrived on the same plate with two generous pieces of pie—lemon meringue and peach. "Thought you might want a slice of each to try them out. No extra charge," she said, topping off my iced tea.

My eyes widened with glee. "Who did you say makes these pies? Mama Mia?"

"Ha! No, it's Mama Mell. She owns Chicky-Pie's. You probably met her when you came in."

"Oh yes! She seemed vaguely familiar. I might have met her when we stopped in here that first time. If it was the same gal, we had an amazing conversation that began through God's leading. But I dunno, that was a long time ago."

"So, you must have visited when Mell's grandmother still ran the place. It was called Millie's Diner back then. Mell was waitressing at the time, but she took over when Mama Millie passed away."

"Hmm, Mell doesn't ring a bell. Seems like the gal's name started with a T. Oh! Do you serve breakfast here?" I asked, changing the subject.

"Yes, we do." Bending down, she half-whispered, "But, honestly, the breakfast at the Good News Café across the street is the best around. Just don't tell Mama Mell I said that." She winked. "They have a collection of books and magazines for customers to read while eating. Most of it is faith-based stuff, which might be up your alley."

"Oh, really? Sounds good ta me. Ya know, I'm an author myself. I'm always looking for inspiration and good readin'."

"An author *and* an artist? Wow! What books have you written? Anything I might have heard of?"

"Oh, a couple of inspirational books, a children's book, and a novel." I beamed at the opportunity to share my work with someone who seemed genuinely interested. Elise made me feel welcome, which was sayin' a lot bein' new to the area and all. I was about to continue when I saw my moving truck pass by the front window. "Oh, sorry. Have ta go. I think that's my moving van goin' by, and I need to meet them at my house. But I'll be back again soon for sure. Can you bring me my check?"

"Of course. It was a pleasure meeting you." Reaching into her apron pocket, Elise pulled out the bill. "I look forward to seeing you again. Bring me one of your books next time you come in; I'd love to read it."

I left enough cash for the bill and a generous tip, then ran out to the patio to get Chiquita. Just as I got to the outer gate, Elise came running up with a small take-out box in hand.

"You didn't finish your pie, so I boxed it up for you."

"Oh, that's so sweet of you. It will be perfect as a late-night snack after some unpacking. See you again soon." I added, "God willing, and the creek don't rise!"

Walking down the front stoop with Chiquita in tow, Mell poked her head out and waved a friendly goodbye. "Thanks for coming. Come again soon."

Waving back, I took a closer look and wondered, *had* we met before? Seems like the gal I remember was named Tamara or something like that.

THIRTEEN

s I said afore, things keep on a changin'. Now, it seems like folks jes keep their heads down in a mobile phone. Seems they don't even like talkin' to they's own chillin much. Everbody who talkin' is talkin' to someone that I cain't see. They's talkin' to that device in their hand.

But I could see some hope when Lily get heah. I could see she an Miss Elise gone be friends. They start talkin' 'bout what's goin' on in both they's life. An when Elise send home some of Mama Mell's pie, well I knowed that gone seal the deal fer sure. She an Miss Elise are sure ta become good friends.

One a my favorite verses in the Bible say somethin' like this: "So I have come ... to bring them ... into a land flowin' with milk and honey." That's in Exodus 3:8 an' it sound a lot like this place.

🐝

Lily

Turnin' my car onto the winding road, I passed a sign: *Entering Nectar Valley.* I rounded another curve and gasped in awe. Flower fields were displayin' a flourish of breathtakin' color across the foothills. I reveled in the community's well-appointed nomenclature. Another sign up ahead read: *Gateway Vistas,* so I turned into the condo complex. Two blocks farther and in full view of a small lake, the voice of the GPS lady announced, "You have arrived at your destination. 77 Wildflower Way is up ahead on your right." Smiling at the thought, I wondered if it was still okay to call the GPS voice a *"lady."* Or had someone assigned a different gender to it now?

Slowin' to a stop in front of the end unit, I gazed upon my new home. White stucco contrasted with aqua shutters. The small, charming porch reminded me of the southern houses of my childhood. That welcoming feature had sold me on the condo. Driftin' back to those days, I remembered how people used to sit on their porches, visiting with neighbors as they passed by. I went to turn off the engine when a familiar and all too apropos song came on the radio—"One is the Loneliest Number." I only listened for a minute. That's all I could take.

"I wonder how friendly my new neighbors'll be?" I asked myself out loud. *I'm suh glad I could find a complex that isn't just for seniors. Being around young people stimulates my energy and makes me feel youthful.* Grabbing my house key and lifting Chiquita out of the back seat, we walked towards the front door together— new opportunities awaiting us.

Entering, I stood silent for a moment, drinkin' in my new home. *The front room is cheerful and bright. And the high ceiling makes the space feel larger.* Imaginin' the design elements and décor, I could add roused excitement within me. "Large enough to invite a few guests but small enough to feel cozy when I'm alone," I encouraged myself.

"Alone," I quietly repeated. "That's gonna' take some gettin' used to. Why's it still so hard even after three years by myself?" *Oh, dear!* I thought. "I better stop talking to myself so much, or they'll be puttin' me in a different kind a home." I laughed at the realization I'd just done it again.

I glanced out the front window at the sound of a car turning into my driveway. "Oh, good! April and Steve are here." The pile of furniture in the bed of Steve's pick-up included some of my favorite pieces—I couldn't let them go just yet. Then, to my delight, my grandkids, Amy and Joey, jumped out of the double cab and ran towards my front door. I dashed out to greet them with warm hugs and tears of joy. *Grandchildren are God's gift for not killing your children.*

Before I could even figure out where to start, chaos erupted; it was a circus! The grandkids raced through the house, examining every nook and cranny, tumblin' around like trapeze artists performing on the floor. Amy and Joey started unpacking boxes while Steve and April rearranged furniture the movers had haphazardly set down. Scott and his wife, Lisa, arrived shortly after, and she found her way to the kitchen with a casserole dish. April and Amy had brought freshly baked brownies and went scrounging through boxes for a knife to slice them. Even the youngest helped by keeping Chiquita busy in the yard and teaching her tricks. This old dog learned a few new tricks that day, too. The best one I learned was staying out of the way and keeping my orders to a minimum!

🐝

"BYE!" I waved as April and her family left. My son Scott and daughter-in-law Lisa tooted a goodbye as they pulled out of the driveway. After their cars were out of sight, I went into the house and slumped down at the kitchen table. With my hands proppin' up my head, I thanked God for all the help my kids had provided. It made me happy to have them here, pitching in to get me settled. I smiled, remembering Chiquita's joyful bark as she took her first romp in the backyard. Her ears perked up, and my little white Mal-ti-poo leaped and bounded across the grass like a happy little lamb frolicking. Her delight anointed our new home. *Chiquita did some actual anointing, too,* I mused.

"It's been a long day but a blessed one," I stated out loud. As if audible words of gratitude would be a supernatural eraser, wipin' away my lingering doubts. But the empty silence quickly swallowed up the cacophony of helping hands and the sweet, tinkling laughter of my grandchildren. Suddenly, it felt like a stark reality check. My tears began to flow, gushing, with no restraint.

"What have I done?" I sobbed. "Oh, Lord, please wrap your lovin' arms around me and let me sense your presence. Give me a glimpse of your purposes for me. Don't leave me alone."

Spotting the brown take-home box still on the kitchen island, I mustered up some courage and wiped my tears. Reaching over, I opened the lid slowly as if it were the most delicate item we had unpacked that day. Inside was more than just the remains of my slice of pie. A simple business card with a short, handwritten note was taped to the inside lid. *Welcome! So nice meeting you today. Hope we can get to know each other better. Elise.*

There it was in plain writin'. God's message of affirmation through a new friend. It was just what I needed.

Elise

My shift ended at four. I considered going straight home but took my time, thinking about the nice lady who'd come into Chicky-Pie's earlier. *Let's see, what was her name? Lily. That's it!* Some of her comments had me wondering about Mell. Was there more to my kind and generous boss than I thought? Or was the new customer just a mixed-up older woman?

FOURTEEN

D id ya'll eva have somethin' happen that you was sure has already happen? Guess we all has, but when my friend Elise had that frightenin' dream again, she didn't know what ta make of it. It's a good thing Mell is there ta help. So, watch an see how she cooks up an answer for her.

Elise

No matter how hard I try, I can't get that dream out of my head. Maybe I could ask Mell's advice on what I should do. I have a feeling she'd be able to give me some perspective.

Since coming to Chicky-Pie's, I observed many things about Mell. I was especially impressed by the limitless joy she exuded. While I didn't know all her secrets, she had alluded to a dark history when she gave me an introduction to how Chicky-Pie's got started. Noticing she was taking her usual afternoon break on the patio, I took the opportunity to ask, "Mama Mell, mind if I sit with you a few minutes before I go home?"

"Not at all. I always like talkin' with you, Elise. What's on your mind?" Mell had long ago learned not to pass up a chance to help someone.

"Well, I was just wondering if you've ever had any troubles that came back to haunt you?"

"You got somethin' that's come back for you, Elise?" Mell looked squarely into my eyes.

"I do," I said, casting my eyes down. "I mean, I think I do. While I know I didn't share much when I first came to Riverview, I have a feelin' you could tell I was runnin' from something."

"Ah, yes. I'll admit there were some telltale signs you were runnin' for your life. You had that look about you."

"That look?" I repeated with surprise.

"Honey, I knew the look 'cause I'd seen it in my own eyes. I'd been there before. I was a runaway too and probably had the same scent of fear on me when I sought out Mama Millie." Mell took a long drag from her cigarette but didn't seem to get much pleasure from it. Thankfully, a cool summer breeze drifted the smoke away from me.

"I suffered abuse as a child … and had been in an abusive marriage after that. When I got pregnant with my baby girl, I knew somethin' had to change. I had to escape. Otherwise, my baby girl would a suffered as I had."

I looked into Mell's eyes, pushing down the tears that threatened to escape my own. "I never would have guessed it was that bad. You always seem so put together and, well, sane." I blanched, "Oh, I'm sorry, I shouldn't have said that." Embarrassed, I slid down into my seat. "I didn't mean to imply anything about your mental stability."

Mell laughed, and we both relaxed. "Don't worry about it. With all I've been through and the crazy stuff that happens 'round here, it's probably a miracle I'm not bananas!" She patted my hand.

After taking another drag from her cigarette, Mell snuffed it out in the ashtray. "Gotta quit this nasty habit." She paused, then began, "Elise, when I came here to my Grandmama Millie's place, I was runnin' from my husband. He'd started beating me, an' it got real bad. If it hadn't been for my Grandmama Millie sendin' me an airplane ticket, I don't know what I would a done." Taking another sip of coffee, Mell continued.

"There was this one night, I was closin' up Mama Millie's place, and a customer came in to eat. She had the same soothing Southern accent my Grandmama Millie had—an' the kindest eyes too." Mell paused midair, coffee cup in hand. "She spoke to me in the most encouraging way. Before I knew it, I found myself pouring out my troubles to her—a stranger! She actually prayed out loud for me. Right there in the middle of the restaurant. Her sweet, gracious prayer struck a needy spot in my wounded soul. The memory of her words sustained me for a long time."

"That's amazing. Ya' know, that new customer, Lily, has a Southern accent. She mentioned she thought she might have met you a long time ago," I pried. "She shared a similar story with me the other day."

"Well, it was a turning point for me. No doubt about it. A moment of transformation that I can truly say was from God. A person doesn't go through the kind-a things I did without having some scars. But her prayer gave me hope an' helped me see myself in a fresh new way."

"I can imagine some of what you must have been through. Sounds like we have some similar history."

Mell glanced at her watch; twenty minutes of her break time left. "I have a feelin' it's time you knew my whole story. Why don't we chat more inside?" She motioned for me to follow.

🐝

MELL STOOD at the counter in Chicky-Pie's kitchen as I found a chair and sat. Pots and pans rattled nearby as the cooks prepared for the dinner hour. The chopping boards were thumping as vegetables were being sliced.

"It was a Monday in 1982 when I realized how desperate my situation was. I had jus' turned twenty-one. Grandmama Millie always used to say, 'Chile, I'm amazed at your energy and upbeat attitude, 'specially since you is only five-foot nothin'.'"

"Ha! Still am!" Mell laughed, and I chuckled, picturing the platform stilettos she wore to greet customers coming in—four inches, no less! I had grown to marvel at her knack for looking tall and slender despite her short stature.

Mell hesitated before continuing. "When I first came to California, it seemed like a good move. I'd fled the horrors I'd grown up with in New Jersey. My mama wasn't right in the head and was very cruel, even when I was just a tiny girl. Grandmama used to say, 'Lord knows what else happen to you when I didn't see it, chile.' She took me in, and I lived with her the remainder of my growin' years. Shortly after she moved to Riverview and started this restaurant, I met Javier. We were both hoping Javier would be the answer to my happiness. He wasn't," she said, tears brimming her eyes with sadness.

"One morning, I woke early with dark, nearly suicidal thoughts. I didn't know what to do. My cheeks were still throbbing from his beating the night before. I sat up in bed and prayed like never before." She touched her cheek as if reliving it. "I asked the Lord to help me. To protect me from Javier and help me get away from him.

"Even though he was snoring away and couldn't hurt me at the moment, it was an awakening for me. The wheels started turnin' in my mind, and I started planning my escape. Then, a wave of nausea come over me. It could'a been from the beating, but in the back of my mind, I knew I was pregnant." She paused before continuing, "The need to vomit passed, but the image of this ragged, battered woman glaring back at me in the mirror sickened me even more. My eye was black and swollen. My cheeks were bright red."

"Oh, Mell," I said, holding my cheek with empathy.

"Seeing the bruises already forming solidified my resolve to get outta there."

"What did you do next?" I asked gently.

"Quiet as I could, I tiptoed into my place of solace—the laundry room."

"The laundry room, a place of solace? Never thought of that room as a refuge before," I teased.

She ignored my comment. "With the door shut and locked, I stood on a box and reached for my most prized possession—my journal. I kept it hidden under a hat on a high shelf so Javier wouldn't find it. When I saw my journal, it felt like I was seeing an old friend again. A friend who was waiting expectantly for me to talk with her."

Mell paused, taking a sip of water. The kitchen had gotten busier, and the noise level gradually increased with the rising bustle of activity. "I sat on top of the washing machine, writing, the whirring of the machine sloshing along under me. It was therapeutic—pouring my heart onto those pages and being soothed by the thrum beneath me. Got two loads of laundry done, too." She chuckled.

"I got to thinkin' that I needed to approach life's obstacles like ingredients in a new recipe. They just needed to be mixed in the right order and cooked properly. My grandmama was such a great cook; maybe that's why she favored me a little more than her other grandchildren. She and I always bonded over good food. It was then I realized that even the best chef couldn't handle the woeful mix thrown my way. I needed some help."

"That's a wonderful ideology to have," I encouraged.

"I wrote my grandmama a letter sharing about what I was goin' through. I'm sure it was hard for her to see the abuse in writing. Even so, she saved the letter in a drawer. I found it after she passed away. I've carried that letter in my pocket ever since, as a reminder not to let someone else's evil bring me down. It's also a reminder of how God protected me."

Mell dug into her right dress pocket and pulled it out for me to read.

Dear Grandmama,

Last night, my past came to visit me again. This time, it came through Javier's hand. I'm worried he will take his anger out on me again, and I think I may be pregnant. Please pray for the Lord to show me His protection and love. Tomorrow, I will start working on a plan of escape.

Love,

Tamara Mell Jackson

"Ironically, God didn't take me away from him. Instead, He took Javier away from me. I can still hear the pounding on the door. The police busted in, slapped handcuffs on Javier, an' took him away. It was hours later before I realized that my plea to God had been answered."

"Oh, Mell." I reached out and touched her shoulder. "Thank you for sharing your story with me. I understand why you are such a compassionate person. You've been through so much. I really admire your strength and courage." I felt so blessed by Mell's transparency that I'd nearly forgotten my own trouble.

Mell sighed and grabbed a Kleenex before turning to me. "Now, Elise, tell me 'bout this problem you're havin'."

"Don't you have to get back to work?" I asked, but she brushed off my comment with a wave of her hand. Taking a deep breath, I began my tale. "Okay. So, just before I arrived in Riverview, I ran away from my abusive home because I had a terrifying nightmare. It was just a dream, but it felt so real, like a premonition or a warning. It's what prompted me to run. Well, just the other night, the dream returned. It's not exactly the same, but it's similar enough that it has me wondering. Maybe something bad is going to happen again."

"Have you told Pete about the nightmare?" Mell asked.

"Not yet." Mell raised her eyebrows a tick. I hurried, "I will. The thing is, I think God wants me to go back there. Like maybe someone—one of the kids even—could be in danger." I gave her a quick rundown of the new dream, and after a moment of silence, Mell stood.

"Speaking of nightmares, if I don't get back to work, we'll have another mess to deal with," Mell declared with finality. Grabbing a knife from its storage, she walked to a chopping table and got to work.

Guess our talk is over. Dumbfounded and hurt at her abrupt cut-off, I sat numb. Mell was chopping away at some vegetables as I approached, feeling a little miffed. "Don't you have a sous-chef for that?"

"Yeah, but with the screw-up on the produce and chicken order last week, I figured might as well do it myself."

Feeling like a bother, I turned to leave, but Mell grabbed my arm and ordered, "Stay. Please. There's more here than you think."

What's that supposed to mean? I rolled my eyes.

"Armando bought way too much chicken and vegetables last week. We tried to fix his mistake with the chicken dinner special we ran, but not nearly enough sold, so now I'm left covering his sins again." She started. I harrumphed.

She looked at me thoughtfully. "Sometimes leftovers can be the start of a tasty new recipe—a kind of redemptive solution if you will. Who knows, perhaps the leftover mistakes and sins of your adoptive parents that still haunt you could be turned into something good—repurposed." She caught my attention with that, and I looked at her quizzically.

"Pete and I have our own term for leftovers," I grinned. "We call it French food."

"French? You cook French cuisine?" Mell asked with surprise.

"No, it's French because leftovers are Déjà vu!" I smiled, and Mell caught my humor and laughed. I could feel the lightening in our spirits.

"So, what do you propose I make with all this *French food?*" Mell looked at me expectantly.

I glanced at the chicken, chopped carrots, celery, and peas, and an idea struck. "How about chicken pot pie?" I suggested. "It's always been one of my favs, and you do so well with pies. Why not add some savory options to balance out the sweet?"

"Never thought of that, but I think you may be on ta somethin'." Mell tilted her head up, contemplating. "Hmm, pie crust and a thick creamy sauce." She considered for a moment. "Yes, that could make the perfect redemptive recipe. Not to mention a delicious way to make use of all that chicken!"

Wiping her hands on her apron, Mell looked at me. "Elise, when you left that house of horrors, it was a courageous and smart thing to do. The harm they were causing you was a sin. No doubt about it. No child should have to undergo the physical, mental, and emotional abuse that you did. And no young woman should be repeatedly raped, especially by someone who is supposed to be her protector. Those actions were their sins, *not yours.* They were destroying you. While you managed to get away, you obviously still have some leftovers to deal with."

"An' I'm not talkin' about dealing with the recovery in your soul. I'm talking about those kids. From what you've told me, they've been dealt a raw deal with those folks as their parents. I believe God sent you that dream so you can redeem the good that is still there before it becomes garbage, too. Before those little ones' spirits are crushed or destroyed."

My jaw dropped. Falling back into a chair, I sat stunned at her wise words. She'd stirred together a recipe for my leftover dilemma. "Mell, you're amazing. You're right as ever. I have to find a way to go back and rescue Bea and Bobby."

"Why don't we pray together about it? You know God's good book of recipes tells us we can always go to Him for wisdom, an' somewhere in there it says, 'Taste and see that the LORD is good.' I'm pretty certain if we bring this to Him, He'll show you the way to go."

So, we bowed our heads and prayed in Chicky-Pie's kitchen —truly an anointed place.

I went home feeling better about the new trouble knocking at my door. Even with my on-an-off-again conversations with God in the past, I had a strong feeling He would guide me through this new challenge. More importantly, I knew I had friends who would be there for me—friends who understand matters like mine.

FIFTEEN

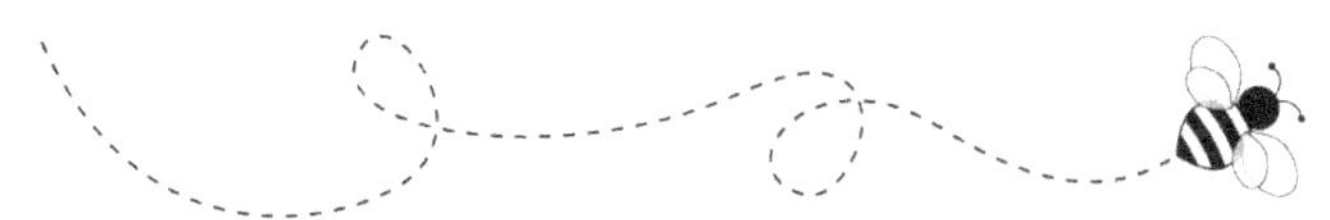

It's been five yeahs since my friend Elise come heah. She doing good now, but new trouble has her worried. An though she handle things betta than she use to, her past still weigh her down. The ugly mire of abuse and the dredge of anger, pain, and loss, still keep a wall round her heart. Ova the yeahs her husband Pete watched everythin' through the eyes of love, but she has a hard time lettin' people all the way inta her heart. She keep it guarded. Yet folks has seen the jewel of truth layin' deep within her jes waitin' to be set free. Fear was the sticky glue that held her back and guilt the weight that pushed it down where it stay.

But Elise is a good mama. She love her little girl and try to do ever-thin' to make her happy. I think she a lot like honeybees that are calt the "nurse bees." They's called that cause they has the job a takin care of all the baby bees in the hive. I think maybe 'cause her husband Pete lost his mama when he was young, Elise is like a mama to him sometime too.

Elise

"Hi, honey! I'm home," I hollered. Arms full of overstuffed grocery bags, I let the garage door slam hard behind me.

"Need any help?" Pete inquired from the den.

"Yes. Thanks. There's two more in the trunk." I set the bags down on the counter and started unpacking.

Pete slid up behind me and placed a warm, wet kiss at the nape of my neck, letting my ponytail tickle his nose. "Mmm. You smell scrumptious."

"It's probably the fried chicken clinging to me," I quipped. "Mell outdid herself today. A lot was left over, so she sent some home with me." I pulled the box from one of the bags and waved it under Pete's nose.

"You know, I think you're right! I thought sure it was the sweet aroma of your perfumed body next to mine. But maybe it *was* the chicken," he said with a sly smirk and a pat on my bum.

I gave him a playful swat on the arm, "Oh, you!"

He pulled me close despite my left hook. We kissed long and slow. His kisses still buckled my knees, and it wasn't because I was exhausted.

"Mommy, mommy!" Little Bella came running in, wrapping her arms around me at kid level.

"Hi, sweetie. Are you hungry? Mommy's got some yummy chicken for us tonight, and I'm gonna make some mashed potatoes and broccoli to go with it." I gave her a squeeze and kissed her on the cheek.

"Yay! But do I have to eat bwoccoli?" Bella asked with fluttering lashes and pursed lips.

"Well, I guess not. But you can't have any peach pie if you don't eat your vegetables," I said, lifting the box top, revealing half a pan of peach pie. Just enough for the three of us.

"Okay, I'll eat the bwoccoli." Licking her lips, Bella responded with enthusiasm.

Pete came back in, holding the other two grocery bags. "How was your day?"

"It was good. Busy but good," I answered with a tired sigh. "There's a new gal in town who seems nice. She just moved to the area. She had the cutest little dog, too. I think her name was Chiquita. The dog, that is, not the lady. Her name was Rose, no, Daisy, or some other kind of flower." Then, remembering, "Oh! I know, it was Lily. She mentioned she's an author. How was your day?"

"Oh, it was fine. We might be acquiring another hotel, and there's a good chance I'll be managing it."

"Really? Where is it?"

"Near Solana Beach. It's not far. Only about twenty minutes south. But it's not a done deal yet." He continued to help unload the groceries and put things away.

"That's good, dear. Bella, would you help Mommy set the table tonight?"

"Okay, Mommy." She pulled the silverware drawer open and counted out, "Three forks, three spoons, two knives. Can I use my Minnie Mouse mat, Mommy?"

"Sure. Don't forget the napkins too. Here." I handed her a couple of napkins before placing two dinner plates in a stack at the end of the table with Bella's small plastic plate on top.

Pete pulled a box of instant mashed potatoes from the bottom of the bag. "Where does this go?" he said with a disapproving frown.

"I'll take that," I said, plucking the package out of his hand. "There isn't enough time to make regular mashed potatoes tonight, so thought I'd try the instant kind." Pete was clearly doubtful.

Dinner was ready quickly, thanks to the ready-made chicken and instant potatoes. Pete said the blessing. "Dear Heavenly Father, we thank you for the many blessings you have given us yesterday, today, and tomorrow. Thank you for providing this delectable chicken, and please help the instant potatoes taste good. In Jesus' name. Amen."

I flashed a disapproving glare his way, but the smile on my face revealed my true feelings for Pete's humor. We all lifted a piece of chicken simultaneously and sank our teeth into its scrumptious, tender crispiness. It was unanimous—the mashed potatoes were pretty good, too.

Bella ate all the meat off a drumstick and every bite of her broccoli, knowing her reward of pie was coming. She managed to spoon a few bites of potatoes in as well. I could only eat part of a chicken thigh and some of the potatoes, mostly picking at the rest. "I had that dream again, you know?" I mentioned nonchalantly.

"That dream?"

"You know the one. The nightmare I had before we met. The one about needing to escape and everything."

"Oh yeah. Guess I forgot about that," he responded. "Can you pass the chicken and the mashed potatoes, please?"

"Well, it's just so weird that I would have it again. I mean, I haven't had it in years. I can't figure out why it would surface now. What's strange is this time, two children were involved and two wacky characters that eerily represented Jack and Jane," I explained further.

"Well, you know, honey, you always were a vivid dreamer. And dreams are just that—dreams. I hope you aren't letting it get to you as it used to." Pete put his hand gently on top of mine. "Tomorrow is Sunday, and I was thinking maybe after church, we could take a little drive somewhere if you're feeling up to it. What do you think?" Pete cleverly weaved in the idea of going to church. It had been a few months since I'd attended.

"Okay. That could be a nice change. It's supposed to be warm. What about going down to the beach?" I said, looking at Bella for her approval. Her brown eyes flashed at us with wide-eyed pleading.

"Sure. Why not? I have somewhere I want to take my girls,

but we can drop by the beach afterward," Pete said with a broad smile.

"Yea!" Bella clapped her hands in glee. "Can I fly my new kite, too?"

"That's a great idea, sweetheart. We still have more chicken here; let's pack a picnic lunch." I was catching Bella's excitement and was grateful for the distraction. The dream felt more real and tangible after talking it over with Mell. Work was so busy I could put it out of my mind while there, but at home, where things were peaceful and mostly quiet, the memory snuck back into my thoughts. I didn't want anything to spoil the joy and restfulness of our Sunday.

After dinner, we all sat in the family room and watched the latest version of *Cinderella* together. Bella fell asleep on the couch halfway through. Pete gathered her in his arms and carried her to bed. He gave her a peck on the cheek and tiptoed out. Following him, I tucked her in. "Sweet dreams," I whispered, bending down and kissing her on the forehead, a flash of Bea coming to mind as I did.

EVENING'S MOON was still rising as final remnants of the sun glowed through the sheer curtains on the window—just the right mood for hunkering down in PJs with a good book and cup of hot tea. I was nearly done reading *Redeeming Love,* one of my favorite novels. I'd read it before but found it even more engaging this time. Its plot gave me hope for my own messy life. As I lifted the book off my nightstand, thoughts of the past seemed to rise up simultaneously. Fuzzy images of my first home skipped through my head. The house I'd lived in before my mother sold me into adoption. Then, the Burrows came to mind.

Pete was flipping through channels in search of something

good to watch as I re-entered the family room. Snuggling close to him on the couch, I drew him into a conversation.

"You know, I was nine years old when Jane had Bobby. I remember being really excited about having a baby brother. But after Jane brought him home from the hospital, I saw her looking into the eyes of her new baby boy with this adoring look of love. I knew it was a look I had never received from her. A look I couldn't remember seeing before—not even from my own mother. My heart was broken. No, shattered." Tears broached my eyes as I began opening up a new part of myself to Pete. Wounds that still lay within my heart and hadn't been fully shared, even after years of marriage.

Pete drew me closer. "You are a wonderful mother. I hope you know that."

"That was when I realized my life with the Burrows was only a mirage of love. Just a picture of a family that would never develop as I had hoped." Wiping at tears and blowing my nose, I continued. "That's also about the time Jane became abusive to me."

Pulling me closer still, Pete put his arm around me, kissed me gently, and brushed stray hair from my eyes. "I wish I could go back there and help you during those terrible days. Be around to stop the abuse. To give you the love you so deserved. Remove you from such pain and heartache."

"You know," I continued, "just about the time I figured things couldn't get any worse, they did." My sorrow turned into sobs, and Pete drew me closer. I sensed the anger rising within him, his desire to fix my past. He longed to fill my wanting soul with his love. I was grateful yet reserved.

Having lost his mother when he was only fifteen, Pete often had his own hurts flair up. But unlike me, he never really talked much about his pain. He never truly opened up about his deep sorrows and regrets. Although very different from my situation, I wondered if he thought his tragic childhood pain paled next to what I'd suffered. By now, Pete knew that Jack began molesting me when I was twelve and that I had given birth to Jack's baby at fourteen.

"After they told me my baby had died, I cried for hours. Even though she was a result of rape, she was a person. She was a part of me. Someone who would have given me the love I longed for." Anger now churned within me.

I watched Pete push his anger down at this reminder of the abuse I had endured. His eyes were on fire.

"Jane had no pity," I went on. "Her pregnancy with Bea was obvious by then, and she happily rubbed it in as a 'proper pregnancy' over and over. But when Jane came home with little Bea, I was actually happy. Happy for me. Bea was so beautiful. Her chubby cheeks and bright eyes brought new life and light to my dark world." I was rambling now.

Pete interjected at this point. "Honey, I am so glad you are free from Jane's influence and abuse. I know these things take time to fully heal. But I also know that God loves you and gave you to me as a wonderful gift. He is using you to bring healing to my own spirit. Who knows, maybe someday God will use you to help other women who have gone through similar troubles."

"I don't know about that." I couldn't grasp that ever being possible. Looking into Pete's eyes, I saw a fresh, deep love radiate toward me. A stronger, more powerful love than I'd noticed before. Was it a glimpse of God's love? While I know Pete had his own deep wounds from when his mother died; he was also thankful for the gift of time he had with her. He knew he was fortunate to have both a mother and father who loved him, guiding him and giving him a good home. His father was still living, and we were blessed to see him often. Pete's love and the love his dad showed me had already brought me some healing.

"Sweetheart. Do you think I'll ever be able to see Bea again?" I asked, wiping away more tears.

"I don't know, honey. We can see about visiting her, that is, if we feel you would be safe." He encouraged my heart with hope.

We both sat silent for a few minutes. The warmth of his body against mine no doubt triggered his question. "Elise, do you think maybe it's time we tried for another baby?" he asked tentatively.

"I'm not sure. Maybe." I smiled and squeezed him tightly. "I would like to have another child, and Bella keeps telling me she wants a sister or brother. I'll think about it."

Yes, I was free from the abuse, just as Pete had said. But my heart was still enslaved by a lifetime of pain. Pete and little Bella had clearly brought me joy and more love than I had experienced before, but I couldn't shake the feeling there was a hole deep within me that would never go away. A hole that would never be filled entirely, until I at least had the chance to see Bea again. But I wondered if the hole was deeper than even she could fill.

SIXTEEN

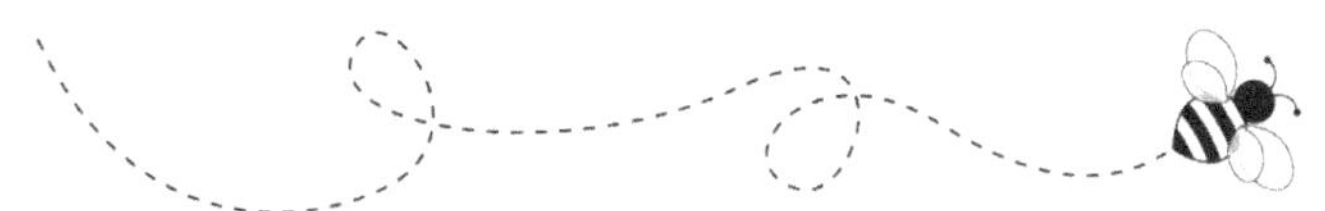

Have any a ya'll ever thought 'bout the fact that the honeybee is the only insect that produces a food eaten by people? Well I has. Maybe 'cause I like ta eat so much.

Lily

It was almost 8:30 in the morning when I awoke. It took a few seconds before I realized where I was. Chiquita stirred at the foot of my bed, whimpering and shaking her collar vigorously to signal that she needed to go outside. It had become Chiquita's service call for getting her dog-gone needs, and as her servant, I obeyed all too compliantly.

"Oh, all right. Come on, girl." I jumped out of bed.

I wrapped my bathrobe around me and jabbed my toes into my slippers. Padding down the short hallway to the back door, I held it open for Chiquita and stood soaking in the beauty of the new day. The backyard was prettier than I remembered, probably because I really hadn't had much time to look at it yet. The lush green landscaping held splashes of color, and large lacy ferns gave a tropical ambiance to its modest size, makin' it feel just right.

"I'm gonna need to hire someone to mow the lawn," *even though it's a pretty small patch of grass,* I decided. *Besides,* I told myself, *I don't own a mower anyway.*

A pergola provided shade from the afternoon's bright sun, and a solid block wall gave me privacy. In the corner, a small natural rock waterfall cascaded into a little pond. Perfectly placed near the spare room window, not far from the kitchen's dining room doors, its trickling water refreshed and soothed my spirit. "Hmm, might get a few koi fish for the pond. Can't wait to set up that extra room as my art, writing, and office space."

Chiquita did her business and trotted back inside, stopping first for an affirming pat on the head. "Are you hungry, Sweetie?" I asked as I lovingly stroked her soft white fur. "Let's go see if we can find some food for you. Guess I better get your doorbells hung so you can let me know when you need to go out."

I hadn't found the bells yet, but finally located the dog food and refreshed Chiquita's water bowl before setting both down near the kitchen door. Scrounging through a few moving boxes that still sat unpacked in the kitchen, I let out a ringing declaration of success. "Hooray! I found it," I said with a good shake of the bells.

Chiquita, uninterested in my celebration, just continued eating her breakfast. I hung the string of bells from the kitchen doorknob, promising myself I'd get something else to hang them from so they wouldn't ding the surface of the pretty French doors with every swipe of Chiquita's tiny paw.

Now, what am I going to eat? I wondered while opening the refrigerator. *Not much here. Gotta get some groceries today for sure.* The clock was still leaning against the wall. *And get that hung before too much time passes.* I smiled at my pun.

"Nearly nine o'clock. No wonder I'm hungry!" I told Chiquita.

Hopping in the car, I found my way back into town, thinking I'd take Elise's suggestion and go to the Good News Café.

I arrived in less than ten minutes, but it was Sunday, and the place was packed. Glancing at the treats inside the pastry display and breathing in the hearty aroma of coffee and sizzling bacon, I asked the seating attendant, "How long is the wait?"

"How many in your party?" the young man wanted to know.

"Just me. One," I clarified, holding up one finger and wishing they didn't have to ask. It only managed to further rub in the loneliness of being a widow.

"About forty minutes."

"Ooh! I'm pretty hungry. Think I'll go somewhere else. Thanks." And without any further consideration, I walked briskly across the street to Chicky-Pie's Café.

The tantalizing aroma of bacon and maple syrup drifted in the air as I entered, but there was definitely no crowd to wait behind. I wouldn't say it was empty, but I think I've seen more chickens gathered around a hound dog than what was here today. 'Course, I got asked the same embarrassing question again, forcing me to admit I was alone. I just held up my index finger this time.

"How about that table?" the young woman pointed to a small table near the bar.

"That'll be fine." Not my preference, but at that point, I just wanted to sit somewhere and eat. I looked over the breakfast menu and waited with hopes of seeing my new friend Elise again. About five minutes later, a different waitress came to my table.

"Hi, I'm Sally and will be helpin' you today. What can I get you this morning?"

"Two eggs over easy with sausage and white toast, please."

"Would you like some juice or coffee with that?"

"No juice, just hot tea with lemon."

"Sure thing," she replied.

A busboy placed a cup and a small carafe of hot water down

a few minutes later. I was happy he included a packet of honey, too. "I like coffee too," I tried to tell him as if he cared. "I've always felt that coffee warms your tummy, but hot tea warms your spirit."

"Jes, miss," he responded with a Hispanic accent but little interest. *Perhaps he doesn't speak English well,* I graciously defended, trying not to feel snubbed.

Might as well talk to the walls. Guess Elise isn't working the breakfast shift. Hopin' to make another friend, I attempted to start a brief conversation with Sally when she returned with my breakfast, but it was obvious the girl was too distracted with her job to talk.

"You been working here for long?" I asked, but Sally dashed away quickly. Looking closer at my plate, I noticed the bread was wheat, not white, and the eggs were scrambled, not over easy as I'd ordered. I waited several minutes, hopin' to catch her eye and get my order straightened out. After about ten minutes of waiting, I resolved to enjoy the meal as it was.

The food was sufficient, but nothin' ta write home about. *I see what Elise meant,* I thought to myself. Glancing around the room, I saw that it was still pretty empty. That seemed unusual for a breakfast joint on a Sunday morning.

Relaxin' a bit longer, I observed the handful of people around me; a family of four sat nearby—two adults and two small children. The kids were both busy on tablets, except when shoveling food into their hungry mouths. The tip-tapping of fingers on cell phones was the only sound the adults filled the void of silence with. A young man and woman about twenty-something sat on the other side of me, both of them with their eyes and heads bowed. *That's nice. Looks like they're saying grace.* But as I shifted in my seat, I realized they were also focused on their cell phones. *Doesn't anyone like to talk to each other anymore?* I wondered.

Finished with my tea, I resolved it was time to get goin.' I started to collect my purse when a man came through the door of Chicky-Pie's. Not just a man. A very handsome man with silver-white hair that flowed over salt and pepper streaks in the back. He had gorgeous blue eyes and a killer smile that I swore got bigger the instant he looked my way. Discreetly sizing him up had me feeling like a schoolgirl. Not too tall. *About five-ten,* I guessed. Fifty-something, possibly pushing sixty. *Better cool it, girl,* I admonished myself as warmth flushed my face.

Sally was back and almost poured coffee into my hot tea. "Uh-uh!" I interfered with my hand just in time.

"Sorry. Anything else today?" she asked, interrupting my delicious train of thought.

"Some more hot water for my tea, please." *Maybe I should stay a little longer after all.*

A good fifteen minutes later, Sally returned with some hot water and placed my bill on the table. "Here. No rush."

"Oh," I drew her attention, "I'm new here and was wondering if you know of a good church here in town," I prompted, hoping we'd have something in common.

"Not really," she replied with a shrug. Placing my money and tip on the tray, I pushed my chair back and started to rise when—

"There's a real good one down near the river." Turning towards the sound of the voice, my gaze fell on the handsome man.

"Oh?" was all I managed to reply. *He must have been sitting behind me the whole time. Good thing he can't hear my thoughts!*

"Sorry to barge in. I heard you ask the waitress about a church in town. My name's Dan. I go to Riverfront Mission Church, and it's been a lifesaver for me." That big smile was back on his face with an extra wide sparkle of joy this time.

Finally, a little excitement around here.

SEVENTEEN

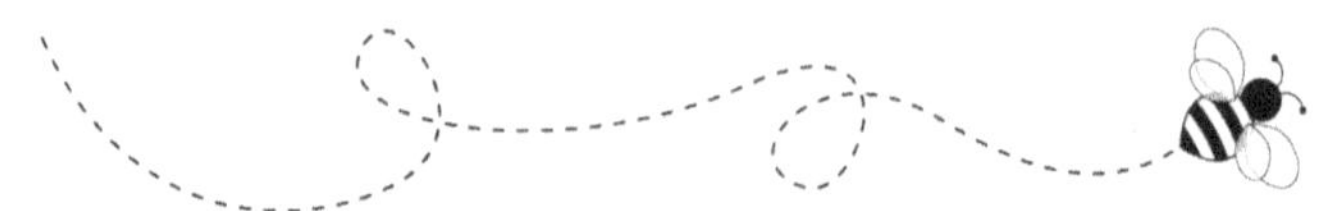

Sunday Morning, Elise

"The car's packed with all our beach stuff." Pete came up behind me softly and wrapped his arms around my waist. "How's the picnic lunch coming along?"

"Done. Just have to put the ice in the chest." I tingled in response to his touch.

"I told Dad we'd pick him up at ten. Think we'll make it?" he asked, turning me to face him.

"Shouldn't be a problem. All I need to do now is get Bella to go to the bathroom. How long of a ride is it? I mean, you haven't said where we're going yet," I nudged.

"Oh, about an hour or so," he answered in part.

"K. Not gonna tell me, huh?" I gave him a quizzical look.

"Sometimes a guy needs to have a little mystery."

We piled into the SUV and drove towards Nectar Valley, where my father-in-law's house was. I was glad Pete's father lived only a short distance away. I knew having him close by gave Pete a sense of security, and admittedly, it made me feel more secure, too.

It was a beautiful day. The temperature was mild, and the

sun shone on the tops of a handful of fluffy white clouds. The stop at Larry's house was quick. He was waiting in his porch rocker as we drove up.

Sliding into the backseat, Bella giggled, "Hi, Papa Lawee!"

"Hello, sweetie. How's my girl?" Larry gave her a kiss on the cheek.

"We're going to have lots of fun today, Papa. We're going on a ride and then we're going to the beach and have a picnic. Do you like picnics, Papa Lawee?"

"Sure do. I even brought some homemade cookies to share with everyone."

"Yay!" Bella said, clapping her hands. "Can we have some cookies now?"

"Now, Bella, you know the rule. We don't have sweets till after our meal. Plus, you know Daddy doesn't like you eating in his car," I reminded my little munchkin.

After about thirty-five minutes of driving, Bella started squirming in her car seat before announcing, "Mommy, I need to go potty."

"Already? I thought you went before we left the house."

"Yes, Mommy, I did, but I have to go big potty now," Bella said with urgency.

"Okay, honey," Pete assured her. "We're almost there anyway. I'll find a place where we can stop."

He exited the freeway and turned onto a small road that appeared to be in the middle of nowhere. There wasn't a gas station in sight. Pointing to the right side of the road, I told Pete to turn at the next intersection. "There's a large park over there. I'm sure they'll have a restroom we can use."

Pete nodded and turned right at the stop light. A sign at the park entrance read *Encinitas Community Park*. "Honey, isn't this the town you were telling me about? The one where the new hotel is that you might be working at next?" I was pleasantly surprised.

"Yep. Sure is. Guess you're on to me now. Thought you guys

might want to see where I'll be working in the foreseeable future. It's a really nice little town, and I thought Bella would especially like the park."

The car had barely stopped before Bella and I jumped out. As we walked towards a community building, a small pond with ducks bobbing up and down greeted us. The path took us past a large white gazebo with a gorgeous array of flowers in bright fuchsia, deep purple, and turquoise. As we circled around the gazebo to the community building, loud cheering indicated a ball game was in progress. The bleachers were full to the max—proud parents, no doubt. I heard the crack of a baseball bat making contact with the ball, and a mental snapshot of Bobby in his uniform slammed into my mind.

By the time I spotted the restroom, Bella was wiggling desperately. Taking hold of her hand, we rushed. I glanced behind us, and Pete pointed to indicate he and Larry were going to watch the game while they waited.

My cell phone lit up as we exited the restroom. It was Ruben.

"Ruben, mi amigo. Como estas?"

"Bien, bien. How are you, my friend?" he replied.

"Good. I've been meaning to call you. It's been a while."

"Thought you want to know I been playing baseball with Bobby ever since you gone."

"Oh, that's wonderful. Thank you. That means a lot to me. Funny timing. I was just thinking about Bobby. We're at a park, and there's a ball game going on."

"Jes, he's got real talent, but Jack, he never have time to help him. But it okay. I like to help."

"Are the kids all right?" I asked, not sure I wanted to know.

"Most of the time, they seem okay. But sometimes it seems maybe things are not good. I not sure, but the new nanny, she say she worried." Ruben sounded concerned.

"Does she say what she's worried about?" Chills ran down my spine in alarm.

"Sometimes Bea seem very sad and Lidia, the nanny, say

she's very shy around Bobby. She also say Bea has been angry a lot and doesn't want to play with Bobby anymore."

I considered Ruben's words, then responded, "Well, they are getting older so might not have as much in common."

"Jes, well, the other day she say she saw bruises on Bea and Bobby that worry her." My heart tightened in my chest as Ruben went on. "But may be nothing. All kids hurt they selves when they play. And Bobby plays so much baseball, he always hurting his self. You shouldn't worry. You have a happy life now and a little girl."

As he fell silent, my heart thundered in my ears, my dream replaying in my mind. "You know, Ruben, I'm really glad you called. Continue to keep an eye on them for me, will you?"

"Jes, I will."

AFTER WE LEFT the park and drove past the hotel property, we spent the remainder of the day at the beach sipping smoothies from our favorite spot, Beach City Smoothies. Bella fell asleep on the way home. I mostly sat silently contemplating all I'd learned from Ruben. Worry crashed in, clouding out much of the beauty of the day. Something was brewing.

EIGHTEEN

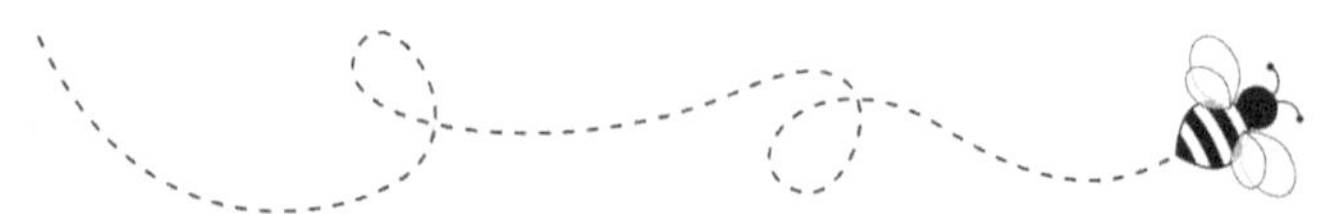

Lily

Gathering a few of my books and flyers, I set off towards
the Good News Café, hoping to get a table this time and
maybe secure a book signing, too. Glancing at my watch, I noted
— *three p.m. Should be a perfect time to talk to management.*

Standing at the pastry counter, I scanned its tempting
contents while waiting. A young man approached and, as usual,
asked how many were in my party.

"One. I'd like to sit over here and just have a pastry and
coffee if that's okay."

"Sure. Sit anywhere you'd like. You can order at the counter
when you're ready."

"Oh," I added, "I'd also like to speak to the manager if
possible."

"I'll see if she's available," he responded with a smile.

Choosing a small table, I placed my purse in the extra chair.
There wasn't anyone at the pastry counter, so I sat waiting for a
server to arrive, drooling. *Those muffins look really good, especially
the blueberry and the almond pastry. Think I'll get that.* I'd almost

made up my mind when a familiar person entered out of the corner of my eye. It took a few seconds to recognize the young woman dressed in blue jeans and a pink sweater. Trying not to be obvious, I looked closer, then she turned towards me, and we both lit up with smiles of mutual recognition.

"Hi!" we both said at the same time and then laughed.

"Lily, isn't it?" Elise asked, her hand outstretched.

"Yes. And you're Elise. Right?" I responded in kind with a handshake. "Would you like to join me?"

"I'd love to. Sure you don't mind? Looks like you're saving a place for someone." Elise cast her gaze downward apologetically, her friendly, outgoing nature disappearing with a shyness I hadn't seen when we'd first met.

"It would be a blessing for this lonely old lady. And no, I wasn't saving a place for anyone. Please sit," I pleaded, removing my purse from the other chair.

"Okay." Elise sat across from me.

As she sat down, I thought I detected a slight somberness. *She seemed so chipper that day she waited on me at Chicky-Pie's.*

"I'm so glad to see you again. Are you getting settled in yet?" Elise began some chitchat, revealing she had truly listened to me that day we met.

"Aah am glad to see you too. Ah'm settling in pretty good, but it's gonna be a darn big adjustment no matter what. Movin' always is, but this time it's without a husband to help and support," I replied with a reciprocal question. "Are you married, Elise?"

"Yes, I am. I have a wonderful husband, Pete, and a beautiful little girl. Her name is Bella." A gleam came to her eyes. "She's three, going on ten."

"Ha!" I chuckled. "Aah know what you mean. My daughter was the same at that age. In fact, she's always been 'bout seven years ahead of herself. How long have ya'll lived in Riverview?"

"I've been here five years now. It's a beautiful town, small but nice. The people here are so friendly. If it hadn't been for a certain ticket man at the train station, I wouldn't have come here at all. I was supposed to go to Flagstaff. I don't know what I would've done if I hadn't met Mell when I arrived," Elise revealed.

"Oh, that sounds like quite a story hidin' inside." My eyes twinkled before catching myself. "Forgive me, can't help the writer in me. I jus' can't turn away from a good story." I apologized.

"It's okay. Guess it *is* quite a story. Maybe I'll put it in writing someday," Elise admitted.

"Well, if ya ever feel like sharing it with me, I'd love to hear it. How long have you worked at Chicky-Pie's?" I asked, changing the subject.

"Mell gave me a job the day after I arrived. She also put me up at the Colony the first year."

"That's amazin'. And you didn't know her before you came to Riverview?" I wondered.

"No. But she has been a godsend from the beginning. When I got here, I had no experience in restaurant work. Hadn't ever held any kind of real job. That is unless you count the years of slavery before that," Elise mumbled at the end.

"Hmm, I don't want to pry, but I did notice you seem a little sad today. Is everything okay?"

"Yeah." She shrugged. "I guess so. It's just…" Elise paused for a moment, seeming to decide if she wanted to share more. "It's just that I got some news yesterday that has me very concerned, and I'm not fully certain what I'm going to do about it. Or if I *should* do something about it."

"Sounds pretty serious." I leaned in, noting tears filling Elise's eyes. "I have lots of time on my hands. If you feel like talking, I'm a good listener, and you can count on me to keep it to myself." Reaching across the table and gently patting the top of Elise's hand, I said, "How about we get some coffee and muffins? Food always helps me cheer up a bit."

"Yeah. Where is Linda anyway?" Elise replied, indicating she knew the waitress on staff.

Just as she said it, a young lady came over and greeted us. "Hi, Elise. Good to see you. Getting tired of the food across the street?"

"Ha! Not yet. Guess that's a curse and a blessing." Elise chuckled.

"Can I get you ladies something?"

"Yes," I responded first. "I'd like a cup of coffee with cream and a blueberry muffin."

"I'll have the same," Elise added.

"This seems like a good breakfast place. I came here the morning after I met you, but the wait was too long, so I went back to Chicky-Pie's. I was hopin' you'd be there. You were so nice ta me that first day I arrived, and I loved the note you put in the pie box. Not to mention the scrumptious pie I got to take home," I said with a smile.

"Oh, I'm usually off on Sundays. I'm glad you saw my note. It felt like we had made a connection that day."

"Yes. And speaking of good food. The pie over there is the absolute best," I winked conspiratorially.

"It most definitely is! Unfortunately for me, I have to fight the temptation of Mell's pies every day I work, and it's starting to show around my waist," Elise said with a hand on her belly. "I can't tell you how often I've told myself to forego the pie and then caved to their seductive sweetness." She let out a chuckle and smiled.

"Well, I don't blame you one bit. It would be hard for me to resist them, too." Linda approached with two cups of steaming hot coffee. The aroma was intoxicating. "Mm-m-m. This coffee smells so good. I could probably get my caffeine high just inhaling it," I said, adding a packet of sweetener. Elise smiled and tilted her cup for a sip. Her countenance seemed to lift as she did so.

A few minutes later, Linda returned with our muffins and some butter and honey on the side.

"Thank you, Linda," I said before turning to Elise and asking, "Do you mind if I say a little prayer over the food?"

"No, that would be very nice. Thank you," she responded.

We both bowed our heads, and I asked the Lord to bless the food, then added, "And Lord, I don't know what's troubling Elise today, but I know that you do. Please comfort and guide her in all things and reveal your precious love for her. In Jesus' name, I ask. Amen."

Elise looked up at me, her eyes clear with yearning. "Thank you so much. I needed that."

"Of course," I said. "If you want, maybe we could meet up for coffee again soon. Here's my cell number. Give me a call when you can."

"I'd like that very much." Then, noticing the books I had brought, she asked, "Are those books you wrote?"

"Yes. I almost forgot I had them. Actually, I came here to ask if I could do a book signing. Do you know the manager here?" I asked hopefully.

"Yes, I do. Her name is Wanda. She's lovely. Let me see if I can get her over here." She waved Linda over to our table.

"Yes, can I get you something else, Elise?" Linda asked.

"Would you see if Wanda can come over for a minute? My friend wants to meet her," Elise asked.

"Sure. I think she's working in the back."

I took a big bite of my muffin, and melted. "O-o-h, this is delicious! Guess ahm gonna have two places of seduction in this town. Better not meet a handsome single man, too, or I'm in deep trouble!" I snickered.

"Lily, you make me laugh," Elise said joyfully.

Wanda came over to our table a few minutes later. We chatted about a possible book signing, and the deal was made. Elise and I chatted for another hour, mostly sharing girl talk and exchanging contact information before leaving.

"Okay," I said with a wave. "Talk to you soon."

I left the café feeling lighter and sensing God's blessing in this unusual friendship that was forming, given our age difference—me at sixty and Elise, I guessed to be in her mid-twenties. I could sense that God was placing Elise in my path for a reason.

NINETEEN

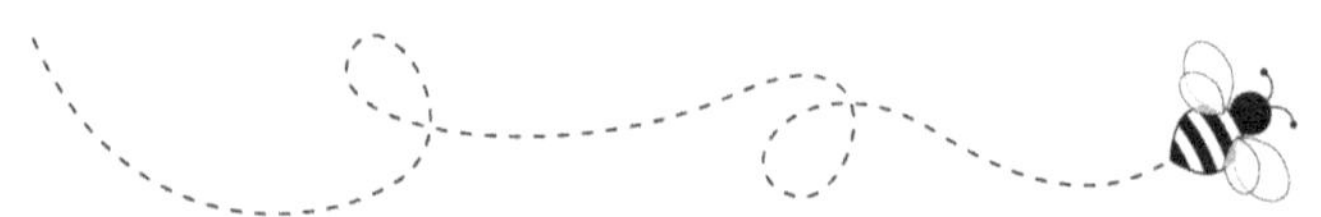

My friend Lily came heah lookin' ta see what new things God had in store for her. Afta her husband die, she was lonely, but she mostly jes feel like there mus be something new, some fresh purpose she sposed to do in her life. She weren't getting no younger either. But she realize she haveta fine folks who cen hep her with things her husband use a do. One a those things were taxes. Miss Lily has lots a talent, but doin' things like that don't come easy fer her.

I read one time that in ancient days, folks in places like Egypt some-time use honey ta pay their taxes with. Sounds like a sweet deal ta me. Miss Lily gone fine sweet honey too jes because of needin' hep with things.

Elise

"Hi, Lily!" I waved as I saw her enter the café. "You can sit here if you want." I pointed to the empty table I was standing by.

Lily's face lit up, and she waved back. It was approaching eight fifteen, and business was slowing for the evening.

Although that seemed like a good thing, Lily looked needy for more than just a snack.

"Oh, good, a booth. Just what ah need tonight." Lily plunked down.

"How've you been?" I asked. "I haven't seen you in weeks."

"Oh, yes. Everything's good, but sometimes it's just nice to have someone to talk to. I'm so glad you're working tonight." Lily grabbed the menu and pretended to look at the selections. "What pies do you have tonight?"

"Peach, apple, and a little chocolate cream pie left," I reported. "My shift is over in about fifteen minutes. If you want, I could join you after I check out."

"I'd love that," Lily brightened.

"Want some coffee?"

"No, think I'd better have some hot tea this late. Got any herbal?" Lily asked.

"Sure. I'll bring you a selection. Do you know what pie you want?"

"Well, that chocolate cream pie sounds awfully tempting. Is it as good as Mell's fruit pies?" Lily asked.

"Maybe better. It's not too sweet and isn't piled so high with whipped cream like most restaurants do."

"Sold. I'll have the chocolate cream pie. Oh, and could yuh bring me a little honey for my tea too?"

"Comin' right up." I dashed off to the kitchen.

Pulling the chocolate cream pie out of the cooler, I saw enough left for two pieces. My mouth began to water at the thought of bringing that last piece home or eating it now.

Indecisive, I held the knife in the air, hovering over the pie with suspension as Mell silently snuck up behind me and shrieked, "WELL, ARE YOU GONNA SLICE THE PIE OR KILL IT?"

"A-A-h-h-!" I screamed. The knife flew out of my hand, sailing past Mell's head and landing point down into the linoleum floor. "Oh, uh, sorry, just trying to make up my mind,"

I mumbled. "I mean, I, uh, was trying to decide if it's big enough for two slices or one big one."

Mell glanced at the pie, over to Lily, then back to me. "Why not just give her the whole thing? We'll be closing soon anyway."

"K," I said in relief before scooping the remaining slice onto a plate.

"Here you go." I returned to Lily's table with a miniature kettle of hot water, an assortment of teas, and the extra-large slice of chocolate cream pie.

Her eyes widened. "Oh boy, does that look good!" Then, peeking at the teas, she chose the chamomile.

"I'm so glad you picked the chocolate pie 'cause if someone didn't take this last piece, I'd bring it home. I'm trying really hard not to give in to temptation," I confessed while turning my head away from the luscious sight. "I'll be back in a few minutes. I have to close out my checks for the evening; then, I can relax and join you. Do you mind paying your bill now so I can take care of it?"

"Not at all. I definitely won't be needing anything else to eat," Lily assured, handing me some cash. "Just keep the change for your tip."

"Oh, thanks. I'll be back in a few." I darted back to the kitchen. Closing out for the evening, I removed my apron, threw it over my shoulder, and then carried my own prefilled mug to Lily's table. She was diving into the chocolate pie and barely coming up for air.

"You done for the night?" Lily asked between swallows.

"Yes, all set." Then, looking up, I noticed Mell coming towards us. "Mell, have you met my friend Lily yet?" I asked.

"Sure have, but it's good to see you again," Mell said warmly.

"Hello, Mell. It's good to see you too. Has business picked up any since we last spoke?" Lily asked.

"As a matter of fact, it has, but who knows how long it'll last?

I could use a little slowing down around here to get my taxes ready in time for the deadline."

"Oh! Speaking of taxes. Do either of you know someone honest and helps old ladies like me with their income taxes?" Lily asked.

"Sure do," I said. "It just so happens my father-in-law is an accountant. He's mostly retired but volunteers at the senior center, helping folks with their taxes every spring. I'll text you his number. His name is Larry Freeman."

"Oh, thank you! I still have trouble getting that stuff done since John died. Numbers and finance aren't my giftings," she said with a chuckle. "I stick more to words and paint."

"Well, I have to get over to the Colony. Heard there's a new girl in town who may need a place to stay. Good seeing you again, Lily." Mell excused herself and left.

"She seems real sweet, and I love her style," Lily commented as Mell walked off.

"Yes, Mell does know how to dress, and she's a great gal, too. I am so blessed to have her as my friend, not just employer," I agreed. "There's no doubt she has a loving and caring spirit." Taking another sip of my coffee, I finally felt ready to open up a bit more. "Mell has helped me in so many ways besides giving me this job. When I arrived in Riverview, I only had a couple-a hundred dollars to my name and nowhere to go. She runs the Colony as well as Chicky-Pie's and sets aside a few rooms for troubled young women. It's a godsend. Unfortunately, there are a lot of women caught up in drugs, human trafficking, and domestic abuse around here, being so close to the border an all. Guess I lucked out."

Lily gave me a puzzled look filled with concern. "Elise, when we met at the Good News Café a few weeks back, you hinted something was troubling you. Do you feel up to sharing? I'd love to help if I can," she asked with tenderness.

"Guess it's as good a time as ever." I sighed, took another sip of coffee, and began, "I have some serious decisions to make, and talking it through might help me figure it out."

"I'm all ears, honey. Let it spill." Lily leaned in with intense interest.

"When I was about six years old, my mother sold me to some men at the border of Mexico and Texas. I was then adopted by a couple. At first, my new parents were nice. I tried hard to please them, but after they had kids of their own, everything changed." Looking down at the table, I mustered my courage to continue. The look on Lily's face reflected she understood where this was going. "The abuse got worse over the years, and I honestly felt like more of a servant than a real daughter. In a sense, I guess you could say I became one of the 45 million who are trafficked and enslaved. I came to Riverview to escape them both."

"Oh, Elise," Lily's eyes gleamed with empathy. "I had no idea."

Pausing for another sip of coffee, I continued. "When I was eighteen, God—I think it was God—warned me through a dream. I was terrified of what the Barrows, my adoptive parents, would do to me. So, running for my life, I managed to escape. Took a train and landed in Riverview."

The café fell silent as I paused again. "When I arrived, I didn't have a plan outside of getting away from that awful house. I was like a scared little mouse wandering around town until I met Mell. She was so kind and not only gave me a room at the Colony, but she gave me a job—my first *real* job."

"Wow." Lily gazed at me with understanding eyes. "I don't quite know what to say." We sat in companionable silence for a few minutes before she continued. "You mentioned you have a decision you need to make now?"

"Yes. I had another dream. Similar in many ways to the first one that prompted my escape." I paused, considering how much to reveal. "I feel like God's giving me another message, one I must obey. But if I do what I think I need to do, it means putting myself back in danger."

"Have you prayed about it, Elise? Asked God what you're supposed to do?" Lily asked.

"Actually, no, but I'm pretty sure what it is." I didn't tell her that prayer wasn't something I did very often.

"Why don't we pray about it right now?" Lily suggested.

"Okay." I shrugged. "Why not?" I said, bowing my head.

"Oh Lord, thank you for loving Elise. And thank you for being her protector," Lily prayed. "Please give her your clear leading to go forward with your plans. Help her to know your will in this and give me an understanding of how I can help."

In my mind, I joined the prayer, but my heart was only half there. I let out a deep sigh and thanked Lily.

"Elise, you may not realize it, but I've been feeling pretty uncertain about my own direction lately. This move to Riverview, all by myself, was out of character for me. But I'm beginning to sense that God brought me here for a reason—and somehow, I think you're a part of that reason." Lily added, "I'd love to hear more of your story sometime. It sounds intriguing."

"You know, I really enjoy talking with you. Don't know how you do it, but you bring things out in me like no one ever has."

"Talking out our troubles is like letting the lid off a bottle of soda. It fizzes and bubbles out for a while, whets our thirst, and lets a lot of gas come to the surface till it eventually settles," Lily responded in her unique Southern style.

"Never heard that one, but it works for me. By the way, have you done your book signing yet?" I asked.

"Yes! Had a signing last week, but ah'm gonna do it again next Saturday morning. This time, it'll be at Chicky-Pie's. Wanna come by and pretend I'm famous?" Lily asked and added, "It's gonna be out on the patio. Thought it might bring attention to Mell's café and put that area to good use all at the same time. We're gonna have some fruit, mini-sized breakfast pies, and of course, lots of good coffee, too."

"Mini pies? Where are you getting those from?" I asked.

"Mell's gonna make them! It'll be a test to see if savory breakfast pies bring more folks in here on the weekends. She's handing out free samples the day of the signing." Lily seemed excited with the idea, and I had to admit it piqued my interest, too.

"That sounds like a great idea. Was it yours?" I asked with a sly grin.

"Well, Mell and I talked it over and came up with the idea together. But I do think it could help her. Maybe be a good draw to folks who need another breakfast spot beside the Good News Café."

Lily's eyes twinkled with glee as she talked, and I knew it must have mostly been her idea. It seemed like Lily would have a significant role as a friend and helper to many in Riverview.

"I'll be there for sure. Might bring Bella too since you have children's books. She loves books and pretends to read." I glanced at my watch. "Oh! Speaking of family, I better get going. Pete will be worried, and Bella will be waiting for my good night kiss."

"Oh! I hope I didn't keep you from your family. That's most important." Lily apologized.

"No. No. Sometimes I stay a few minutes after anyway, just to wind down a little before I go home." An idea struck. "Say, would you like to go to the park with Bella and me tomorrow? I'd love for you to meet her, and we could continue our conversation."

"I'd love to. How about letting me pick you up?" Lily offered. "Should we pack a lunch too?"

"Yeah. That would be great! Not sure what all I have in the fridge for lunch fixin's though."

"If you both like egg salad, I could make sandwiches," Lily said.

"Yes. That would be perfect. Bella loves egg salad. I'll bring some chips, beverages, and brownies."

"Sounds like a plan. Ten-thirty a good time for you?"

"Perfect! See you then."

We rose from our chairs and hugged. Our meeting was good for both of us. Not wanting to leave a single bit of leftover pie, Lily took her plate to the kitchen and asked for a take-home box. I grabbed my apron and dashed out the back door with a newfound joy in my step. Memories of my friend Betty brushed my emotions at the prospect of a new friendship.

🐝

"HI, HONEY," I said, entering the kitchen. Pete was sitting at the table having milk and cookies.

"Hello, sweetheart. D'ya have a good day?" He stood and walked toward me.

"An excellent day. Is Bella still awake?" I kissed him.

"Maybe, but not likely. She was a busy bee today, so I'll bet she's already fallen asleep."

"You must have worn her out at the park again. You look a little tired, too." Drawing close to Pete, I started bragging proudly. "Oh, by the way, you'd be proud of me. I want you to know that today, I resisted temptation."

"Really? What happened? Did Matthew McConaughey come into Chicky's or something?" Pete grinned slyly.

"Oh, no! I wouldn't have resisted that," I quickly shot back. Pete lifted an eyebrow, and I let things sizzle for a minute, then finished. "No, it was chocolate cream pie."

"Oh really?" he questioned, laughing at my humor.

"Yeah, it was calling to me, but I didn't give in. In fact, I made sure there wasn't any of it left, so I couldn't bring it home," I retorted.

"That's great! I'm proud of you. Perhaps I can offer you a more slenderizing enticement," he said, pulling me close and planting a long, warm kiss on my lips.

I never made it to Bella's room for a good night kiss that night.

<h1 style="text-align:center">TWENTY</h1>

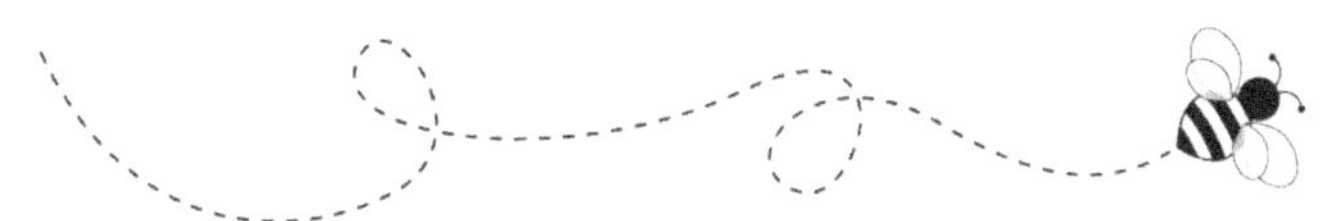

Lily tooted her horn as she pulled into my driveway. Opening the front door, I stuck my head out and waved. "Be out in a minute!"

"Come on, Bella, let's go. Got your sandals on?"

"Yes, Mommy."

Dashing out the door, I brought Bella's car seat out and placed it in the back seat, put the picnic basket in the trunk, and went back in for her.

"Hi, Lily." I jumped in the front passenger seat after buckling Bella in. "Thanks so much for driving. It's a little hot for walking to the park today."

"Glad to be invited along." Lily was upbeat as usual. "The beach park should be nice today. Wanna go there?"

"Good idea. Like your purple hat. Perfect on this sunny day."

"Can't be too careful, especially with my fair old skin," Lily self-deprecated.

"Lily, you always look far younger than your years. How do you do it?" I asked sincerely.

"Must be the Oil of *delay*," she quipped, purposely misnaming the famous face cream. We were at the park less than ten minutes later. Finding a table, I set our picnic provisions down. Lily and I were happy to find a large shade tree and bench next to the playground where we could watch Bella while visiting.

"Thank you again for inviting me today. It means a lot. I've been getting so lonely lately. Just can't seem to get used to not being married," Lily began.

"It must be tough after so many years with someone by your side." I couldn't help but remember the years of loneliness I endured, even with a so-called family surrounding me. But I sensed her loneliness was vastly different, having lost a spouse.

"It surely is. But ah'm glad to get to know you better, Elise. Have you had any more thoughts about your dream since we talked last night?"

"Only the pressing need to make a decision. Pete is supportive, but I don't think he knows what to do with it either."

"Well, dreams can be tricky. Even though God uses them sometimes, it's always a good idea to check with His Word first to make sure you don't do anything that contradicts what it says."

"Well, if God really cares about us, He wouldn't want little girls to be molested and abused like I was. That said, I feel confident that God gave me the dream that prompted my escape five years ago. Which makes me think this dream is from Him also." I was a little skeptical about letting things go too far into religious talk. I just wanted someone to listen to me.

"Sounds like the truth to me." Lily cut to the chase. "God surely doesn't like anything that harms little children. It says in the Good Book that 'whoever causes one of these little ones ... to sin, it would be better for him if a millstone were hung around his neck, and he were drowned in the depth of the sea.' I think that's in Matthew 18," Lily enlightened me.

"Wow, that's pretty damning."

"Sure is. Elise, God never intended men or women to do such terrible things to children, but sadly there are a lot of people who don't care what God thinks. Many times, the very people who harm children were abused similarly when they were younger. It gets handed down from generation to generation." Lily looked at me with compassion and question in her eyes. *Does she wonder if I abuse Bella, too?*

"I don't even spank Bella." I tried convincing her, just in case.

"Elise, I never would suspect that you would hurt her. But I hope you are also able to fully give her your love. Withholding love or discipline can be another way parents who have experienced abuse harm their children. They fear inadvertently abusing them and overcompensate by withholding healthy love and discipline."

"I love Bella with all my heart!" I felt insulted.

"I'm sorry, Elise. Please forgive me if I've hurt you. It's just that it took me a long time to figure out why my mother had such a hard time demonstrating her love for me. She said that she loved me but always seemed emotionally detached," Lily confided.

"I get that. My adoptive mother never gave me any love, that's for sure," I empathized.

"It wasn't until I was married with children of my own that I understood why she kept me at arm's length." Lily explained, "Mother saw me disciplining my daughter one day and got extremely angry with me. Ugly accusations spewed out of her mouth, unlike anything I'd heard from her before. When she finally calmed down, she told me about the abuse she had endured as a child and that it was why she never spanked or disciplined me. She saw spanking and discipline as the same thread of abuse. The truth is, there are healthy boundaries and consequences that provide children security, so withholding it can prove harmful."

"Oh, Lily. I am sorry to hear that. You seem so at peace and happy. I would never have guessed you had a difficult childhood."

"Oh, we've all had difficult childhoods in one way or another." She chuckled. "I think my sense of humor has always been a defense mechanism that's helped. But faith is what ultimately led me to find peace and joy. Good counseling made a big difference, too. It helped me understand my mother better, so I could eventually forgive her."

"You are so right about counseling. I used to see a counselor, thanks to Mell, and it helped a lot."

"I'm so glad you did. Mell is a wise and caring friend to have suggested it."

"Maybe you're right." I hung my head. "I hadn't given it much thought before, but sometimes I feel fearful just being alone with Bella for long periods of time. I don't know why. And Pete is always telling me I don't let him love me like I should," I admitted.

"Trauma is never easy to fix, even with years of good counseling. My Aunt Myra came alongside me, helping bridge the gap of love I felt was missing from my mother. If it hadn't been for her, I probably wouldn't have been blessed to know the fullness of love with my husband. But it took years before I fully understood and received the love she poured into me."

Just as she finished, I saw Bella reaching for a monkey bar that was too far for her little arms. Jumping up, I ran and caught her just in time. "Be careful, honey; these bars are pretty high for you to manage on your own. But if you want to try again, I'll help you," I told Bella, smiling at Lily as I said it.

"Good catch, Elise," Lily hollered out. "I'm going to get our lunch set up now."

"Good idea. I'm famished!" I helped Bella reach onto the monkey bar again, then encouraged her to let me push her on the swings for a while.

"Thanks, Mommy. I'm tired of just going down the slide." Guess I hadn't noticed that was mostly what she'd been doing the whole time Lily and I were talking. "Can I go play in the sandbox now?" she asked just as Lily called out, "Lunch is ready when you are."

"Let's go wash our hands and have our lunch first," I replied.

"But Mommy, I want to play some more. Please, please?" Bella pleaded.

"No, you'll get too dirty. We should eat first," I insisted. She continued pleading with me, nearly succeeding in getting her way as she usually did. I was about to give in when the realization of Lily's words sank in. Standing in awe, I looked Bella in the eyes and firmly said, "No!" The shock on Bella's face said it all too well—I *have* been afraid to discipline her.

"How about we all go wash our hands together?" Lily said with a smile as she walked over.

Taking Bella by the hand, we all walked to the community building where the nicest restrooms were. Something caught my eye as we came out, shaking the water off our hands. A man stood under a tree about twenty yards away. A woman lay on the ground at his feet. I squinted to see better as something seemed a little off about them. Lily came up beside me, stopping short with a curious stare towards the couple, too.

"Any idea who they are?" She asked.

"No, don't believe I've ever seen them around here before. But something seems wrong with that young woman," I said, trying not to stare at them too obviously.

"Yeah, I get that feeling too."

We watched a while longer as the young woman, looking to be in her mid-teens, lay on the grass, writhing and convulsing as if in pain. The man standing nearby rubbed dirty fingers through his greasy black hair. Grey-brown strands at his roots and the nape of his neck indicated a lousy dye job growing out. He looked much older than her, with deep wrinkles marring his complexion. Even more surprising was that he simply stood over the girl. Watching. Doing nothing to help her. Then he got down on his knees and began touching her inappropriately. It was an unsettling sight, to say the least.

"Wow!" I said, glancing at my watch. "Didn't know it was nearly twelve. No wonder I'm so hungry." I pulled Bella's hand and turned her away from the scene, not wanting her to witness what we saw. Heading back to our table closer to the pier, I felt a twinge of guilt for not doing anything to help the girl, *but what help can I provide anyway?*

"Yes, let's mind our own business," Lily agreed, quickly following. As we sat to eat, I could tell she was as disturbed as I was.

Could that girl have been drugged? The man with her was clearly a shady character. My thoughts wandered back to the scene in the empty outlet mall parking lot years earlier. *Hmm, why would that come to mind right now? Could there be a connection?* "Maybe we should call the police or something," I suggested.

"I don't know. He looks pretty scary," Lily said with a pointed look at Bella. Neither of us wanted trouble, especially while she was present.

Gratefully, our picnic was in a busier park area, providing a sense of security. Even so, we ate quickly before heading home. As we drove away, I couldn't shake the sense of unease and the bitter taste it left in my mouth. It remained like a penitent sin demanding a confession.

TWENTY-ONE

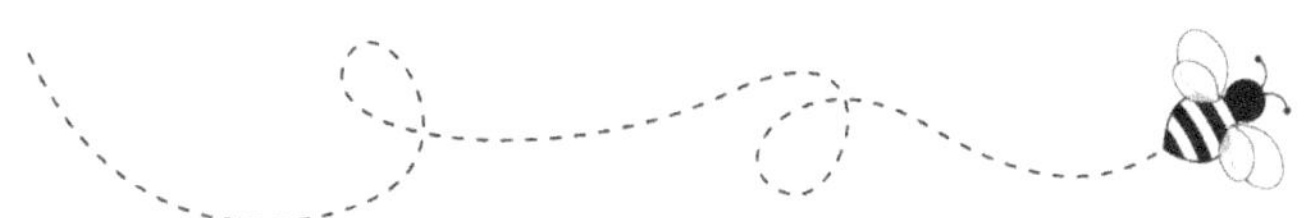

Now, it seems troubles are always comin' in. Tragedies keep own happenin' and sometimes fall nearby. But no matter how they come, somehow, I've had the blessin' of seeing them work-out for the good. At least most of the time. Oh, they's lots a folks that may not see it my way. They only knows the outside lookin' in. They only hear the mockin'bird's chatter and see his bird's-eye-view. But the folks that look from the inside know better. They knows that comin' to visit me oft enough, and knowin', really knowin', the heart of me, makes all a differ-ence in a world. 'Cause, in the heart a me, folks fine nourishment. They get fed. They grow. Oh, I don't mean jest in size, though I've been known ta encourage that too. No, I mean they grow in strength. In character. In relationship with one 'nother. An' that's the kine a' growin' that mean the most.

March 13, 2012, Elise

A darkness fell over the small town of Riverview. Spring flowers which should have begun poking their heads out of the soil, remained hidden underground. Birds that normally would be singing joyfully to the awakening of springtime remained mute. Even nature seemed to sense something was amiss. A somber foreboding spread quickly through town. People woke up that morning. They went about their business, but an air of anticipation and angst was tangible. As if everyone knew something had happened or was about to. Storm clouds rose from the east, with Riverview their target.

The Riverview Daily News hit the stoops and driveways with disproportionately loud thumps. Residents with no reason to rise at the break of day got up anyway. An extra hour or two of morning slumber wasn't going to change or evade this malady. What kind of sorrowful, disturbing news lay waiting within the thin pages of the newspaper? No one knew. Should they bother to pick them off their lawns and porches? Would removing the rubber bands holding the pages together release this darkness into their souls? Had someone, some prophet, failed to warn them to mark their doorposts the night before so the plague couldn't affect the inhabitants?

I sensed it like everyone else. Something was going to happen. Something big. Something dark and foreboding already had its tendrils growing beneath the unsuspecting morning dew. Yet they did open their newspapers. They turned on their cell phones and the television, hoping to find out what was wrong. Most folks, at least. As I stuck my thumb under the band of my paper, about to remove it, my phone rang. It was Mell calling.

"Mell, is everything okay?" I asked tentatively.

Lily

I sat at the kitchen table with my morning cup of Joe in hand, the same way hundreds of other Riverview residents were doing. I hoped the morning jolt of caffeine would scare away the unsettling feelings that were creeping in.

"Spur-r-rt!" I spit the coffee back into my cup. "Ugh! Must've put too many scoops of coffee in the filter." Even my coffee was infused with bitterness. Chiquita cocked her fluffy head at me in puzzlement. Neither of us knew what to make of the ominous feeling in the air.

"You must want your morning walk," I answered her perplexed expression. "In a few minutes, honey." Reaching across the table for the morning paper, I caught a glimpse of my Bible. Pushing away from the table, I rose and retrieved the leather-bound book instead.

"Come on, sweetie," I called Chiquita. "Let's go out on the patio for a while." Following close behind, she happily trotted out the back door and dashed to the small patch of grass. I sat at my bistro table next to the pond. It was still a little cool, even for a Riverview morning, but this felt like just the spot. "Yes," I confirmed out loud. "Think I'll do my morning devotions out here every day."

Opening the Bible, I let the pages fall open where they willed. Immediately, my eyes were drawn to a passage, and I read: "Making the most of every opportunity because the days are evil."

Chills went up my spine. I had read that verse many times before, but it seemed especially prophetic on this day. Bowing my head, I approached God in prayer. "Oh Lord, most Holy and powerful, blessed are you, God, above all. I pray, Oh Lord, that you will strengthen and guide me through this day and whatever it may bring. Protect me, Lord, from the evil lurking like a roaring lion...." My prayer continued until I became engulfed in a covering spirit of peace that I can only recall experiencing a few times in my life. When I closed with amen, Chiquita was curled at my feet and fast asleep. The sun was farther up on the horizon, and my wristwatch indicated I'd been praying for twenty minutes. Though it had been a long prayer time, it felt like only a nanosecond. A verse came to mind, "...With the Lord, a day is like a thousand years."

"Rr-r-ring. R-r-ring." My cell was ringing from inside the kitchen. A sense of urgency filled me, and I dashed in to catch the call just in time. It was Elise.

"Elise. How are you this mornin'?" Sobs sputtered from the other end of the line. She couldn't talk for several seconds.

"What's goin' on?" I prodded her. "Are you all right?"

"I'm sorry. I – I can't help it," Elise choked out. "Did you hear what happened?"

"No. What is it?" I asked with trepidation.

"She's dead!" Elise sobbed.

"What? Who's dead? What are you talking about?"

"The girl we saw next to that strange man in the park," Elise explained.

"You mean the brunette with the red plaid shirt? The one who seemed to be writhing in pain?" I asked.

"Yes, that's the one. It's terrible, just terrible. We should have done something. We should have helped her." Elise sounded angry now. Angry at herself.

"Was it drugs?" I asked. "Did they get the guy who was with her?"

"No!" Elise nearly shouted now. "She jumped in front of the train!"

"Ugh!" I gasped in shock. "Oh, my God! No!" My whole body felt weak and sick all at once. I could hear Elise sobbing again.

"Where are you?" I asked.

"I'm at Chicky's. I'm supposed to work the breakfast shift today, but I don't think I can. Mell called me early and asked if I'd come in. She's pretty upset, too."

"I'll be right there." I grabbed my jacket and keys. Before dashing out the door, I took a quick peek at the newspaper head-line. The story was tastelessly splattered all over the front page of the Daily News. *DRUG ADDICT JUMPS IN FRONT OF TRAIN! Riverview police reported a woman committed suicide by train near Tyson Oceanside Park early yesterday morning.*

Quickly scanning further, it read, *Riverview had its latest suicide by train when Ms. Tracy Dunlop jumped in front of the Coaster early this morning. Sheriff's department reports finding drug paraphernalia near the tracks along with her wallet, ID, and a plaid shirt. Reports are sketchy as to whether or not drugs were in play. A man was seen running from the scene, but witnesses say they couldn't identify him... This was the fourth such death in over thirty years. Authorities are piecing together information to help with the investigation. Witnesses are encouraged to report to the sheriff's department.*

It had to be the same girl we saw at the park. Even though we had sensed something was wrong, really wrong, we'd chosen to walk away. Now, she was dead. Smashed to a thousand pieces by a powerful high-speed train. Had the man pushed her? Did she have drugs in her system that dulled her senses so much that she didn't know what she was doing? Whatever the case, another tragic example of a lost sheep and Satan's evil victory had struck with deadly force.

Elise

Lily arrived at Chicky-Pie's in record time. She found Mell and me sitting at a booth near the kitchen. My shaky hands were barely able to prop up my distraught head. Mell attempted to blink away signs that she'd been crying, yet still welcomed Lily with a warm hug.

Seconds after Lily sat down, Mell jumped out of her chair and dashed to the front door. She'd spotted a patron approaching the entry, no doubt there for breakfast. Stopping him at the door, Mell quickly turned the *Open* sign back around to *Closed*.

"Sorry, we're closed for breakfast in respect for the town tragedy." She pointed to the newspaper stand by the door. "We'll be open for dinner at 5 p.m. Hope you understand." Seeing the customer's disappointed face, she continued, "All dinner entrees will be $5 off tonight."

Lily and I were crying as Mell rejoined us. It was clear that everyone was deeply affected by what had happened despite the fact that none of us knew the young woman. Although no one had met her, we had all seen her in the faces of many other women who had streamed in and out of town over the years. Each carried their unique story, but all had the common thread of hopeless despair that comes from abuse, human trafficking, drugs, or all of the above.

"I should have known better. That was me not too long ago. Why didn't I do something?" I scolded myself.

Mell placed a comforting hand on my shoulder. "Honey, that could have been any one of us. That's what makes this so hard. We can see ourselves in her face, in her fate."

Lily did a double take, then looked deep into Mell's knowing eyes.

"All of us have known struggles and have had times when we didn't do what we should have," Mell continued. "We live with our regrets, but we have to move forward, using those moments to teach us what to do differently next time." Mell's surprising candor and wisdom got our attention, and the conversation took a new direction.

"She's right, Elise," Lily affirmed. "Instead of blaming ourselves, we have to look to God and see how He can use this terrible thing for His good purposes."

"Are you saying that God wanted this to happen?" I asked.

"Of course not! God is 'not willing that any should perish, but that all should come to the knowledge of His salvation,'" Lily explained, a Scripture rolling off her tongue. "What I'm saying is, the world is full of evil. Terrible things happen no matter how strong our faith is. But when we trust in God, He can take those terrible things and work them together for good. He can turn them into good, godly purposes."

"She's right," Mell confirmed. "Do you remember the

colorful oval rug that was in the room you first stayed in when you came to the Colony, Elise?"

"Oh, yeah. I do. I'd never seen a rug like that before. It was kind of old-fashioned and had lots of different colors, but was so pretty," I remembered.

"Yes, well, in a way, life's a little like that rug. It was made from a whole bunch of rags." Mell explained further, "My grandmother made it. I watched her weave those rag strips back and forth when I was just a small girl. At first, I wondered why she was even wasting her time with all those ugly pieces of cloth. Then, I began to see how she wove them all together into a pattern. When she was done, the rug was breathtaking." Mell could weave a tale of redemption as I'd never heard before.

"Years later, when I was out on my own, and troubles came my way, I found myself thinking about that rug," Mell continued. "When someone showed me a verse in Romans 8:28, it was like an epiphany. The verse revealed how our mistakes and troubles are like old rags that aren't very pretty or useful. But when we put them in God's hands, He weaves them together for His purposes. In His hands, troubles can become useful, even beautiful."

"That's lovely, Mell. I've never heard a better example than that," Lily commented. "I'm the oldest in this circle, and I can tell you I've made a lot of mistakes in my life. But I can also remember times when God used those awful mistakes and turned them into something beautiful. We should ask Him right now to forgive us for our blunder in this incident and ask Him to guide us on what to do next."

Casting my eyes downward, I hung my head, feeling a mixture of sorrow and shame. Everyone must have thought I was about to say a prayer because as I looked back up, their heads were bowed and eyes closed.

"Before we pray," I interrupted, "I need to tell you guys something." Both women lifted their heads and gave me their full attention. "I know you're aware of a little bit of my story, but there's something I've never opened up about. It's been weighing heavy on me lately." I continued, "So, you all know I escaped from an abusive family. You know that the man I once called Dad molested me. But I never told you that he fathered a child in me."

Mell and Lily sat in stunned silence. The heaviness in the air was palpable.

"I was only fourteen. And even now, it's hard for me to think about," I confessed. "What made it even worse is they gave me anesthesia during the birth, and when I awoke from the C-section, they told me I'd had a girl. And—" My voice choked, "And they told me she died." It was the first time I'd ever poured out my sorrow to someone besides Pete about my baby's death. Tears streamed from my eyes. Through my blurry vision, I saw tears glistening on Mell and Lily's cheeks as they listened to my story.

Lily reached out to me and put her hand on top of mine. "Oh, dear. That's terrible. I can't imagine how awful you must have felt."

Mell came over and gave me a gentle hug. "Honey, I've known you for almost five years, and that's the first I've heard you mention that piece of your life's puzzle. I am so glad you feel safe enough to share that with us today." I nodded, attempting to swipe at the flow of tears running down my cheeks. I looked at my hands as if they were the most interesting thing in the world. *Who knew it was so difficult to unburden your soul?*

As she sat back down, Mell opened up, too. "When I first came to Riverview, I, too, was a lost soul looking for solace. My husband continued the abuse I'd received all of my growing years. If it hadn't been for my grandmother, Millie, I don't know what I would have done. That's, in part, why I feel a kinship, or connection, with young women who come to our town looking for a second chance at life," Mell confessed. "I found a second chance at Chicky-Pie's, and I believe God has called me to help other women find theirs. It's devastatin' to think that this young woman came to Riverview but didn't ever realize her second chance."

"Mell, you always seem so together and confident. How'd you manage to turn out so well after such a rough beginning?" Lily wondered out loud.

"Well, it's been a journey, that's for sure," Mell said with a soft chuckle. "But I thank God for His strength and direction. He sent so many wonderful people into my life to help me along the way. He protected me from danger more times than I can count." She paused with a deep sigh, "So, I guess that's why learnin' 'bout that sweet soul run over by the train yesterday… well, it hit me really hard. We'll never truly know what happened with her to bring her to that point. But I hope that God will reveal how to weave this tragedy into His beautiful rug to stand on— not only for us but for the town and all the women who come to Riverview after us."

Lily nodded and said, "Let's pray now, ladies, and ask God to direct us all." So, all three of us bowed our heads and asked God for comfort and guidance. As we lifted our heads back up, a strong sense of relief washed over each of our spirits.

The heaviness in the room had lifted, and as if on cue, the sunshine broke through the clouds and streamed in through Chicky-Pie's front window.

When Lily and Mell glanced over at me with concern in their eyes, I hardly noticed. Staring into space, an idea flooded my mind. Then, breaking my silence in a most irreverent way, I pounded the table with my fist, stood up, and made a declaration. "That's it!" I said emphatically.

A little startled, Lily asked, "What's it?"

"Yes. Tell us, chile. What did God reveal to you?" Mell queried. "Maybe we cen help."

Starting to pace, I gulped hard and began, hoping it wouldn't scare my friends away. "You both know a terrifying dream drove me to leave my home when I was eighteen." I continued as my two friends leaned in with interest. "Bea was about four then, and even though I knew that God was warning me to get out of that house, leaving Bea behind was the hardest thing I've ever had to do. Even harder than living under constant abuse." My breaths came in heavy. I was onto something; I just knew it.

"So, exactly what do you think you're supposed to do now?" Mell asked.

I swallowed hard, sat back down, and answered, "I think I'm supposed to go back to the Burrows' house and rescue Bea—maybe Bobby too."

Mell and Lily looked at me in stunned silence.

"A few weeks ago, I talked with an old friend. He does the landscaping for the Burrows and has kept an eye on the kids after I left. Well, he said some disturbing things were going on. He made it sound… I mean…" I fumbled a bit for words. "It sounded like Bea's behavior, well, it may indicate she's being abused as I was." I inhaled air all the way down to my diaphragm, then let it out slowly.

"Going back there sounds pretty dangerous," Lily cautioned.

"Yes, it's not going to be easy, that's for sure. I'll have to go about this very carefully." I absently started tapping my nails on the worn tabletop. "Last night, I had the dream for the third time. Only this time, it was interrupted by a loud crashing noise. The explosive sound woke me up and gave me an urgent sense of danger. I'm pretty sure the loud noise was the sound of the train's screeching brakes and the crash that killed that young woman. The timing of the crash with my dream felt intentionally coordinated. I mean, it was too interconnected to be a coincidence." I looked at Lily and Mell, "I have a pretty good feeling that God was trying to get my attention. I need to stop waffling and obey. I must go back and rescue little Bea from the evil that's present in that home before it's too late for her. It might be risky, but I have to go."

Lily and Mell continued in their state of quiet shock until Lily ventured, "That's remarkable. Just plain remarkable. Elise, I'll help you in whatever way I can."

"I'll help you too," Mell declared.

Their conviction sent a feeling of warmth through me like I'd never known. *So this is what family feels like,* I thought to myself. *People who stand by you even in the most difficult times.*

"That is so sweet of both of you. And I appreciate it, really I do, but don't feel like you have to get involved. It's my burden to figure out."

Lily jumped in, "Hogwash! Where I come from, that's what we do—we help one another. We care 'bout one anotha' and if one of us is hurtin', we all hurt too. And if somebody needs help, we help."

"Lily's right, Elise. We're all family here. An' families help one another," Mell agreed.

I grasped both of their hands with a wide, grateful smile. "I can't begin to express how much this means to me. Thank you."

"Okay," Lily sat up straight, "let's get to figurin' out how we're gonna do this."

TWENTY-TWO

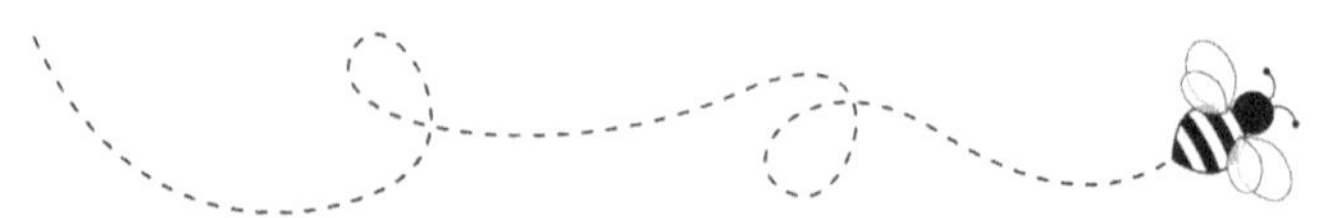

A *low hum, or buzz, emittin' from a tree or bush prolly means a beehive live in it. Things were surely hummin' on one particular day. All three a my friends, Miss Lily, Miss Elise and Mama Mell, were jes beside themselves ova the death of a young woman. It were one a the worst days I cen remember. But I had a feelin, things would get betta, afta they meet heah cause the good book say: "Where two or three are gathered together in My name, I am there in the midst of them." An, tha's how things is heah, ya know.*

Half an Hour Later, Elise

The morning's gloom, while not entirely dissipated, morphed into an animated discussion with a sense of purpose as Mell, Lily, and I began planning the rescue of Bea Burrows. Barely thirty minutes into our discussion, Chicky-Pie's door opened with a jingle. Mell jumped up and greeted her daughter, Allie, as she entered the restaurant and headed toward our table.

"Hi, baby." Mell hugged her daughter and then pulled another chair over to our table.

"Hi, Elise. Good to see you again," Allie greeted me with a brief hug. We'd seen each other off and on over the past few years when she'd come to Chicky-Pie's to see her mother.

Mell introduced her to Lily, "Allie, this is Lily. She recently moved to Riverview and has already become a good friend."

"So nice to meet you, Lily," Allie greeted her with a handshake and her mother's infectious smile.

"Were your ears burnin'?" Lily said with a grin. "Mell was just tellin' us you're an attorney. Is that right?"

"Yes, I'm a dependency attorney."

"What exactly is a dependency attorney?" I asked.

"I represent children at risk of abuse and neglect," Allie replied. I perked up and glanced at Lily with a knowing expression.

"Really? That sounds like tough stuff," Lily commented.

Allie responded, "It's definitely not easy work, that's for sure. But it's rewarding when you can help kids get out of abusive homes and find freedom from their abusers."

My heart started beating faster as I listened to Allie describe her work. *She could be a big help in figuring out how to get Bea and Bobby away from Jack and Jane. The timing of her arrival couldn't have been more perfect.* My mind whirred with the opportunities that working with Allie could open up. Breaking from my internal thoughts, I went back to focusing on what Allie was saying.

"There are hundreds of cases our law firm handles every week. And that's just for this county. Sadly, all around our nation, thousands of kids are abused and neglected by the very people who should be most protective of them—their parents."

Lily shook her head sadly as Mell jumped in, "You know, Allie, we were just discussing the recent tragedy with the girl jumping in front of the train."

"Yes, such a sad situation," Allie replied. "I don't know about that case, but it could be related to drugs or human trafficking. We see a lot of that here in Southern California, being so close to the border of Mexico and even in the families of citizens. But sadly, it can be a revolving door for these kids. We get them taken out of a home to protect them, only to see them put back in harm's way a year or so later."

Lily spoke up, "It's heart-wrenching to think of what all those children go through. As a mother myself, I can't even imagine what would drive a person to treat their kids in such a way."

The conversation was really picking up now as Mell commented, "Actually, Allie, we've been made aware of a situation that could involve child abuse." Mell gave me a swift glance, and I turned my head a bit, asking her with my eyes not to share too much about Bea and Bobby. "You might be able to help us with some of the logistics and legalities of a plan we're puttin' together," Mell hedged, not going into too many details.

I could tell Allie's interest was sparked, so I chimed in, "I was thinking the same thing. Mell, why don't we get our plan together first? Then we may have a few questions for you, Allie. If you're open to helping, that would be tremendous."

"I'd be glad to help in any way I can," Allie offered, nodding in the affirmative. "I'm going to be on sabbatical soon, so I'll have more time on my hands."

"All right. Sounds good," I smiled back. *Maybe this timing was a sign from God.* Somehow, I sensed that His blessing was being revealed to me. *Huh, perhaps I can trust Him with this.*

"That would be great, honey. We sure would appreciate it," Mell agreed.

"Sure thing. Is the kitchen open? I thought I'd grab a bite while I'm here." Then, with a lift of one disapproving eyebrow, Allie glared at Mell and asked, "Is that another new outfit, Mom?"

Mell's face turned slightly pink as she hemmed and hawed before answering, "Uh, yeah. It was on sale, and I couldn't resist. Do you like it?" Turning toward us gals, Mell sought our approval with her eyes.

"Looks great!" I praised.

"Love it!" Lily said. "You always look so stylish and pretty. I don't remember eva' seein' you in the same outfit twice."

"You probably haven't," Allie said in a slightly scornful tone.

Mell glanced at her watch and swiftly changed the subject. "We need to wrap up pretty soon. You said you wanted somethin' to eat, Allie? I'll fix somethin' for you. Need to get things ready for the dinner crowd anyway."

"Oh, yes," I agreed. I should be heading home. "Why don't we plan to meet again in a few days?"

"How about the Monday after next?" Mell suggested. "I've been thinking about closing for breakfast on Mondays for some time now. So, we can meet right here if you want. Coffee and rolls will be on me."

"Well, I can't turn that offer down!" I said joyfully. While the day had started on a sour note, I was grateful for a renewed purpose and felt the nervous twinge of excitement and fear bubbling up in my belly. "I'll start thinking through our options for how to move forward."

"I'm in," Lily concurred. "Don't have anything special goin' that day except laundry. And ahm sure it'll wait like all housework does." She gave me a wink before a shadow crossed her face. "But before we go, Elise, there's one more thing I think we should do," Lily added tentatively.

"What's that?" I wondered.

Lily looked at me and spoke. "I think we should go to the police and report what we saw the other day at the park. We can tell them everything we observed and give them a description of the man we saw with that girl. We didn't help her then, but we can do the right thing now. Maybe it will help them piece together what really happened. If that guy had a hand in her death, we could be doing a good thing by helping get him off the streets."

"Yes. You're right. Let's go while our memories are still fresh," I agreed. "In fact, why don't we go right now?"

"That's a good idea," Mell encouraged.

"No better time than the present." Lily and I gathered our things and hugged Mell and Allie goodbye.

I felt lighter as we exited the café. As if a big weight had been lifted from my shoulders.

⚇

Elise

Arriving at the Riverview police station, Lily and I looped our arms together and walked to the door feeling a little like Laverne and Shirley, that old television show. It felt a little silly but gave us a sense of courage and strength like we were in this together.

As we approached the front desk, Lily spoke up on our behalf. "We'd like to talk to the sheriff regarding last night's train incident."

"Okay. Have a seat over there, and I'll see if he's available," A female police officer sternly directed. "What are your names?"

"I'm Lily Phillips, and this is my friend, Elise Freeman."

The policewoman walked over to the sheriff's office door and knocked lightly. "Two women here to see you about the train incident."

"What're their names?" Sheriff Willis hollered through the door.

The officer opened the door to address him further. "One is Lily Phillips, and the other is Elise Freeman."

"Don't know any Lily Phillips. Did you say, Elise Freeman?"

"Yes, sir."

"Hmm. Pretty sure she's the friendly waitress at Chicky-Pie's. Has she got light blondish-brown hair and bright turquoise eyes?"

"Sure does."

He sounded more interested now. "Tell them to come on in." With the door slightly ajar, we watched Sheriff Willis lean back, feet on his desk. A thought bubble over his head couldn't have said it any clearer than the salivating look on his face—he was probably imagining the prospect of free lemon meringue from Chicky's.

"Hello, ladies. Have a seat, please." Willis swung his feet off the desk and stood to greet us. Shaking my hand, his big smile confirmed his recognition of me. "What can I do for you?"

"We think we saw the girl who was killed by the train. Before the accident, that is," I began.

"All right. Why don't you tell me all about it?" Willis grabbed a pen and paper and started to take notes.

"Well, we were at Tyson Park near the pier two days ago, and we noticed a girl who matched the description of the one in this morning's news. When we saw her that day, she was with a really creepy guy. We both sensed something was wrong." I glanced at Lily and saw she was bobbing her head in agreement. "Then that night, the train's screeching brakes woke me up, and I just knew something terrible had happened."

"Yep! Sure was loud. Woke me up, smack-dab-middle of a good dream," the sheriff agreed rather insensitively. We continued describing all we had observed the afternoon before the train incident. Sheriff Willis took a few notes and listened intently.

"So, about how tall would you say the man was?"

Lily and I looked at each other to confirm. "About six-foot-two or three and lanky," Lily spoke up to my nod of agreement.

"Yes, and he looked like his hair was dyed black, but his natural color was starting to grow out with some greyish-brown tones. He seemed quite a bit older than the girl. Maybe about forty to forty-five. And he just seemed, well, creepy. Right, Lily?"

"Yes. Very creepy. Not only that. The young woman was clearly in pain. It was so strange. The man just stood over her, watching her. Then, at one point, he knelt down and appeared to touch her inappropriately as she rolled on the grass. It was very unsettling," Lily concluded.

Sheriff Willis reached for a large book on a nearby shelf and plunked it down on his desk. "Take a look at these photos and tell me if any of the men in here look anything like the guy you saw. Can I get you ladies some water or coffee?"

"No, thanks," Lily responded.

"I'll have some water, please."

We sat for quite a while, flipping the pages. Finally, the sheriff handed me a water bottle and a glimpse of recognition flickered across my mind. "Wait!" I shouted. "Turn back to the last page again."

Lily flipped back to the previous page, and we both took a closer look at one of the photos. The man in the picture had slightly shorter brown hair, but there was a strong resemblance to the guy we had seen that day. "I think that's him," I proclaimed, pointing to the middle picture.

"Yeah. It sure looks a lot like him, I'd say," Lily agreed.

Sheriff Willis examined the photo and made a note. "That's interesting. We haven't seen that guy here since his drug arrest about three years ago." Then, punching a number on his desk phone, he picked up the receiver. "Kanistra, come in here for a minute, would you?"

Lily's eyes perked at the name with a look of nervous excitement I hadn't seen before. *What could that be about?* A distinguished-looking officer entered the room, and Lily's eyes blinked with immediate recognition. He was an attractive man I'd seen at Chicky-Pie's several times. Lily and I both stood to greet him. I could see Lily's knees starting to wobble. She sat back down quickly, no doubt to prevent falling.

"Dan, these two ladies may have some critical information regarding the recent train incident." Turning to us, he began with me. "This is Elise Freeman, and this is…"

"Lily," Detective Kanistra filled in before Willis could spit it out and shook Lily's hand warmly.

"Hello, Dan, I mean Detective Kanistra," Lily stumbled, her hands trembling and knees going weak. A small smile played on my lips. I was starting to enjoy this new friend of mine even more now.

"Nice to see you again," they said simultaneously.

"Oh, you two already know each other?" Willis asked the same brain-scratching question that I had.

"Well, we met recently at Chicky-Pie's," Kanistra explained. I could tell Lily had more to say about that.

"So, ladies, Sargent Kanistra is my top detective. Can you please share with him what you told me?" We recounted what we saw at the park and showed him the photo we thought looked like the man in question. As we stood up to go, Sheriff Willis shook our hands. "Thank you, both. You've been very helpful."

"Can I get a phone number for both of you in case I need to ask any more questions?" Detective Kanistra asked.

"Of course," I answered for both of us. Lily was too tongue-tied to speak.

Feeling satisfied and relieved at having done the right thing, we left the police station with our heads held high. It felt good to have done something important. Something that could potentially help the community be safer. But soon after I got home, a phone call quickly dashed my prideful high spirits with startling interruption.

"Ruben? Como estas?" I began. "Is everything all right?"

"Si, I am doing good, but we may have a problem starting, too," he mentioned.

"A problem?" I asked.

"Jes. I think there is a beehive somewhere near one of the new bushes. And you know how Mrs. Jane feels about that."

"I sure do." The picture that came to my mind was comical. "Why don't you tell Jane to call a bee service?" I suggested, curious why he would be calling me about bee trouble. He must be calling for a different reason. "Is everything okay with Bea and Bobby?"

"Yes, I think so, but Bea, she don't seem very happy. She look sad all the time and sometimes I hear Mrs. Jane yelling at her and saying bad things to her. And Mr. Jack, he don't take Bobby to his games, so I've been taking him."

"That's so sweet of you, Ruben."

"I think it make him feel better. But I don't know how I can help Miss Bea." I sensed he was worried beyond words. "I think maybe it time for you to come for a visit," he continued.

"I think you may be right. But there are some things I have to put in order before I can make a trip. I promise I'll keep you posted," I tried to reassure him.

"Okay, I will pray for you. And I find a good bee company to help with the beehive, too. That way, when you come, you only have to worry about Mrs. Jane's sting." His words sounded almost prophetic. An idea began to form in my mind. Maybe I could use this bee problem to my advantage.

"Hold off on calling the beekeeper service just yet. I just might know of a good company that could help in more ways than one. I'll get back to you soon," I promised.

"Okay. I will wait."

"Thank you, Ruben." I hung up with a stirring within me that was unsettling.

TWENTY-THREE

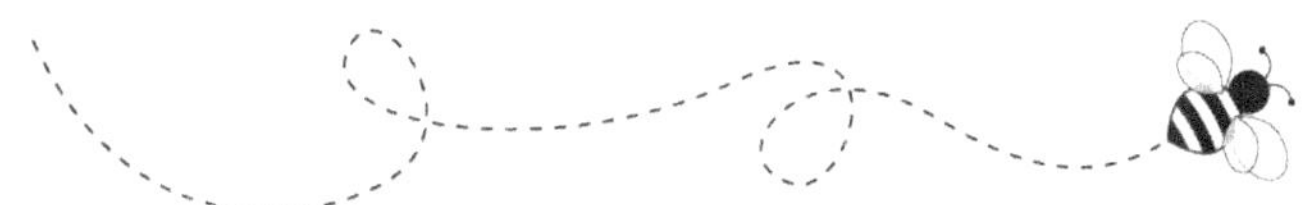

Winter was jes about ova, an things was mostly quiet heah in town, not too much activity goin' on. Honeybees cluster together in the cold winter months and their activity is kept to a minimum too. But not fer my friends. No siree, oh they was clusterin' tagetha all right, but it were ta figure out what Elise ought'a do next.

Elise

At the door of Chicky-Pie's, I lifted my hand to knock, then, noticing the window sign, hesitated and left it hanging mid-air. The café was closed. The door flew open at that same instant. My fist almost hit Mell square on the nose. Surprised, I jumped back right in the nick of time.

"Hi Elise, right on time." Her bright smile greeted me.

"Good morning, Mell. Glad to see you did it—you closed Chicky-Pie's for breakfast?" I greeted her with a hug and returned the smile.

"Yeah, think I'll just do mini pies on the weekends and see

how that goes." Mell motioned for me to come in. "Lily should be here soon. Go on back to our table near the kitchen. I'll bring the coffee over."

Sitting down, I fumbled through my satchel full of papers. Then, pulling out a pile, I stacked them neatly and thumbed through the top five documents, looking for the one I needed. "Ah! Here it is!" Holding it up for inspection, I placed it face down next to the pile.

Mell approached the table with the coffee cart just as Lily arrived at the front door. "Go ahead and help yourself to coffee and pastries. I see that Lily's here. Gotta get the door. I don't dare leave it unlocked, or somebody will walk in no matter how big the closed sign is."

"Oh, for sure," I agreed. "Thanks, Mell." Nerves punctuated my every word with an obvious staccato.

Sensing my anxiousness, Mell commented, "You know, I was thinking, since we're closed this morning, why don't we go shopping after we're done with the meeting? A cute little boutique just opened up down the street where Pinky's used to be. I'm dying to see what they have."

"That sounds like fun, Mell. I'd love that," I gratefully agreed. "And since my wonderful boss let me have the day off today, I can go," I winked.

"Did somebody mention shopping?" Lily bounced in and placed a large shallow box on the table. "Count me in."

"Great! Let's aim to end our discussion at nine-thirty. That way, we'll have time to shop, and I can be back in time for lunch hour set-up with my crew," Mell instructed. "What you got there, Lily?"

"Oh, just a little something I baked last night," she answered. "Thought you gals might like to try it." Opening the box, Lily revealed a large pecan pie. Everyone's eyes lit up with glee, especially Mell's.

"That looks amazing!" I crowed. "Guess having pecans for

breakfast would be a way of getting some good nut protein. So, it's healthy, right?"

"Right!" Mell agreed. "And you took out all the calories, too?"

"No," Lily answered, "but when you get to the last bite, there's a gym membership." We all laughed and dug into our slices of pie. I took the first bite. "M-m-m. This is delicious, Lily!"

"Aahh, yes," Mell savored. "Would you mind letting me use your recipe for Chicky-Pie's? Customers would line up clear 'round the block for a taste of this goodness."

"I would be honored, Mell," Lily said proudly. "I'll email it to you. There's quite a bit left in the pan, too, so if you want to try it on your patrons today, that would be fine with me."

"Oh, I don't think we should let her do that," I said with feigned seriousness. Mell raised an eyebrow, and I gave her a sly smile. "Because we want it all to ourselves, don't we, girls?" I said, slicing another piece for myself.

"Absolutely!" Mell agreed.

Mouth full of pecans, Mell got us on track. "Well, I say we get started. What do you have so far, Elise?"

Clearing my throat and glancing at my notes, I tried to organize my thoughts. "So, this is going to be tricky for sure, but I've compiled a list of steps we'll need to take. We'll first need to get some information on the family's current habits and schedules. I have an inside connection for that. His name is Ruben, and he's the landscape gardener for the Burrows. He's a good guy and was instrumental in my escape five years ago."

"Is he the one who told you about possible abuse happening now?" Lily asked.

"Yes. He called me a couple of weeks ago while at one of Bobby's baseball games in Arizona."

"Whoa! Arizona? I forgot that's where you came from, Elise. That's not a short drive away," Mell pointed out.

"No, it's not. But it's doable. I thought we could take a train to Phoenix, and if Ruben is willing, maybe he'll let us borrow his van for a few days. If not, we can rent a car, but I'm pretty sure he will."

"Okay. What next?" Mell asked.

Over the next hour or so, our conversation grew into a buzz of excitement. Before we knew it, the clock struck nine-thirty. "Ladies got ta stop now," Mell announced. "I need to talk to the staff for a few minutes, and then I can join you for shopping at the boutique. We still goin', right?" she asked.

"Yes. We sure are!" Lily winked at me. As I gathered my notes, I felt a release of some of the tension in my chest. Maybe things would work out after all. And even if they didn't, it sure was nice to have some friends to help carry the burden.

THE BOUTIQUE WAS NICE, but I found myself occupied with how I could remake some of the dress designs to give them more flair and style. On the other hand, Mell and Lily cooed over everything they saw and proceeded to buy new dresses. Mell left promptly after shopping to return to Chicky's before the lunch rush. Lily and I wanted to stretch the fun a little longer, so we went for beverages at the nearby coffee shop. Choosing a shady table out front, we sipped our iced coffees contentedly. After a few minutes, I glanced at Lily and broached a subject I was curious about.

"Lily, you seemed a little flustered at the police station the other day. Were you nervous about giving our report?" I asked in a half-hearted attempt not to intrude.

"Sort of. Well, not really. Aah was actually a little nervous around Detective Dan," Lily responded.

"Detective Dan? Why? Do policemen intimidate you or something?" I questioned. "I mean, he seemed very nice to me."

"Well, no," Lily fumbled as she picked up a napkin, wiping the condensation from her glass. "I mean, yes, he is nice." She took another moment to collect herself, then continued, "It's just that I think I may know him from long ago. I mean, I met him at Chicky-Pie's a few weeks ago. But I have this strange notion that I met him years ago. I don't know if he remembers me from way back when or not."

Glancing at Lily, I saw she was blushing. "Were you romantically involved with him back then?"

"I guess you could say that. We hadn't been out on many dates, but I had a mad crush on him. And suddenly, one day, he just stopped calling and writing. He was in the Navy and would be at sea for long periods, so I never knew if it was because of that or if he was just over me. Then weeks turned to months, then to years, and I never heard from him again. I was just a silly teenager, but it broke my heart," Lily confessed.

"Oh, Lily, I'm sorry. Are you sure it's him?"

"Yeah. Pretty sure. I mean, there aren't too many guys with the last name Kanistra, let alone with the same first name. Plus, the more I see him, the more he looks like the Dan I knew back then. But, hey, it's been forty-three years or so. I doubt he even remembers me; never mind, recognizes me now."

"Well, who knows? Maybe that's why God brought you here. I mean, wouldn't that be something after all those years? That's pretty amazing that moving here meant seeing him again." I was excited for Lily.

"I suppose you could be right. But it makes me all kinds of nervous. I don't know if I'm ready to date again or get serious about someone like that. Who knows? Maybe he was just a jerk and left me hanging all this time. Besides, I had a long and wonderful marriage to John. That's enough blessing for any gal," Lily reassured herself. "Want to shop a little more? I need some shoes, too." She changed the subject.

Looking at my watch, I begged off. "Oh, no, I need to go. I've got to run a few errands before it's time to pick up Bella at preschool. You know, I was thinking maybe you and I could do some painting together one day soon."

"I'd love that, Elise," she agreed, and we hugged goodbye for the day.

PULLING my car into the local post office, I parked and went to the trunk to fetch two packages. One was the paper-wrapped package I brought to Riverview five years ago. The other was a new package of the same size, shape, and weight. I took them inside to get weighed and posted, then returned to my car with a feeling of lightness. The rest was now up to the postal service and Ancestry.com.

One Week Later, Elise

It was a blue-sky kind of day. The world seemed to sparkle in greeting as I entered Chicky-Pie's.

"Good morning, Lily! How are you today?" I chirped.

"Good morning, Elise. I'm doin' just fine. You're looking especially happy today."

"Yes, I am feeling good. Mell busy in the kitchen?" I asked.

"Yeah, I saw her a minute ago. Some problem with the cooks, I think. She'll be right out. Why don't you help yourself to some coffee and pastries while we wait?" Lily offered.

"Oh, yum!" I said, pouring myself a cup and grabbing a chocolate-filled crescent roll. As I sat, Allie walked through the back door.

"Hi, ladies. Is it okay if I join you today?"

"Absolutely!" Lily replied. "Good to see you, Allie. How's everything going with you?"

"Pretty good, but this week has been more stressful than most." She sighed as she poured a cup of coffee and took a seat at the table. "We've got a huge load of child abuse cases rollin' in. It gets overwhelming at times. We put so much time and energy into helping these poor kids, only to wind up back in court a year or two later, with them sent right back into the same abusive situation we'd gotten them out of. The system doesn't always help. It's truly heartbreaking."

"Oh, Allie, that has to be hard. How do you stay positive through it all?" Lily asked.

"Prayer, faith, and a clear sense of purpose," she answered. Then, eying the tasty goodies on the coffee cart, she exclaimed, "Whoa! Look at those pastries. Don't remember those bein' on the menu."

"That's 'cause I got them across the street. Thought it wasn't right for Mell to provide food for us every time. Help yourself," Lily offered.

Just then, Mell walked up. "Hi, girls. Thanks for waiting for me. Nick was having some issues. Had to get it straightened out. Where'd these come from?" Mell grabbed a chocolate-filled crescent.

"Lily brought them," Allie told her.

"Mell, you look great," I noticed. "You're wearing the new dress you got at the boutique, right?"

"Yeah. Do you like it?" Mell twirled like a little girl showing off her new prize. Her smile was radiant.

"Another new dress, Mother?" Allie asked. "I can't believe it! I thought we agreed no more shopping for clothes unless you *really* need something." Allie's tone dripped disapproval. "I don't think you needed that dress."

"I know, honey, but it was so cute. And everybody liked it. I tried it on, an' it fit perfectly, an' everybody said it looked real good on me. So-o-o, I just couldn't resist the temptation!"

"Well, you should have told Satan to get behind you," Allie scolded.

"I did. I did!" Mell confessed. "But he said it looked good from the back, too."

Everyone broke into squeals of laughter. Thawing a bit, Allie couldn't help joining in. "Okay, ma, you win!"

Wiping a tear of laughter from my eye, I tried to bring things back to order. "Okay, ladies, I guess we better get to work. Allie, I wanted to ask you about something." Allie gave me her full attention. "What is the protocol for reporting child abuse? I mean, how long does it usually take for authorities to check on children when a report has been made? Do they move pretty quickly?" I asked.

"Most counties require the Department of Child Protective Services to follow up on child abuse reports within twenty-four hours. But even if they see evidence of abuse, they may have to make several trips back to the house over a long period to confirm the extent and danger level before removing the child."

"Really? That's pretty disturbing. Doesn't that keep the children in danger?" I asked.

"Yes, it can. Unfortunately, many caseworkers have such heavy caseloads that it's inevitable a few cases slip through the cracks," Allie reported.

"What if it's something like molestation?" I asked.

"Those cases are even more difficult to address. When authorities are notified about sexual abuse, the procedure is to acquire a warrant and act quickly to remove the child from the home. Trouble is," Allie took a sip of coffee and then continued, "even after it goes to trial and evidence is clear and abundant, the child may change their mind and take back their testimony. They fear being taken away from their parents more than the abuse they endured. It's even worse when other family members turn against the victim." Allie set down her cup and finished her thoughts. "That rejection compounds things, adding to the pain they're already enduring. But many kids recant and beg to go back home."

"That's hard for me to hear," I confided. Overwhelming sadness spread through me. "Thanks, Allie. We are so lucky to have your expertise in these matters."

"Glad to help. I have to take care of some business now. Let me know if you have any more questions." Allie excused herself.

Thanking her again, I gathered my thoughts and went forward. "Okay, so we'll need to have a plan A and a plan B. I had an interesting idea come to me last night that I could use your help on, Mell."

"Whatever I can do," Mell agreed.

"Did you find out anything from your friend? What was his name? Rudy?" Lily asked.

"Ruben. Yes, I talked to him a couple of days ago. Turns out it's perfect timing for us to use his van. He's getting bought out by a large landscaping company and was thinking about selling Old Blanco, as he calls it. So when I mentioned we may want to use it, he offered to sell it to me for $500."

"$500! That sounds like a steal. Is it in good shape?" Lily asked.

"It's old and a little beat up, but it's got lots of mileage left on it if I remember correctly. I'm sure it'll come in handy. But, before we go further, we need to determine how we can pull this off in a legally sound way and still effectively bring the kids to safety. That, my friends, is not going to be easy. So, however we do it, this thing's gonna need thoughtful preparation."

Mell placed a small three-ring binder in front of me on the table. "Elise, this is something I put together a long time ago. I wonder if it's helpful." Opening the binder, I began reading Mell's outline for escape. The top of the first page was dated:

March 12, 1975

THE PLAN

1. File an abuse report with the police
2. Make a schedule so there's no interruption
3. Pre-pack
4. Arrange transportation
5. Bring cash
6. Have a plan B (in case something goes wrong)

"I know it isn't very detailed," Mell began, "but maybe that's a good thing. It could serve as a basic outline of action. It was something I put together when I was trying to get away from Javier. As things turned out, God took care of the situation for me. Javier was arrested and thrown into jail, effectively taking him away from me and my baby. Yet even though I didn't need the plan then, I remember feeling sure God had given it to me. It helped me feel prepared. So, maybe it can help you prepare now."

"Mell, that's extraordinary." I was overwhelmed with gratitude and wonder. "I love the simplicity of it, and it can certainly work as a starting point."

"Did you guys notice it's dated March 12? Here we are, in March now—only thirty-plus years later," Lily added.

"Oh, you're right. Hadn't noticed," Mell acknowledged.

"Why don't we start filling in the details according to this outline? Here's what I have so far." Handing them my notes, I was amazed at how almost all of my notes fit exactly into the same basic order of Mell's plan.

About ten minutes later, Mell said, "I'm sorry, girls, but I have to get back to the kitchen. Anything you want me to do at this time?"

"Yes, I'll talk to you about it when I come to work tomorrow. You go ahead," I excused her.

Lily chimed in, "I hate to break off our time together, but I need to take care of some things at home. Are we going to meet at the same time next week?"

"No worries, Lily. Mell, would it be okay if we meet again next Monday, but maybe a little earlier to get more done?"

"Sounds fine with me," Mell agreed.

"After all Allie has told us, I sure hope we can get this done legally," I fretted.

Lily must've sensed my reservations. "Elise, don't worry; this is going to work out. I know God is directing us and will help us get those children to safety."

"Thanks, Lily. And thanks to all of you. Keep praying," I asked.

"Of course. Oh! By the way, how about lettin' me watch Bella sometime? I'm sure you and Pete would enjoy some time away once in a while," Lily offered.

"That would be wonderful. I'll ask Pete. He might want to go for dinner and a movie."

TWENTY-FOUR

Lily

"Hello. Is this Lily Phillips?"

The man's voice sounded familiar. "Yes, this is Lily," I replied.

"This is Detective Kanistra. Do you have a minute?"

"Oh, hi. Uh, sure," I answered, suddenly a little nervous.

"I have a few more questions for you and Elise. Would it be possible to meet with you or, I mean, with both of you in the next few days?"

"Let me see." I paused as if checking my calendar. "Oh, I think I could meet you on Tuesday or Wednesday this week if that's good. But I'll have to check with Elise about her availability."

"Tuesday at three p.m. would be perfect if that's okay," Dan confirmed.

"All right, I'll give Elise a call. She may be working that day, but perhaps we could meet at Chicky-Pie's. If she's working, that might be easier for her."

"Sounds good," Dan replied. "Let's meet at Chicky-Pie's even if she's not working. It's more comfortable than the station," he suggested.

"All right. Sounds good."

"Wonderful." Dan continued, "Call me if anything changes. You can reach me at the number I'm calling from."

"Okay. Will do. See you then, Dan. I mean Detective Kanistra." I felt myself blushing and was glad he couldn't see it.

Why would he call me instead of Elise? Probably just thought I would be more available since I don't work. But wait, he doesn't know if I work or not. Least, I don't think he knows. Oh, this is so silly. I'm arguing with myself over nothing.

Elise

I was waiting tables when he walked in. "Hello, Detective. It's good to see you again." Dan nodded in greeting. "Lily will be here in a minute or two. I saved a good booth in the back; it's pretty private. But if that won't work, we could go out on the patio."

"Hi, Elise. No, that will be perfect. Would it be possible to get a cup of coffee?" Dan asked.

"Coming right up. Black or with cream?"

"Black, please. What pies do you have today?" he sat and continued.

"We have a delicious pecan pie, new on the menu. It's Lily's recipe, actually," I said with a gleam in my eye. "We also have our staples, apple or cherry."

"Well then, gotta try the pecan."

Lily came in just as I returned with his coffee and pie. Her hair looked freshly coifed, and she wore a new lavender dress that complimented her blond hair and fair coloring.

"Oh, there you are," Lily said nonchalantly as she strolled

towards the booth, a sweet fragrance following her every step. She chose a seat opposite Dan.

I set the pie down and poured his coffee. "Here you go, Dan. Pie's on the house. Can I get you anything, Lily?"

"Think I'll have hot tea today. Got any chamomile?" she asked.

"Think so. I'll take a look. I'm just about to go on break, so your timing is perfect."

Lily

Dan forked a bite of pie but stopped midway to his mouth. "Oh, excuse me. I should at least wait until you have your tea," he apologized.

"Oh, no. Don't be silly. Go ahead and start." I brushed it off. "Do you come ta Chicky's often?" I poured on a little Southern charm, letting it ooze out slowly.

"Yes. Don't think there's a soul in Riverview that hasn't made this a usual haunt. They have the best chicken and pie for miles." He took a bite of pie, and a look of divine pleasure spread across his face. Before he finished with the first bite, he took another. "So, tell me, how long have you been living in Riverview?" His fork flew to his mouth before I could answer. "M-m-m.! Oh! This is good. This is really good." His mouth was still half full, the words a little garbled.

"Glad you like it." I blushed. "I've only been here about two months now."

"Heard it's your recipe. Is that true?" he asked with another bite aimed at his mouth.

"Yes, in fact, it is," I smiled. "I brought Mell one of my pecan pies a week ago, and she put it right on the menu. I grew up on fresh pecans… My grandparents had an orchard of pecan trees in Georgia, ya see, so anythin' with pecans was a staple. I never quite liked those store-bought versions 'cause they never put enough nuts in. Most people make it with lots of syrup and just a sprinklin' of pecans, but not me." As I spoke, Dan lifted his gaze to me as if hanging on every word. I found myself blushing again.

"Well, it's delicious!" he gushed.

Hmm, is he just tryin' to earn some points? I wondered.

"Why, thank you, Officer Kanistra. I mean, Dan. Or is it Detective Kanistra?" I stumbled.

"Oh, don't worry about it. Just call me Dan. But if you happen to be at the police station, you probably should call me Detective Kanistra. Sheriff Willis might not like it if you get too familiar there." His mouth full, he continued, "So, tell me, are you and Elise good friends or just acquaintances from Chicky-Pie's?"

Goodness, does he always talk with his mouth full? Or is my pie so good it took away his table manners? Brushing aside the thought, I replied, "We are friends, though we did meet at Chicky-Pie's. We immediately hit it off when I first came to town and quickly became good friends."

"She seems like a nice gal. It's a little unusual, though, isn't it? I mean, and please don't misunderstand, it's just that, well, you don't appear to have much in common. I'd say there's a bit of age disparity between you."

I let out a small laugh and glanced at Elise to see if she'd heard his comment. "Yes, we've both said the same thing ourselves. But we truly feel that the Lord brought us together."

※

Elise

Dan and Lily seemed to be getting along fine when I joined them at the table. But, as I sat, Dan got down to business, and the conversation quickly turned to the train incident. He asked, "So tell me, ladies, have either of you remembered anything else, any other details since you made the report about the girl you saw at the park?"

"I don't think so," I said. "What about you, Lily?"

"No, not really," Lily paused, then mimicked Dan's repetitive sentence starts. "So, tell us, Dan, what other details are you hoping to hear?"

The jab whizzed over his head. "Oh, even the smallest observation can be helpful. It's common for folks to have additional memories resurface after providing a statement. Those new pieces of info can be beneficial to an investigation." He paused to wipe a bit of pie off his lip. "I wondered if either of you had seen the man you described before the incident or afterward."

"I'd never seen him before that day or since then," I affirmed.

"Nope, don't think I saw him before or after either," Lily said thoughtfully. "But, you know, one thing about him comes to mind now that you bring it up. Seems like there was a mark of some kind on his left hand," Lily added.

"Wait! You're right." I lit up. "There was a tattoo on the backside of his left hand. It was like a long arrow or sword and went up the back of his hand to his elbow."

"Yes, a tattoo, that's what I thought it was," Lily agreed. I could feel my eyes glaze over, and my mind was transported to another place in time.

"That's an important detail, to be sure. Elise, are you okay? Is there something else you remember?" Kanistra pried as he gave me a curious look.

Shaking off my fogginess, I took a moment to respond. "I must be remembering wrong. It couldn't possibly be the same man."

"What is it, Elise? Tell us what else you remember," Lily prodded now.

"Well, maybe I'm crazy, but I'm pretty sure I've seen a hand with that same tattoo before. I can see this image of a man sitting in a big truck, his elbow resting on the door of the truck's cab window, his hand on the steering wheel."

As I started to tell them the memory, my nerves kicked in. Taking a minute to regain my composure, I took a drink of water then tried to explain more clearly. "I could be crazy," I repeated, "but I think it might be the same man who drove the truck they put me in when my mother sold me to the Burrows. I was very young, only six, but I remember being dragged around to the back of the truck and catching a glimpse of the tattoo when we passed the cab. It was so frightening; I fought even harder to get away." My body started trembling all over.

"Oh, Elise! How awful!" Lily got out of her chair and gave me a comforting hug.

"You know Elise, I've been a detective with the police force for a long time. It's common for people to recall details of an event for years after, especially if the event was traumatic in some way. So, this memory is likely accurate and could make a big difference in our investigation," Dan assured me. His calm, sensible tone helped me relax, my shoulders unclenching a little at a time. "If I'm not mistaken, the person you identified in the police photo book also had a tattoo on one of his hands. I'll check it out when I get back to the station."

I could tell from his expression that my revelation had Detective Kanistra's mind whirling. The sheriff had hinted that the man we identified had been a part of a larger ring of criminal activity. My admission just now may prove helpful in connecting this criminal to more than just one offense. Furthermore, it could be a piece of the puzzle in my own life. It could lead me to answers for why my mother sold me in the first place.

I could tell Detective Dan suspected there was more to my story, but I think he restrained himself from asking more questions. Glancing at Lily, a look of total admiration for his sensitivity spread across her face like butter on a bun. Her eyes sparkled with a new respect for him, and I think he gained a couple of notches on her list of contenders.

"Thanks, Detective," is all I could say at that moment.

"You're welcome, Elise. I think you've both given me more than enough for the day. Thank you for meeting with me. I'll be in touch. Please don't hesitate to call if anything else comes to mind." He stood and excused himself.

Lily and I looked at each other in astonishment. Then, hugging again, my trembling started to calm.

⚱

Lily

My cell phone rang as I was leaving Chicky's. "Hello, Dan. Did you forget something?"

"Hi, Lily. No, I was just wondering if you like hiking. There's a beautiful rock formation and waterfall in the hills above Bear Creek Road. It's supposed to be nice weather this Saturday, and I thought maybe we could pack a picnic and hike it," Kanistra inquired.

"Uh, not sure. Sounds like fun, but is it a difficult hike?" I wondered. "I'm not getting any younger and don't want to take a fall."

"No, it's pretty tame, but you should wear some good sturdy shoes and bring plenty of water in case it gets hot. We could get an early start to avoid the heat. Say, maybe eight or nine a.m.? What do you say?"

"Okay, but let's do eight thirty, so I have time to walk my dog first. Would you like me to make some sandwiches? I make some mean pimento cheese," I bragged.

"That would be great. I'll bring some chips, drinks, and cookies. Oh, and you probably should wear a hat, too," he added. "Okay, so it's a date, right?"

"Yes, I'll go." With some hesitancy, I agreed but added with gusto, "See you then. God willing, and the creek don't rise!" I was both excited and nervous. *Hope I'm not getting myself into trouble with this guy. Maybe I should ask if Elise can come along, too. Then again, Dan might not like that.*

🐝

Elise

My shift ended at six that evening when Sally came in for her shift to start. She and I nodded a polite hello. Then, after removing my apron and counting my tips, I looked for Mell to say good night. Trying the kitchen first, I found Nick, the head chef, talking to Armando, the new sous chef. They seemed to be sharing a private joke about Sally and were laughing boisterously.

Slipping back out, I stifled my laughter, hoping no one had noticed me. It was embarrassing to hear them joking about one of the servers, but admittedly, I'd also noted how many times Sally seemed to get orders messed up.

Mell poked her head in, her timing for ethical matters as good as with her baking. "All right, that's enough. Get back to work." She wasn't smiling.

"Yes, ma'am. Sorry." Nick put his head down, and Armando apologized profusely.

I stepped back for a minute to let things simmer down, then took a breath and approached Mell. "I was just looking for you, Mell. Sally is here for her shift, so I'm done for the day. Do you have a minute?"

"Sure, Elise. What's up?"

"I heard you know quite a bit about beekeeping. How hard is it to remove a beehive? I mean, is it necessary to hire a professional?"

"Why in the world do you want to know about that? Do you and Pete have a bee problem?"

"No, heh, but I've had a tip-off that the Burrows have a hive acting up."

"Aah. That's what you was talkin' 'bout the other day when you said you had somethin' I could help with."

"Exactly," I smiled. "I know it sounds weird, but I think helping with the beehive could work as a cover for us."

"Sounds interestin'. I'll walk you out, and we can talk about it."

Following Mell, she began again. "By the way, I know you must have heard the guys joking about Sally. It hasn't missed my attention that she hasn't had an easy start. She's been handed a raw deal in life, and I want to give her a chance."

"You know, I noticed that Sally seems good at organizing things; maybe she'd be good at doing the schedules and things like that," I suggested.

"You may have a good point there. I'll give it some thought. Now let me tell you what I know about bees."

TWENTY-FIVE

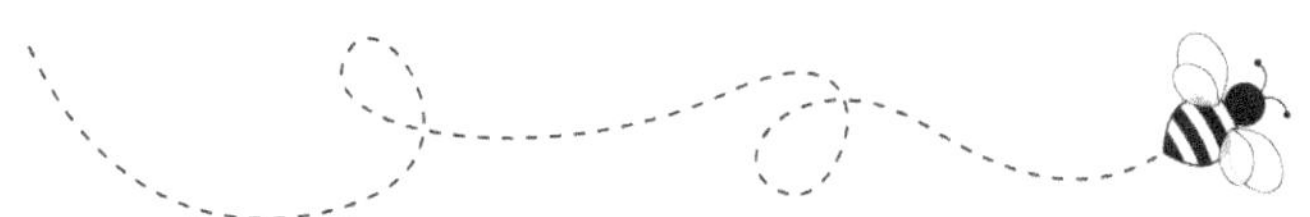

I hear tell that in a colony of bees, there aren't very many males. They say that's cause the male bees is only there for special mating purposes. It's a good thing Miss Elise has her husband all a time to hep her an give her love. But sometime she don't spend enough time with him an that's not good.

Elise

"Hi, honey." Pete came in from work and gave me a quick peck on the cheek. "Did you have a good day today?" he asked.

"Yeah, pretty good. Bella had a little tummy ache and didn't feel like playing dress-up or tea party like usual. So, I mostly did chores. How about you?" I answered.

"Well, I found out I *will* be managing the hotel in Solana Beach. I start in two weeks."

"That's great! You're excited about it, right?" I asked.

"Yeah, but it'll mean more time going back and forth on the road. I'm not gonna be available to stay here with Bella while you're working. So, we'll have to get that figured out."

"Well, I just might have a solution for that. Lily offered to watch Bella for us so we could have a date sometime." I wrapped my arms around his neck and snuggled close to his body. "And if it works out, maybe she would want to watch Bella more regularly."

"Oh really? You're okay with that?" he questioned, knowing how hesitant I'd been of anyone else watching Bella.

"I trust Lily. And I know you've wanted to go out on a date, so I told her we'd come up with a day and let her know." I beamed.

"All right then. What about this Friday?" he suggested. "I heard there's a new 007 movie out; I think it's called Skyfall with Daniel Craig."

"Yeah, that sounds good. I'll call Lily and see if Friday works for her. Do you want to get some dinner first? I was thinking maybe Norte's Mexican or Coyote's." I could tell Pete saw my sincerity.

"Honey anywhere with you would be perfect. I'm so glad just the two of us will have time together." Pete beamed and gave me a sweet kiss on the mouth.

I melted into his embrace.

🐝

THE MUSIC WAS LIVELY and had me dancing in my chair. "The chicken tacos are always so good here." I talked over the booming music. "And I love that they have a live band every night. It makes the restaurant feel so festive. I keep telling Mell she needs to have the jukebox playing more at Chicky's. Guess she just gets too busy with everything else she has to do."

"Well, as I understand it, the restaurant business is one of the most difficult to run. Owners hardly have any time for their own families. But Coyote's seems to have it down good for bringing the crowds in," Pete observed.

Minutes later, the waiter, Marcus, came towards our table,

holding a large tray of plated food. Hot steam lifted off our plates as he set them in front of us.

"Be careful. It's hot," Marcus warned, using a napkin to shield his hand.

"I'm sure you're right about restaurant ownership being a challenge, but sometimes I wonder if that might be something I'd like to do one day. I mean, it would be satisfying to put my own touches on a place where people could come and enjoy a meal and conversation," I continued my train of thought.

Minutes later, Marcus was back. "How's everything? Can I get you anything else?"

"The food's delicious!" I said a taco halfway to my mouth.

"Actually, can you bring us our check now? We have a movie to catch after this," Pete asked.

"Sure thing!" Marcus replied.

"Hey, Marcus, you've worked here for a few years, right?" I jumped in before he had a chance to leave.

"That's right. It'll be two years and three months tomorrow," he counted.

"Do you like being a server? I mean, you always do such a good job; I wondered if this was what you're passionate about or if you have some other dream," I pushed further.

"Honestly? I want to become a professional singer. Sometimes they let me sing with the band here, but I want to make a name for myself as a vocal artist," Marcus confessed.

"Wow! That's wonderful. I hope you're able to reach that goal," I encouraged.

"Thanks."

As Marcus walked away, I continued the point I was making. "I bet most servers would rather do something else. But with tips, the job is a decent financial stepping-stone for other professional endeavors."

"You're probably right," Pete agreed. "So, you want to start a restaurant, honey?"

"Maybe. I'm not sure. Sometimes, I think I want to be a dress designer and other times, I think it would be fun to own a place like Chicky-Pies." I looked down at my hands. "But I don't think I could ever do anything *really* important in life."

"You're doing something significant now." Pete put his hand over mine. "You are my beautiful wife and the mother of our daughter. That's very important. Especially to Bella and me." He gently rubbed his thumb over my knuckle.

"I know it is, but somehow, it feels like I should be doing something—oh, I don't know, something more meaningful. Don't get me wrong, I love you and Bella. But life just seems to fly by, and pretty soon, we'll be old, and Bella will be out on her own. What then?"

"Honey, I want you to be happy. So if there's something you want to do, just tell me. We'll work together to make it happen. But no matter what we do in life, the only things that have true meaning and lasting value are those God values. Everything else will one day turn to rubbish," Pete did his best to explain.

Changing the subject, I interjected, "Speaking of God, Mell informed me that I *need* to be at church this Sunday for Easter. I've been working on new dresses for Bella and me. Hopefully, they'll be finished in time." Just talking about sewing stirred joy within, and a smile played on my lips.

"Honey, your eyes just expressed what really excites you. You love sewing and dressmaking. Furthermore, you're good at it! It seems to me that's maybe what you should pursue." Pete returned my smile.

"Thanks, honey. You're right. I do love to sew."

"Elise, how is everything going with your plan to get Bea and Bobby away from the Burrows? I'm a little worried about what you might be getting yourself into," Pete asked, settling us back into the booth.

"It's coming along well, but I'd be lying if I didn't admit I'm a little nervous, too. I've been talking with Allie about the legalities of filing a report and involving the child protection agency.

She said proving molestation isn't easy. Sometimes, it's hard to detect."

"You have to be careful, Elise. I don't want you putting yourself in an incriminating position. Let the authorities handle it. That's their job, not yours." Pete paid our bill, saying, "We'd better get going, or we'll miss the movie."

Before he could stand up to leave, I spoke, "I don't want to do anything illegal. But I can't stand back and do nothing. I *have* to do something, or I'll never forgive myself. Mell said I need to pray about it. But I'm still uncertain how I feel about God. How can I trust Him when He let my mother sell me? When he let the Burrows hurt me?"

"Honey, Mell is right. Pray about it, and let God's Spirit guide you in what steps to take. I know how hard it is to trust Him when your circumstances don't make sense. A verse that has helped me over the years says, 'With Christ, I can do all things.' My dad often quoted it to me, especially after Mom died. I was so angry with God for taking her away from me, so I didn't fully understand what Dad meant until years later. Eventually, I let God take my anger and heal me from the pain of losing her. And I know He can do that for you as well if you allow Him to." Pete's eyes now glistened with emotion. I sensed there was more to the story but didn't push.

"Oh, Pete, I'm so sorry! Sometimes, I get so caught up in my troubles that I forget about the pain you've lived through. I've never experienced the kind of love you've had, the love of a father and mother who cherished you. So, it's almost impossible for me to imagine that kind of care."

Squeezing my hand in his, Pete shared, "You've got that kind of love and more from Bella and me. God brought us together. He isn't only present in the blessings. He's there in the trials as well. You know I love you very much, but sometimes it feels like you only let my love go so deep. It's as if you won't allow yourself to accept all I want to give you. You love us, but you don't fully give yourself to us. I know the Burrows hurt you deeply, probably in ways I don't even understand. But the thing is, Bella and I aren't like them. If you would just let us into your heart, you'd know what it feels like to be truly cherished." Pete's depth of understanding and grace flowed freely, and I tried my best to receive it.

"Honey," I began timidly. "I *do* love you. It's just that rejection has been part of my life since I was little. First, my mom, then the Burrows. If you were to stop loving me. I mean … I just… I can't help imagining one day, you're going to wake up and realize I'm just not worth the effort. There's something inside me that pushes people away, and," tears streamed down my face at the vulnerability I'd unleashed, "I'm afraid of being hurt again, and I know it would kill me. I just can't seem to get past that fear. I try so hard, but I just can't do it."

"I know, you do, honey. That's one of the things I love the best about you. You sincerely try your best at everything. But that's the beauty of faith. When you actually believe God loves you so much that He died for you. That He could and would never leave you. When you fully let Him into your heart, He will give you the power and strength to do all the things you've been trying to do on your own. I believe that when you surrender to Him, your fears about Bella and me will ease as well."

Giving me a moment to wipe my tears, he gave my hand another squeeze. With a warm smile, he rose from his chair and held out his hand. "Come on, I think we can still make the movie if we hurry." Taking his hand, I returned his smile, and we walked out of the restaurant together.

※

THE MOVIE WAS GOOD, but the ending made me feel like *my sky was falling. I just don't think I can handle seeing Jack or Jane again.* Fear was creeping, threatening to drown me, but I pushed the feelings aside, trying to focus on being present with Pete.

"Thanks, honey. It was fun getting out of the house, just the two of us. Daniel Craig was even better in this movie than the last." I linked arms with him as we headed to our car.

"Yes, it was good."

I glanced up at the stars. It had been ages since I'd been out on the town so late. "Hope I sleep well tonight." I'd almost forgotten Lily asked me to join her on a hike with Dan tomorrow morning.

"Maybe I can help with that," Pete gave me a sly smile. I returned it with a kiss.

BELLA WAS STILL NAPPING, and Pete seemed anxious to get off to work when I arrived home. The hike with Lily and Dan was beautiful but hot and exhausting, so I jumped in the shower. As the water flowed over me, all the showers I'd taken after Jack had ravaged me darkened my thoughts. I wished the water would wash away my shame and the dirty feelings that lay deep beneath my skin, but that never seemed to happen.

Wrapped in a towel, I rummaged through dresser drawers, looking for shorts, when something caught my eye. Hiding underneath a stack of socks was the photo I'd kept of Bea on her 4th birthday. Staring at it, emotions welled within me, heightening to a crescendo as I remembered my promise to her. The blue teddy bear I'd given her was hanging from Bea's right hand. Her curly blond hair fell in ringlets around chubby cheeks, and her beautiful smile looked back at me as if to say, *when are you coming back?*

Smokey leaped up on top of the dresser. As she did, another memory jumped into my mind—a happy one. I remembered going to a carnival with my dad, my *real* dad. He was throwing balls at a game board and won a prize—a pink teddy bear. An intriguing sensation came over me. This was more than a memory; it was a revelation of some kind. But I couldn't quite piece it together in a way that made sense. The only thing that stood out was the pink teddy bear.

As I finished dressing, Bella came in, rubbing sleep from her eyes. "Hi, honey. You took a nice long nap, didn't you? Mommy did, too. Guess we were very tired. Would you like a snack now?"

"Okay, mommy." She dragged her blankie as she came up to me and snuggled her warm cheek against mine.

"After our snack, let's play in the backyard for a bit. It might help us wake up. Then I want to work on our new Easter dresses."

"Okay," she said sweetly. "Can I have animal cookies?"

"Sure, honey." We walked to the kitchen, and Smokey also followed us in for a snack. *I swear, sometimes that cat can read my mind.*

The afternoon was chilly, so I put a sweater on Bella and got a light jacket for myself. The fresh air felt good, and my mind started to clear. As Bella played on her gym set, I stood watching her sweet joy at play. A chilly breeze swept in, and my hands dove for the warmth of my pockets. Feeling a piece of paper in the left pocket, I pulled it out to see what it was. To my surprise, it was the slip of paper my friend Betty had written her number on all those years ago.

Wow, guess I haven't used this jacket much in the past five years. Oh, Betty, how are you doing? I hope you have forgiven me for disappearing as I did.

Flipping the paper over as I returned it to my pocket, revealed the license plate number of the big rig in the outlet mall parking lot—another reminder from the past. *I need to give this to the police,* I thought.

Better get inside and start dinner now.

AFTER BELLA WAS IN BED, Pete and I settled in to relax. Sitting in the big easy chair, I spotted a paper Mell had given me to read, so I jumped up to fetch it off the credenza. Relaxing back into my seat, I unfolded it and read: *Elise, I know what it's like to live in fear. For many years, I was plagued with fear and scared to step out in faith on anything. I had so much pain and abuse in my past that it was hard for me to feel secure about anything. Then, one day, I read this verse, and it helped me. Hebrews 13:5-6.*

I decided to see if I could find it in my Bible. Pete looked up and saw what I was up to. "Can I help you find a verse, Elise?" We started in Chapter 13 at verse 4 instead of 5. *"Marriage is honorable among all, and the bed undefiled; but fornicators and adulterers God will judge."* I took a deep breath. That struck a nerve as I considered my marriage to Pete compared to Jack's ravaging of me.

Continuing to verse 5, I read: *"For He Himself has said, 'I will never leave you nor forsake you.'"* There it was again.

I looked at Pete, "Honey, all this talk lately of my mother and the Burrows has had me dwelling on the people who've abandoned me over the years. I just realized that I've been putting God in that category, too. Isn't it amazing that Mell would send me a verse that answers my heart's question about God?" He smiled as I continued, "Do you think it's possible that God hears our thoughts?"

"Of course it is, honey. How many times have I heard you say you think the cat can read our minds? If a cat can do that, surely God can. Besides, the Bible tells us that God is all-knowing and includes many instances when God acknowledges the thoughts of people. He must be trying hard to reach you."

Then, we read verse 6. *"So, we may boldly say: The Lord is my helper; I will not fear. What can man do to me?"*

"Wow!" *That can't be a coincidence!* I thought. It was as if God was personally answering my fears about returning to the Burrows'. He promised to go with me as my helper. I pondered this new revelation for a few minutes, then turned back to Pete.

"Pete, I haven't kept my promise to Bea. I told her I would come back someday, yet it's been almost five years. I've been so full of my own fears about Jack and Jane and so angry with my mother that I've been taking my sweet time responding to the threats Ruben shared about possible harm to Bea and Bobby."

"It's not too late to do what God is leading you to, honey. Just be sure you aren't letting your emotions guide you," Pete advised.

With sudden excitement, I sprang up and proclaimed, "I need to finish those dresses. They're almost done; just a few finishing touches. I'm going to wear mine to the Easter service tomorrow!" Pete looked at me in shock. There had been way too many Easters that I'd made excuses for not attending. Just that morning, I said I couldn't go because I hadn't finished my dress yet. Fresh conviction filled my heart. Tomorrow would be another first—my first time at an Easter service.

⚜

FINISHING THE LAST SEAM, I trimmed the excess threads and sat for a minute, soaking in the joy of accomplishment. Then I got up and made a phone call.

"Ruben, I think it's time. I've been going back and forth for a while now, but I'm certain I need to come back for the kids. Have you managed to gather any information on their schedules and routines yet?"

"Si. But when you plan to come?"

"I was thinking about coming at the end of next month. So about five weeks from now."

"Okay, good. Do you still want my van?" he asked.

"Yes, but how's the clutch and starter these days? The clutch was a little jumpy the last time I drove it, and I will need it to bring me all the way back to Riverview. Do you think it will make it?" Before he could respond, I jumped ahead, "Oh, and can you give me the number of a place where I can get it painted? I don't have a lot of money, but I want it to look good, so not too much dinero."

"Oh, jes. My friend Jose, he is very good. He will give you a good price. I make sure. You will see. I'll text you his number. I will check on Old Blanco and see if the engine she is good, too."

"Gracias, mi amigo. Can you text me Jane and Jack's schedules once you have them? Also, I need to know what days and times Bea is at home." I made sure he understood.

"Jes. Okay. I will tell you after I go there this week," Ruben reassured me. "I think Lidia, the nanny, will help with some of the information you need."

"Okay. Oh, and tell Jane to call the "Bumble Beekeeper Company" to help with the beehive problem. I'll text you the number in a couple of days. Thank you, Ruben. I look forward to seeing you soon." I hung up, feeling a mixture of relief for my decision and angst at what could happen next.

TWENTY-SIX

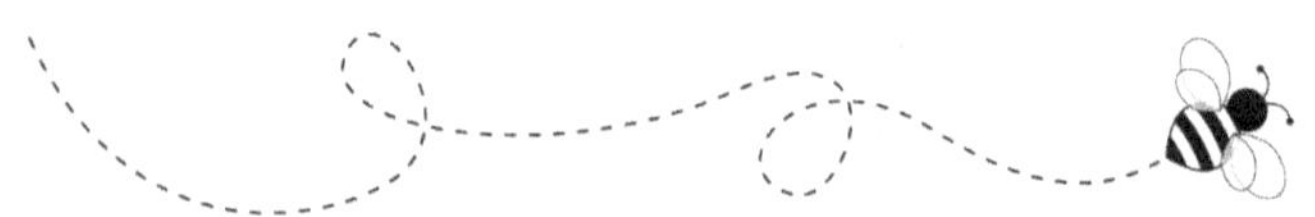

Springtime is my favorite time a yeah. I think it must be the favorite time fer bees too, cause tha's when all the flowers is bloomin'. A course they likes that cause they get mo nectar then. But even tho I likes all the flowers and the sunshine in the spring, it's my favorite 'cause it's when Easter come. An the Lawd reminds us that He die for us an come back ta life again. I think he use this season cause it's so much like the meaning of what the Lawd done fer us. You know, how all the flowers seem like they dead in the winter, then they come back ta life in the spring. Like when we borned again too.

🐝

April 8, 2012, Easter Sunday

"Hi, Daddy. Do you like my new dress?" Bella lifted the edges of her skirt to show him better.

"It's very pretty. Did Mommy make that for you?" Pete gushed.

"Yes. I love it so much. See all the pretty flowers on it?" She twirled around. "And my new shoes match, too. Are we going to see the Easter Bunny today?" Bella asked. "He brought me a big basket of candy and a pink bunny, and I want to tell him thank you."

"Well, I don't think we'll be able to see him today. I'm sure he's really busy. But I think he knows you are thankful. Is Mommy ready yet?"

"I sure am." I came around the corner, feeling like a spring flower myself.

"Wow! Honey, you look gorgeous. Is that the dress you made?" Pete seemed genuinely impressed.

"Sure did. Designed by yours truly!" I couldn't help beaming.

"I knew you had it in you. It's beautiful. Can't wait to show you off at church today." Pete beamed, handing us plates of scrambled eggs, toast, and bacon. "We only have a few minutes to eat in order to get there in time. Don't forget we're picking up Dad, too, and we need to be there a little early to get a parking space. It's bound to be busy."

"That's right, so hop to it!" I told Bella and gave her my best bunny smile.

Bella laughed. "Mommy, you talk like the Easter Bunny. He says hop to it, too."

"Well, maybe *I am* the Easter Bunny," I teased and wiggled my nose like a bunny.

"How did you do that, Mommy?" Bella said in wonder as she tried to imitate me.

Lifting my fork to eat, a picture came to mind of my father showing me how to twitch my nose like a rabbit. "The Easter Bunny taught me a long time ago."

"He did? How come you didn't let me see the Easter Bunny then?"

"Because it was before you were born. Let's eat our breakfast now, honey."

"Mommy, aren't we going to pray first?" She already had her hands folded and ready.

"Yes, let's ask God's blessing." Pete began, "Lord, thank you for this food and nourishment. Thank you for Easter and for giving us faith and new birth."

I lifted my head after he said amen. "Faith and birth?" I gave Pete a curious look.

"Yes, the new birth of springtime, and it's my prayer for all of us to have faith." Pete gave a short explanation.

"Oh," I said, feeling a little lost. As I ate, I thumbed through mental files of all the sins I'd committed. *I had sex with a married man. Even if it was forced on me, I'm sure that's still wrong. I've lost count of all the lies I've told. I stole money from the Burrows.* As the list grew in my mind, guilt and fear fed that old desire to flee. Recognizing the dark cloud sweeping across my face, Pete gently took my hand. Gazing into his eyes, love restrained me.

"Honey, are you all right?"

I couldn't answer. Just nodded and pulled my hand out from under his. *How could he love me? How could anyone love me?*

Standing up and walking over to me, Pete put his hands on my shoulders and began praying out loud. "Heavenly Father, thank you for my wife, whom I love so much. I know that you love her even more than I do. Help her to see your love and know her worth. I pray you will come against the powers keeping her from you. In Jesus' name, amen."

"Thank you, honey," I said as I jumped from my chair. "Let's go before I change my mind." I grabbed my purse and nearly ran out to the car. Pete gathered Bella, his sports coat, and his Bible, leaving the table uncleared. This would be the first Easter church service I had attended. The darkness of guilt and fear had kept me away every previous Easter.

The fifteen-minute drive there dragged by so slowly, magnifying my anxiety. *Why should I go to church and hear about everything I've done wrong? It's just going to make me feel worse about myself.* Trying to remain calm, I thought about Riverfront Mission, set on a gentle hill of rolling green grass. The church overlooked the river's beach. Pathways meandered along the bank's edge. Benches allowed folks to sit and gaze at the river's beauty. Over the years, during the few services I'd managed to attend, I'd duck out partway through the sermon and go to the river's sandy shore. The sloshing water licking the wounds of its shoreline was calming.

Maybe I'll slip out again.

§

"GOOD MORNING, ELISE. HAPPY EASTER." Lily waved as we walked by. "You look beautiful. New dress?" She was getting out of the passenger side of Detective Dan's car. He was holding the door for her, both looking sharp in their crisp Easter clothes.

"Thanks. Yes, just made it yesterday. Happy Easter to both of you." I glanced back at Larry as he and Bella caught up with us. Had he seen Dan with Lily? While Lily and Dan were still out of earshot, I asked, "Larry, has Lily reached out to you for help on her taxes yet?"

"Yeah. Thought I'd mentioned it to you. She seems like a great gal. Might have me help her with a remodel, too." He smiled as if remembering the experience with eagerness for more. *I hope he won't give up on her too easily.* I vaguely remembered Lily telling me something about meeting up with him at her condo complex and giving him a slice of her pecan pie. Apparently, it must've made an impression on him. But she hadn't expounded on it enough for me to know how she felt about Larry. I'd begun to warm up to the idea of Lily and Larry getting close.

As Lily and Dan fell into step with us, she remarked, "Look at you, little princess. So pretty in your Easter dress." Bella beamed and slid shyly behind me. "Thank you, Miss Lily."

"Elise made both of their dresses," Pete bragged.

"Elise, you are so gifted. If Pete hadn't told me that, I would've thought your dress was from some famous designer," Lily poured it on. Pete shook hands with Dan.

"Happy Easter!" Larry greeted Dan and Lily graciously.

As we entered the church lobby, Mell and Allie came into view. Lily sidled up behind Mell, saying, "Mell, your new dress looks really cute from the back."

Mell turned with a questioning look, "Uh, thanks, Lily," Mell replied, a little puzzled.

"Thought I'd tell you, so you don't have to ask the devil his opinion this time."

"Oh, you!" Mell wagged her finger at Lily, laughter sparking in her eyes. As we embraced hello, the three of us burst into hearty laughter, easing some of the tension in my shoulders. The guys stood there baffled.

I winked at Pete's curious glance. "Just an inside joke."

We stepped into a sanctuary blooming with lilies—the fragrance nearly toxic with their perfume. I chose an aisle seat and let Pete, Larry, and Bella slide into the pew first. *Easier to escape this way,* I thought. Glancing over my shoulder, I saw Lily and Dan seated at the back of the sanctuary with Allie and Mell.

The room filled quickly. Excitement and anticipation hung in the air. A choir and small orchestral ensemble opened the service with several joyous songs of praise. The congregation stood, singing along with vigor. The cross on the wall had no figure of Jesus, only lilies and a banner proclaiming: HE IS RISEN! As the final praise song tapered off, Pastor Shawn took the stage.

"He is risen!" he began.

"He is risen indeed!" everyone echoed.

"As you might expect, I'm going to tell you the story of Easter today. But I wonder, how many of you know how far back the story goes? You see, Easter didn't start when Jesus was nailed to the cross. It didn't start in the manger when he came as a baby to Mary and Joseph. No, the story of Easter began thousands of years before then. It first began in Genesis, chapter one, in the Garden of Eden with Adam and Eve.

"Now, before you all get nervous and think I'm going to recite the whole Bible today, I want you to know I'm not. I can't. The fact is, it would take too long. And my wife warned me she has a roast in the oven, and I can't go over two hours today." Everyone around me laughed, knowing he was kidding about preaching for two hours. I chuckled halfheartedly, looking for the nearest exit.

"Just kidding," he said. "My wife can't cook. So, *I* took care of the roast, and it'll probably take three hours 'cause I forgot to thaw it out yesterday." The snickers turned to a roar. Pete joined in and wrapped his arm around my shoulder. *Wants to keep me put, no doubt.*

Shawn chuckled as the laughter died down. "All jokes aside, it *is* true that the Easter story begins with Adam and Eve. You see, when they ate the forbidden fruit, God's plan of redemption was set in motion. Does anyone know who the first person was that killed a living creature?"

A few names were shouted out, and some people raised their hands. "Cain killed first," one said. "Noah," someone else said. "Able," shouted another, getting the brothers mixed up.

"No," said the pastor. Then, spotting Lily's raised hand, he called on her.

"It was God who killed the first living creature." Hushed whispers followed as Pastor Shawn replied, "That's right! You see, when Adam and Eve disobeyed the Lord by eating the forbidden fruit, they became ashamed of their nakedness and sin. When God showed up in the garden, they covered themselves in leaves they'd fashioned into clothing. They tried to hide, which, of course, didn't work. He found them huddled in shame, clothed in the autumn colors of fallen leaves.

Now, there's a unique dress design. I laughed to myself. *Too scratchy and seasonal, though.*

"God killed an animal, providing not only more suitable clothing than the leaves, but the first sin covering required the blood of a living being. So, that was the first creature killed. That was the first sacrifice provided by God to cover the sin of man and woman."

He continued, "You know, if you read Genesis, you will see

that the Garden of Eden was perfect. It had everything Adam and Eve needed. It wasn't necessary for any hard work or strenuous toil. That is, not until they sinned and got kicked out of the garden. Isn't it amazing that bad things still happen even in the most perfect setting? And isn't it interesting how the sin of two people caused pain and suffering for all of humanity?"

I thought the Burrows were going to give me a perfect home. They were rich, and at first, it was perfect ...until it became hell.

"You see, sin never affects only the one or two persons who commit it. No, it always affects many others. You may be sitting here today thinking that your sin only affected you. That it's your own business. If so, you are just fooling yourself," Pastor Shawn pointed out.

A battle raged within me, blocking the full reception of the message, a nugget of truth periodically finding its way through the internal clashing.

"...You may say, I didn't do anything *that* bad. I just stole a little money, or it was just one kiss, and their spouse will never even know. That's my business, no one else's. But no matter how big or small the sin, it still brings shame and separation from God."

"Think about it: Adam and Eve ate a piece of fruit. *Just* a piece of fruit," he repeated. "How many times do we tell ourselves what we did wasn't a big deal? We think, 'It was just a little fib,' or 'I only took a dollar from the expense box at work,' or whatever it may be. When you consider that it was *just* a piece of fruit that Adam and Eve ate, look how it affected everyone in the world for the rest of history."

Pastor paused, letting his words sink in. *Oh, great. Now I'm supposed to feel guilty about the small stuff, too.* I rehearsed my sins like a lottery wheel, and every error and every mistake tumbled around in my head. Which one would be the lucky winner—sexual sin, stealing, lying? Slumping down, I glanced at the exit again.

"I want to skip ahead now," he began, as I thought, *I want to skip out.* "I'm sure most of you have heard the story of Moses. You might have even seen the movie *The Ten Commandments*. There within the plagues…we see another link of sacrifice…"

I remembered seeing the movie. *Entertaining, but hardly real, I* thought. *God doesn't do miracles. If he did, why doesn't he do anything like that today?*

"If you remember the story, you will recall that the last plague that fell on the Egyptians was the death of all the first-born…" He continued, and I zoned out again.

"…also remember what God did to save His chosen people. He told them to put the blood of a lamb on their doorposts so the angel of death would pass over and they wouldn't die. The blood of those lambs saved their firstborn children. So, this is one of the next stories we are given about sacrifice and covering.

"The Passover story, just like the first animal sacrifice in the Garden of Eden, was merely a shadow of the ultimate sacrifice. A prophecy about the covering Jesus gave us with His blood. The good news is that Jesus' sacrifice paid the price for *all* of our sins, big and small. All we need is to accept His gift by believing Jesus died for us and rose again from the grave." A vague memory of my friend Betty, back in Phoenix, surfaced. She told me that gifts aren't something we earn or pay for. The last time I saw her, she gave me two wonderful gifts. One of them was a cell phone. *Hmm, that phone provided me a way to liberation. The other was a Bible.*

Pastor Shawn seemed to be wrapping things up and caught my ear again. "…Sin, whether it seems insignificant or unforgivable, makes you a slave to it, but Jesus said, 'If you abide in My word, you are my disciples indeed. And you shall know the truth, and the truth shall make you free.'"

Wow! God must be reading my mind again, or maybe Pastor Shawn is. The timing of that verse couldn't have been any closer to my thoughts.

The war continued raging. I felt it all the way from my heart down to my feet. My heart thundered in my chest. Everyone around me stood to sing the Hallelujah chorus as I prepared to bolt down the aisle and through the door. Just then, Pete took my hand in his, halting any attempt.

"Before we close, I'd like to give an invitation to anyone here who has never taken that step across the bridge of faith to do so. Remember, today, if you hear His voice, do not harden your hearts. You may never hear him call you again, so don't put that step off any longer."

My heart was pounding so loud I was sure Pete and others around me could hear it. How could the pastor know that last night, I dreamt about standing on a bridge and being afraid to take that first step? Or about the verse Pete read, "I'll never leave you"?

I need to get out of here. I panicked, closing my eyes. But instead of running, I prayed, *God, help me do what you want me to do.* I was overcome with the need to confess my sorrow to God for every sin I'd ever committed. Tears trickled down my cheeks, leaving streaky white tracks in my foundation. Unseen to others, the weight of shame I had carried all my life felt like a heavy iron-laden sack on my shoulders. *I have been in prison all my life. Please take this weight off me, Lord. Forgive me. Set me free.*

"Let's all stand and sing an old favorite hymn together," Pastor Shawn invited. "And if anyone here wants to take that step of faith in Jesus today, take a physical step now and come down to the front. There will be folks here who will pray with you."

My legs felt like lead. There was no way I was walking down the aisle in front of everyone. The song began. *Just as I am, without one plea, But, that Thy blood was shed for me, And that Thou bidst me come to Thee, O Lamb of God, I come, I come. Just as I am and waiting not To rid my soul of one dark blot, To Thee whose blood can cleanse each spot, O Lamb of God, I come, I come...*

Voices rose around me as I closed my eyes tightly. Tears streamed down my face. The words rang so true, and the melody drew me to my feet. My eyes still closed, I lifted my right foot then felt a strange sensation. When I opened my eyes again, I found myself at the front of the church with two ladies praying over me. I had no memory of walking. But somehow, I was there.

Pete, Mell, Lily, and Dan joined me at the front, hugging and encouraging me. My sweet Bella came alongside Larry. In tears, they expressed their love and joy for me. More hugs were exchanged as we went out together. I felt a sense of relief like never before. It was as if a fifty-pound weight had been lifted off my shoulders. I felt like I could fly. Yet, deep down, something still niggled at my spirit. Something that wasn't quite settled. *Lord, what else do you want me to do?*

Two Days Later, Phoenix, AZ

Ruben arrived at the Burrows' house for their landscape work. As he parked, a *For Sale* sign caught his attention. The anxious whimper of a dog diverted his gaze toward the street, where he saw Bea walking Skippy.

"Hi, Bea!" Ruben waved. As they approached, he asked, "You sure are growing up fast. How old are you now?"

"Hi, Ruben. I'm going to be nine in a few weeks," Bea announced proudly.

"Wow! That's hard to believe. I remember when you were only four, and Elise was your nanny." Looking closely, he saw a spark of recollection cross her face. "Are you going to have a birthday party?"

"Yes, I think we'll have it in the backyard the Saturday after my actual birthday, April 28th. It's going to be an art party, and everyone gets to paint a picture." She sounded cautiously excited.

"So, you still like to paint?"

"Sometimes. But I miss having Mom… I mean, Elise, to paint

with. And Jane keeps forgetting to get me more colors. I'm almost out of red and blue." With that, Bea cast her eyes downward, looking a little sad. Ruben noticed she'd referred to her mother as Jane, not Mommy.

Bea tugged Skippy's leash towards the house. Ruben tried to catch her as she walked off. "Don't give up hope, little Bumble Bea." She stopped short in her tracks and turned her head back towards him. A startled look flashed across her face. She hadn't been called Bumble Bea since Elise left.

Ruben walked to the sideyard to join his crew. A small swarm of bees buzzed by, nearly hitting his face as he rounded the corner of the house.

"Oh! Looks like they do have a problem." *Better tell Jane to call that beekeeper service so they won't have any issues at the party.* He found the text I had sent him with the number.

TWENTY-SEVEN

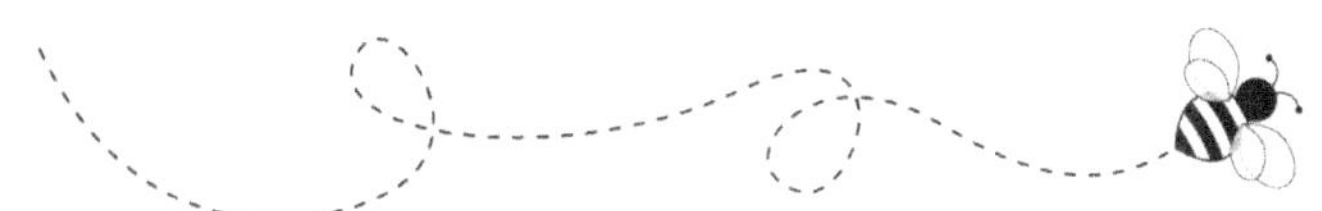

I learnt that worker bees is usually females. They'll do everthin' they cen ta protect the queen and the hive. If they has to, they will sting, but when they do, they give up their life an die.

☙

"GOODBYE HONEY, DRIVE SAFE." I kissed Pete. We both needed to get to work by nine a.m. "I get off at four, and Lily's going to stay with Bella till then, so don't worry about rushing home early.

"Okay, honey. I'm so glad you worked things out with Lily." Pete kissed me again and held the door open for me.

"Yeah, she seems thrilled to let me make some dresses for her in exchange for watching Bella."

Pete had a thirty-minute drive to Solana Beach. I let him go, then rushed to finish getting ready for work.

☙

"WOULD YOU LIKE SOME DESSERT NOW?" I poured some more steaming hot coffee into Larry's cup.

"Got any of that wonderful pecan pie?" he asked.

"You mean Lily's pie recipe? Sure, do," I clarified with a smile.

"Lily's recipe? You mean to tell me Mell is using her pecan pie?" Larry asked in surprise.

"You didn't know?" I said with a twinkle in my eye. "Mell's been using her recipe for several weeks now. Pretty darn good. Wouldn't you say?" The smile in my eyes likely revealed my motives. I wasn't giving up on a relationship between Lily and Larry and knew my father-in-law's biggest soft spot was his appetite. *Looks like she used the old get-to-his-heart-through-his-stomach routine, and I don't mind helping with that one bit,* I thought.

"Well, I'll be! She never even mentioned it the last time we met up. Yes, bring me a slice."

"You met up?" I asked with an eyebrow raised.

"Oh, yeah, I helped Lily with her taxes, remember? After we finished business at the community center, she invited me into her condo for some pie," he explained.

"You know, Larry, I think Lily is very fond of you. You might think about asking her to dinner sometime."

"She seems like a wonderful woman. But I think she and Dan are getting pretty close these days," he said with a thoughtful look in his eyes. "And I wouldn't want to come between her and any man who carries a gun."

I laughed unrestrained, a little surprised and impressed at my father-in-law's sense of humor. It wasn't something I'd seen him display often.

"Well, I wouldn't blame you for being a little *gun* shy," I quipped back. "But maybe you shouldn't assume anything either." I walked to the kitchen, grabbed a slice of pecan, and brought it back to the table.

"Here you go." Setting his pie down, I nudged a little more. "Didn't you tell me Lily wanted you to help with a remodel at her place?"

"Yeah, I haven't heard any more about it though. She probably changed her mind."

Handing Larry his bill, I mentioned, "I have to close out in a few minutes. Lily's actually watching Bella for us today, and I want to get home on time. The pie's on me today."

"Really? You don't have to do that, Elise," he said earnestly.

"Why don't you think of it as insurance for watching Bella while Lily and I go to Phoenix next month?" I offered.

"Well, okay. But I may need more than one piece to be sure," Larry said in jest.

"I don't know about that. Maybe you ought to ask the creator of the original recipe." I came back quickly, "But seriously, Larry, Pete, and I are so glad you can watch Bella for us during my time away. I know Bella will be thrilled, too."

Walking back to the kitchen to close out for the day, my cell phone lit up. A text from Ruben came on the screen. *Call me pronto!*

"What's up, Ruben?" I asked as I walked out to my car.

"Elise, so glad you answered. I think we may have a problem."

RUBEN'S PHONE call was fresh on my mind as I got home from work. I greeted Lily a little bluntly as I entered.

"Hi. Everything go okay?"

"Everything went wonderfully. Are you okay, Elise?" Lily sensed something was wrong.

"I'm sorry, didn't mean to barge in with an attitude. I just got off the phone with Ruben, and we have a bit of a problem." Putting my purse down on the entry credenza, Bella came skipping to the door with her gleeful welcome.

"Hi Mommy. Lily and I had a lot of fun. We painted pictures. See?" she held up a colorful painting for me to see. "It's you and me and Daddy," Bella explained.

"Oh, that's beautiful. But who's the other girl in the picture?" pointing to a simple figure standing next to the girl that was supposed to be Bella.

"That's my sister that you said I might have someday," she said happily. "I think she looks like me, so I made her hair like mine. Do you like it, Mommy?"

"I sure do. Can you go and play in your room for a few minutes so I can talk with Miss Lily for a while?" I bent over and gave Bella a hug, then sent her off.

Sitting in the kitchen, Lily asked, "What is it, Elise?"

"I got a call from Ruben a few minutes ago. He said it looked like the Burrows were planning to move soon. They've put out a For Sale sign in the front yard, and Lidia, the current nanny, confirmed it with Ruben yesterday. He thinks we may need to move up our trip out there." I could feel my anxiety building as I voiced my concerns out loud.

"Oh, dear! But selling a house usually takes weeks, even months. We should have enough time to get there before that," Lily tried to reassure me.

"Lily, when we moved to Phoenix from Texas, a sign went up only two weeks before we left. I never even saw a sold sign or any indication that it had sold before we moved. I barely had time to pack my things, and I have no idea what happened to my cat." My voice was frantic now.

"Oh! Well, I can leave whenever you're ready. I say we pack up and go ASAP. But, you know, the Good Lord will be with us in this change, so don't worry. Everything will work out okay. Don't forget His timing is always best," Lily continued, trying to reassure me, but my mind was spinning.

"But I still have so much to get settled and set up, and I haven't heard back from Allie's friend at the child welfare services yet. What if Mell can't drop everything and leave the café this quickly? I didn't say anything to her about the call before I left tonight. I was too upset and wanted to talk it over with you and Pete first."

Pete walked in at that moment. "You wanted to talk *what* over with me?" he asked, bending over to kiss me on the cheek. "Hi, Lily. Hope our little munchkin didn't give you any trouble."

"Not at all. She was a doll," Lily answered as Bella came bounding into the kitchen.

"Daddy!" she squealed, opening her arms for a hug and kiss.

He picked her up and swung her around. "Hi, sweetie. Did you have fun with Lily today?"

"Yes, we played games and painted pictures. Can Miss Lily stay for dinner, too?" Bella asked.

Pete glanced at me with a questioning look, then back at Bella. "If Miss Lily likes Chinese, it's all right with me." He held up the take-out bags.

"Honey, you picked up Chinese food?" I was delighted. I hadn't even thought about what I was going to make and certainly didn't feel like cooking. "That's great! Lily, we'd love to have you stay if you want."

"Please, please, please!" Bella jumped up and down, pleading.

"Well, okay, if it's all right with your mommy, I'd love to," Lily asked me with her eyes and a tilt of her head.

"I insist. Besides, it will give us all an opportunity to talk about the new development," I confirmed.

🐝

"GOOD NIGHT, SWEETHEART. SWEET DREAMS." I kissed Bella and tucked her in for the evening while Lily filled Pete in on the latest development.

"All settled in now. Are you sure you don't mind staying a few more minutes to talk, Lily?"

"You know, I do have to get home soon to feed Chiquita and make sure she goes out. It's already been more than four hours, and she can't get out without someone opening the door. Larry said he'd let her out at noon, but I didn't ask him to feed her dinner, too," she explained.

"Why don't you give him a call and see if he wouldn't mind? He lives so close, I'm pretty sure he'd be glad to help out." I was happy to know Lily and Larry were still on friendly terms.

Lily left the room to make the call to Larry. I only heard her say goodbye to him, but it sounded endearing.

"He said he would, but only if I baked him a pecan pie." Lily chuckled and joined them in the kitchen for some more discussion.

"Lily, did Dan give you the name of his policeman friend in the Phoenix area yet?" I asked.

"Oh, sorry, been meanin' to tell you. His name is Detective Carl Lewinsky. Here's his number." Lily texted his contact information to me.

"Thanks. Got it. I'll give him a call tomorrow."

The three of us talked for another hour, and then I called Mell. She was surprised at the news of a date change, yet calm and assuring. "I'm sure I can work something out," Mell assured me. "The manager, Rita, at Coyote's, is a good friend of mine, and she might be willing to fill in for a few days. Allie might be able to help a little too. I'll get Nick to set up as much as possible ahead of time just to be sure. But I won't be able to be gone more than five days at most."

"That would be plenty of time, Mell, thank you. Could you have Allie give me a call ASAP? She was working to connect me with someone she knows at Child Protective Services in Phoenix," I said gratefully.

We talked a little longer, and Lily excused herself to go.

"Lily, thank you so much for watching Bella today. I'm so grateful you were here to catch me so I wouldn't fall. Know what I mean? Don't know what I would do without your friendship and support," I said, sending Lily on her way with a hug.

Pete and I stayed up late talking for hours after she left. I could tell he had something on his mind and wasn't feeling good about whatever it was.

*

"SO, what's going on with you?" I asked Pete as we settled in.

"Oh, nothing."

That could only mean *something,* so I pushed. "Pete, what's bothering you?"

He sighed. "I'm concerned about the schedule Cavenaugh has me on for the next few weeks. If I do everything he wants of me, I'll be a zombie just trying to keep up with the hours it would take to do it all."

"What are you gonna do?" I asked.

"Dunno yet. If I complain, he'll probably just replace me. But we need the extra income this new hotel position is giving us," Pete said, concern written all over his face. "And, I have to say, honey, that I don't feel real good about you going back to Phoenix. Especially since I'm gonna be working more hours and can't be there to help you."

There it was.

"What do you mean? Are you saying you don't want me to go?" I asked, feeling emotions rise within me.

"I don't think it's safe, that's all." He tried to smooth over his true feelings, and it was showing in his demeanor.

"Honey," I said, "you know I have to go. We already discussed this. I'm going to be careful, and we are looking at every legal avenue possible. Allie's friend Michelle is already working on the case, and we shouldn't have to do anything but watch it all come together."

"Elise, you are in total denial. You think you can just wave your magic wand, and everything will go fine. Well, things are never that easy. You could end up in jail or worse." Anger was building in Pete's voice. "Do you really want to risk that? Do you really want to take a chance on something that could mean being separated from Bella and me?" He got off the couch and paced in front of me.

"Do *you* really want me to sit by and watch Bea get abused and molested like I was?" I raised the volume of my voice above his. "How can you be so insensitive about her situation? How can you sit there and start ordering me not to leave now? If they move away as quickly as they did when I was there, the Burrows will get away, and the authorities may never catch up with them. Then, what can I do?" I was nearly shouting now, my emotions running on the edge.

"I'm not *ordering* you to do anything. I just think maybe you're putting Bea's problems before our family's needs and not looking at this with a clear mind." He calmed a little, but I could tell he was still upset. So was I.

"That's not fair. What am I supposed to say to that? Bea is my family, too. She may not be my real daughter, but I love her just as I love Bella. You know, ever since we've been together, you have told me I should trust in God and let him lead me in things. Now that I am trying to obey God, you want to pull the rug out from under me. Have you considered that maybe you're being a stumbling block to what God has directed me to do? I mean, I just don't get you sometimes. Are you just looking for a reason to leave me? Isn't that what men do?" I was boiling with anger and hurt now. I could picture him walking out the door and never coming back, just like my father did.

The look of pain in his eyes pierced through my stirred-up feelings of abandonment. Covering my face and walking away, I started sobbing. Pete held back a while, then came up to me softly. "Honey, you know I would never leave you. It's just that I am worried about you. I don't know what I'd do if I lost you. And..." he paused, swallowing hard before finishing, "sometimes it feels like you are falling back into a mindset of bondage. Like maybe you feel enslaved again and just want to escape from Bella and me. But you're right. If God is truly directing you to go back and get Bea, I don't want to hold you back."

He put his hands on my waist, drawing me to him. "I'm sorry, honey. Guess I'm a little stressed. Maybe it's all the extra work I've been putting in lately that's got me on edge." He looked me straight in the eyes with tenderness. "And I am *not* going to leave you as your father did."

I pulled away, and he spun me back around and kissed me in a way that said what we both couldn't speak—I love you.

Lingering into the embrace and still feeling raw with emotions, hurt and pain turned to passion as we found comfort in one another's arms. Gently taking my hand, he led me to the bedroom. I hadn't realized how long it had been since we'd made love or how much I needed him until we came together in divine bliss once more.

We lay together for several minutes after, entwined in one another's arms, letting the release fill our spirits. Making love to Pete always brought me a sense of closeness. It was a demonstration of true love compared to what I'd known with Jack. It gave me trembles just thinking about the scars Jack had left me with compared to the joy and pleasure Pete gave me.

How could I have ever dismissed his love so easily? My heart felt deep conviction and sorrow now, and I sincerely poured out my confession to him. "Oh, Pete, I am so sorry. Please forgive me for saying those terrible things. You were right. I've been so distracted lately that I have been acting like a child of captivity again."

Thinking on it further, I knew he was more right about my attitude than I had wanted to admit. For many weeks now, my mind had been so distracted by my dreams and the memories they released that I had taken on a mindset of bondage without realizing it. I was looking at things through the lens of my childhood and projecting impressions and expectations onto Pete that didn't fit. My own emotions were keeping me more captive than I'd ever been during my childhood.

Would I ever truly be free from that feeling? I was exhausted just thinking about what was coming next.

TWENTY-EIGHT

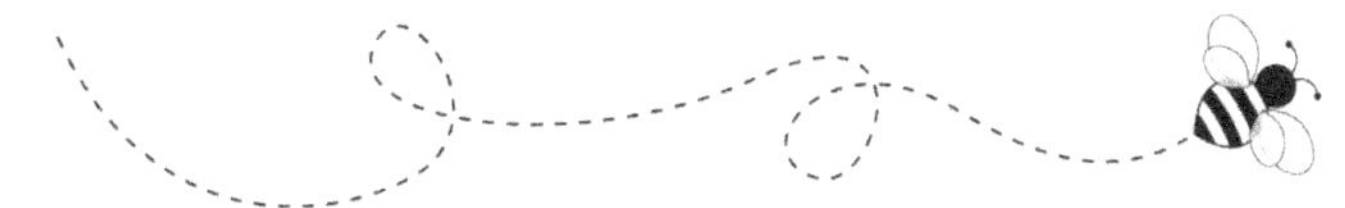

Did ya'll know that honeybees will travel several miles to find the nectar they need for makin' honey? Mama Millie tole me bout that since her folks use a raise bees an' she know a thing or two 'bout them little critters. Elise, Lily and Mell is goin to travel by train more than 380 miles to get ta Phoenix, but they will have each otha which should help pass the time.

This rescue they was plannin' was gone be the thing that bring new purpose to all three a them. An all three a my friends was gonna be doing something they neva' did before.

I bet ya'll don't know that bees change they jobs and try new kine a duties as they get older. An scientists know that bees has a protein that is like one in humans. They say that when a bee learn ta do new job, it hep their brain become like a young bee's brain does. An people cen do the same thing by trying somethin' new. So guess Mell and Lily gone be like new afta' this adventure.

Very Early Monday Morning

With our departure time moved up by three weeks, I was a mess. But at least I didn't have to pack under duress this time. *Got real luggage, too.* I'd put a lot of thought into our rescue plan, and everything was set to go three days after our arrival. Despite all the careful planning, jitters rattled my insides.

Pete drove me to the train station with Bella in the back seat. Larry was to pick up Lily at her house, then stop to get Mell at Chicky's on the way to the station. "Have you got everything? Your ticket?"

"Don't worry, I'm going to be all right. Got my ticket." I patted my purse.

"Honey," Pete continued, "remember the Lord is with you. We'll all be praying for you night and day. But be careful." Pete's eyebrows furrowed with worry.

"Be sure Bella gets to bed on time and brushes her teeth. I made you a big pot of spaghetti with meatballs on the side. It's in the fridge. That should hold you both for a couple of days." After giving Pete a big kiss, I bent down to say goodbye to Bella.

"I love you, sweetie. Be good for Daddy and Papa Larry. Mommy will be back home soon. I love you so much." I gave Bella a big hug and another kiss.

Larry wished us well and promised to be a good grandpapa, then gave me a hug. Lily stood by, eyes fixed on Larry. Then, to my surprise, she walked over and hugged Larry warmly, "Bye, Larry." Blushing, she started to move away, but turning her chin, he kissed her.

Pete and I exchanged smiles. Then, putting on a brave face, he walked over for another goodbye kiss. Looking into his eyes, it was evident he wasn't feeling as confident in the whole rescue thing as he pretended to be. "I'm so glad Lily and Mell will be with you." His words of encouragement were as much for him as they were for me. "And even more," he went on, "I'm over-joyed the Lord will be with you now too."

As we stepped onto the train, my thoughts drifted to the email I'd received that morning. *What could it mean?*

＊

PLACING MOST of my luggage on the rack, I kept one bag with me. The three of us settled into our seats, adrenaline running high. I was grateful we were able to get a spot on the train where we could all sit together with a modicum of privacy. The horn sounded, and the train lurched to a start and then picked up speed.

For several minutes, we all sat as still as mannequins. Except for Lily, that is. She must've shifted position four times in the first five minutes alone. I was in a world of my own, lost in thought while fumbling my locket. Mell started fiddling with a stray strand of hair that wouldn't stay put out of her eyes.

After waiting ten minutes more, Lily broke the ice. "So, Elise, how about we go over today's plan?"

"Oh, sure. Sorry if I've been in la-la land. I received a strange email this morning and can't get it out of my mind."

"You want to tell us about it?" Mell pried.

"I received my DNA results from Ancestry.com. I sent samples into them several weeks ago," I explained, hoping to leave it at that.

"A-n-n-d?" Lily prodded.

"Oh, it's nothing. Probably some mix-up. It said my mother's maiden name was Kelly, which has to be a mistake. My mother was Mexican, and Kelly is an Irish name—it just doesn't add up. It did have my father's last name correct, though—Dupree. I'm still waiting on some other results; maybe they'll clear things up."

Trying to drum up some enthusiasm. "So, this is exciting, huh?" My hands were shaking violently, so I clasped them together and wedged them between my knees, hoping to stop the trembling.

Naturally, Lily came to my rescue with her humor. "Excitin'. Ya mean like when Forest Gump meets President Kennedy right after drinking a lot of Dr. Pepper and says, 'I gotta pee?'"

We started to giggle like a bunch of schoolgirls—my nervousness momentarily dispersed.

"Lily, having you on this caper is sure to keep us in good spirits no matter how nervous we all are." I thanked her.

"Yeah!" Mell spoke up. "We might all end up in jail, but at least we'll laugh all the way there."

After we all settled in once more, I started my pep talk again. "Seriously, ladies, I can't tell you how much this means to me having you by my side. If either of you gets cold feet, even in the slightest way, please don't hesitate to drop out. I could never live with myself if anything happened to either one of you."

"Mell, is Sally watching over things at Chicky's while you're gone?" Lily inquired.

"Heavens no. My friend Rita is."

"Speaking of Sally, how's she workin' out?" I jumped in.

"Well, it's not been easy," Mell replied. "I've given her about every chance I can, but I'm not sure she's cut out for restaurant work."

"Didn't you say she did okay with the schedule last week?" I asked.

"Yeah, but can't say what else she could do."

"Well, I don't mean to be critical, but last week, I was in there for dinner. After waiting to order about twenty minutes, she finally came back to my table and asked if I wanted dessert now," Lily told us.

"You hadn't gotten your meal yet?" Mell asked.

"Hadn't even been able to order it." Lily quickly changed the tone. "Oh, speaking of food, I made us all some pimento cheese sandwiches and a few PB&J's, too. Thought we'd need lunch and wasn't sure what all they'd have on board."

"I brought us some berry pie as well." Mell brightened things further.

"My, my, that sounds good." Lily lit up. "Ya know, I'm fairly excited. About the rescue, that is, not the pie. I mean, it's probably the biggest and most excitin' adventure I've eva had, except maybe the alligator incident. I am so thankful God brought me here and let me connect with all ya'll."

"Alligator?" Mell said, raising her eyebrows. "What do you mean, alligator incident?"

"Oh, it was nothin'. I'll tell you later. But honestly, who would a thought an old church lady like me would be doin' such a thing as this? It's bringing me a new purpose, just like I prayed for," Lily declared with nervous bravado.

"Thank you, Lily. I think you're right. God sent you here for a purpose, and you have helped us fulfill our purposes, too."

Mell nodded in agreement, then asked, "So, Elise, what's the plan for today again?"

"I've rented a car. We'll pick it up next to the train station. Ruben's van will be ready in a couple of days. I've arranged to have it painted—that way, Jane won't recognize it. Our hotel is about fifteen minutes from the station and ten minutes from where we tango. Ruben's gonna meet us for dinner at a nearby BJ's tonight," I started explaining.

"What about Allie's friend, Michelle?" Mell asked. "Have you been able to set up a meeting with her?"

"Yep. Tomorrow morning at 9:30. Detective Dan's friend, Carl, will meet with me sometime tomorrow too, but we haven't finalized a time yet," I told them, noticing the look in Lily's eyes at the mention of Dan. "Speaking of Dan. How's that goin' for you, Lily?"

She blushed. "Oh, not sure. It was quite a rodeo the night he took me out to dinner," Lily said, some consternation showing.

"Rodeo? What do you mean?" Mell asked.

"Well, I was all gussied up in a new white lace dress for our dinner date, and wouldn't you know, he took me to the Rotary Club Barn on 3rd Street." She rolled her eyes. "For some silly reason, I figured he'd take me somewhere nice for our first real date, maybe even somewhere we could dance. And when I saw where we was goin', I just about died in my Sunday best. I mean, talk about rustic," Lily started, and we knew there was more coming.

The picture I had in my head of Lily dancing wasn't a pretty one. Not really sure why I thought ladies her age didn't dance, but as usual with Lily, it brought a smile to my face.

"I was a little miffed, to say the least, but when we went inside, I was pleasantly surprised." She started up again but was distracted by something she saw outside. "Isn't it gorgeous out there today?"

"Lily, sometimes you have the attention span of a flea," I teased.

"Hah!" She laughed. "Guess you got me pegged. So, about the barn, the décor *was* rustic but chic, and the live band was actually very good. They played a mix of music from the 60s and 70s, as well as some more contemporary music. We ended up having a good time, but, of course, I did manage to get BBQ sauce on my white dress."

"Well, isn't there some kind of scientific law about that happening? You know, something like red sauce plus white equals stains to the tenth power," Mell joked.

"You got that right, Mell," we all agreed.

Mell pried further. "Didn't you go on a hike with Dan recently too?"

Lily started blushing again. "Uh, yes. Elise came with us for most of the hike, so it wasn't so much a date as a group of friends gettin' together. It was a real pretty hike. If you haven't been to Pulpit Rock, you should go. The waterfall is gorgeous, and the view is spectacular."

Lily seemed a little embarrassed, so I jumped in for support. "Lily's right; the waterfall and the view are amazing. I have to say, seeing the valley from a birds-eye-view gives you a new sense of perspective on life. It's kinda like getting a glimpse of God's view on the world and on us."

"So true," Lily piped up again. "Especially after the snake incident."

"You had a snake incident?" Mell asked.

"Oh, yeah. A rattlesnake slithered up behind us. Dan got there in the nick of time. He said it was coiled up and ready to strike, so he shot it with his pistol."

"Oh, my! That must've been frightening." Mell seemed a little shocked.

"It was! I nearly peed my pants at the sound of the gunshot. But it was kinda cute how Dan was so protective. He also gave me lots of tips on hiking. He's very knowledgeable about nature and the trails around the area." Lily beamed, obviously impressed in more ways than one.

I was still hoping she and my father-in-law might hit it off, especially with that goodbye kiss we just witnessed. "I guess we both learned a little bit more about Dan, the man, not just the police officer up there in the hills," I affirmed. "He demonstrated both manly grit and gentleness."

"Yes, something I've always admired in a man. When we got to the other side of the trail, well, it was heaven. The waterfall was amazing as it cascaded all around us. Standing behind it felt so immersing, almost like being baptized. We had our picnic in a cool, flat area where we could gaze at the waterfall while we ate. And guess what?" Lily said, eyes sparkling. "We finally had the talk about knowing each other years before."

"Oh really? That must have been after I'd gone on ahead of you," I told her. I had a feeling Dan had kissed her, too. Mell looked a little puzzled. She didn't know that Lily had met Dan many years earlier.

"Well, I don't know about you gals, but your story got my appetite goin'. How about some sandwiches and pie now?" Mell offered.

"Sure! Sounds good ta me," I said.

"I brought some paper plates, but not sure if I brought

enough napkins for you, Lily. You *are* wearing a white blouse today," Mell teased.

"Yeah, perfect for a little statistical research," she shot back as we dug into our lunch.

Speaking of the laws of probability— last week our new mayor, Bob Filner, came into Chicky's, and wouldn't you know he got Sally as his waitress." Mell shook her head in disbelief. "When he asked Sally what the soup of the day was, she said, 'Du jour... See, it's right there on the menu—soup *du jour*.'"

"You should've seen the baffled look on his face, especially when she added that it was 'just a fancy name for all our soup.'"

"You know," Mell flashed a sheepish look. "About Sally, she may not be the dumbest girl in the world, but she better hope that *that* girl doesn't die."

Mell's unexpected zingers had us chortling. "Yesterday, just for fun," Mell continued, "I told Sally our special of the night was shark's legs served in a lemon caper sauce with parmesan risotto." Mell paused, letting the idea of a fish having legs sink in. "She asked if the fish was farmed or wild caught." Taking a breath, she continued, "I told her, 'Neither one... it walked up on shore.'"

We lost it. Uncontrollable laughter had us spitting pimento cheese.

"Then, Sally said, 'You're kidding me, right? Because...'" choking out the rest, tears of laughter rolling down Mell's cheeks, "'because I've never heard of risotto.'"

That did it! We all busted up in howls of hilarity. Mell's sarcastic humor caught us all off-guard.

"Mell, you really got us now. I think I just wet my pants." Lily roared with laughter. We heartily agreed, and then all of us got up to go to the restroom.

THE TRAIN SLOWED DOWN, and so did we. More relaxed now, we all settled down for an afternoon nap, our mirth rightfully dissipated, smiles replaced by a somberness of conviction. We'd made merry at the expense of a sister.

After an hour or so, I awoke and saw Mell and Lily stirring. Glancing out the window, the scenery was beautiful. Rolling green hills with spring flowers were sprinkled in colorful patterns. A lagoon and the ocean in the distance reminded me we were nearly out of San Diego County. But, picking up speed changed everything into a blur of color. The horn blared a warning to all, fully rousing Mell and Lily. Unlike the scenery that continued to whiz by, pictures in my head slowed to a memorable pace. I saw my grandparents' house, clear as could be. I sat straight up, pondering the memory the horn had triggered. Lily must have seen the perplexed look on my face.

"Thinking about something, Elise?" she asked.

"Yeah. I just remembered something from long ago about my grandparents."

"Your grandparents?" Lily seemed surprised.

"Yes," I confirmed. "Even though I couldn't have been more than three or four, I remember some things about them. Their farmhouse was so close to the railroad tracks the whole house shimmied when the train roared by. It was small but boasted a nice porch with rocking chairs on it. I remember putting pennies on the tracks and waiting for another train to roll over and flatten them. Funny thing is, I can picture their faces, and neither of them looks Hispanic."

"Well, maybe they were your father's parents. Didn't you say his name was French? Du-something."

"Yes, Dupree. You could be right."

"So, Elise, what's in the big bag next to you?"

"Oh," I said, pulling it close and sliding it out. "It's a magnetic sign. What do you guys think?"

"I like the name *Bumble Beekeeper* and the little flowers and bees you have on it, but are we really going to remove a beehive?" Lily asked, noting it also said *Beehive Removal*.

"Only if we have to," I answered. Seeing the worried look on their faces, I added, "Don't worry, I'll do the removal if need be. I wouldn't want you to get hurt."

"That's a relief. But are you sure, Elise? It sounds dangerous." Lily expressed concern.

"Well, I can do it," Mell said, standing and grabbing her suit-case off the rack. We watched curiously as she pulled out a bulky white suit, yellowed with age, with a semi-attached protective head covering.

"This was my grandmother's bee suit. I've had it for about twenty years now. Guess it's time to dust it off and use it again," Mell declared.

"Mell, that's amazing. Do you know how to remove hives?" Lily asked, and we both awaited her response.

"Think I know enough. We probably won't have to remove one anyway. Many beehives and colonies are vacating by the end of spring, so any swarms are probably just on the move, looking for new sites."

"Wanna see the suit I made?" I asked, pulling it out of my bag. "What d'ya think? Mell?"

"You made that, Elise?"

"Yes, I had to rush it a bit since our date got moved up, so I used some fabrics I already had on hand and a jacket I've had for years. The netting I used in the face cover is leftover tulle from a bee costume I made for Beatrice right before I left. Pretty ironic, isn't it?" I held it up for them to see.

"Wow!" Lily praised. "I am impressed."

"So, Mell, will it work?"

Mell examined it closer, staying silent the whole time, which made me nervous. Finally, she responded, "I think this suit is not only sufficient for the job, it's marvelous. Mama Millie would be proud of you, Elise. But remember, there's a lot more to removing a hive than having a protective suit. So, I think I should be the main one to handle that if necessary," Mell insisted.

"Okay with me," I said. "Lily, you can be our driver and business rep."

"Yes! That sounds more like something I can handle," Lily exclaimed with a sigh of relief we all heard.

"Ladies, I really hope we don't have to resort to this, but let's just pray God will guide us every step of the way. And mostly that little Bea and Bobby will be removed from the hive of danger they live in," I waxed on.

THE TRAIN SPED UP AGAIN, and our hearts picked up speed in time with the whirring motion of its wheels. The reality of being amid a daring rescue grew closer every minute. Thankfully, all of the anecdotes and laughter we shared had a calming effect on our nerves. We were able to get back to business and iron out some of the details of our plan, but mostly, we tried to stay positive. I was probably the only one with nerves still battling it out in my gut. *Hmm! Never did hear the alligator story.* Just imagining Lily's possible story made me smile and relax.

TWENTY-NINE

We arrived in Phoenix right on time. Tired and a little bedraggled, we gathered our luggage and headed toward the car rental. As we trudged over to it, my cell phone rang. It was Pete.

"Hi, honey. Perfect timing. We just got in, and we're heading over to get our car now."

"Oh, good. Everything go okay with your ride?" he asked.

"Yes. It went great. We even got naps." I was feeling pretty pumped, and I think Pete could tell.

"Well, you sound good. I wanted you to know that Dad and I are praying for you. And Bella too. Please stay safe. I love you."

"Love you too, honey. Kisses to you and Bella. I'll call you tonight after our meeting with Ruben." As I hung up, a name popped into my mind that I hadn't thought about for a long time —Betty. We hadn't spoken since I left Phoenix five years ago. *Maybe I should give her a call while we're here.*

Getting the rental car took a lot longer than it should've. Lily insisted on being signed on as the key driver, then had a hard time finding her insurance card. We managed to get to the hotel by five in the evening, and I called Michelle. We arranged to meet the next day around ten. It was just as well since we were all a little bushed and needed another quick nap before meeting Ruben at BJ's.

"RUBEN!" I waved him over as he entered the restaurant. "It's so good to see you." I welcomed him with a hug. "Come on, I want you to meet my friends."

"Jes, jes. Sorry I a little late." His English as rustic as ever, and his smile as genuine.

"Mell, Lily, this is my friend Ruben."

They greeted him warmly, and we sat chatting about the weather and figuring out what to order. After the waitress went to get our drinks, I got down to business. "So, Ruben, were you able to get Old Blanco in for the prepping and paint job?"

"Jes. *Yes*. It should be ready for the color now. I will take you there to see. I took it in to get the engine, the clutch, and the starter checked last week, too. Everything is good, except the starter needed to be fixed, and my friend Carlos get that done for you. I did some work on the clutch before I bring it in, and he say it is good now."

"That's great. Let me know how much I owe you for those repairs. Did you bring the pink slip?"

"Oh, la nota rosa está en el vehículo ahora." *The pink slip is in the vehicle now.*

"Okay, thanks. So, you said Bea should be home by 2 p.m. this coming Thursday, right?" I asked.

"Jes," Ruben replied.

"What about Bobby?"

"He has a baseball game. I will be with him from 2:30 till about 5 p.m. Lidia say Miss Jane will be home with Bea on Thursday. Lidia say she has to go to the doctor, so that's why Miss Jane will be home with Bea." Ruben had done his homework.

"Thank you so much, Ruben. That's very helpful." I was so

grateful to have him helping once again. I knew Lily and Mell were able to see firsthand what a good friend he was to me. Then, handing him a wrapped package, I asked him for another favor. "Ruben, would you mind giving this to Bea tomorrow when you go to do the gardening at the Burrows'?"

"Sure, no problema. I think that will make miss Bea happy. Should I tell her who it from?"

"No, just tell her it's from a friend who remembered her birthday." For his protection, I hadn't told Ruben about us going there in the van disguised as a beekeeper service. I didn't want him involved any more than necessary.

The burner phone I'd purchased began ringing. It was Jane. I excused myself and went to the back of the restaurant, where it was quiet.

"Hello, Bumble Beekeeper. Can I help you?" I said in my deepest voice. She asked about removing a beehive. "Yes, we do that. We have an opening this Thursday if that would be good for you." I cleared my throat and answered her next question. "Prices range anywhere from $150 to $300 depending on the hive, where it is, and how tough it'll be to remove. I'll bring my team, and we can give you an estimate then."

Jane added that it was "very important" we come "because my daughter might have a party this Saturday, and I don't want any of the kids getting stung." We set a time of three thirty p.m. I hung up, noting she'd said, "*might* have a party."

I started shaking inside. Things were starting to get real now.

⚜

THE WHITE MINIVAN was now a flat grey from the prep work. I handed the shop owner, Jose, a small sample of paint color that I'd brought and asked if he could match it. "Si, no problema." I looked at the soft yellow I'd chosen and thought about the sign and the little curtains I still had. They were going to look good together.

"Jose," I asked, "I wonder if you could do a special job for me? Could you paint all of the van black except the driver's side? On that side, I want the recessed area to be yellow, like this color sample, outlined with the black on the rest of the van." My hand pointed out what I meant. "And if I could borrow some of your paint, I'd like to paint a picture on the yellow part after it's dry. Reaching into my pocket, I pulled out the watercolor painting that Bea had given me. It was her version of a garden and a bumblebee on a flower.

"Oh," Jose said. "This is very beautiful. We will need to put a clear finish coat on after, so maybe I have it ready Saturday."

"We have to have it by Thursday. What if I came in right after the yellow and black is done and painted the picture?" I pleaded as pitifully as I could.

"Okay. I think it will be good. We do the yellow and black tomorrow, and it will be ready for you on Wednesday for the picture," Jose promised. "The cost is $900. It usually more, but Ruben is my friend and he say you need it and it very important. So we give you good price."

"That's great! Thank you so much. I'll see you Wednesday morning."

Nine Fifteen, Tuesday Morning

Lily had an errand to run, so she dropped Mell and I off at the nearest Coffee Bean. The aroma of freshly brewed coffee brightened our senses as we entered. Choosing a table in a quiet corner, we sat drinking our lattes and watching for Michelle while the caffeine awakened us further. Mell seemed pensively quiet, then blurted out, "Elise, if we have to remove a beehive, we'll need a beehive smoker!"

"Oh, didn't know that. Do you think they'd carry those at a hardware store?"

"I doubt it. We'll also need a bee box or two, so the bees have somewhere to go if they do leave their hive." She filled in further. "One of the boxes needs to have a queen bee inside; otherwise, the bees won't vacate their current hive and go to another."

"Oh, okay. I think Lily said something about visiting a bee farm on her errand. Do you think she would be able to buy those things there?"

"I'll give her a call and explain what we need in case she can," Mell offered.

Just as Mell finished talking to Lily, I looked up and saw an attractive young brunette enter holding a briefcase.

"Michelle?" I asked, standing as she came in.

"Yes. And you must be Elise?" She put her hand out for me to shake. "So nice to meet you."

"You as well. This is Mell, Allie's mother," I introduced.

"Oh, of course. Great to finally meet you, Mell. I've always enjoyed staying in touch with Allie. She is such a special gal," Michelle raved.

"Thank you, Michelle; I've heard a lot about you, too," Mell said.

"Can I get you a coffee, cappuccino, or latte?" I offered.

"A latte sounds good. Thanks."

"Michelle, I was never clear about how you and Allie met?" Mell asked. "Was it while she was in Phoenix for law school?"

"Yes. We met at Arizona State University of Law. I dropped out when I became pregnant with my first child but have kept in touch with Allie ever since," Michelle said.

"So, you studied law too?" Mell asked.

"At first, yeah, but after my baby was born, I realized my heart was really more in line with helping kids in abusive situations. After my son turned four, I trained to work with Child Protective Services. But I'm so grateful for the time I spent in law because it gave me a strong foundation for my work now."

"Oh, that makes sense." Mell commented, "It sounds like

God brought you to a place where you could serve and take care of your little boy at the same time."

"Yes. That is so true." Reaching into her briefcase and pulling out a paper, she got right to business. "So, Elise, we've been looking into your concerns about the Burrows' kids. At this point, we have some strong suspicions but haven't been able to establish any firm evidence that would allow us to remove Bobby or Bea from the home."

Not having a good poker face, I'm sure my expression revealed disappointment. "Have you been able to talk to Bea when she was alone?" I asked.

"Only for a short talk. Mrs. Burrows insisted Bea had a dentist appointment, so it wasn't sufficient. We're trying to set up another meeting and hope we'll be able to get a doctor's report, too," Michelle added.

"What about Lidia, the nanny?" I asked. "Have you spoken to her?"

"Every time we try to connect with Lidia, she's gone some-where. A doctor's appointment, or out shopping for groceries, or some other excuse given. So, we'll try to catch her at home as best we can." The barista called Michelle's name, letting us know her latte was ready. As she sat back down, she continued. "You know, we have to get a warrant from the court in order to remove children from a home. And in order to do that, we must have enough evidence to prove our suspicion of abuse."

Feelings of dread started to filter in. I pictured Jack and Jane packing up and leaving before the next visit by Child Protective Services. It would be just like when we moved from Austin, Texas, to Phoenix. Bobby and Bea would barely have time to pack their things or say goodbye to their friends at school. Even more dreadful, I feared we might not get there in time. The aroma of coffee suddenly took on a bitter note.

"If we are able to remove them on a warrant, they will be temporarily placed in an approved home. Soon after that, there'll be a court hearing, and depending on what the ruling is, the children will either be placed in a foster home or released to go back to the Burrows'," Michelle explained, and my spirits dipped further down. Hope was turning dismal.

"Ask Ruben, the landscaper I told you about. He may be able to help you get a meeting with Lidia. I'll ask him and get back to you as soon as I do," I told her. "Michelle, I'm concerned the family is planning to move out of town very soon. They have the house up for sale, and I know they have a history of fleeing before a sale even goes through. I wouldn't be surprised if Lidia is also being molested or abused in that household. So be sure to investigate that, too."

"Oh, that's good to know. As for getting a warrant in the next day or two, I can't promise you when or if that's going to happen. The sooner we can talk to Lidia, the better," she stressed.

"You might want to check Jack's computer too. You'll probably find some child porn on it. Don't know if that will affect a warrant or not. But thought I should mention it."

"Thanks, Elise. I'll make a note to look into that once we get the warrant. Don't worry, if any kind of abuse is going on in that house, we'll move like lightning to get the kids out of there. And Lidia too, if needed," Michelle assured us.

"Thought you might want to know I'm meeting with a detective here in Phoenix also. It's regarding some criminal activity that could potentially be tied to Jack Burrows. If it does, it could play into this situation."

"Well, that certainly could. Who are you meeting with, Elise?" she asked.

"Detective Carl Lewinsky."

"Oh, he's a good guy. If we do go to remove the kids from the home, we'll have an officer assist with it. It's typically a police officer that works closely with Child Protective Services. Not sure who would be assigned to this case. Once we establish cause, it shouldn't take more than 24 hours to get the warrant," Michelle informed us.

"Okay. Thanks so much." Guessing she thought that would be quite fast, my nerves kicked in again. I couldn't tell her we needed to have it done by Thursday.

Michelle got up to leave. "I'll keep you both posted as things progress," she paused to tell us as the door to the coffee shop opened and Lily walked in.

"Thanks so much, Michelle." I waited till she had left, then gave Lily a nod. *No need to introduce Michelle to everyone who's involved in our backup plan.*

"Hi, guess what I got today?" Lily said, holding up a paper bag. She marched over and placed it on the table, then pulled a jar out. "Honey!" she declared, holding it up.

"Hmm," I said, noting the label said *The Natural Honey Company*. "That looks like quality honey."

"It's the best!" Lily declared with confidence. "I tried some of it back home in California recently and loved it. Thought we could use it as a gift to Jane when we arrive. After all, you can catch more flies with honey than with vinegar."

"Where'd you find it?" Mell asked.

"Well, ya'll ain't gonna believe this, but the guy who owns the same honey company in California happens to be right here in Arizona working on a bee rescue. You can't miss his bright red and yellow B11 Rescue vehicle, and it was parked in the shopping center where I went for my errands." Lily reached into the bag. "Got all of us a jar, too."

"That's so sweet. Thank you, Lily," I said.

"*Sweet* for sure," Mell punned. "Thank you, it reminds me of the unfiltered honey my Grandma Millie used to make. I love that they left the honeycomb inside. "Were you able to get a bee smoker and some boxes?"

"Sure did," Lily responded. "Dael Wilcox, the bee rescuer guy, gave us two boxes for free. One has a queen bee inside it to attract the other bees. And he sold me his extra smoker at a good price. They're in the car."

We filled Lily in on the latest from Michelle and left to go back to our hotel. As we got to the car, my cell phone rang. It was Detective Lewinsky. "Hello, Elise. Could we meet at eleven-thirty?" he asked.

"Sure, how about at the Cracker Barrel on Front Street?" I suggested.

THIRTY

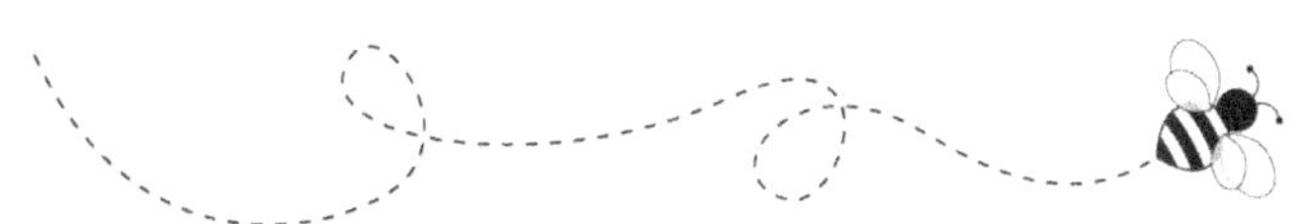

I'd barely arrived at the restaurant when a tall, mature-looking police officer walked in. "Hi. You must be Detective Lewinsky?" I asked, sticking my hand out. With silver grey hair, he looked to be about sixty, but deep wrinkles creased and crinkled his face, making it hard to determine. His soulful brown eyes revealed an unexpected tenderness and compassion that seemed incongruent with the many years of detective work and horrific crimes that he'd likely dealt with.

"Yes. Elise, right?" he confirmed as we found a table in the back of the dining room.

We both ordered cold sodas. "Mind if I get a little lunch, too?" he asked politely as the waitress approached.

"Not at all. I'll be meeting some friends later, so I'll hold off till they arrive," I briefly explained.

"I'll have the roast beef special, please," he told the waitress.

After she left, I got started. "So, let me tell you why I wanted to meet with you." I took a sip of my Dr. Pepper and began. "I lived here several years ago, and the people who were my adoptive parents were very abusive to me…" Without going into too much detail, I gave him some context for my history with the Burrows. "While I lived with them, I witnessed some unusual behavior that made me suspect they might be involved in human trafficking."

"Tell me what you saw, Elise."

I proceeded to describe the scene with Jack, his neighbor Jim, and the big rig near the closed outlet mall that day five years ago. I went on to explain that I was working with Child Protective Services for the sake of Bea and Bobby. "It's my hope they will remove the kids from the Burrows' home before they pick up and move out of town like they did with me." To his credit, Detective Lewinsky listened thoughtfully, taking notes as I shared my story. It was obvious he took me seriously, and that fact alone calmed some of my anxiety.

Taking a deep breath, I told him the worst of it. "To give you an idea of the abuse I endured, I gave birth to Jack's baby when I was only fourteen. Sadly, the baby died." Detective Lewinsky shook his head in disgust. "I realize that Child Protective Services will likely not look into the criminal behavior I witnessed, as it doesn't necessarily apply to removing the kids from the Burrows' custody. But I couldn't stand by and let Jack and Jane hurt anyone else the way they hurt me and could possibly be hurting Bea." I shuddered at the thought, though considering the possibility strengthened my resolve.

"I'm so sorry to hear what you went through. Adoption can be a lifesaver for many children, but it sounds like yours wasn't a good story," he commented with sincerity.

"Far from it. In fact, I'm pretty sure the Burrows paid my mother in order to get me. I don't know if that was the case with their other live-in nannies over the years, but some of the coincidences in our stories lead me to believe they may have been trafficked as well. I was only six years old when it happened, but I remember that day vividly." The heat of shame flamed up the sides of my face as I admitted my suspicions out loud.

"Do you want to tell me what you remember of that day?" His sensitivity and concern were evident and made it a little easier to open up.

"Well…" I paused a moment, sipping my soda and collecting my thoughts. "I was living in Mexico with my parents. Then, one day, while my father was gone on a long trip, my mother, Carmen, drove me up near the border of Texas. Two men were waiting for us along the side of the road. I didn't understand what was happening. Mama was silent when she got out of the car. She walked over to them, talking in whispers. Then…" As I spoke, my breath started constricting in my throat. Tears welled up in my eyes, and my chest heaved as the memory poured into me.

"It's okay. Take your time." The detective gracefully looked down at his notepad, providing me space to continue when I was ready.

"I … I saw them give my mother a wad of cash. She ran back to the car and opened my door, yanking me from my seat. I started crying, asking her what was going on. She said something about me going with the men, and I struggled to get out of her grip. I didn't want to go. I told her over and over that I wanted to stay with her. But when I looked up at her face, her expression was so hard… so unrecognizable."

Tears were streaming down my face by now. The emotions still bottled up from my six-year-old soul longed to escape from inside me. But I knew I had to get through this. If not for me, for other children who had endured the same rejection. The countless women who had experienced the seams of their lives being ripped apart, unable to fully be mended back together. I could do this for them.

The waitress brought Lewinsky's meal, so after a few deep breaths, I continued. "In the end, she forced me to go with the strangers. I never saw my mother again after that." I hung my head in shame but continued. "Next thing I knew, I was dropped off at the Burrows' house. They were nice at first. But, as you can imagine, that didn't last long."

Sensing I'd come to the end of my story, Detective Lewinsky

took a bite of his roast beef and reviewed his notes before asking, "How and when did you move to California?"

"When I was eighteen, I ran away from the Burrows', took a train to Riverview, and tried my best never to look back. That was in 2007."

"And you're sure you lived in Mexico before you were placed with the Burrows family?"

"Positive," I said. "I clearly remember the border road sign saying we were entering Laredo. I got a glimpse just before they threw me in the back of the truck. Hmm… guess that would've been about 1995."

I paused a minute to gather my emotions, then changed the subject to a brighter note, hoping it would help. "Oh, would you like to see a picture of the little girl named Bea that I am worried about? I couldn't find my photo of Bobby," I said, handing him the picture I'd kept all these years.

The color drained from Detective Lewinsky's face, his expression slowly turning to shock. Silence hung in the air like a giant helium balloon about to be popped. Sweat gathered on my forehead, threatening to drip to my brows. Maybe the Arizona heat was just getting to me. He looked closely at the photo, peered into my face, grunted, and then reached into his pocket, pulling out his wallet.

"You said 1995, right?" He held a photo up. "Does this little girl look familiar to you?"

I jerked back in surprise. The girl looked to be about three. "Is that Bea? How did you get her picture?"

"Look a little closer," he said, handing it to me.

Gasping in disbelief, "It… it… it can't be!" I stuttered. "But how? I mean, where did you get this?" The photo showed a little girl with soft blondish-brown curls holding a pink teddy bear and wearing a red polka-dotted dress. In the background was a giant Ferris wheel, as you'd see at a carnival. My mind began spinning in confusion. What was going on? How could he possibly have this picture? Examining the photo closer, the evidence glared back at me—a locket hanging too long for a young child—my locket.

"I've been carrying this picture around in my pocket for the past twenty years, hoping that one day I would find you, Mary." He gazed at me with arched eyebrows and a lopsided smile, one corner of his mouth lifting, the other straight and serious.

"Mary? I told you my name is Elise."

"That's right," Lewinsky admitted. "Your full name is Mary Elise Dupree."

The room around me whirled and blurred before my eyes. Heat rose to my head, then dropped suddenly. Everything went black.

WHEN I CAME TO, Lewinsky was sponging my forehead with a damp cloth. A small crowd was gathered in the outskirts of my vision. "What the…? Where am I?"

"Are you all right, Elise?" Worry was written all over his face as recognition came over me.

"Detective Lewinsky?"

"Yes," he said with a kind smile. "Let's put your feet up a little." He gently lifted both of my feet and put them on top of his rolled-up jacket. "You just had some shocking news. You're going to be okay."

It took me several seconds, but reality began to sink in. Sitting up, I remembered him saying my name was Mary Elise. The photo swam before my eyes. "The picture. It *is* me, IT'S REALLY ME! ISN'T IT?" I nearly shouted. The detective shooed the curious bystanders away as he helped me settle back into my chair.

"Yes, Elise, I believe so. I can't be absolutely positive, but it certainly adds up." His tone was gentle. "That photo was given to me by your mother when your father took you and disappeared. I've been searching for you, on her behalf, all these years. Your mother never gave up looking. She was convinced you were out there somewhere. Every once in a while, she calls to see if I have any new evidence of your whereabouts."

Shaking my head, I questioned, "I don't understand. Why would my mother sell me and then have a detective look for me?" *This makes no sense,* I thought.

"Elise. Your mother's name isn't Carmen; it's Kathleen Kelly Dupree. She goes by Katie. She never lived in Mexico. You were born here, in Phoenix. The last time I heard from her, which was about two years ago, she was still living here." My questioning look had him explaining further. "When they divorced, your father took you and ran to Mexico because your mother was granted full custody."

"Oh, my. Oh my." It was all I could say. I sat frozen, unable to move, think, or speak. Everything around me seemed cock-eyed, out of place, and surreal. "This must be a dream… must be a dream…" I repeated the words over and over, finding solace in their consistency. I thought about my father and me at a carnival and the pink bear and the DNA results saying my mother's maiden name was Kelly. It all began to add up.

⚜

OFFICER LEWINSKY MADE sure I got to my hotel safely. He wanted to drive me, but it was close, and I insisted on walking, so he accompanied me. At the door, he said goodbye and turned to walk back to his car. I searched the righthand pocket of my jacket for my hotel key, then found it in the left one. Jerking it out, a familiar piece of paper came with it.

"Wait!" I hollered back at him, then ran to catch up. "I think you might want to check out this number. It's the license plate from the big rig that the young girls were getting out of at the outlet mall."

⚜

COLLAPSING on a chair inside my room, I reached for my cell phone and called Pete. "I don't know what to think about all of this. I mean… this means… that Carmen wasn't my mother. I just don't know what to think. Everything seems so upside down."

Silence on the other end spoke of his shock. He finally responded. "Honey, it certainly is a surprising development. But how amazing is it that the officer had your picture after all these years? I mean, what are the chances of that happening without divine intervention? We need to pray and ask God for guidance, let Him take things where they need to go." We kept our conversation short and then said our goodbyes. It had been an exhausting day, and something told me the coming days weren't going to be any easier.

🐝

THE WHOLE ORDEAL had drained me. I took a long nap, and Lily and Mell came in just as I was waking. I had heard the concern in their voices when I called to let them know I wouldn't be able to join them for lunch. Now it was four in the afternoon, almost dinner time. Muffled chatter filtered through the hotel door as it opened. "Hey, girl. You okay?" Mell came alongside me, giving me a hug in greeting.

"Better than expected, under the circumstances, I suppose." The look on their faces told me I'd better explain pretty fast. I told them about my meeting with Detective Lewinsky and the startling news we'd uncovered. Naturally, they were both dumbfounded. Couldn't say I blamed them. That's how I felt.

"But I thought you said your mother was from Mexico?" Lily puzzled.

"That's what I thought," I shrugged.

"Well, I'll be a monkey's uncle!" Lily said. "If that ain't the wildest story I've ever heard."

"Yeah, Lily, makes some of your stories sound tame!" Mell quipped.

I appreciate the levity my friends brought to the situation. As my stomach rumbled, I stood and stretched, loosening the kinks in my neck from my nap. "Well, I don't know about you girls, but I am famished. Especially since I skipped out on lunch today."

WE ORDERED pizza delivery and stayed up for hours chatting like teenagers at a slumber party. It felt unexpected. Strange, yet perfectly natural, to be enjoying myself, especially after the shock of the morning. Like God had planned this out, these friends, just for me. Just for this moment.

It wasn't long before the day began to take its toll. After the lights were out, I lay on my back, silently praying. Asking God's guidance for the coming days and for Him to watch over Pete and Bella while I was away, but mostly asking Him to help me understand all I'd learned that day. Questions darted back and forth in my mind but finally settled in on the gift I'd asked Ruben to give to Bea. Today was her actual birthday. I pictured her looking at the painting of flowers and bees, a spark of recollection flashing across her face as she realized it was the picture she'd painted and given to me. I wondered what her reaction was when she read my note. *Dear Bumble Bea, Happy Birthday! I hope to see you very soon. Watch for <u>the Bumble Bee.</u> Love, E.*

I hoped Bea would understand my clue and that it wouldn't cause trouble if Jane happened to see it. *Will she be happy to see me? Will she want to go with me?* Thoughts and fresh worries swirled in my heart and mind. *Lord, help her to be brave.*

Wednesday

The blazing desert sun rose before the earth had a chance to prepare for its early morning heat. Its bright rays rudely pried our eyes open, preempting any attempt at sleeping in. Lily, Mell, and I dashed out, grabbing a quick bite of breakfast before heading to the auto shop for our painting project. "Sure am glad I brought old clothes to paint in." I made the best of things.

"I turned my blouse inside out," Lily chuckled.

Mell dropped us off at Jose's shop. He greeted us as we approached. I was relieved to see Jose had done a good job. The striking black against the yellow recessed area of the van was stunning. Pulling out the photocopy I'd made of Bea's painting, I showed it to Lily. "This is what we are going to paint in the yellow area."

"Is that something you painted?" she asked with diplomatic restraint.

Knowing she must've thought it looked very childish, I smiled and explained it was a copy of the painting Bea had given me when she was four. "We aren't going to paint it exactly like that, but I want it to have a flavor of Bea's picture—something she will be able to recognize. I think we can give it a whimsical style of happy bees and flowers that will make folks smile. After this is over, I can easily remove the magnetic sign and repaint this side to indicate a mobile seamstress business or a Chicky-Pie's delivery service, whichever we want to use the van for next."

"That's brilliant, Elise." Lily brightened.

BY ONE O'CLOCK, we were nearly finished painting. I stood back, admiring how cute the van looked. We'd painted the flowers and bee near where the sign would be placed, giving it a cohesive, intentional look. We'd managed to capture the essence of Bea's painting yet also make it look professional. Once finished, we took a break for lunch. Neither of us imagined this would be the painting day we'd planned several weeks ago, but despite the reasons, it had been a fun and creative experience.

JOSE TOLD us there was a good Mexican restaurant within walking distance, so we decided to try it. Spotting the restaurant as we rounded the corner, I was surprised to see it looked more like an old church. A large stained-glass window let colored hues of light into the foyer, confirming my suspicions.

"There's two of us," Lily announced proudly. "You have no idea how good that felt to say *two*," she winked.

Taking a table near the entrance, we were glad there was no wait. "Don't know about you, Lily, but I'm starving." We both ordered tacos, and Lily decided to get a margarita. I settled for water. "Want to share some guac and chips?" I asked.

"Love to," she replied. "Seems to me the folks that turned this church into a restaurant went to a lot of trouble just so they could say they have *Holy Guacamole*."

Lily laughed at her own pun. I chuckled and rolled my eyes. Minutes later, our food arrived, and coincidentally Ruben entered. "Ruben!" I waved him over. "What a surprise. Please join us."

"Oh, thank you. Ju sure it okay?" he asked humbly.

"Yes, yes. Please. Sit down." We caught the eye of the waitress to take his order.

"We just got back from Jose's shop. The van is looking really good. It should be all done by tomorrow morning. How did it go with Bea? Were you able to give her the gift?"

"Jes, it went very good. She was happy, and I told her it was from a good friend."

"Oh, good. Thanks, Ruben. I really appreciate everything you've done for me."

"Oh, I think you want to know; it look like they going to move very soon," Ruben told us. "I saw some boxes stacked in the kitchen when I was there yesterday. It was my last day to do their gardening, and Mrs. Jane tell me to come inside to pay me. I also see some boxes in another room when I go in. I told Mrs. Jane I had a present for Bea because I knew it her birthday. I think she believe it was from me because I asked if I could give it to Bea myself. When Bea came in the kitchen, she asked her mother if she could pack her toys."

Lily and I stared at one another, a look of worry etched on our faces.

MELL BROUGHT US BACK. Out of words as we approached our hotel, Lily and I went to the room we were sharing, and Mell walked to hers—all three of us tired and quiet with anticipation of the next day.

A text came in from Michelle as I entered the room and flopped on my bed. *"Good news. We'll be serving a warrant and removing B kids 2morrow @ 3. Not sure who the policeman will be. Will keep U posted. Michelle."* My heart was full, with a mixture of both gratitude and insecurity. What if they didn't go through with it, and we left town assuming everything was taken care of? We have to go to the house regardless. No more planning, no more stalling. It was now or never.

ALTHOUGH IT WAS time for bed, we were both a little jittery. Lily accidentally knocked over a cup of water, making me jump higher than a bullfrog. My nervousness was starting to drive both of us batty. The slightest noise made me jerk, and my left eye wouldn't stop twitching. I had tried meditating on a few scripture verses while sipping my glass of wine. Nothing worked.

Settling into bed, try as I might, sleep avoided me. My eyes refused to stay shut. Worries, combined with Arizona's stifling desert heat, fought against me. "Mind if I turn on the air conditioning?" I called out to Lily, hoping not to wake her.

"Please do. This heat's worse than hot flashes."

"Okay." I jumped up and found the thermostat. "Think I'll step outside for a few minutes to clear my head." I pulled a long shirt over my pajama top and made sure I had my room key.

Finding a pathway near the backside of our room, moonlight brightened its winding route. The night birds paid no attention to my angst. They continued singing their joyous goodbyes to the day while the man-in-the-moon smiled from his perch high in the blackened sky. Was he God's appointed watchman, looking down on all of us minuscule humans, reporting back to his maker about our stupid blunders? No, I decided, he looks too friendly.

Stopping at the crest of a slight hill, I gazed upwards as a breeze caught the leaves of a tree nearby, blowing a cool freshness into my spirit. Looking up, I knew the cloak of darkness around the moon couldn't dim its shine on this night—nothing could. Our creator was with me. And even if I lose my freedom or my life, saving Bea's, it will be to God's glory. Yet, the push and pull within me somehow seemed related to the moon's same effects on the ocean tides. Then, as if listening to my thoughts, a hoot owl in a nearby tree probed me with a repetitive "who." "Who"— *is going to help you?* "Who" — *do you think you are?* "Who"— *will win this battle against evil?* My mind slid back and forth with the fullness of each question.

Back in my room, I lifted up another prayer before falling asleep.

THIRTY-ONE

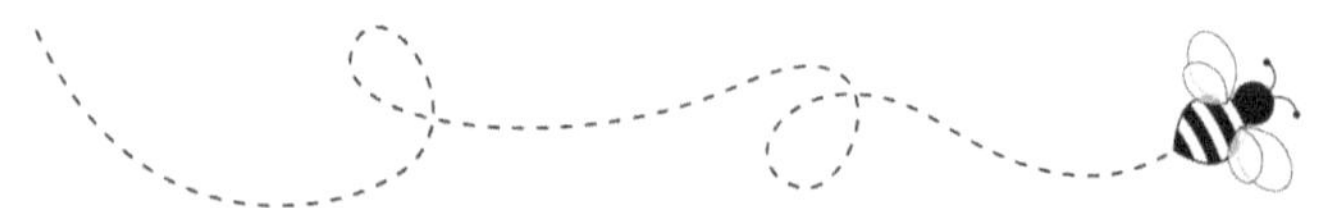

As things start comin' tagetha for Elise, it make me think of a *Bible verse that was a prophecy bout the Messiah. It in Isaiah chapter 7 an it say: "Curds and honey He shall eat, that He may know to refuse the evil and choose the good ... And it shall come to pass in that day that the Lord will whistle for the fly that is in the farthest part of the rivers of Egypt, and for the bee that is in the land of Assyria."*

Now, idn't that the mos interestin' thing you ever heard from the Bible? I really like the part where it say, the Messiah gone eat "curds and honey" an "the Lord will whistle for the fly... and for the bee."

Six a.m., Thursday Morning

I awoke feeling rested and solid. Walking to the window, I drew the drapes open. As if parting curtains on a stage, they revealed a dark, brooding sky full of threatening clouds. Not quite the mood I was hoping for Act 1 of today's drama. In the past, such weather would drench my spirit in a deluge of gloom. But not this time. Today, I wouldn't allow it. Whispering a prayer of thanksgiving, I felt a bright stirring of hope and assurance only the Holy Spirit could impart. Like a shadow chased away by the sun's rising, all doubt dissipated, letting light permeate through every part of me. At that moment, I knew that everything was gonna be all right. I might end up in jail—or worse, but I knew deep down that God was in control. No matter what happened today, everything would work together for His good purposes. It was a feeling so solid and sure. So unlike anything I'd felt before. It made me fearless. A bolt of lightning lit up the sky, and thunder quickly followed, as if God was adding punctuation to His heartening message.

LILY AND I took turns using the bathroom to shower and get ready. She insisted I go first, maybe because she wanted a few more winks of sleep. As the water pricked my skin, moving too slowly from freezing to warm, I considered the day's events. *Let's see, we'll pack up, grab some breakfast, and head over to the detail shop to pick up the van. Lily will follow Mell and me and can park the rental car out of sight near the green waste dump. Then, she'll drive us all in the van over to the Burrows' house. Hopefully, I'll at least get a glimpse of Bea.* My mind raced almost as fast as the shower spray.

Then, a thought popped into my head—*Call Betty.* It was more like a voice than a memory or thought, so I carefully peeked around the shower curtain just to be sure I was alone. Relieved to see no one there, I tried to continue with my agenda, but my mind was now muddled.

Toweling off, I dressed and dried my hair. *Think I'll put it in a bun on top. That'll help with my disguise. I never wore a bun when I was living there.* As Lily took her turn in the bathroom, I dialed Pete. "Hi, honey. You guys doin' okay?"

"Morning, honey. Yes, Bella's still sleeping. You're up early. Ready for the big day?"

"Surprisingly, yes. It's stormy here, but believe it or not, I'm not afraid. In fact, I feel courageous. And good news—Michelle texted me yesterday and said the warrant will be served this afternoon," I announced heroically.

"Oh, that's a relief." Pete sighed loud enough for me to hear. "What will happen then?"

"Well, they'll put the kids in protective foster care until the trial. I'm sure it will take at least several weeks before that happens, so we'll head back home. No need to hang around waiting." I intentionally omitted our plan, which was still on for the beehive removal. He'd just worry.

"Oh, that's good." He sighed again, and I heard the sweet little voice of Bella.

"Are you talking to Mommy?" she asked.

"Yes, honey, you want to talk to her?" Pete handed her the phone.

"Hi, Mommy. Are you still in Zona?"

"Yes, honey, I'm in Arizona. I should be coming home very soon. Are you being a good girl for Papa Larry and Daddy?"

"Yes, Papa Lawee is going to take me to the park today. He said we can feed the ducks."

"Oh, how fun! I love you, honey. Remember that, okay?"

"Okay, Mommy, I love you too."

Tears threatened to spill, but holding them back, I said goodbye and hung up quickly. I heard Lily drying her hair and started to gather my things when *Call Betty* came like a loud whisper in my head again. This time, I heeded the call.

"Hello! Is this Betty?" I asked timidly. An affirmative answered on the other line. "It's me, Elise, your long-lost friend. Hope I'm not calling too early."

"Oh, my goodness! Elise, it's so good to hear from you. How are you doing?" I was glad Betty answered cheerfully. It had, after all, been five years since my abrupt departure.

"I'm doing very well. How about you?" I asked.

"I'm doing good: a few aches and pains these days, but

nothing to complain about. Joe and I are getting ready for a vacation. I'm excited to be taking a break from work for a while."

"Well, I don't want to bother you. I know it's been a long time, but I happened to be in Phoenix and felt a strong urge to call you. Are you sure everything's all right?" I asked, wondering if she was hurt or in trouble, trying to determine why God wanted me to call her.

"No, everything's fine. I'd love to see you. Can you come by and visit while you're in town?"

"I'm not sure I'll have time. Got some business to take care of, but I'll try. When are you and John leaving for your vacation?" I asked, hoping it wasn't too soon.

"We're supposed to leave on Monday, but our dog sitter had to cancel last minute, so we're scrambling to find someone to watch her."

"Okay. In that case, I might be able to come by for a couple of hours. Can I give you a call if my schedule opens up?" I asked, knowing it was highly unlikely. "I would love to reconnect. God has been helping me in so many ways since we last spoke. In fact, I finally gave my heart to Jesus over Easter."

"Oh, Elise! What wonderful news," Betty said joyfully.

"I don't have time to go into details, but would you please pray for me? I have some things to take care of over the next few days, and even though I know God is with me, it's going to be tough."

"I'd be honored to pray for you. In fact, the funniest thing is I was just thinking about you a few minutes ago, Elise. Please come by if you possibly can. I know it would be a blessing for both of us."

"I'll try my best. Sorry to chat and run, Betty. I gotta go, but I promise to call again soon." We said our goodbyes and hung up.

"HI MICHELLE, it's Elise. I wanted to check in and make sure everything is lined up for the warrant and removal today." A ball of worry settled in my stomach.

"Elise! I was just about to give you a call. It's all set for three this afternoon. I'm preparing the paperwork now and making sure the foster home is ready. Looks like we have two potential homes for the kids. One is a nice lady who started fostering a few years ago. I think she would be a perfect fit for Beatrice," Michelle filled me in.

"Oh, that's great! I may swing by just to watch from a distance. If that's okay?" I tacked on the question, not mentioning our Beekeeper plans. I just had to see Bea, no matter what Michelle's reply.

"That's not a good idea, Elise. You never know how volatile things may get. It's really better if you stay away from the house for the time being," she cautioned.

"Oh? Hmm, okay, well, please let me know if anything changes. I'm only planning to be in town until tomorrow morning, but I could stay one or two more days if I have to. I'd rather not leave until I know the kids are safe. Could you please give me an update later this evening?"

"Of course. I know how stressful this must be. I'll follow up with you later on," Michelle replied. The understanding in her voice made me feel a little bad for not being fully honest with her.

"Do you know who the police officer is that's going with you?"

"I thought it would be Officer Cody, but I think they are pulling in Officer Ruiz. I'm not 100% sure. Don't worry, Elise, it'll be fine. Oh! Detective Lewinsky gave me a call. He said he had a very enlightening talk with you. Sounds like pieces of your own puzzle might be coming together for you," she commented. I let it pass without comment.

"Yes, thanks for everything, Michelle. Please keep me posted." I hung up with the name Ruiz on my brain. *Ruiz, why does that name ring a bell?*

Lily stepped out of the bathroom and saw the look of panic on my face. "What's going on?" she asked.

"I just talked to Michelle. They're going to serve the warrant today at three. They're putting the kids in a foster home," I told her in part.

"Well, that's great news. So, why do you look scared out of your wits?" *Ugh, I've never been good at hiding my feelings.*

"Oh, it's probably just my worry-wart self." I'd already made up my mind to ignore Michelle's warning not to go near the house. *Besides,* I told myself, *no one will know it's us. They'll just think we're beekeepers doing our job.*

⚜

Eight Thirty a.m.

Like a steam iron, the overloaded rain clouds pressed down upon us with a stifling unusual mugginess for Phoenix. With predicted temperatures of 90 degrees, we dressed in lightweight clothing. I grabbed my bee suit, the sign, the curtains, and a bottle of water. Lily wore a smart-looking pantsuit that gave her a professional appearance as our Bumble Beekeeper representative. Mell was waiting just outside the hotel entrance when we walked out. She had the bee smoker and a stack of white boxes at her feet. Her bee suit was slung over her arm. "Good morning, Mell. Ready?" I asked.

"Ready as I'll ever be!" she replied.

We decided to grab breakfast at a nearby café, then head over to the shop to pick up the van. As we stepped out from under the hotel porte-cochere, a torrent of rain burst out of the sky, nearly drenching us. Poor Mell got the worst of it. We all quickly scooted back under the covering and watched, hopeful it would stop as quickly as it started. "Oh boy. Hope this isn't a bad sign for today," Mell spoke her worry.

"Sounds like something I might say, especially under the circumstances. I don't like this weather either, but I'm not giving up that easy. Let's go back inside and wait it out." I tried to be optimistic.

WE ALL GATHERED in Mell's room, the rain a torrential downpour outside the window. Our spirits dampened with every drop. I'm pretty sure we were all thinking the same thing. *Is God sending us a message?* With this quiet moment together, Mell spoke up. "Ladies, something has been bothering me ever since our laugh fest on the train." She cast her eyes downward. "I know I apologized at the time, but I need to ask your forgiveness. I sinned against a sister and set a bad example to both of you with backbiting and slander against Sally. She may not be cut out for restaurant work, but that doesn't excuse my judgment against her."

We sat quietly with our own convictions. "You're right, Mell. Of all people, I shouldn't have joined in. God knows the mess I was at waitressing when I first started."

"I'm the oldest here and should've known better," Lily chimed in. "Instead, I laughed louder than all of you. Mell, you're absolutely right. We should never make fun of other people, telling stories at their expense," Lily agreed.

"I have an idea. Got any wine?" Lily asked as she opened the room fridge. "Aah!" Pulling out a bottle of Cabernet, she plunked it down on the small table we sat around. Since Mell's room had only one twin-size bed, there was a cozy sitting area that was perfect for our impromptu gathering. "Why don't we go to God in prayer and confession and have communion right here and now?" She held up a box of crackers.

We agreed wholeheartedly, and Lily added, "This morning,

God laid a word on me from James 4:7-12, and Mell, you just affirmed it." She picked up her cell phone to look up the verse. "Beginning with verse 9, 'Grieve, mourn, and wail. Change your laughter to mourning and your joy to gloom. Humble yourselves before the Lord, and he will lift you up. Brothers and sisters, do not slander one another.' Ladies, we need to turn our laughter into mourning."

"Yes, Lily, you are right." Mell then blurted out, "'A little yeast...'" She left the rest of the verse hanging incomplete. The blank expression on my face must've shown my confusion. Lily obliged, filling in the blanks: "'...leavens the whole bunch.'" I nodded with understanding now. We remained silent for a moment, giving our souls time to ingest the words.

AFTER PRAYER AND A CLEANSING COMMUNION, we felt revived, and the rain had settled down to a light mist. I suggested we drive by the house and scout out the area where we were going to park the rental car. "Good idea," Lily agreed.

Taking it slow, we drove past the Burrows' house. "Oh, no!" I hollered as a moving van pulled out of their driveway. "This is terrible!" Panic laced my voice.

"Isn't that a light on in their kitchen window?" Lily noticed. "Maybe they're still there. Let's not panic just yet."

A figure standing at the window appeared to be Jane, but we were too distant to tell. I drove a few blocks away, dialed Jane on my burner phone, and in my deepest voice, said, "Hello, this is Bumble Beekeeper. Just want you to know we'll be there around two this afternoon."

To my relief, Jane answered, "Oh, okay. That will be fine. Glad you called. I forgot you were coming today. With the rain, we've postponed our move for a few days," Jane confirmed, noting she hadn't mentioned the birthday party.

"Okay. See you then." We all took a deep sigh of relief.

The sun broke through the remaining clouds, and the storm began clearing as we headed for Jose's auto shop.

※

APPROACHING from the back side of the van, then circling around to the yellow-flowered side, we beheld our shiny new mode of transport. "Oh, my goodness, it's stunning!" Mell proclaimed as we all stood in awe at how beautiful it looked.

Placing the magnetic sign at the top of our design, I stood back to admire the total effect. Our painting looked even more charming alongside the sign, giving it a finished, professional look. "Jose, you did a beautiful job." *Even Ruben wouldn't recognize Old Blanco now.* "Is it okay for us to take it now?"

"Jes. It good you come a little late. It better now because the rain, she stop and it not good to get wet before the paint fully dry."

"Thank you so much, Jose. It looks great!" I thanked him and paid in cash, adding an extra $75 for a job well done. I drove the van while Lily and Mell followed close behind in the rental car to our pre-arranged spot. Once there, Lily took the driver's seat, and Mell and I loaded all the bee equipment in the van, donned our beekeeper suits, and jumped in, ready to go.

※

Two p.m.

"Ready or not, here we go," Lily said, an anxious giggle coming through. She handed me the jar of honey we were gifting to Jane to soften her up. "Can you hold this for me?"

"Good idea, Lily," I said, remembering her idiom about honey. I added, "We're off to catch some stinking flies!" We all took a deep breath and shot off toward the Burrows' house.

Lily backed into their driveway so we'd have an easy

getaway. This way, the signage was visible as well. Glancing back as we pulled in, I noticed the garage was open, revealing only Jane's car inside. Lily put the van in park, leaving the key in the ignition. *Smart,* I thought. As she was about to get out, a car drove in and parked in front of us. I nearly panicked, but looking closely, I reassured everyone. "It's Ruben. Probably here to pick up Bobby for his game." We all sighed in relief. "Best not to reveal ourselves and blow our cover. Remember, girls, Ruben doesn't know what his van looks like now and has no idea we are here today."

After waiting for Ruben and Bobby to leave, Lily got out, holding a clipboard under one arm and the honey jar in the other. She walked to the front door while Mell and I sat waiting in the van, feeling as hyper as a couple of bees at a picnic.

Mell looked directly at me. "Can't even tell that it's you behind your dark netted veil, Elise."

"Oh, good. I was hoping it would hide my identity."

Lily came up to our window. "She wants to show us where the hive is."

"I'll go, Elise. You stay in the van until I come to get you. I'll answer any questions she may have," Mell insisted, taking her helmet off as she got out.

"Okay," I agreed. Then, just as Mell got near the front door, it opened, and Jane walked out. A slender young girl with shoulder-length, light brown hair followed behind her. The girl turned her glance towards me, catching a ray of sunshine that gleamed in her bright blue eyes and highlighted a handful of freckles that dusted her nose.

Bea. It's got to be Bumble Bea! My heart skipped.

The urge to jump out and run to her was hard to restrain, but I held back. I sat another minute or two, then couldn't wait any longer. Jerking the door open impatiently, I got out, grabbed a box from the back of the truck, and walked over to a row of bushes, acting as if I was looking for a hive. Jane was pointing something out to Mell, and Lily had gotten back inside the truck.

Keeping my head down, I tried not to be obvious as I inched closer to the house.

Then, to my horror, I saw a police car pull up and park against the street curb. I hollered at Mell, speaking in Spanish. "Mira, mira, una colmena de abejas," *look, look, a beehive of bees,* and waved for her to come over as if I'd seen a beehive. Mell excused herself and quickly came over to me. Although I had spotted some bees, the real reason I'd waved her over became obvious—the policeman was strolling over to Jane, and Michelle was nowhere in sight. I glanced up and looked at his face as Jane greeted him with inexplicable friendliness.

"Manny! It's so good to see you again. Everything well with you and Tina?" Jane greeted him warmly.

Manny! Manny Ruiz! Recognition struck me with a shocking revelation, and the name echoed in my mind. *The dirty cop I met at Jack and Jane's party that night.* Hearing my gasp, Mell sensed my panic and gave me a questioning look. Whispering in her ear, I explained. Her expression told me she understood all too well what this could mean. We carefully slinked a little closer to hear what was being said.

"Hi, Jane. Yes, doing good, and Tina's fine. Here on some official business." He handed her a paper, and she glanced at it, then back at him with alarm. "Sorry about this, but I'm sure that Bobby and Beatrice aren't here now, are they?" He winked.

She nodded assent, "No, they aren't here." Even though Bea was standing just a few feet away.

"That's what I thought. Don't worry about anything. I know you're planning to move. The sooner, the better, in my estimation."

She glanced again at the paper he'd presented, her lips pursing into a scowl. "That would probably be a good idea."

I gasped in disbelief. "Oh, my goodness. He really is dirty. He won't look for the kids, never mind removing them. And he's warning her to move quickly," I quietly muttered, wanting to scream. Mell held me back knowingly. By now, Lily was out of the van and standing with us. She must've sensed something was wrong.

"Oh. Thanks, Manny. You've been a big help, and we won't forget it. Do you think a departure by Saturday would be fast enough?"

"Maybe, but if I were you, I'd leave no later than Friday morning. "I'll do my best to stall things in the meantime."

"Jack will be home soon. Do you want to stay awhile and visit?" she asked timidly while my heart jumped into my throat.

"No, not a good idea. I have to go." He waved and headed back towards his police car. As he walked off, I saw him glance back at us and wondered what he was thinking.

I took a deep breath. "No question, we have to do something," I whispered. "There's no way we can risk waiting until Michelle gets another warrant and a different cop. It's time for plan B, so let's move on it. Mell, did Jane show you where the hive is located?" She nodded yes. "Okay, you start checking out the hive. And Lily, you need to get back in the van and be ready to roll quickly."

"Okay," Lily walked with long strides of determination. "But if you're sure about removing a beehive, I will get our payment first. I'll tell her we have to leave immediately after we get the hive in a box, so we need the check ahead of time," Lily suggested. I loved her style. *Good thinking. Might as well get paid for our trouble and make the entire operation look legitimate.*

"Okay. We'll make our move as soon as we see you back in the van. Mell, get the smoker ready; I'll hold the box for you when you're close to getting it done." I checked my helmet and netting, then put some gloves on. Mell put her helmet on for protection now, too.

"You'll need to get the box with the queen bee inside. It's marked with a red X so you can identify it easily," Mell informed me.

Grabbing the correct box from the truck, I saw that it

contained a queen bee and a small honeycomb. "This the one?" I confirmed with Mell.

"Yep," she said and headed towards a tree with a hollow in it near the sideyard. "I think this tree is the one," she said, pointing. "The bees you saw are probably just out scouting for nectar."

I started following Mell when I spotted Bea standing on the front walk. She was staring at our van, then looked my way. I wanted to run to her right then and there but looked away. She came closer, and everything within me screamed for action. Yet I stood frozen in my tracks. Then, fearing she might disappear back into the house, I set the box down near Mell and walked over to her slowly, whistling a tune as I did. Bea looked back at the van again and inched a little closer to me. On impulse, I started singing the lullaby I used to sing to Bea when she was little. "Roses and bows, butterflies, and toads. These are the things that a baby sees. Soft whispered breeze, and kisses on the knees, tell of the love that they know..."

Did she recognize it? I couldn't tell. A look of revelation on her face gave my heart hope. Then she glanced once more at the van and its flowery bumblebee picture. I stood motionless, waiting further for some kind of clear signal. But she suddenly turned and ran back into the house. My heart sank like a steel ball. I was devastated. She must've known it was me but didn't want to see me or be with me. *Guess I can't blame her after all these years.*

Mell was shouting something about a hive in a hollow and to "come right away." I picked up the box and ran to hold it for her. She had the smoker going pretty strong, and bees started flying out of the hollow of the tree.

"Hold it down near the base of the tree," she ordered. I obeyed, feeling my nerves tingle within me. It didn't take long for the bees to buzz over to the box we'd brought. I sighed, grateful that part of our job would be over soon. Without warning, Jane came running out of the house, blustered with anger.

"Elise! It's you. Isn't it? What the hell do you think you are doing? I'm calling the cops, and you better know they'll catch you this time," she hollered and trounced briskly towards us.

Dropping the box, I ran towards the van, then stopped dead as I saw Bea again. Rolling something beside her, she looked straight at me. We both froze. Why had she come back out? Had she told her mother I was here and come outside to see what would happen next? Or did she sense I was there to help her get away and wanted to go with me? Glancing at Jane, I mumbled something in Spanish, hoping it might work to keep her guessing. Then, looking back and forth between them with tennis match breakneck motion, I started whistling again. Not sure why, but I kept the lullaby tune going, all the while feeling my legs turn to lead.

My heart continued to race, time stood still, and things seemingly moved in slow motion. Jane got closer and closer. She raised her right arm up, revealing a long metal tool. Then, baring her big teeth, she bellowed like a wild animal and charged toward me, screaming. "Aa-a-h!"

Simultaneously, Mell cried out in victory, "Got the beehive!"

I stayed put. It took every ounce of restraint within me not to grab Bea and run. All thoughts became a blur, but beyond my mental fogginess was a dark cloud the size of a small person. A low humming buzz followed it. The cloud drew closer, and the noise emanating from it grew in volume and intensity—a loud, feverish buzz charging directly toward me. It was a swarm of bees—thousands of them. I could hear little bee bodies thumping as they hit my soft helmet and suit. Jane was only seconds away from me. I wanted to run in panic but couldn't budge.

Once more, I was frozen, but this time with fear of the bees. Somehow, the reverberating sound they made broke through the wall of fear that encased me. My head grew dizzy with the noise as I was covered with bees from head to toe, and my vision went black. *Lord, help me! Tell me what to do!* I prayed with all my heart.

The swarm was thickly covering every inch of me. My veil and suit a thin wall between them and me.

Then, just as suddenly, something snapped within me, almost like a whip had struck its tip on the edge of my soul. A soft new melody rose within my spirit. It grew in tone and rhythm, becoming a song flowing through my veins. I started humming along, then singing with lyrics that flowed from within. *You are my covering, oh Lord; you are the sacrifice for me. Hide me in the shadow of your wings, and my redemption be.* With each measure came a feeling of sweet assurance. Then came a low whispering voice. "This way," it said, repeating three times. It felt like the longest minute of my life until a shrill whistle pierced through the buzzing. The dark swarm pulled away from my body as if obeying its call and flew toward the sideyard.

And I followed.

All common sense said to do otherwise. Yet I followed. All fear gone. The dark cloud had lifted. Bea's beautiful face was all I saw. She was trembling, her hand grasping the handle of a small suitcase, a glint of light shimmering on something around her neck. Was it the bee pendant I'd given her for her birthday? I was sure it hadn't been there when she'd come out a few minutes earlier.

From the corner of my eye, I saw Mell standing in stunned shock, Jane statuesque. Then, as the swarm and I neared the side of the house, Jane rushed toward me again. Dashing by the forget-me-nots and running through the red apple ground cover, I raced ahead. Jane followed close behind. The bees swooped up and away.

Stopping to catch my breath, I looked back at Jane. For some reason, she paused, too, probably thinking she had me now. But just as she started back in pursuit, her body jerked backward. She squealed and fell to the ground, her foot stuck in something. As she tried desperately to pull it out, she screamed, and her arms flailed about, swatting at something—hundreds of bees suddenly swarmed around her. She was trapped.

"She must've stepped in a ground hive!" Mell yelled out. "Quick! Get in the van, Elise," she hollered while running towards the van, carrying the box of bees she had just removed.

Instead of following her, I ran to Bea, who was still standing nearby watching the whole scene. Drawing close to her, I pulled off my protective helmet, revealing my face, and called out, "Bea, it's me, Elise. Quick, get in the van away from the bees before you get stung!" I took her hand in mine, put my netted helmet on her head, and grabbed her suitcase with my other hand. Together, we raced to the van. All the while, Jane screamed as the bees continued to surround her.

Mell reached the van at the same moment we did. Lily had already opened the two back doors. Covering the box with a gunny sack to keep the harvested bees inside, Mell set it down at the rear of the van, leaving the back doors open. I hoisted Bea inside. "Go to the front and lay down on the blanket behind the white boxes," I told her.

"But what about Jane?" Bea asked timidly.

"Don't worry. I'll see if I can get the bees to go away. Do you want to come with me, Bea?" I asked, fearing she might say no but feeling it was important to confirm that she wasn't afraid of me now. That she *wanted* to come with me. She sat on the end of the van, cowering and shaking, tears running down her cheeks. I began to cry with her as memories stirred within my soul. Memories of a mother who'd sold me to strangers. Memories of Bea's sweet face as I said goodbye to her years ago. Was I doing the right thing? Had I let my own feelings interfere with her safety and well-being?

"It's going to be all right," I assured Bea. "If you trust me and want to go with me, scooch back into the van. I promise I'll take care of you. But we need to leave right now, or it'll be too late." With glistening eyes, Bea looked straight at me, then put her arms around my neck, hugging me tightly.

"Mommy, I'm so glad you came back. Please take me with you this time." Her words were honey to my wounded heart.

"Okay. Let's go. Stay in the back by the cab till we tell you it's safe to come out." I kissed her on the cheek and hugged her back, then noticed Mell was hosing the bees off Jane. Slamming the doors, I grabbed the hose from Mell and motioned for her to return to the van quickly. Lily revved the engine. A glance confirmed the bees were leaving Jane alone, at least for now. I dropped the water hose leaving the water still gushing out, and ran to the van.

Just as I reached it, a car approached the driveway, slowing to turn in. It was Jack. "Get in quick," Mell hollered.

I opened the door, jumped in, and yelled, "Step on it, Lily!"

Lily peeled out before the door was fully shut. Jack's car nearly hit us as we barreled out of the driveway. Thankfully, he came in on the black side of the van, so he didn't see the sign. "Get us to our rental car and quick!" I told Lily.

Lily gunned it again, and we took off like a race car on its final round. Talk about a fast getaway driver. Lily could give the best of them a run for their money. *Who is this little old lady anyway?* I smiled, grateful for my brave friends.

Mell told us the bees attacking Jane looked different than most bees she'd seen before. She'd heard tell that Africanized bees were prevalent in parts of Arizona when the weather warmed up. I cringed, knowing they were deadly, and unlike regular honeybees, many of them would likely sting her. Despite the fact that I abhorred Jane and was thankful the bees had provided a way of escape, I never intended for her to be harmed. *Oh Lord, you know I still struggle with forgiveness, but please don't let Jane die from the bee stings.*

Lily pulled up against the curb next to our rental car and threw it into park. She and Mell scrambled out of the cab and ran to the rental car as I scooted over to the van driver's seat.

Seconds later, a tap on my window startled the heck out of me—it was Lily holding a bundle of cash. Quickly letting the window down, she thrust her hand in. "Here," she said. "Jane paid us in cash for the beehive removal." Shocked, I saw it was three hundred dollars. "I offered her a discount if she gave cash instead of a check; otherwise, it would've been more," Lily explained.

"Lily, you are really something, but this should be divided between the three of us," I insisted.

"Nope, you take it all. And don't argue with me 'cause we're in a hurry. God bless you, Elise. See you back at the ranch." Lily hurried away to the rental car and blasted off as I screeched away, too.

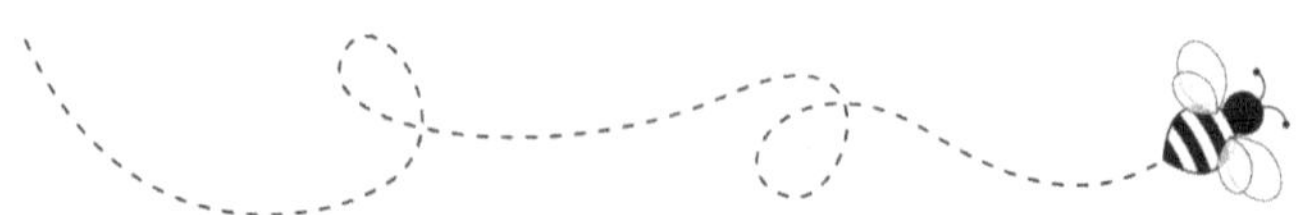

I raced to the green waste dump as they returned to the hotel. Hiding the van behind a clump of trees and bushes, like before, I turned the motor off and looked behind my seat to check on Bea. "Are you okay?" She didn't answer, so I jumped out and went to the back. I opened the doors and repeated, "Are you all right, Bea?"

"I'm scared, Mommy," Bea timidly admitted.

"Oh, honey. I know. I'm a little scared, too. But I know God is with us. With Him by our side, we'll be all right." Removing the box with the hive inside, I placed it outside on a pile of weeds near the trees. I was grateful it had been secured and tightly covered with the gunny sack, so there was no chance Bea could have been stung during our wild escapade. "Thank you, my little buzzing friends. You saved my life," I said, hoping they'd find a new home to settle into. I carefully removed the gunny sack, freeing them from the box, then dashed back to the van.

Taking off my bee suit, I carefully placed it inside a black garbage bag, knowing it was likely saturated with bee pollen. Tying the end of the bag brought a flashback of my escape in Ruben's van with all of my worldly goods inside a garbage bag. Funny how things come around. Then, hopping into the back of the van, I wrapped my arms around Bea in a hug. "Oh, Bea. I've missed you so much."

"I've missed you too, Mommy," she replied.

"I know you probably have lots of questions, but for now, we need to get somewhere safe. Will you be okay back here just a little while longer?" I looked at my Bumble Bea with a warm smile. It felt like a missing puzzle piece had just fallen into place. Like I was home.

"Yes, Mommy, I'll be all right." Bea hugged me back; then I helped her get settled out of sight.

Once she was safe and secure, I removed the magnetic sign and switched out the license plates so the current registered one was in place. Then, dashing back to the cab, I jumped in and caught my breath. Counting to sixty twice before taking another deep breath, I put the burner phone in the glove box, grabbed my regular cell phone, and dialed Betty.

"Hi, Betty? It's Elise again. Hope I'm not catching you at a bad time." I greeted her with the calmest voice I could summon.

"Elise, good to hear from you again. It's a perfect time," Betty chirped.

"Oh, good. I was wondering if maybe I could come by for a while and visit. I have someone with me you'd probably like to see." I tried not to sound as anxious as I felt.

"That would be great! Do you remember how to get here?"

"Couldn't forget. See you in about ten minutes." I hung up and leaned over the seat again. "Bea, you know what? Why don't you come up front now? You'll be more comfortable that way." Bea nodded, climbed into the front passenger seat, and put her seatbelt on.

"Do you remember my old friend Betty? The one who used to work at the fabric shop?"

"Uh, sort of. Is she the one who came to see me in my school play the day you left?" Bea asked.

Not realizing Betty had done that, gratefulness swelled

within me. She must've sensed I wasn't going to be able to go. "Yes, that was her," I responded with a smile.

PULLING INTO BETTY'S DRIVEWAY, I parked next to her SUV. Thankfully, it blocked the van's decorated side, making the all-black side visible to street traffic. I helped Bea out and gave her another comforting hug of assurance.

"Elise. It is so good to see you." Betty's smile and the smell of freshly baked cookies greeted us as she opened her door.

I hugged her tightly. "I can't tell you how happy I am to see you, Betty. Do you know who this is?" I said, nudging Bea out from behind me.

"Oh, my goodness! This can't be little Bea." Betty hugged her gently. "You have grown so much. The last time I saw you, you were dressed in a bee costume."

Bea managed a shy smile, and Betty invited us in. "Come on in, you two. I've got fresh lemonade and cookies." Her gracious welcome astounded me. Her hospitality shone despite my rude departure and sudden reappearance in her life. Her house was as beautiful as I remembered it.

"Thanks so much, Betty. We'd love some lemonade. Are you sure we're not interrupting you? I know you're trying to get ready for a trip."

"Not at all. I'm just so glad you could come by while you're in town. Guess you must've stopped by your old house to visit there too."

"Yeah, kinda. Would you mind if we used your bathroom? We've had an exciting ride getting here today." I looked knowingly at Bea as I asked.

"Of course. Down the hall on the left, as you might remember. Oh, and Bea, you can use the other one next to the bedroom on the right if you want."

I desperately needed to have a minute to calm myself. Taking deep breaths, I lingered a few extra minutes in the bathroom and prayed silently. *Lord, thank you for protecting us today. Please continue to watch over Mell and Lily and guide me in all things.*

Bea was already in the kitchen when I got back. "So, were you able to get someone to watch your dog?" I asked, steering the conversation away from Bea and me. I needed a distraction from the chaos of the altercation with Jane and the bees.

"Well, I still don't know about the dog sitter. The gal I talked to yesterday is supposed to call me today to let me know if she can." Betty grabbed a few napkins and small plates. "We can't wait for the trip, though. We are looking forward to some time away. You both want some lemonade? Or can I offer you something else, Elise?"

"Lemonade is perfect. Thanks. Is that okay with you, Bea?" I asked, hoping to see her cheer up a bit and relax.

"Sure." She kept her reply brief, but her eyes lit up when Betty placed the plate of chocolate chip cookies in front of us.

"So, Elise, tell me what you've been up to these past five years." Betty was direct as usual.

"Well," I took a deep breath, "where do I begin?" I chuckled, rolling my shoulders to release some of the tension. "I'm married and live in California now. I work as a waitress in a restaurant called Chicky-Pie's and…" Looking at Bea, I hesitated, realizing I needed to be careful how much I revealed. I'd have to ease into things with Bea. "And…" I began again but was rescued by Betty's Shih-Tzu puppy yapping loudly at the back door. Apparently, she had just realized visitors had arrived.

"Excuse me. I better let Twinkie inside, or she'll drive us nuts with her barking." Betty got up and opened the sliding door. "It's okay, girl, now hush." The fluffy little dog went directly to Bea and started wagging her tail. "It's okay, honey. She won't bite," Betty assured Bea.

Bea was thrilled to meet Twinkie. "Can I hold her?" she asked politely.

"Yes, she loves to be held. But let her sniff you a little first."

Betty got up and came back with a doggy snack. "Here. Give this to her. She'll love that."

Bea and the dog took to each other immediately. "Betty, would it be okay for Bea to go out back and play with Twinkie for a little while?" I asked with pleading eyes.

"Sure. You can take your cookie outside, too, if you want." Betty carried Bea's lemonade and cookie plate outside and put it on the patio table, then shut the door behind her. I whispered a silent prayer of thanks for the opportunity to talk more freely, then glanced nervously out the front window, looking for any sign of a cop car.

"So, you were saying?" Betty didn't waste any time.

"Yes. I have a little girl now, Bella. She's three and the sweetest little blessing ever. My husband, Pete, works in hotel management and is such a wonderful man." I took a deep breath and got to it quickly, knowing I may not have much time before Bea returned inside. "Betty, God has been so good to me in recent years. But I need to confess something. I was at the Burrows' house just a few minutes ago, but it wasn't for a friendly visit."

Betty leaned in.

"You see when I lived with Jane and Jack, they were very abusive. It got so bad that I believed my life was in danger. The last time you and I saw one another was only a few days before I left. I've been in California ever since. Gratefully, they never found out where I had gone."

"Oh, Elise. I knew something wasn't right when we met up that last time. I've been praying for you ever since." Betty gave my arm a gentle squeeze, a look of deep concern in her eyes.

"God's put some wonderful, caring people in my path there in Riverview. My friend Mell gave me a great start with a place to live and a job. I recently made another friend, Lily, who's been so kind too. In fact, along with my husband, Pete, they've all been instrumental in leading me to faith." I stopped and took a sip of my lemonade and a bite of cookie.

"Oh, Elise. I'm so happy to hear that. I've never stopped praying for you, and I often prayed for your mother, too. I wondered what had happened after the last time we got together. So, it sounds like today was pretty rough. Do you want to tell me what happened?" I could sense she wouldn't push if I wasn't ready to share.

"Betty, the truth is," I swallowed hard and began, "I came here this week with the express purpose of rescuing Bea from those terrible people. I've been talking to Child Welfare Services as well as the police for several weeks now, trying to get both Bea and Bobby removed from that house. I'd had reports that some of the abuse I had suffered was also being brought down on them. Things were all set for CWS and the police to serve a warrant for their removal today. But, while I was there, watching in disguise, the policeman arrived early. He turned out to be a dirty cop who personally knew the Burrows and only came to warn them."

Taking a deep breath, I continued, "I was at their house posing as a beekeeper when the cop arrived, so I saw and heard the whole thing. It gets a little complicated after that, but let me say that Bea came with me willingly. I drove off with her in my van while Jane was trying to escape a swarm of bees." The look of shock on Betty's face gave me pause. So, I started mounting a defense.

"The Burrows were going to move out of town. I knew they'd get away before child welfare could send someone else. So, I *had* to take her with me immediately." I looked down at my hands. "Bobby was at a baseball game, so I couldn't bring him."

Tears brimmed in my eyes from the day's stress and the seriousness of the situation. "So, Betty, I'm on the run as we speak. And I don't want to get you in trouble, so I'll leave right now if you want. I just needed a place to stop and breathe. A chance to consider what God wanted me to do next." I paused again, taking another sip of lemonade. Betty remained quiet and patient, waiting for me to continue.

"There's one more important thing," I said, glancing nervously out the front window again.

"Go ahead, Elise. Your secrets are safe with me," Betty assured me.

"I don't think I ever told you, but when I was twelve, Jack started molesting me. When I turned fourteen, he'd gotten me pregnant. My baby died at birth, but Bea has always been my heart's replacement for that child. I just couldn't let them hurt her the way they hurt me. I haven't had a chance to tell Bea anything about my new family or that I have a daughter back in California. I want to be sensitive. She's been through quite a lot today, and I don't know what may happen next now that the police will probably consider me a kidnapper.

"On top of that, I found out just a few days ago that my birth mother wasn't who I thought she was. Carmen wasn't my mother at all. My birth mom lives here in Arizona." I couldn't hold back anymore. Sobs came pouring out of me, and Betty hugged me.

"Does your husband know what happened today?" I shook my head no. "How were you planning on getting home?" Betty asked.

"When I talked to Pete this morning, the officials were supposed to issue the warrant and remove the kids this afternoon. When things changed, a bunch of bees threatened Bea and all of us. I left in a hurry and came straight here. I haven't had a chance to tell Pete what happened yet. The original plan was to head home in the morning. Two friends came with me and are probably back at our hotel by now. I should call them to tell them where I am so that they won't worry. We were planning on driving the van home together," I explained.

After a moment in thought, Betty suggested, "Well, before we go any further, why don't we both pray about what to do and let God help us?"

"Yes, I would like that," I replied.

"Okay, let's go to the Lord now." Betty began, "Oh, Lord,

thank you for watching over my friend Elise and for her heart in helping Bea in this terrible situation. We ask that you guide both of us about what Elise should do next. We also pray for your continued hand of safety on Bea, Bobby, and Elise. In Your name, we ask and pray. Amen."

I lifted my eyes, wiping the tears that continued to flow. "Thank you, Betty. You set me on the path toward faith all those years ago. I know God used you to bring me where I am today."

"Thank you for telling me that, Elise. It blesses my soul." Just as she started to speak again, her phone rang. "Hello? Oh, yes, Nadine. Is it going to work out for you to watch Twinkie?" I heard her ask.

As she spoke on the phone, I checked on Bea in the yard. "Mommy, Twinkie is so smart. She will chase the ball when I throw it and bring it back to me to throw again. Watch!" And with that, Bea picked up a tennis ball and tossed it to the end of the yard. Sure enough, Twinkie ran to get it and returned to her, dropping it at Bea's feet. "Good girl!" she praised the dog.

"That's great, Bumble Bea," I reverted to her old nickname. "I need to make a few calls. You can stay outside a bit longer and play if you want. Looks like Betty has a nice swing set, too. I'm sure she wouldn't mind if you also played on that." I was relieved to see that Bea seemed happy and relaxed.

When I came back into the kitchen, Betty had finished her call. "Everything work out with your dog-sitting arrangements?" I asked.

"Unfortunately, no. Nadine can't watch the dog for the entire two weeks we'd planned to be gone. So, it isn't going to work. She can only watch her the second week," Betty explained.

"Oh, that's a shame. What are you going to do?"

"Well, I was just thinking. Would you be interested in staying here with Twinkie for that first week? It would allow you to spend time with Bea, think things through a little more, and let things settle with the police. And if the police do track you down and find you here, I won't be around to get in trouble. Joe and I could leave tomorrow instead of Monday." Betty surprised me with her idea, but I had to admit, it sounded good.

"Are you sure? I mean, I'd be happy to stay and watch Twinkie, and I know Bea would love it too. I just don't want to get you wrapped up in my problems." I took a moment to consider further. "Then again, it would give me a chance to talk to the police detective. Maybe they'll go easy on me if I come clean up-front."

"Okay, then. As long as you and your husband agree, and my husband is okay with it, then that's what we'll do. I'll call Joe now, then you should call your husband and friends."

"Betty, I don't know how I can ever repay you for all your kindness. I promise I'll take good care of Twinkie while you're gone. Since I'm staying longer than expected, would it be okay for me to park in your garage? That is if you have room in there."

"We sure do. I'll move my car out right now, and you can pull it inside. We'll also need to get you some groceries to have on hand. That way, you don't have to be out driving through town. Find out what Bea likes to eat while I call Joe." Betty had caught on quickly to why I wanted to hide the van.

"Oh, yes, thanks!" I said, glancing nervously out the front window as Betty left the room to call her husband.

As she made the call to Joe, I called Lily. Picking up the burner phone, I dialed. "Hi, Lily? It's me."

"Elise! I'm so glad you called. We've been worried sick. Is Bea all right? Have you talked to Pete yet?" She peppered me with questions.

"Yes, I'm okay, but I won't be coming to the hotel. I'm at a friend's house and might stay here for a few days before heading home. Bea seems to be doing well so far. But I haven't had much chance to really talk with her yet. I'll call Pete in a few minutes. I'm waiting to make sure things are all set for me to stay at my friend's house. She needs to get the okay from her husband first. You and Mell all right?"

"Yes. We're doing good. A little frazzled still, but okay. Are you sure you're all right?" Lily asked thoughtfully.

"Yes. You know, Lily, I just realized it's a good thing you're listed as the driver on the car. That way, the cops won't be able to trace the rental car to my name and won't know about your involvement. Are you still planning to leave in the morning?"

"I think so. I know Mell is anxious to leave soon, so probably early tomorrow. I'm a little worried about her, though. She's been coughing quite a bit. I think she might be coming down with something," Lily said.

"Oh no. I sure hope she's not getting sick, but I'm so glad you guys are all right. Thank you both again for everything. Please continue praying. We're not out of the woods yet."

"Absolutely!"

"Okay, I'll call you again when I know what my next steps are."

I hung up the phone as Betty walked into the room. "Well, it's all set. Joe says he's fine with you staying here as long as you don't throw any parties," Betty joked with a smile. "Is your suitcase in the van?" she asked.

"No, it's still at the hotel. Ugh, I should have asked Lily to bring it over." I cringed at the oversight. "No problem, I'll ask her after I call Pete."

"All right. Why don't you call him now, and I'll check on Bea?"

Pete was upset, to say the least. He wanted to drive to Arizona immediately. I had to convince him to wait until tomorrow. "Pete, honey, I'm scared, there's no question about that, but I'm at peace at the same time. It's hard to explain, but I *know* the Lord is at work. Everything is going to be okay."

"What are you going to do, Elise?"

I took a moment to consider my options. "You know, if Betty doesn't mind, why don't you and Bella come stay with Bea and me while she's on vacation? I would love to have you both by my side. It would help keep my courage up." I tried reassuring

Pete without getting choked up at the same time. I knew he was worried, and rightfully so.

⚜

LATER THAT EVENING, after Lily dropped off my luggage, Bea and I set the table while the tantalizing scent of Betty's home-made meatloaf, potatoes, and fresh vegetables saturated the room. Bea and I inhaled the savory aroma, letting it soothe our spirits. Betty was perfectly fine with Pete joining me at their house. In fact, she encouraged it. I forked a bite of parmesan broccoli, savoring its crisp freshness, and began, "I'm going to call Detective Lewinsky tomorrow after Pete arrives. Maybe he'll give me a little space before the gig is up, if you know what I mean," I mentioned cryptically, hoping to avoid upsetting Bea.

"I am really proud of you, Elise. You're showing such maturity and wisdom. And having Pete here will be a great way for everyone to get acquainted if you know what *I* mean." She winked at me. "We'll wait to see what the detective says before Joe and I leave, just in case things change with the dog-sitting."

⚜

AFTER DINNER AND A LITTLE TV, I helped Bea settle into bed early. I was so glad she'd been able to bring some of her clothes and a few toys. It dawned on me that if the Burrows hadn't been planning to move that very day, she wouldn't have been packed and would have left their house with nothing. As she was putting on her pajamas, I noticed a dark bruise on her back.

"Bea, what happened to your back?"

"It's nothing," she tried to dismiss it. "I didn't clean up my room very good, and Jane was mad at me. But it's okay. I shouldn't be such a bad girl." Seeing my look of alarm, she shrugged. "She hit me with the big metal spatula." At the admission, shame spread across her face. I was well acquainted with the feelings that came from being overly disciplined. I had carried the same misplaced sense of shame for years.

"The metal spatula?" I asked.

"Yeah, it's the one Jack sometimes uses when he BBQs. You know, the one Jane had when she was chasing you today?"

So, that's what it was. Guess I lucked out more than I knew. Then I pictured this innocent, sweet girl standing before me, beaten with that spatula, and tears pricked at my eyes.

"Oh, my. That's not right, Bea. No one should ever hit you or any child in that way. No matter how badly you may have behaved." I sat in the nearby chair to be at eye level with her. "Bea, I want you to know I will never harm you." She looked at me with such unassuming trust in her eyes that I embraced her tightly. She melted into my arms and sat across my lap as an infant would, even though she was much too tall for that. I treasured the moment. Soaking in her warmth and her sweet, child-like scent. It was the perfect time to tell her a few things.

"Honey," I started. "I know it's been a tough, long day. It's been hard for me too. I… I know you've probably wondered why I waited so long to come back for you. I am so sorry that it took so long. I want you to know I never stopped thinking about you. I prayed for you every night." Tears slid down her cheeks as I tried my best to explain the impossible. "Oh, Bumble Bea, you are growing up to be such a beautiful girl—inside and out. I love you so much and want you to live in a safe home where you don't have to fear metal spatulas or worry about making simple mistakes. I'm doing everything I can to make sure that happens."

Bea turned her head to look up at me. "I love you too, Mommy." We sat embracing the healing moment.

"There is so much I want to tell you, and I want to hear everything about your school and your friends. But first, I have some exciting news." Lifting Bea off my lap and onto the bed, I started to tuck her in under the covers. "I think you heard me mention earlier that I'm married to a wonderful man named

Pete. Well, Pete and I have a little girl. She's three years old, and her name is Bella. She doesn't know about you yet, so it'll be a surprise for her too, but she has been longing for a sister. I know you two are going to like each other. Tomorrow, Pete and Bella are going to come here from our home in California to be with us. So, you might get to meet them. Would you be okay with that?" I asked carefully.

"Yes, Mommy," Bea smiled. "I always wanted someone to play with who wouldn't treat me mean like Bobby does." Her expression had me wondering how bad things had gotten between her and her brother.

"Oh, I know big brothers can sometimes be mean. I hope he never did anything really bad to you, Bea." I phrased it with an opening in case she wanted to tell me more.

"Sometimes Bobby calls me mean names and hits me, and he never wants to play with me anymore, so I don't have anyone to play with. I was supposed to have a birthday party this Saturday, but Jane canceled it again. She always says she's going to have a party for me, then cancels it for some reason." She rambled from one thing to another. "But thank you for my present. I love the necklace you gave me and the teddy bear, too." She showed me she was still wearing it and had the teddy bear cradled in her arms. I gave her another hug and a kiss on the cheek.

"Bumble Bea, I know all this is a lot for you to take in. Let's get some sleep, and we'll find something fun to do together tomorrow. Maybe we could paint pictures. Would you like to do that?"

"Yes. That would be fun. I remember when you used to paint with me, and I liked the picture that was on the van. It was just like the painting I did for you. When I saw that, I knew you were there for me, and then I heard you singing the roses song, so I knew for sure it was you."

"Oh, Bea, you have made me very happy today. Let's say some bedtime prayers together, okay?" She gave me an uncertain look and nodded a timid yes. With that, I guided Bea in her first prayer. Until that moment, it hadn't even occurred to me that prayer and faith in God were things I'd never discussed with her.

Friday

Pete and Bella arrived late in the afternoon. By that time, Betty had a meal ready in the crock pot. She and Joe were gracious to Pete and fussed over Bella as if they were her grandparents. I was overjoyed to see Pete and Bella again. When I introduced Bella and Bea, Bella started talking up a storm, her excitement at having a new friend evident. Bea was shy at first, but little Twinkie quickly broke the ice between the girls. It wasn't long before they were both playing outside and throwing the ball for the dog.

While the girls played and the guys talked, Betty walked me through everything I needed to know about the house and caring for Twinkie. When we all sat down for dinner, it felt a little like a family reunion. At least as close to one as I could guess, having never actually had a family or a reunion to go to.

"We'll be staying at the Marriott in Phoenix tonight and tomorrow before leaving for the Grand Canyon, so if you have any problems or questions, don't hesitate to call," Betty shared.

After dinner, Betty and I hugged tearful goodbyes, realizing the fullness of what may come next. Pete and I finally had some private time to embrace each other and assess my precarious situation. We agreed that I would call Detective Lewinsky and Michelle first thing in the morning to explain what happened and let them know I had Bea with me. It was probably the hardest thing I ever had to do, but I knew it was right, even if it meant going to jail.

THIRTY-THREE

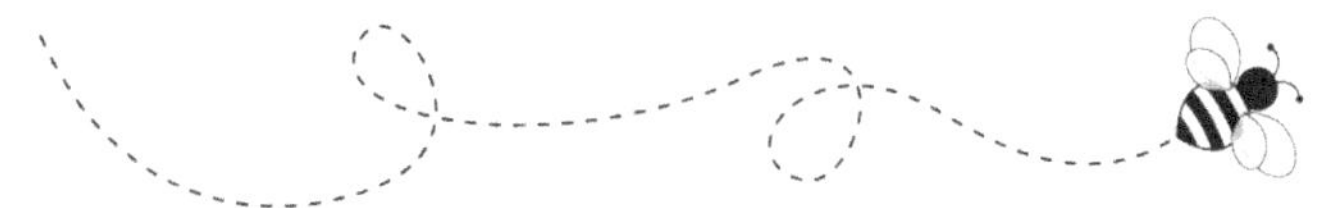

Now, you gone see that Elise has ta go through more hard things, but she now knows she gots ta trust in the good Lawd, no matta what. An jes like I say way back at the beginin', maybe some things gone work out for the good like it say in Romans 8:28. But only the Lawd know that fer sure an right now, she in a big mess.

Saturday

"Good morning, you two. Did you sleep well?" Bella was holding Bea's hand as they walked into the kitchen in their PJs. I nearly cried just grasping the magnitude of seeing them together. "I'm making pancakes and bacon. Does anybody want some?"

"Yay!" they squealed at the same time. Twinkie came running in, wanting to know what all the excitement was about. She barked as if in agreement, and we all laughed.

"I haven't had pancakes since you left, Mommy," Bea revealed with wide-eyed excitement. My heart sank a little, realizing how much she'd missed in five years, even something as insignificant as pancakes.

Pete wandered in a minute later, looking a little downtrodden. "Hi, honey. You okay?" I asked him.

"Yeah. Didn't sleep much. But it sure smells good in here. Want me to make some bacon while you finish the cakes?" he offered.

"That'd be great. Girls, can you help me set the table?"

PETE HELPED CLEAN UP, and the girls fed Twinkie before running to their shared room to get dressed. I heard Bella ask Bea if she'd help her pick out clothes to wear. As they trotted off, everything crashed down on me. I turned to Pete, nearly breaking down. "Honey, I just don't think I can handle it. I had to leave her once already; how can I possibly do it again? She'll never trust me if I let her go this time."

"It's gonna be all right, honey." He took me into his arms and hugged me tightly. Detective Lewinsky told us to be ready by one o'clock. "At least you'll have time to really explain things to her. Plus, she's older now and should understand well enough. Remember, God will be with you through this part as well, and Bella and I will be here waiting for you."

Walking slowly toward the girls' bedroom, old voices taunted me to *just run*. I whispered a prayer instead. As I did, my cell phone rang. "Hello? Yes. Yes. Oh, that's wonderful!" I ran back into the kitchen to share the good news with Pete. "Honey, Detective Lewinsky just called. He said that Bea can stay with us one more day. He talked it over with Michelle, and they both agreed it would be better to wait another day before she goes to the foster home. They are going to come tomorrow at four o'clock instead." My heart leaped in my chest. *I'll be able to talk with Bea and spend some time with her. That just might make a difference.*

IT TURNED out that explaining things to Bea and Bella was tougher than I thought, even with the extra day together. I couldn't tell which one of them was upset more, but when I peeked into their room that evening, I saw them sitting together on the bed and Bea comforting Bella. *Goodness, they're already acting like sisters,* I thought.

"I have to go somewhere else for a while," Bea consoled my three-year-old. "But I hope I can come back soon, and we can be together forever then."

"I will wait for you, Bea, and I'll pray for you too." *Guess I couldn't ask for better than that, Lord.*

MICHELLE PULLED INTO THE DRIVEWAY, with Detective Lewinsky and another police officer parking on the side of the street. I sent the girls to play in the backyard as Pete answered the door. Michelle waited until the officer joined her, and they all entered together. Officer Lewinsky introduced me to the other policeman, Officer Robert Cody.

"Elise," Michelle said, "Officer Cody is a good man and has worked with me for several years. He was the policeman who went with me to serve the warrant to the Burrows after things fell apart with the other police officer."

I was tongue-tied, so Pete bought me some time, suggesting we talk in the living room.

"Elise, I am glad you called me," Lewinsky started. "I want you to know I will work hard to ensure you are treated justly. I've already been sniffing around and feel good about what I've discovered. I will recommend that the judge let you out without bail since you turned yourself in and in respect for what you've been through. Even so, you're going to need a good lawyer. Know anyone?"

"I'll call my friend Allie. She may know someone out here." I paused briefly before asking the question that had been on my mind. "What happened with Jane? Is she all right? I know she got stung pretty badly. Were they Africanized bees?" I raced through the words, my nervousness evident.

Detective Lewinsky responded first. "She's fine. Swelled up like a balloon but only got stung on the face once and a few other places. They think they were hornets, not bees, which can be pretty nasty. I understand hornets are carnivorous, so they sting *and* bite. I think she had to stay in the hospital one night, and that was it. Oh, speaking of hospitals, can you tell me the date you had Jack's baby and in what hospital it was?"

"Yes, it was April 21, 2003, at 9 a.m. at St. Joseph's Hospital," I answered with surprising clarity.

"And do you remember the name of the street you lived on in Austin?" he asked. *Why does he need to know that?* I wondered.

"Uhh, yeah, I think it was Collins Street. But I was pretty young, so I may not have that right."

"Okay, that's great. Michelle?" He nodded his go-ahead to her.

"Elise," she began. "I know this must be hard for you, but we'll have to take Bea to a foster home. Bobby was taken to a home yesterday. I think you'll like the home Bea's going to." Michelle paused and glanced at Detective Lewinsky. "I can't tell you where it is, but she's going to stay with a lady who has been fostering kids for about four years now." She took a deep breath and continued, "There's something else you need to know."

At this point, I felt flush. Something big was about to come down on me. I could see it in Michelle's eyes and feel it as she touched my hand. My heart raced in anticipation, and it felt like I might faint, but I willed myself to be calm. *What could it be? Would I never see Bea again? Are they going to put her back with Jane and Jack?* I asked for a drink of water, and Pete went to get it for me.

Taking a big swallow, I couldn't look directly at Michelle as she began. "Elise," Michelle started gingerly, "the woman that Bea will stay with has a wonderful reputation for fostering. And —" Michelle paused again, her words hovering in the air, making me even more nervous. "Her name is Kathleen Dupree."

"Dupree?" My mouth flew open in shock. "You mean my mother? My *real* mother?" I could hardly believe my ears. I felt lightheaded, and my heart filled with questions, excitement, and dread. *How could this be?*

"Wait. This can't be true. I... I don't know what to think. I mean, Detective Lewinsky told me she was here somewhere in Arizona. But... this just doesn't make sense." A fresh realization dawned on me. I jerked my hand from under Michelle's. "How can you be sure she's a good foster parent? I mean, she lost me once." Anger and fear started welling within me, but Michelle continued before I could say more.

"It's true. I wish I could take you to meet her now, but it would be stretching the law even further. We've already had to pull a few strings to give you this extra time with Bea. But you can be sure that Katie is a capable, caring foster parent. Ironically, it would have been a different person entirely if Officer Ruiz had done his job right the first time. So, this little leeway time, along with some help from Detective Lewinsky, made it possible for Katie, your mother, to have Bea instead."

"I don't know what to say." I felt numb. Rushing through this rollercoaster of emotions in such a short time had winded me. I couldn't tell if I was happy, angry, or sad, but an inner peace washed over me. It was going to be okay.

Pete put his arm around me and then addressed Michelle, Detective Lewinsky, and Officer Cody. "Thank you for all your help. The extra time with Bea and finding Elise's mother... it's come as a bit of a shock. But we are grateful for all you've done."

I perked up at that. I was still trying to sort out the shock from the joy, but Pete was right. "It's amazing, just amazing. Isn't it?" I looked up at Pete, a little dazed.

"It *is* amazing," he repeated, then added, "I'm wondering...

Michelle, would it be okay for Bella to visit Bea at Katie's home? I know they just met, but they have already become close friends. I think it would help them both to have each other to connect with during this difficult transition."

"Well, it would be unusual." She sat for a moment, a thoughtful expression on her face. "You understand that Elise will not be allowed to interact with Bea during this time. But if she maintains her distance, I think it would be all right for the girls to see each other. Of course, we'll have to confirm that Katie is okay with it, but I have a feeling she'll agree. I'll talk with her when we get Bea settled."

At her words, a new turmoil churned within me. I wouldn't be allowed to see Bea, at least not at first. And … I shuddered, considering what might come next—jail. I didn't have time to ruminate further as the girls jostled in from the backyard.

Bea took one look at the uniformed police officer and turned pale. Her eyes bloomed wide with fear, and her gaze darted around the room, landing on the front door. She was about to bolt, and we all saw it. I rushed towards her, adrenalin pumping in my ears, ready to race after her. Reaching her first, Michelle interceded. Gently taking Bea's hand and crouching down, she looked her straight in the eye.

"Bea, Elise needs you to be brave. She has to take care of some things so you can be safe. I know this might be scary, especially leaving Elise right after connecting with her again. But I promise you, the home I'm taking you to is safe." Bea didn't appear convinced, so Michelle added, "We thought that Bella might come to visit you there. Would you like that?" Bea gave a little nod. Taking Bea's hand firmly, she helped her with her suitcase and guided her to the door. "I hear you like to paint. The lady who you'll be staying with is an artist, too."

I stood frozen, not knowing what to do. Watery pools filled my eyes as I struggled to hold in the sobs that threatened to spill out of me. My arms begged to hug her again, but fear held me at bay, not wanting to make things worse. As they walked out the front door, Bella ran up and gave Bea an unrestrained hug. "I promise to ask Jesus to watch over you," she said with the perfect faith of a child.

Like a coward, I ran from the room crying. Pete followed after me, and we embraced, letting our emotions blend, his arms enveloping me in a comforting peace. Detective Lewinsky assured me things would work out okay and left us with Officer Cody while he escorted Bea and Michelle to the car. I gathered enough composure to call a friend for help.

"Allie, do you have a minute?"

"Elise, everything okay? I heard things with the Burrows didn't go as planned," she asked anxiously.

"Yes, I'm all right. Did your mom and Lily get back there in one piece?" I asked first.

"Yes, they're fine, a little tired, though. Mom took another day off to rest after she got home. Can I help you with something?"

"Yes. I wondered if you know a good criminal attorney in the Phoenix area. Looks like I'm gonna need one ASAP."

"Well, I do, but I thought I could represent you. Even though my expertise is focused on child abuse and neglect, not kidnapping, from what you've told me, you have a strong case for child abuse against the Burrows, which could work in your favor. I practiced in Phoenix briefly before going to California, and I still have the required licenses. How soon do you need an attorney?" Allie asked.

"Like, now. They'll be formally arresting me in about ten minutes, and although Detective Lewinsky said he will put a good word in for me, I may be locked up for a while."

"Oh my. Tell you what, I'll call my friend Andy Cole and have him meet you at the police station. Wait for him and keep your mouth shut. If you feel confident in me and Andy agrees, I'd gladly team up with him. In the meantime, don't say anything to the police. Just give them your name and remain silent till Andy gets there."

The idea of having both Andy and Allie on my defense was a significant relief. I thanked her profusely and then rushed to get ready before they carted me off. I started to freshen my makeup and put on a nice outfit when Pete walked in. "Honey, what *are* you doing?"

"Oh!" I blushed. "Acting stupid, I guess." I cringed, realizing just *how* stupid. Number one, I'd be in jail for who knows how long. Number two, I'll probably cry all the makeup off. Three, why worry about what to wear? I'm sure they'll provide some kind of fashion statement—something with stripes. As silly as I was acting, I was grateful Officer Cody would allow me to say goodbye to Bella before arresting me. Pete arranged to take Bella out for ice cream and give hugs and kisses first so she wouldn't see me get carted off in handcuffs.

"I'll be home soon," I assured them while swiping the tears streaming down my cheeks. "I love you so much!"

🐝

AFTER A FULL NIGHT in jail and the most sobering 24 hours of my life, I was released on $300 bail. So, the money from the bee job came in handy after all. Pete came to pick me up.

"Honey, you doing okay?" Pete asked. I nodded yes. "Bella's at Katie's. She's going to bring her home around three. Michelle is staying with Bea so that you can meet Katie," Pete explained. "That is if you're sure you're okay with meeting her today?"

"I think so. I mean, it's hard to know how I feel about meeting her." The very idea of having a mother in this town, one who hadn't sold me or abandoned me, was a lot. And knowing that Katie had tried to find me all these years made me joyful and scared witless. I was still trying to wrap my head around it all.

My mother didn't sell me. But she must have caused my father to take me away like he did. Thoughts collided in my mind, bringing with them a sudden nauseousness. Whether hunger or revulsion, I couldn't tell. I wasn't sure if I would ever be ready to meet her. Yet, I also knew there was no way I wouldn't. It was a "now or never" and "at long last" battle of emotions playing tug of war within me. *Oh Lord, help me! I'm so confused right now. I know I should be thrilled. I just don't know what to feel or what to say to her.*

"Honey," Pete saw the struggle raging within me. "I know this is an enormous weight on you. So much has happened in the past few days, and it's okay if you're not ready to meet her. I think she'll understand." He kissed me softly and took my hand in his.

"No, I want to meet her. I *have* to meet her. It's just so unexpected. Like I'm in a dream and can't wake up. I can hardly explain it to myself." I shook my head, attempting to clear my mind.

"Maybe take it one step at a time, not all at once. I'm sure she's harboring some pretty deep regrets as well. Can you imagine if you lost Bella and didn't know what happened to her? Waiting 20 years to know if she was still alive? She must be filled with questions and yearning like no mother should have to carry." Pete wisely helped me see another perspective.

"You're right. Tell her I'll be waiting."

I AWOKE FROM A LONG NAP, splashed cool water on my face, and applied a little makeup. As I entered the family room, Pete was sitting on the couch reading the newspaper. "Feel better, honey?" he asked.

"Yes, sure do. Do we have any cookies in the house?" I was suddenly hungry for a snack.

"We have Oreos and milk."

"Sounds perfect." I found the cookies and poured a glass of milk just as the doorbell rang.

The front door flew open, and Bella came bursting in with a

clatter of excitement. "Mommy!" she cried out, running to my open arms.

We stood hugging for a minute, and then I saw her—Katie. My mother. She was standing in the doorway with sunlight glinting on her silver-streaked hair. We both froze in the magnitude of the moment. She was younger than I'd pictured, weathered around the eyes, but her resemblance to me was striking. Except for her lighter complexion, it was like looking at myself in a magic mirror, reflecting how I'd look in twenty years. "Come in, come in." I finally spoke.

Bella raced to her bedroom, grabbing a couple of cookies on the way. I gave Katie a questioning look. "Did she already have a snack?"

"No, no snack yet," she answered.

"Would you like some iced tea or milk?" I asked, setting the plate of Oreos on the table.

"Iced tea sounds great. Pretty hot today." She started the small talk, and Pete joined us in the kitchen.

"Hello, Katie. Thank you so much for watching Bella for us today. It was a great help."

Pete grabbed a cookie off the plate. "Honey, I have some work to do, so I'm gonna let you gals visit if you don't mind." He graciously excused himself, knowing we needed some space.

Bella ran back in, grabbed another cookie, and raced out the door with Twinkie close behind. I brought her milk outside and placed it on the patio table before settling in the kitchen with Katie.

"Beautiful roses," she commented.

"Yes, Pete is so sweet to me. He had them on the table when I got home." I took a sip of my milk.

"The girls got along well today," Katie mentioned.

"Oh, yes. They seemed to hit it off right away," I managed to say, then took another sip, wishing it contained a little courage in it, too. My insides began to shake as emotions rose within me. I had long gotten past the hope of seeing my mother again. That is, the mother I thought was mine. By now, all thoughts and feelings had moved miles away from imagining a joyful reunion with her. My false memories of who my mother was and that she'd sold me had my emotional gauge stuck in *raging anger* for too long.

We looked at each other, quickly jerking our gazes away with embarrassment. Katie brushed away a tear on her cheek, and my brief glimpse revealed a storehouse of deep pain and longing in her eyes. Silence hung in the air as if captive. Too many years, too many questions, and too much pain between us. It was a chasm too deep to cross with no bridge in sight. She brushed away another tear and opened her mouth to speak, only to close it again just as quickly. I fiddled with my locket, then the placemat under my plate, trying to push its corner down flat the way it belonged, then took another sip of milk while staring at the uneaten cookies in front of me.

"Mary," she finally began, "I mean Elise. I know this must be so hard for you. I can't imagine what you've been through all these years. But—" her words hung precariously; her tongue stuck to her throat with emotion. "But…" she tried to start again, "I hope you'll find a way to forgive me."

Tears were quickly gathering, and storm clouds swelled within me, ready to burst at any moment. I waited, then pounced as I'd never done before. "Why? Where were you? What took you so long?" my voice elevated close to a scream. "And what happened to my father? Why didn't he come back? Did you even care that he left me?"

I must've continued ranting and raging for at least ten minutes before I realized what was coming out of my mouth. Hot with anger and pain, tears squeezed out of the small slits of my intense glare. "I thought my mother was Carmen. Did you know that?" My angry outburst became even more vile with every word I shouted. "Did you know she sold me into a household of strangers?" I breathed and forced my tears to stay put, not caring that she was bent over, sobbing in deep devastation.

"That the family I lived with most of my life abused me? Hit me? Molested me? How could a mother do that to her child?" I exploded, then stopped abruptly.

Closing my eyes and gathering myself, I prayed. *Lord, help me to see. Help me to forgive.* My heart pumped loud and fast. I heard Katie's soft cries across from me. Raging pain moved through me with a paralyzing sting that was more emotional than physical. Everything within me wanted to scream, yet somewhere from deep within came a swelling. It grew stronger and stronger as if a crescendo of music was building to a climactic thunderous crash of cymbals, drums, and horns. A memory began to form in my mind. It was a mental snapshot of the moment when I saw Bea right after the swarm had lifted off me. Then, as if a dam within me had broken and all the pent-up pain that had been held back since I was a little girl had finally been let loose, tears started to gush out. The poison of bitterness and anger flowed out, and a sense of humbling shame and sorrow poured in. "Oh dear God, forgive me!" I cried out.

I opened my eyes and looked at my mother. How could I stand here railing at her for leaving me when I had left Bumble Bea and taken so long to return to get her? How could I be angry at her for not finding me when I knew where Bea was all along? She had tried to find me and even hired Detective Lewinsky to look for me for years. "She never gave up," he'd said. But I had. I was too afraid, too chicken to go back to the Burrows. All the while knowing Bea might be abused like I was. Katie didn't even know what kind of home I was in or whether I was alive. But she kept on trying after all these years.

"Oh, Mommy!" I cried out. "I am so sorry. Please forgive me. Please! I am the worst for talking to you that way, for even being angry at you."

Katie looked up at me, tears glistening. "You still have the locket I gave you!" Touching it, I gasped in realization. Rushing to her, we embraced in an all-encompassing hug of forgiveness.

"Well," she broached with a hint of humor, "that was a good cleansing for us both."

We hugged again, wiping our tears and blowing our noses. "Yes. More like a flood. Let's have some cookies now. Sugar always helps a wounded heart feel better," I proclaimed while washing my hands.

TIME FLEW by as we talked about what happened from the beginning of our separation to our reunion. I learned that my father had been put in prison for kidnapping me. He'd tried to track me down after he got out and lost his life in the process. The similarity with my situation with Bea was astonishing and had me wondering what my fate would be. "Mother," I said, "if I end up going to prison for kidnapping Bea, would you continue to look after her and allow Bella to visit often?" I asked with hopefulness.

"Elise, I don't even want to consider that you will go to prison. It just can't happen. I know that God won't allow it. He's brought you back to me miraculously now, and I know in my heart that the Lord will see you through this trial."

"Are you a believer?" I ventured to ask.

"Yes, honey. For about five years now. Guess someone must've been praying for me, allowing God to get through my Irish hot-headed stubbornness." She looked at me with a twinkle in her blue-green eyes.

"Oh, don't tell me you think I have any of that Irish stubbornness in me, too," I came back with a sly smile, and we both laughed knowingly.

"Sometimes I wonder if I would have ever come to faith if it hadn't been for your disappearance. I was pretty messed up when your father and I split. I'll tell you that it was probably a lifesaver for you that he took you and left the country. My life fell apart after I had kidney surgery. I couldn't manage without the pain medication, and it just took over me. Half the time, I wasn't there for you; the other half, I was becoming abusive. That's why your father ran to Mexico with you. After trying everything else, I finally asked God to help me."

"You sound exactly like me. All my life, I've tried to be perfect. I've tried to outsmart every challenge that came my way. Sometimes, it worked out, but I mostly ended up with another big problem to solve. Guess that's how I got into the mess I'm in now. I did give my life to Christ, but I'm still figuring out how to let Him guide me in all things."

"Sweetheart, spiritual growth takes time, and we all need to work out our salvation, but eternity is within our spirit because of His work and grace." She gave me another big hug.

"Mom," I said, the word sounding strange as I spoke it, "I can hardly believe we are finally together." It was clear that the joy of a shared faith added another layer of bonding and forgiveness that may not have happened without it.

Hopefully, my faith would also get me through the trial that loomed ahead. I fingered my locket for the hundredth time but with new appreciation now.

⚜

PETE and I snuggled into bed early that night. The closeness I felt for him was stronger and more secure than ever. We came together with sweet release and a sense of oneness that was uncharted in my experience. It was as if I'd been holding back some of my love for him all our married life. The explosive exhilaration of completion that came seemed to be the culmination of so many hurts being set free. As we lay in each other's arms, breathing in the aftermath of our ecstasy, a poem sang within my heart.

The Sweet Slumber of Summer

Oh, sweet slumber of morning's summer grasses,
The scent of honey's nectar to my wanting arms

lay thick and slow as it passes.
But drips with ease
With summer's warm breeze.
And slides by quickly near the end of our days.
Come to me, my love.
Linger here once more.
Taste the day that still remains.
Drink of us, beloved and let love's gift restore.

I SLEPT PEACEFULLY but awoke to the realization that my fate was at hand. A fleeting thought came that I should just run off somewhere again. But, no, it was in God's hands now—and the courts.

THIRTY-FOUR

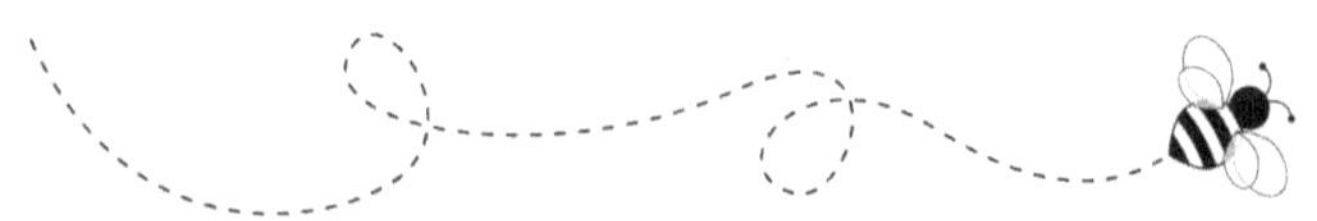

Things was goin' good heah, while Elise was away. Chicky-Pie's got busier then eva, an Mama Mell had ta hire two mo waitresses ta keep up with things. I think lots a folks is comin' heah 'cause they love Miss Elise an wanna know what gone happen ta her. Sally finally seem ta get the hang a things as a waitress too. But, everbody miss Elise an they keep own prayin' fer her, 'specially now that she's in big trouble.

Miss Lily and Mama Mell call Elise ever week to see how she doin' an give her they wisdom bout trustin' in the Lawd.

Lily

"Hi, Elise. How you holdin' up?" I asked, knowing she must be feeling a lot of turmoil.

"I'm doing okay, all things considered," Elise replied.

"Mell had to hire two more waitresses to take care of the crowds of people comin' in. 'Course it's prolly 'cause it takes that many ta fill your shoes."

"Well, you got that right, girl," Elise joked.

"Hah! For sure. You know, folks around here are truly concerned for you. We're all praying, and the whole town is rooting for you. Talk about a buzz at Chicky-Pie's. This court case is big for Riverview. But the gossip's startin' to wear on me. I always say that getting a good recliner is like finding a chair that'll take you all the way to the therapist. An afta all this hoopla 'round here, we all gonna need one-a-those kind-a chairs."

"Lily, you always know how to cheer a girl up. It humbles me to know so many are concerned for me. My hearing is in two days; they'll set a date for the actual trial then, so keep those prayers coming."

"We sure will. Keep looking at the Lord during all of this."

"Lily, you are such a treasure. Thank you for all your kindness. I sure hope you and Mell don't get dragged into this trial, too. I'm doing everything I can not to let that happen," Elise promised.

"Don't give it a second thought. I'd do it again in a heartbeat. If I have to come out there to testify or be charged as an accomplice, then so be it. We did a good thing by getting that sweet little girl out of there, and I know the Lord will reward us for that."

"Thanks, Lily. I'll pray for everyone in Riverview, especially the crew at Chicky-Pie's."

⁂

May 7, 2012, Elise

"Please rise for the Honorable Ivy G. Dawning," a thundering voice commanded. I obeyed and rose to my feet, my knees feeling like they'd buckle any minute, sending me to the floor. Only a handful of people were in the courtroom, but it felt like thousands, and all eyes were on me.

We'd barely sat down when the bailiff announced, "Court is

in session for the hearing in the matter of the State of Arizona against Elise Burrows Freeman. Miss Freeman, will you please stand?"

A rush went to my head as I stood, and my legs felt like rubber. I thought I might faint, but Allie caught me by the elbow. The judge addressed me. "Miss Freeman, you are hereby charged with kidnapping a minor and endangerment of a minor in the course of said crime. How do you plead?"

I tried to open my mouth, but it felt like it was glued shut with dry paste. Allie gave me an encouraging smile that finally freed my tongue. "Not guilty, Your High…uh, Honor," I finally responded. Glad I didn't say *Your Highness* like I almost did.

"The defendant pleads not guilty. I am setting the trial date for Monday, August 27, 2012." BANG! Her gavel went down heavy, and I flinched. "Miss Freeman, you are hereby ordered to report to this courtroom on Monday, August 27, 2012, where you will be tried for the crime of kidnapping and endangering the life of a minor. Does the prosecution have a request regarding Miss Freeman's release on bail?" The judge's words hung heavy on my heart, and everything became a blur of noise after that.

BANG! The gavel startled me back to reality. "Mrs. Freeman, you are hereby released and ordered to remain in Maricopa County for the entire time of the trial."

Sleep was scarce for most of that night. My tossing and turning no doubt interfered with Pete's restfulness, too. His boss had arranged for us to stay at a cozy hotel with a small kitchen and room for Bella and us. It wasn't the same as home, but it gave us a semblance of normalcy while I needed to stay in Phoenix. I was grateful I wasn't being kept in jail throughout the trial.

⚜

AFTER BREAKFAST THE FOLLOWING DAY, we walked out by the pool, and Bella squealed with excitement at the play area and pool with a slide. She hadn't yet learned to swim, but I figured it would be the perfect time to teach her. To my delight, the recreation room offered game tables, a small library, and a large-screen TV.

"Honey, would you mind running to the store for groceries?" I handed Pete a short list.

"Sure." He said, pointing at the list. "What's this?"

"A legal pad and thesaurus. I was thinking I might do some writing to pass the time."

"Hmm. Doubt the grocery store will have those." He smiled teasingly. "But maybe with a little encouragement during Bella's nap, I just might be able to find them." He wrapped his arms around me and drew me to his chest.

"Looks like someone besides me has conniving ways. Throw in some lemon meringue pie and BBQ takeout, and I'll see what I can do," I said with a wink.

My phone rang, interrupting our embrace. "Hello, Elise?" the voice asked.

"Detective Lewinsky!" I said in surprise.

"Hello! Wanted you to know I'm continuing to work on your case, helping Michelle and Allie. We may have found some strong evidence that could help you."

"That's great. I really appreciate your support. Are you able to tell me anything else?" I asked.

"Not now. But don't worry, a pathway to justice is forming."

I hung up, feeling a mixture of hope and fear.

***

Monday, August 27, 2012, Trial Day

Knowing I needed extra strength for the day, I woke early and grabbed my Bible. Ironically, it fell open to Psalm 25:1-2. I read, *"To you, O LORD, I lift up my soul. O my God, I trust in You; Let me not be ashamed; Let not my enemies triumph over me."*

"ALL RISE for the Honorable Richard Solomon." *Good name*, I thought. *Hope he's as wise as the one in the Bible.* The courtroom was at total capacity. Pete sat right behind me, and to my delight, I turned to see Lily and Mell in the spectator gallery. My legs were shaky again, but not as much as the first time. Allie and Andy stood on either side of me, offering support. The judge entered, and the charges against me were read, again putting a heavy weight on my shoulders. *Guess I did a foolish thing*, I thought. *Maybe we should have stuck to our original plan.*

Prosecuting attorney James Stonewell stood proclaiming his case against me. He seemed the epitome of a perfect devil's advocate with his greying black hair slicked back, manicured mustache, and dark arching eyebrows. His demeanor was calm and calculating as he addressed the jury. When he looked directly at me, his piercing stare went deep. My eyes veered to his left, where I caught sight of Jack and Jane Burrows two rows behind him. Jack glared at me, and Jane kept her gaze straight ahead, avoiding all eye contact.

"Ladies and gentlemen," the prosecutor began, "through the evidence we will present to this court, you will see that Mrs. Elise Freeman risked the safety of a nine-year-old girl for her own selfish purposes. You will also see she went through a great deal of premeditation and planning in her endeavors to kidnap Beatrice Burrows."

My heart sank, and I hung my head in shame. *Oh, Lord, please forgive me*, I prayed silently. Allie touched my shoulder with a gentle nudge of encouragement.

I tuned out the rest of Mr. Stonewell's charges against me. There were snippets of truth in his words, and despite turning a deaf ear, shame and guilt wriggled their way in. *I deserve to go to prison. I shouldn't have taken justice into my own hands.*

"Mrs. Freeman was adopted by Mr. and Mrs. Burrows and given everything a child should need or want. Yet she betrayed their loving generosity by kidnapping their natural daughter out of jealousy. She wanted to hurt them for not being the center of their attention," Mr. Stonewell vilified me further. "We can only guess what harm may have come to Bea if she still had her."

Roiling with anger, I wanted to jump out of my seat and give him a piece of my mind. But like a dam holding back a torrent of water, Allie's hand gripped my arm with gentle restraint.

Next, Andy stood and gave an eloquent defense statement to the court—so convincing I nearly let myself relax. *Lord, please help me get through this trial and not have to go to prison. I want to be with Pete, Bella, and Bea,* I prayed silently. At that moment, it hit me like a ton of bricks just how much they meant to me, the fullness of the risk I'd taken weighing me down further.

Mr. Stonewell rose again and proceeded with the state's case against me. "Your Honor, I'd like to call Mrs. Jane Burrows as my first witness." Jane gave me the side eye as she went up to testify.

"Mrs. Burrows, are you the adoptive mother of Mrs. Elise Burrows Freeman?" Stonewell asked.

"Yes."

"And before today, when was the last time you saw Elise?"

"About six years ago, before she left us without a word," Jane coldly replied.

"Did Elise run away?"

"Yes, I guess you could say that."

"Can you tell us what happened on the day your daughter Beatrice was taken from your home?"

"Well, I had called a bee removal service to take care of a beehive in our yard. After they arrived that Thursday, I went back inside the house. When I came out later, I saw one of the beekeepers remove her helmet and recognized her as Elise. She was talking to my daughter Beatrice, and my daughter seemed upset, so I ran toward Elise. My foot got caught in some kind of trap-like thicket of weeds, and I fell. Then a bunch of bees started swarming around me and stinging me."

I sat frowning, shaking my head at the version of things Jane had just given.

"What happened next, Mrs. Burrows?"

"I was on the ground screaming, trying to swat the bees away from me." She glared in my direction when she said, "Elise just left me there and took Bea away."

"That must've been terrible for you. Did anyone help you?" Stonewell asked.

"When my husband Jack came home, he helped me get to the hospital."

"How did you feel when you found out Bea was gone?"

"I was so upset I could barely breathe, just thinking about how scared Bea must've been. I couldn't believe Elise took her after all we did for her." Jane covered her face and started sobbing loudly. So loudly it was almost comical.

"I know this is very upsetting for you, Mrs. Burrows. That's all I have for you now."

"Defense, you may cross," the judge nodded toward Andy.

Andy stood and approached the stand. "Mrs. Burrows, can you tell us why you hired beekeepers on that particular day?"

"We were going to have a birthday party for Bea that weekend, and I was worried that all the bees might interfere with the children's fun," Jane replied, suddenly calm again.

"You mentioned you went inside for a while after the beekeepers arrived. What were you doing when you went inside the house?"

"I was packing up for our move on Saturday," she replied quickly. Too quickly.

"Oh, I know moving can be a lot of work," Andy looked sympathetic. "Now, you said you were planning a birthday party for Bea that weekend. If the incident happened on Thursday as reported, and you were moving on Saturday, how were you going to host a birthday party on the weekend or on Sunday if you were moving on Saturday?"

"Uh, I... I... I think we decided to cancel the party but forgot to cancel the beekeepers," she answered, blushing bright red as she stuttered.

"And was that the first time you canceled a birthday party for your daughter Beatrice?" Andy prodded further.

"Oh, guess maybe we had to cancel a few others too," she looked down at the admission.

"I see. You also stated that you were attacked by a lot of bees. That must've been terrifying. How did you protect yourself from being stung in the face?"

"I covered my face the whole time. A few bees or I guess they were actually hornets, stung my hands as I did."

"That was smart. Now, you told us Elise had taken Bea away. How were you able to see Elise take Bea away if your face was covered the whole time you were being stung?" Andy asked.

"Uh, I don't know. It was all so terrible, and I just couldn't take it." Jane began sobbing loudly again.

"Thank you, Mrs. Burrows. That will be all for now," Andy excused her.

Mr. Stonewell got up and called his next witness. Officer Robert Cody stepped up to the stand wearing his police uniform and a look of reluctance.

"Officer Cody, can you tell the court your role in this case?"

"Yes, I accompanied the child protection officer, Miss Colby, to the Burrows home at four p.m. that Thursday. The plan was to serve the warrant and take young Bobby and Beatrice Burrows for placement in a foster home. I was also the arresting officer of Mrs. Elise Freeman a few days later and brought her in for booking," Robert Cody answered politely.

"And did you collect any evidence at the time of Mrs. Freeman's arrest?"

"Yes, sir. We searched her van, gathered things inside it as evidence, and had it impounded. Also, Miss Colby talked to Beatrice and checked for any signs of injury to her," he answered.

"Is this a picture of the van you got the evidence from?" Stonewell held up a large photograph to the witness.

"Yes, that looks like it."

"And could you describe the van for the court?" Stonewell asked.

"Yes, it was shiny black, but one side had a yellow rectangular section with a picture of flowers and bees."

"Did it look freshly painted?" Stonewell inquired.

"Yeah. I'd say so. It was very striking, and the van looked almost new."

"Was it a new van?"

"No, sir, it was a 1995 Chevy van."

"And did Miss Colby find any signs of injury or harm to Beatrice?"

"Yes, she saw that Beatrice had a large bruise on her back," Officer Cody reported with reservation in his voice.

Mr. Stonewell reached inside a large cardboard box and pulled out my bee suit. "Officer Cody, is this one of the pieces of evidence you seized from the van during your arrest of Mrs. Elise Freeman?"

"Yes."

Embarrassed, I slid down in my seat. *Looks like they've got everything on me.* Even though I never hurt Bea, I don't stand a chance. The next suit I'll probably be wearing will be prison blues.

"Thank you, Officer Cody. I have no other questions for this witness. Your cross, Mr. Cole."

Andy stood and asked, "Officer Cody, when you went to arrest Mrs. Elise Freeman, did it appear that Beatrice was afraid of Elise?"

"No, she seemed very content with Mrs. Freeman. In fact, when we first saw them, Beatrice gave Elise a big hug. She ran and hugged her again just before we took her for placement in the foster home."

"When you went to arrest Mrs. Freeman and pick up Beatrice, were they at Elise's house?" Andy asked.

"No, sir, they were both staying in a home in Phoenix owned by someone else."

"And how did you know where to find Elise?"

"Detective Carl Lewinsky phoned and told me where they were. He said Elise had called to turn herself in and give Beatrice to child services. Detective Lewinsky also met us at the house that day to ensure everything went well."

"When you arrived, did Mrs. Freeman resist arrest or give you any kind of trouble?" Andy asked.

"No sir, none at all. But I could tell she was upset about having to let Beatrice go."

"One more question, Officer Cody. When you removed Bobby Burrows from his residence on Friday, did his father, Jack, resist you in any way or try to talk you out of taking him?"

"No," Cody commented. "I thought it was sad that he didn't object at all. I felt bad for the boy."

"Thank you, Officer Cody. That will be all." Andy excused him. My emotions were a roller coaster from the guilt of taking Bea and leaving Bobby. It must have been devastating for Bobby that Jack didn't stand up for him.

"Your Honor, I call Mr. Jack Burrows to the stand," Stonewell boomed.

Jack passed by, and I cringed as he lobbed a look of detestable anger my way. I held my cool. *Wonder what kind of lies he's going to tell.*

"Mr. Burrows, can you tell the court what you saw when you arrived home on the day of the abduction?" Mr. Stonewell asked.

Andy stood up, "I object, Your Honor! The word *abduction* implies guilt for my client."

The judge responded, "The defense is correct. The jury is instructed to disregard that term."

"Mr. Burrows," he started again, "tell the court what you saw when you arrived home on the day your daughter was taken."

"Yes. As I drove into my driveway, a black van blasted out. I heard my wife screaming and saw her lying on the lawn, swatting at a swarm of bees. I ran over and grabbed her arm, pulling her away from the bees. She'd been stung pretty bad, so I took her to the hospital," Jack said.

"Did you see Bobby or Beatrice as you helped your wife to the car?" Mr. Stonewell asked.

"No, I didn't see them. But that's not unusual. I figured Bobby was at a ball game, and maybe Bea was at dance class or something," Jack replied.

"When did you discover that Bea had been taken?" he asked.

"About twenty minutes after we got to the hospital, Jane told me that the beekeepers had taken Bea. I didn't know what she was talking about. I thought she was delirious from the bee stings. But when we got home, I realized she must be right. There was no sign of Bea anywhere, so I called the police," Jack reported.

"Did you know who may have taken your daughter?" Mr. Stonewell asked.

"Yes, Jane told me it was Elise who took her. She said she was dressed like a beekeeper and put Bea in a van, then drove off."

"Were you surprised to hear your wife say Elise took your daughter?"

"Yes."

"And why were you surprised?"

"Because we hadn't seen Elise in several years. She disappeared when she was eighteen, and we'd been searching for her ever since. We didn't know if she was dead or alive. My wife and I were devastated. Just worried sick about it." Jack looked down as he made the last statement—no doubt to hide his lying face.

I felt restless and claustrophobic. Every ounce of me wanted to run. Knowing that wouldn't be wise, I scanned the room, looking for something or someone to focus on. My eyes settled on a phrase hanging on the wall—*In God we Trust*.

"Was your wife injured as a result of the bee attack?"

"Yes, she was stung and bitten several times. The doctors said they were hornets, not bees."

"That must have been terrifying for both of you," Mr. Stonewall pressed.

"Yes. I was very worried about my wife." Jack feigned a look of deep concern. "It was so hard on her after Elise disappeared, and now this."

"I have no other questions, Your Honor."

Andy stood to cross-examine. "Mr. Burrows, when Elise went missing at eighteen, did you report it to the police immediately?"

"No, we kept thinking she was just being a temperamental teenager and would come home soon. But then, after a couple of days, we did get concerned and called a police friend to see if he could locate her," Jack said.

"And what is the name of the police officer you called?"

"I, uh, think it was Manuel Ruiz. But it's been several years now, so I may be wrong."

"How long have you been friends with Officer Ruiz?" Andy pressed.

"I'm not sure, probably about eight years," Jack squirmed in his seat, "but I wouldn't say we're close friends. I mean, we don't see each other often." He looked sideways as he answered.

"When you arrived at the house the day Beatrice was taken, was anyone else with you in the car?" Andy asked.

"Yes. Our nanny, Lidia," he replied.

"And why was Lidia in the car with you?"

"I had taken her to a doctor."

"Oh? Was she sick?"

Jack looked a little sick as he answered, "Well, she, uh, hadn't been feeling well for several weeks, so I drove her to get checked out."

"Mr. Burrows, isn't it true that you didn't just take Lidia to the doctor but took her to a clinic to get an abortion?" I gasped, realizing that Lidia was likely being molested like I had been.

"I object, Your Honor. This is irrelevant, and Lidia is not a witness or on trial here," Mr. Stonewell declared.

"You are right. The defense must withdraw the question," the judge ordered.

"Sorry, Your Honor, I withdraw the question. Mr. Burrows, how old is Lidia?"

"I object! I don't see the relevance in this, Your Honor."

"Your Honor, it's foundational to my case that I continue this line of questioning," Andy reasoned.

"I will allow it," the judge declared.

"So, again, how old is Lidia?"

"She is seventeen," Jack answered. "Uh, I mean eighteen."

"Eighteen? Are you sure about that, Mr. Burrows?" Andy questioned.

"Well, when she started working for us, she said she was thirteen." She's been working for us about five years now." Jack shrugged in reply.

"So, Lidia started working for you when she was only thirteen, soon after Elise disappeared? Correct?"

"Yes," Jack answered.

"And what are her main duties?" Andy prompted.

"She makes lunches for the kids, helps with laundry, cleans the house, and cooks our meals. When she started driving, we had her take the kids to school and pick them up. The usual stuff," he answered.

"Wow. That sounds like quite a lot for a young girl," Andy commented.

"Your Honor, I object. I don't see the relevance," Stonewell declared.

"Counselor Cole, I agree. Get to your point," Judge Solomon directed.

"Yes, Your Honor. Just one more question regarding Lidia. Mr. Burrows, when Elise left, you must've missed her. I mean, she probably helped with all the same things Lidia does now. And with Lidia pregnant and unable to complete her chores, you must have been worried." Barely coming up for air, Andy continued, "Worried that people, especially your wife, will find out you are the father of the child Lidia was carrying?"

"Your Honor, I object! This is outrageous and irrelevant!" Mr. Stonewell shouted. Judge Solomon struck his gavel with a bang as a loud murmur spread throughout the courtroom.

"Counselor Cole, that is enough. If you continue along this line of questioning, you will be reprimanded and held in contempt. Jurors, you must disregard Counselor Cole's questions and statements regarding Miss Lidia's condition and his accusations against Mr. Burrows regarding any pregnancy."

"Yes, Your Honor. I withdraw the question." Unphased, Andy continued. "Mr. Burrows, how old was Elise when you hired her?" Andy looked straight at Jack, a smirk sneaking through.

"She was six," he started, then corrected his answer. "I mean, she was six when we adopted her."

"And how old was Elise when she started doing the laundry, cleaning, and caring for your other two children?" Andy asked.

"Well, I don't know exactly, but I think she started helping out more when she was nine or ten." Jack looked at his watch and then at me with a glare of impatience.

"Mr. Burrows, isn't it true that Elise was doing all of the things Lidia does and more by the time she was twelve or thirteen, except for driving the kids places?" Andy pressed.

"Probably."

"And how much did you pay her?" Andy went on.

"I think it was about $50 per week since she was a family member," Jack lied.

Ha! You didn't pay me anything until you started molesting me and paid to keep me quiet about it. I was fuming inside. Surprisingly, my ears weren't letting out steam.

"Wow! Sounds like a good deal for you and your wife. Especially if there were other *services* you expected her to provide." Andy emphasized the word *services*, leaving no question exactly what kind of assistance he was referring to. Andy waited a few seconds, letting the implications of his insinuation settle into the jurors' minds.

"Mr. Burrows, did you actually see Elise put Beatrice in the van and leave with her that day?"

"Uh, no, I guess not," he admitted.

"Thank you. Tell us, Mr. Burrows, you said Elise was six years old when you adopted her. Do you have possession of the adoption paperwork for Mrs. Freeman?"

"Uh, no. I mean, we can't find the paperwork. It got lost when we moved last time." Jack's eyes shifted to Jane and back.

"Mr. Burrows, isn't it true that you don't have adoption papers for Mrs. Freeman because you never had adoption papers for her? In fact, isn't it true that you bought Elise from a man in Mexico commonly known for human trafficking?"

Gasps filled the courtroom as Jack's face drained of all color. He looked like a fish out of water. Before he could speak, Mr. Stonewell jolted out of his seat.

"I object, Your Honor. Counsel is badgering the witness. His questions are irrelevant to this trial."

"Agreed. Mr. Burrows, you do not have to answer that question."

"I withdraw the question, Your Honor. I have no other questions for this witness."

Mr. Stonewell stood and, to my relief, announced, "Your Honor, that completes my witness list. Prosecution rests."

Judge Solomon tapped his gavel and spoke up. "It's eleven forty-five now. Let's take a lunch break. We will reconvene at two."

Andy looked at me, his face brimming with accomplishment. My head was pounding. I couldn't wait to get out of there. Besides a full bladder, I couldn't stand to hear any more of Jack's lies. I shot out of my seat and nearly stormed out, but Allie caught me by the arm. "Cool it, Elise. You have to stay calm," she whispered firmly.

Taking a deep breath, my shoulders relaxed some. "Jack's lying through his teeth. Why shouldn't he answer that last question?" I whispered back, then stopped in my tracks, numb with realization. "It's true. Isn't it?" My mind reeled as questions erupted, like a fireworks show making my head throb harder.

Allie leaned in and whispered, "Honestly, we're still looking into it. But we must display a calm attitude, or it will not read well to the jury. Remember, they don't know you or Jack but are watching your every move. Right now, you don't want to give them any reason to believe that what the prosecution is saying about you is true," Allie wisely advised. Andy nodded in agreement.

We swiftly headed towards the courtroom cafeteria, but my mind still reeled from this revelation. I had been trafficked.

FINDING a table in the back of the court cafeteria, we made sure no one was sitting nearby. I was hungry and ill simultaneously, that last question still ringing in my ears. After some light-hearted chit-chat, I managed to eat most of my sandwich.

Andy turned to me. "Elise, would you feel comfortable taking the stand?"

Alarmed, I looked up from my plate. "Oh! Uh, I dunno!" Truthfully, I was terrified at the prospect. "What would I say?"

"Well, after I call Michelle to the stand, I'll call you up and ask about the day you left the Burrows and why you left. If you feel ready, you can tell them about the abuse you endured." He paused a moment, allowing his words to sink in. "After that," he continued, "I'll ask what your intentions were the day Bea was set to be removed from the Burrows' home. We'll describe what happened that day and why you took Bea. You can tell everyone about the swarm of bees and how you protected Beatrice with your helmet and got her to the van." I nodded in rhythm to his words, trying to swallow the lump in my throat.

Andy hesitated, then said, "But before I put you on the stand, you need to know what to expect from Mr. Stonewell when he cross-examines you," Andy explained. "After you're done eating, we can find a quiet room and go over things more clearly. We won't make you take the stand unless you're comfortable. Okay?"

"Okay. I guess so. Yeah, that would be okay." Surprising myself, I agreed.

"Elise," Andy glanced at Allie, then back at me, "I don't want to upset you, but I need you to read this document. It could play into our case." He slid a small piece of paper across the table. I felt the blood drain from my head as I read it to the end.

"Are you sure this is real?" I asked.

"Positive!" Allie answered. Andy nodded in agreement as my world suddenly shifted.

THIRTY-FIVE

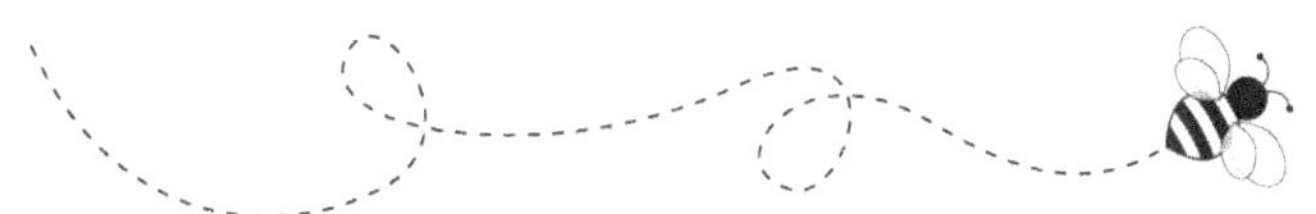

I t was a short walk to the courtroom, yet my usual quick stride felt sluggish as my mind raced ahead. The realization that I'd soon be on the witness stand and emotions stirred by the new and revealing document kept turning in my mind. Fear, doubt, anger, hope, joy, and elation somersaulted repeatedly without settling. I stepped inside, taking a deep breath and sending up a quick prayer for strength.

"All rise for Judge Richard Solomon," the bailiff ordered.

"Mr. Cole, you may proceed with your defense," Judge Solomon directed.

Andy stood, looking taller than ever, and called his first witness. "Will Miss Michelle Colby come to the stand?"

After she was sworn in, Andy proceeded. "Miss Colby, would you please tell the court how you know the defendant?"

"Yes. I work for Child Protective Services here in Phoenix. Elise contacted me several weeks ago with concerns about the safety of Beatrice and her brother, Bobby. She reported to me the abuse she had suffered while living with the Burrows and was worried that Beatrice and Bobby may also be getting abused by Mr. and Mrs. Burrows," Michelle stated.

"Can you tell the court if you investigated her suspicions and what you found?" Andy asked.

"Well, I can't present evidence here because that will be done at the hearing for the children's welfare, but I can tell you there was enough evidence found during our investigation to warrant the removal of both children."

"And on the day in question, were you in the process of removing Beatrice and Bobby with the sole purpose of protecting them?" Andy asked.

"Yes, we had secured a warrant, and it was supposed to be done that afternoon," Michelle answered.

"And can you tell the courts what happened?"

"Yes. Officer Manuel Ruiz was supposed to accompany me to the house. However, he went earlier than was arranged and claimed the children weren't home when he arrived."

"So, let me get this straight. Are you saying that Police Officer Ruiz was supposed to accompany you to the Burrows' residence on the day of the abduction, but he disregarded protocol and went there ahead of time without you?"

"Yes. We were supposed to go at three that afternoon, but he went to the house earlier without me," Michelle testified. "We also saw a moving van and boxes and were concerned about the possibility of the Burrows moving away before we removed the children."

Then Andy asked, "Can you tell us about the day Elise was arrested and you went to get Beatrice?"

"Yes. Mrs. Freeman called me Friday, the day after Beatrice was taken. She told me she had Beatrice with her and wanted to turn her over to Child Welfare Services. She also mentioned..."

I tuned Michelle's testimony out as the trauma from that day washed over me. I still worried Bea would never forgive me for leaving her again.

Andy's voice broke through my thoughts. "...So let me get this straight. The police hadn't tracked down Elise or Bea? In fact, Elise was the one who called and told you and Detective Lewinsky where she and Bea were. Is that right?

"Yes, sir."

"And, Miss Colby, can you tell the court what happened when you went to the house to get Bea on Friday? Did you observe Bea showing signs of fear or mistrust towards Elise Freeman during that visit?"

"The process went smoothly. Mrs. Freeman cooperated entirely. And no, the only fear I sensed in Beatrice was towards the police officer, which is understandable. She started crying when we told her we had to take her away from Mrs. Freeman...."

Tears brimmed my eyes as the memory of that moment came clear to me again. The next thing I knew, Andy asked Michelle about the bruise on Bea's back.

"Yes, it looked like some kind of hard object had caused it," Michelle answered. I held my breath.

"And did you ask Beatrice how the bruise got there?"

"Yes. Bea said that Jane Burrows hit her with a large metal BBQ tool because she hadn't cleaned her room well enough," Michelle explained.

"And did you have a doctor examine the bruise?"

"Yes, that same day, we took her to a doctor who commonly assists us with abuse situations," she testified.

"And what did the doctor say about the bruise?"

"He determined that the bruise had to be more than a week old and, therefore, couldn't possibly have been caused by Mrs. Freeman since Beatrice had only been in her presence for two days," Michelle answered as I exhaled. "I have his report right here if you want it." She held it out to him. Andy retrieved it and gave it to the judge, asking that it be admitted as evidence.

"Thank you, Miss Colby. That will be all for now," Andy said. Mr. Stonewell, you may cross-examine now.

Stonewell approached Michelle, dropped his jaw open a few

seconds, then clamping it shut again, proclaimed, "I have no cross for this witness, Your Honor."

"Miss Colby, you may step down," the judge excused her.

My hands started shaking, knowing I would be called to the stand next. *Lord, give me wisdom and strength,* I prayed silently. Andy stood and called me up to testify. It took me a minute to respond, but I managed to walk. Putting my hand on the Bible as they swore me in brought an unexpected sense of calm and strength.

"Mrs. Freeman, how long have you been married?" Thankfully, Andy began with an easy question.

"For four years," I replied.

"And you have a little girl named Bella. Is that right?" he asked.

"Uh. Yes, she's three."

"Is Bella the only child you have given birth to?" Andy followed the line of questioning we'd discussed.

"No, I had another baby when I was fourteen."

"And can you tell us a little more about that child?" Andy prodded.

"She was a baby girl, but I was told she died at birth."

"I'm so sorry. Were you still living with Mr. and Mrs. Burrows when that occurred?" Andy asked gently.

"Yes."

"Mrs. Freeman, can you tell us what things were like growing up with Jane and Jack Burrows as your parents?" He switched gears.

"At first, they were nice to me. I was only six when I came to live with them, and they treated me kindly for a few years. But things started to change when I was eight and Bobby was born. Jane constantly yelled at me and started forcing me to do all kinds of chores. I took care of Bobby while Jane went out with friends, shopping, or playing bridge. I didn't mind watching the baby because I loved him and still do. But at eight, I didn't really feel equipped to carry all that responsibility."

"Mrs. Freeman, did you feel loved by Mr. and Mrs. Burrows?" he asked, and to my surprise, I began to tear up.

"No." Casting my eyes downward, my self-esteem fell too. I became that scared little girl I was when I first went to live with the Burrows—the girl who didn't feel worthy of anyone's love. My voice softened to a whisper, and Andy had to ask me to speak up so everyone could hear. Looking at him, it finally came out more clearly. "I tried to be a good girl. I truly did. Maybe they would've loved me if I'd been good enough." I swiped at a tear.

Andy looked at me with encouragement in his eyes, so I continued. "When Jack started molesting me, and Jane began beating me, I knew neither one loved me. They hated me." As I spoke, it felt like someone else was speaking for me. "At least Jack only hit me when I wouldn't cooperate with him in bed. Then he'd pay me so I wouldn't tell Jane about it. It was the only time I got *any* money for all my work." Shame and guilt filled me as if I'd just admitted to prostituting myself.

Something deep within me seemed to shake loose. With each detail I spoke out loud, knotted emotions that were restrained within me came untied. Like a helium balloon, they were let loose. Set free. A feeling of weightlessness came over me. I wanted to go on and on forever.

Andy brought me back with another question. "Mrs. Freeman, according to Jane and Jack Burrows, you disappeared when you were eighteen. Can you tell us what happened and where you went after you left the Burrows' house?"

"After Beatrice was born, the abuse got much worse. I knew my life was in danger, so I escaped." Rambling on, I left out the town name but told the court about getting a job as a waitress, getting married, and having Bella. Then, to my surprise, I boldly added, "God helped me start a new life."

"Elise, why did you come back to Phoenix?"

"I've wanted to return ever since I left. I missed Bobby and Bea. And I worried they might be abused the way I had been.

When a friend told me about recently seeing suspicious bruises on the kids, I felt an even greater urgency to return."

"How did it feel to be near the Burrows again, Elise?"

"I was terrified. That's why I dressed in disguise when I went to their house. I couldn't take a chance of them recognizing me."

Andy prompted, "So why did you return?"

My eyes welled with tears again. "I needed to see for myself. To know for sure that Bea and Bobby were okay. That they were safe."

"Elise, what was your plan when you went to the Burrows' house that day?"

I wiped away my tears and focused on Andy to remain calm. "I just wanted to see the kids. I knew there was no way I could step foot near that house without Jack or Jane coming after me, so I bought a used van and had it painted to look like a beekeeping business. I knew from my time living there that they had a lot of problems with bees, so I made myself a beekeeper suit with a helmet and veil to protect me from the bees. I figured it would work well as a disguise, too."

Andy continued the line of questioning with, "Elise, would you tell us exactly what happened the day Beatrice was taken away from the Burrows' house?"

"Well, a moving van was leaving when I arrived. Soon after, I saw Officer Ruiz go to the door without a Child Welfare Service representative. I knew they were supposed to go to the house together and was alarmed when I heard Officer Ruiz warn Jane to move away quickly. I decided to remove the beehive as a distraction to stall so Child Welfare Services could get there before the Burrows left."

I continued my story, purposely leaving out Ruben, Lily, and Mell's participation. The jury seemed mesmerized when I got to the part about Jane chasing me with a large metal tool while the swarm of bees covered me from head to toe. I noticed two jurors shudder.

"When the bees finally lifted off of me, Bea was standing

nearby. Jane started running after me again but suddenly stopped and fell backward. Apparently, she'd caught her foot in a hornet's nest in the grass. At least that's what they told me later on. She couldn't get it loose, and hundreds of hornets swarmed around her, and she started screaming. I wasn't sure what to do, but when I saw Bea cowering in fear, I ran to her, took my helmet off, and put it over her head to protect her. Then I helped her get into the van to get away from the danger," I explained the best I could.

"When you took your helmet off, were you concerned that Jane Burrows would recognize you?" Andy asked.

"Yes, of course, but at that point, I didn't care; I just needed to protect Bea from the bees," I answered.

"Did you do anything to help Jane with the bees?"

"A water hose was nearby, so I tried to hose them off. I think it helped some." *Does anyone know I left out my accomplices, Lily and Mell? Will I get in more trouble for not being totally forthright? Please, Lord, don't let them bring Mell and Lily into this.*

Andy looked me in the eyes and then asked something I didn't see coming. "Elise, why didn't you stay behind and try to help Jane more or call 911?"

Thinking quickly, I said, "Because Jack drove up just as I got Bea in the van. I knew he'd take care of Jane and…." I took a steadying breath, "…and I was afraid he'd come after me."

"That's understandable," Andy nodded. "One more thing, Elise. Did Bea try to get away from you or in any way demonstrate that she didn't want to go with you?"

"No, she was very willing to go with me. In fact, I asked her if she wanted to leave with me, and she said yes. Even gave me a hug." I wiped another tear from my eye, emotions stirring wildly within me now.

"No more questions for now. Your cross, Mr. Stonewell."

Approaching me, Stonewell's stature was imposing and grew more intimidating the closer he got. "Mrs. Freeman, you testified that you pretended to be a beekeeper, fixed up a van to make it look like a business, and even wore a beekeeper suit that you made yourself. That seems like an awful lot of trouble to go through if you were just going to *see* that authorities removed Beatrice and Bobby. Why go through all that trouble?" he asked.

"I was afraid of Mr. and Mrs. Burrows. I had to disguise myself so they wouldn't recognize me. But I wanted to see Bea and Bobby again and knew I wouldn't...." He cut me short.

"Only answer the question, please," Mr. Stonewell scolded. "Mrs. Freeman, isn't it true that you didn't do this beekeeper thing all by yourself?"

"No, I didn't," I answered his questions directly this time.

"Mrs. Freeman, it certainly *sounds* like you've had a rough childhood, but why should we believe anything you said today? Especially when you didn't tell us everything. Why don't you tell us who helped you remove Bea from her home?"

"Oh, I'm sorry. I thought you only wanted me to answer your specific question." A couple of low chuckles sprinkled the room. "Now that you asked, I will tell you that two friends came with me to help with the bees. But none of us planned to take Beatrice that day." I started to explain further, but he squelched the full answer again.

"Okay, Mrs. Freeman. So, tell me, again, why would you go through all that trouble if you didn't plan to kidnap Beatrice?"

"Objection, Your Honor, 'kidnap' assumes guilt that hasn't been proven!" Andy came to my defense.

"Counselor, you have been instructed not to refer to it as an abduction or kidnapping. Strike it from the record."

"Sorry, Your Honor. It won't happen again." Without pausing, Stonewell continued, "So, Mrs. Freeman, why would you go through all that trouble if you didn't intend to take Beatrice away?"

The repetition prompted guilt to well up within me. *Jesus, I know I didn't go there to take Bea. But I did want her to come with me.* I suddenly felt unsure of myself, why I did what I did, and if I deserved God's mercy and grace. I gulped hard, closed my eyes, and prayed silently. When I opened them, my eyes fell on Ruben and Betty, who, until that moment, I hadn't realized were in the courtroom. Betty smiled and lifted up a Bible. She was sitting next to Pete, who smiled at me supportively. He threw me a kiss, and Mell and Lily gave a gentle wave as I glanced their way. There were so many people who helped, supported, and encouraged me. So many who had led me towards faith in God and gave me hope. It was an epiphany that buoyed me like nothing I'd felt before.

Mr. Stonewell cleared his throat with irritation and spoke louder. "Mrs. Freeman, isn't it true you went to the Burrows' house that day to remove Beatrice from their care because *you wanted her for yourself?*"

A sudden surge of power grew within me. I looked him straight in the eyes and proceeded with courage I didn't know I had. "Mr. Stonewell," I began, "have you ever had a dream so strong you couldn't forget it? A dream that was clearly from God. One that directed you to do something that terrified you? Well, I did—twice."

I saw Andy's look of surprise, yet he nodded his head, egging me on. "The first nightmare came when I was eighteen. It made it clear that my life was in danger so long as I stayed at the Burrows' house. So despite my fears and insecurities, I made a creative plan and escaped." I was on a roll.

"For every day of my life since leaving the Burrows' house, I wanted to return and get Bea out of that house. But despite my worries for both Bea and Bobby, I procrastinated. Helping them meant going back into that house of horror. I was terrified of Jack and Jane and what they might do to me."

Taking a quick breath, I proceeded. "A few months ago, I had another dream. One that was just as scary and just as surely from God, only this time, He told me to return and rescue Bea and Bobby. They were in danger, and this time, God gave me extra courage. So, I got even more creative in my efforts. Being creative was how I'd survived all those years of abuse. Being creative provided me with a refuge. It took me to a place of peacefulness, of mental escape.

"God protected me when I escaped six years ago. God has shown me His overflowing love, refuge, and redemption through the people He brought into my life. How could I not follow His lead again? How could I disappoint all the people who've helped me over the years? Furthermore, how could I not want Bea and Bobby to be safe and whole, to protect them as I never was? What I did was not for me, Mr. Stonewell; it was for Bea and Bobby, and more importantly, it was for God's purposes."

I inhaled deeply, receiving another dose of God's courage. *Hmm, maybe God brought me to this trial to give me a platform to proclaim His love and help to all who are in this courtroom today.* Oddly, Mr. Stonewell hadn't interrupted me even once. In fact, he seemed lost for words. I glanced at Mell and remembered Jeremiah 29:11, the verse on her bulletin board six years ago. It led me to Mell and Chicky-Pie's Café. It was about God having good plans for us, not to harm but to prosper us. I smiled.

"Mrs. Freeman, I... uh," Stonewell stammered and cleared his throat again. "If you didn't plan to take them that day, why didn't you call the police rather than risk danger to yourself or Bea?"

Tilting my head in baffled wonder, I grinned and answered with a tinge of sarcasm. "W-e-e-l-l, since I had just witnessed a policeman encourage Jane to flee, somehow calling the police didn't seem the thing to do." I wobbled my head in disbelief, then answered his question further. "But I truly hoped the authorities would remove Bea and Bobby for me. And, no, I did *not* plan to take them that day. But I couldn't leave Bea surrounded by angry hornets and the cruel woman who'd beaten and abused me for years."

Seeing a blank look on Stonewell's face, I continued. "I couldn't let one more moment of danger threaten Beatrice again. So, I risked being identified by Jane. I took my helmet off and put it over Bea's head. I risked my own life and the consequences that might follow to get her out of there. Fear drove me away from my love of Bea and Bobby, but *love* kept me from leaving them in danger." I sighed with heavy release as a stunned prosecutor stood silent before me.

"Mrs. Freeman," Mr. Stonewell snapped back but stumbled over his words as he proceeded. "Uh, I uh, wanted to ask you about when you lived with the Burrows. You said you had a child, but the baby died. You're an attractive young woman, Mrs. Freeman," he started to pick up steam now, "you must've had boyfriends in your teens. So, although I don't condone the kind of abuse you claim to have had, was it possible that one of your boyfriends got you pregnant, and maybe that's why Mr. and Mrs. Burrows were so angry with you?"

"No, no!" I shook my head. "That's not true. I didn't have any boyfriends. I had no friends because they wouldn't let me go to school in my senior year. And I never liked Jack; I despised him. He repulsed me, but I was too small to fight him off." My resolve began to break when Andy came to my rescue.

"Your Honor, counselor is badgering the witness," Andy pleaded.

"Mr. Stonewell, get yourself in order, or I will charge you with contempt." He banged his gavel with vigor as if he was on my side now.

"Yes, Your Honor." Mr. Stonewell stood glaring at me when I caught sight of a man entering the courtroom and walking up to Andy. He whispered something in Andy's ear and handed him a paper. Allie and Andy seemed to be consulting with one another as Stonewell charged into me unfettered now.

"Elise, I think you wanted revenge. You wanted to hurt Jack and Jane Burrows. You planned to leave Phoenix with Beatrice that day."

"No!" I cried out, but he cut me off.

"You knew things weren't going to go your way, and you took matters into your own hands, didn't you? You grabbed

Beatrice, shoved her into the van, then took off with lightning speed. You got out of there like a bat out of hell, didn't you, Mrs. Freeman?"

"No. No! I…mean, yes, we left quickly, but I just tried to save her from the bees, and I… I didn't know what else to do. I was trying hard to do everything by the rules, but…" I stuttered, "Yes, we left in a hurry. We had to." I covered my face and started crying.

"That's all for now, Mrs. Freeman," Mr. Stonewell said sternly as the judge surprised us both by handing me a box of tissues.

Andy stood up and began, "Your Honor, permission to redirect?"

Judge Solomon nodded yes, and Andy proceeded. "I have a copy of the actual plan that Elise and her friends had laid out before the incident. I'd like to submit it for your and Mrs. Freeman's inspection." Andy handed me a piece of paper. "Elise, can you please tell the court what this document is?" Andy asked.

Surprisingly, it was the document we'd used with my scribbled notes on it. *How did he get this?* I thought, then responded, "This is the plan we outlined for helping Bea and Bobby," I confirmed.

"And are there places on this document that are in your handwriting?" Andy asked.

I pointed to places I had written. "Yes. Right there and there."

"Elise, I noticed that you have a plan A and a plan B described in this outline. Would you read the final sentences of plan A and plan B for the courtroom to hear?"

"Yes. The last lines of Plan A state: 'If there is no evidence found of abuse of either of the children, we will <u>not</u> continue to seek to have Beatrice and Bobby removed from the household.' For plan B, it says: 'Stall if needed, but only use legal avenues to remove the children if abuse is evident to authorities.'"

"Thank you, Mrs. Freeman. Is there anywhere on the document indicating anyone intended to take matters into their own hands?"

"There is not."

"Is there any mention of a plan or desire to capture or abduct either of the children or to remove them from the property on the day in question or any day after that?" Andy asked.

"No, there is not," I replied with confidence.

"Thank you, Elise. Your Honor, I'd like to submit this document into evidence for the jury's inspection." The bailiff passed the page to the judge, then after a moment, retrieved it and gave it to the jury foreperson for review. "Ladies and gentlemen of the jury, you will see nothing included in this detailed outline to indicate that Elise intended to abduct or take Beatrice or Bobby away from the Burrows without the legal permission to do so."

While the jury members passed the paper around, Andy returned to me and asked, "Mrs. Freeman, you mentioned that you overheard Officer Ruiz advise Jane Burrows to move as soon as possible. How could you hear what Officer Ruiz was saying?"

I wasn't expecting this question from Andy and was caught off guard. I sat stunned momentarily, then replied, "Well, I was standing about twenty-five to thirty feet away. Officer Ruiz was speaking loudly, and he told Jane, 'If you're planning to move, you should do it as soon as possible—no later than Saturday morning.' It was obvious he was trying to warn Mrs. Burrows."

"I object, Your Honor. This is hearsay," Mr. Stonewell stood and interrupted.

"Agreed. Counselor?" Judge Solomon said.

Andy acknowledged the judge's admonition and continued. "Okay, let me ask you, Elise. Had you ever encountered Officer Ruiz before that day?"

"Yes. When I was still living at the Burrows', they hosted a party. I served the appetizers, and Officer Manuel Ruiz was one of the guests. They introduced him to another couple as their 'friend Manny.'"

"Elise, earlier, you mentioned that Mrs. Burrows chased you with an object. Can you please describe that object?"

I took a moment, re-imagining the scene in my mind. "Well, it's hard to say for sure. At first, I was covered with bees, but when they lifted, Jane screamed and charged me with a large metal tool. It was about 12 inches long with a wide flat piece on one end that glinted in the sun."

Andy held up a large metal BBQ spatula and asked, "Is this the tool she had when she was chasing you?"

Surprise lit my face. "Yes," I responded, "sure looks like it."

"Your Honor, this was found by police investigators in the grassy area where the hornet's nest was on the day of the incident. I'd like to submit it as evidence."

Andy gave me an affirming smile as if to say *here we go*. Then he took things up a notch. "Elise, I'd like to go back to your earlier statement. You said that at fourteen, you gave birth to a baby girl. You also said you were told she died at birth. How long after you gave birth was it before Mrs. Burrows came home from the hospital with her baby girl?"

"It was about a month later," I answered.

"Did you notice anything different about Mrs. Burrows' pregnancy before she brought baby Beatrice home from the hospital?"

"Well, Jane wasn't showing a baby bump or any symptoms until she told me she was six months pregnant. That was the first I'd even heard she was expecting a child."

"How unusual," he commented. "And have you learned anything recently about the baby you gave birth to at fourteen?"

Looking straight at the jury, I proceeded firmly. "Yes! I found out just *today* that my baby didn't die. She is alive and well and living right here in Phoenix." Filled with emotion, I continued, "My baby was, and is," I gulped, "Beatrice Burrows! The same baby girl Jane Burrows brought home from the hospital a month later, claiming *she* had given birth to." A collective gasp could be heard throughout the courtroom. "...the same child I rescued that day. The same little girl I loved from the start." My breathing was heavy, the shock of the news still fresh. I looked at Jane. Her face turned pale as a ghost, her mouth open, slack, her eyes glazed over. Jack flared red with anger.

Andy asked if I was surprised to learn about Bea being my daughter. "Yes, it was a shock at first. But, inside, I think I always knew. Bea and I always had a connection, and when I saw her again that Thursday, her resemblance to my other daughter and myself was unmistakable. I had suspected it for some time. I think, as a mother, you instinctively know," I said with pride. "But it wasn't until today when it was confirmed and documented that I fully believed she is my daughter. The one I thought I'd lost." Tears of joy trickled down my cheeks, touching the corners of my broad smile.

"Mrs. Freeman, can you tell the court who Beatrice's father is?" Andy looked me in the eyes, giving me the strength to answer.

"Yes, her father is Jack Burrows," I said emphatically, looking straight at Jack as another loud gasp swooped through the courtroom.

"And is he the same Jack Burrows here in this courtroom?"

"Yes! He's right there," I said, pointing to him. Jane's eyes rolled back into her head like she was about to faint. Jack closed his eyes tightly and swore under his breath. A low buzzing mutter grew in intensity through the room. Judge Solomon hit his gavel, calling for order.

"Thank you, Elise." Andy smiled. "Do you have any proof that you are the birth mother of Beatrice Burrows?"

"Yes, several weeks before I came to Phoenix, I gathered hair samples from an old baby brush of Bea's and a pacifier I still had and sent them in for DNA testing through Ancestry.com. As I mentioned, I'd had my suspicions. The test results arrived this morning, revealing I have a relative named Beatrice Burrows." I aimed my beaming joy and pride toward the prosecutor now.

"There's just one more thing I'd like to submit to the court before I call my next witness," Andy said. "Your Honor, I have the birth certificate of Miss Beatrice Burrows. You will see that her birth date was April 21, 2003, at nine a.m. Elise, will you read for us who is named as the father and the mother of the child in question?" Andy handed me the small document.

I nervously read, "The father is Jack Burrows. A-a-a-nd, the mother is Elise Burrows."

A loud rumble of chatter erupted now.

"Your Honor, if Mr. Stonewell has no further cross-examination for Elise, I would like to excuse Mrs. Freeman from the stand.

"I have no questions," Stonewell's broad shoulders slouched now.

Andy addressed the judge. "Your Honor, that completes my examination of all witnesses. If it pleases the court, and the prosecution agrees, I'd like to request a break to prepare for closing comments."

Mr. Stonewell agreed, and the judge declared a twenty-minute break. As we filed out, Allie guided me toward a conference room, my whole body trembling. Andy approached the prosecutor, and I heard him ask, "Mr. Stonewell, shall we meet in the conference room?"

"Sure. Let me talk with my client first," Mr. Stonewell responded.

⚜

"ALL RISE." The bailiff called the court back to order as Judge Solomon entered. All were seated, and then the prosecutor rose to speak.

"Your Honor, permission for myself and counsel for the defense to approach the bench?"

"Granted," Judge Solomon declared.

Tension grabbed my gut, twisting it into knots as I watched them whisper back and forth. What was going on? Was Andy trying to cut a deal? Can he do that without talking to me first? When Andy and Mr. Stonewell returned to their positions, Mr. Stonewell continued standing and faced the courtroom. I could hear the thrum of my heart beating in my ears.

He cleared his throat and began. "In light of the evidence presented to the court today, the State of Arizona moves to dismiss all charges against Mrs. Freeman," Mr. Stonewell proposed.

Sighs of relief and shouts of joy could be heard throughout the courtroom. Some of the jurors and audience clapped in approval. I slumped into my chair, tilting my head up at the ceiling, with my heart in praise to God. Another weight had been lifted from my shoulders.

The judge hit his gavel, but it was the celebratory bang of victory this time. "Case dismissed! Justice has been served, and the defendant is free to go," he declared.

I gasped, my heart still racing in my chest but full of all-encompassing joy. Turning to Andy and Allie, I gave them big hugs of appreciation. Pete found me quickly, and we embraced tightly. In the hall, Mell, Lily, Betty, and Ruben congratulated me and enveloped me in hugs. We decided on a restaurant for an early evening celebration before going home.

Heading outside, Katie walked towards me. Her eyes were wet with tears, but a bright smile decorated my mother's face with joy. We hugged as if never wanting to let go. The flashing clicks of reporters' cameras captured our moment for the newspapers, their voices rising with question after question. But I paid no attention to them even as bright cameras flashed. I was in my mother's arms. I was finally home.

THIRTY-SIX

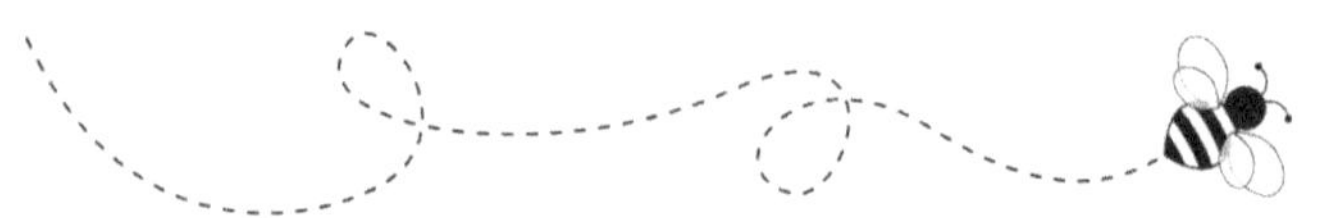

They say that walls cain't talk, but soon as Mama Millie done built my walls, an folks start comin' in heah, I started talkin'. I tole them they is loved with warm hospitality an lots a evidence a God's Spirit. An when Mama Mell come an spruce things up, I spoke through her warm and welcoming smiles, cheerful music, an wise food fer the soul. An the evidence of heppin' folks has spoke louder than a train's horn tootin' its way into town.

TO CELEBRATE, we went to the local Cheesecake Factory, where our conversation buzzed with the excitement of freedom—not only for myself but for Bea and Bobby. I sat down beside Allie with relief. Pete sat on my other side and slid his arm across the back of my chair. His presence helped to calm my lingering jitters from the ordeal of the past few days. Glancing at Allie, I asked, "Have you talked with Michelle about what's next for Bea and Bobby?"

"Yes, I caught up with her on our drive to the restaurant. The children's trial date has not been set yet, and until the trial is concluded, there is no guarantee they will be removed from the Burrows permanently."

I sighed upon hearing this, though I wasn't surprised.

"However," she continued, "now that we have established you as Beatrice's birth mother, that will help. I understand you wish to gain full custody of Bea?" She looked at me expectantly.

I glanced at Pete, and he gave a quick nod. "Yes, I want to be legally recognized as her mother and guardian."

"Okay. We will work to do that. For now, we will seek to garner visitation rights for you to see Bea. As her father, Jack might continue to have parental rights to visit, even if they reward you with custody." Allie gave us a dose of reality. It was hard to swallow.

"I don't mean to sound ungrateful. I know the trial's purpose was to review my actions in taking Bea. But I can't help but be disappointed that Jack and Jane won't be held accountable for all they did to me," I mentioned while glancing across the table at Lewinsky.

"I'm sorry about that too, Elise, but at least you won't have to worry about prison time now," Lewinsky offered. "I have a hunch Jack and Jane will be in court soon for serious charges against them. Just leave it to me." Looking at him with curiosity, I caught a gleam in his eye. There was something he wasn't telling us, but a sense of peace washed over me. I knew he'd fill us in when the time was right.

🐝

BELLA RAN to me as we entered Katie's house to pick her up. Beatrice followed close behind, and they hugged me, the warmth of which would last indefinitely. We shared our great news with the girls. Bella squealed with joy and exclaimed, "Oh, Mommy, I am so happy. I knew Jesus was going to help you stay with us."

Bea gave me a tentative smile, saying, "That's so good, Mommy." She gave me another hug, but I sensed she knew her worries weren't quite over yet. "Does this mean I can come live with you now?" she asked.

Katie and I looked at each other with joyful realization. Bea has been and will continue to stay with her true grandmother during the interim.

"Not just yet, my Bumble Bea. But we're doing everything we can to make sure that happens very soon." I gave my daughter, the first daughter of my heart, a smile and took her hand. *Oh, my word, Bea is my daughter! No wonder I felt such a connection to her from the moment she came home from the hospital.*

BACK AT THE HOTEL, Pete and I slumped onto the couch, weary from the emotional rollercoaster we'd been on.

"Well, all's well that ends well, right, honey?" Pete wrapped his arm around me. I stiffened and picked up a sewing project I'd nearly finished.

"Yep," was all I said while clipping the loose threads still hanging from the blouse I'd been working on.

"Is something wrong?" Pete nudged.

"Nope. How could there be? I mean, after all, I didn't have to go to jail, and Bea might be able to live with me." My reply dripped with bitterness, betraying the questions still unsettling me.

"With *us*, Elise, Bea will be able to live with US! So, what's the deal? You should be ecstatic." Pete seemed annoyed with me, and I couldn't blame him.

"You're right. It's just that after all the proof of what Jane and Jack did to me came out in the trial, I don't understand why Jack isn't in jail. And what about Manny Ruiz? We proved he didn't do his job. In fact, his actions could have enabled Jack and Jane to continue abusing Bea and Bobby. And what about the whole trafficking thing that's probably still going on? I mean, there are other victims out there. Will justice be served?" The words tumbled out of my mouth. "I guess I'm feeling a little vindictive," I said with a shrug.

"Honey, I don't blame you for feeling that way. It's understandable. But we need to trust those things to the Good Lord. Today was a victory, but it doesn't mean it was the last time the Burrows or Officer Ruiz will see the inside of a courtroom for the part they played. It could take a long time for justice to be fully served, so for now, we need to focus on all the good that *has* come out of this—to count our blessings, not our worries. God can handle the rest."

I sighed in resignation. "You're right, of course. I will just continue to stay on my knees in prayer. That's all I can do." I leaned over to face Pete. "I am so glad I'm free to be with you and the girls." My good night kiss expressed my sincerity.

THIRTY-SEVEN

A big shoutin' holler went up when everbody at Chicky-Pie's heard 'bout the charges bein' dropped against Elise an that she was actually Bea's real mama. We was all overflowed with joy like a river without a dam. Mama Mell gave a big shindig when they got home an there was music an dancin'. An a course lots a good food.

Ya, know, it was jes like when the bees get back from foraging nectar — they all do a dance calt the waggle." Maybe that's what everbody was doin' at the big party. I know one thing. There ain't never been a buzz in Riverview like the one tha's been goin' on at Chicky-Pie's. An now that things is goin' well fer Miss Elise, it time to waggle our booties an celebrate.

Mama use a read a verse in the Psalms that say, "But you will be fed … with honey from the rock." Well, the gatherin' of friends was surely sweeter than honey on my lips. The party brought in nearly the whole town of Riverview. Folks lined-up at the big yella' door with they feet tappin' to lively tunes of my jukebox, an they mouth's salivatin' at the 'roma of fried chicken an sweet pie.

The excitement continued long into the night with a celebration that will keep this heah town buzzin' for weeks ta come. It truly was a night ta remember. An I ken bet they's gonna be more ta buzz bout if the Good Lawd let it happen.

So ya'll keep comin' back. Ya heah!

Three Weeks Later

It was time to go back home. I'd put the last few items in my suitcase when Mell called, insisting she host a celebration for me at Chicky-Pie's. "We could have it on Monday night. We'll clear out some of the tables so we can have a dance floor, too," she suggested.

"That would be amazing! We have something else to celebrate now too."

"Oh? What's that?" Mell asked expectantly.

"The court gave me full custody of Bea. And Ruben is going to foster Bobby until he can officially adopt!" A chorus of joyous hoots and hollers came through the phone line.

"Is Lily there with you?" I asked with glee.

"I sure am, honey!" Lily confirmed. "Mell's speakerphone is on, and we're so happy to hear the good news."

Laughter and joy bubbled up within me as well. "God *is* good!" I joined in.

"Well, I'm even more excited about a party now," Mell was nearly shouting into the phone. Pete peeked his head into the room, wondering what all the commotion was about. "So, when do you want to have the party?" Mell asked.

"Well, my mother, Katie, will want to come too, so let me see when she can make it down there. I'll give you Betty's contact info as well. I'd love for her to be there."

THE TRIP back to Riverview was an adventure. Pete had to fly home early for work, so Lily came to Phoenix to accompany me, Bella, and Bea, on the drive home. Lily and I took turns driving the van and had a great time catching up while the girls mostly napped in the backseat. We must've sung that hit from the 60s, "Hit the Road Jack," at least four times and Lily kept us in stitches with her silly jokes.

THE DAY'S warm air lingered into the early evening as hundreds gathered at the door of Chicky-Pie's. Blown away at how many cared enough about me to come, I searched the crowd for familiar faces. Lily was escorted in by Dan *and* Larry. *Interesting,* I thought. Katie and Betty made it down for the party, and naturally, the entire Chicky-Pie's staff was there, including Sally. Even Ruben surprised me by showing up with his wife Camila, and Bobby.

EXHAUSTED, my head fell heavy onto my pillow. But it was a good kind of tired. Considering my journey over the last few months, I smiled. The thrill of the party continued to sing in my mind. God's hand was evident, and the dear souls who'd been instrumental in bringing me to this point? Well, they encircled me like colors on a palette. Admittedly, there were some bitter colors mixed in—Jack, Jane, and Officer Ruiz. These unresolved, muddy colors remained. As did my worry. Would they continue to go unpunished? But as quickly as the thought came, I shook my head, breathing a prayer that God would release me from anxiety. I thanked Him for being in control of the situation. I had no reason to worry. I knew God was on my side.

All things considered, God's grace and mercy towards me were more than I deserved. The friendships he'd put in my path —Mell, Lily, Allie, even Sally—these women were dear as a family to me. Their sweet friendship had turned my dismal life into a song.

And far greater was how He returned me to my real mother —Katie. Oh, how God has painted bright colors over the dismal grays of our family tree! We are still getting to know one another, but I see the joyful colors of love wet on the palette, shimmering in the sunlight, our story being painted anew.

My thoughts turned to Pete, my beloved Pete. Who stood by me and loved me when I didn't even know how to love myself. *Thank you, Lord, for so many blessings!* My sweet Bella's wish to have a sister was granted in the most wonderful of ways. I could still picture her holding hands with Bea as they fell asleep next to one another in their new shared room.

And my Bumble Bea, buzzing back into my heart and my life again. Bringing the sweet nectar of joy with her radiant smile. *God is so good,* I thought as I drifted into a peaceful sleep.

THE LOUD RINGING of the phone woke me way too early. "Yes, who is this?" I mumbled sleepily.

"Good morning, Elise. Sorry if I woke you." Lewinsky sounded too chipper for seven in the morning. "Just thought you'd want to know we found skeletal remains of a woman buried near the Burrows' house." I shot up, suddenly awake.

"What! Who is it?"

"Don't know yet, but I'll keep you posted. Call you again soon." He hung up, leaving my mind whet with curiosity. A memory flash came to me with a clear and troubling image— Skippy wildly digging near the property line of the Burrows' and Jim's yard, a wide-eyed girl in a blue dress standing next door, and the disturbing question I had that day about why I hadn't seen their nanny, Alejandra, for several days. My skin now tingled with fear and uncertainty.

ACKNOWLEDGMENTS

As I consider everyone who has contributed to this book, I bow myself in praise and thanksgiving first and foremost to my Lord and Savior Jesus Christ, who inspired it from its' inception. The daunting task of writing a complete novel was something I never imagined accomplishing. Yet God continued to encourage and inspire me towards perseverance in the goal. One moment continued with heartening reassurance. I awoke in the middle of the night to the startling awareness of His word speaking in my mind; "Being confident of this, that he who began a good work in you will carry it on to completion..." (Philippians 1:6).

Coming in with a close second is my soulmate and husband, Larry, who has stood by me during the long process with understanding and faithful support despite enduring some lonely evenings. His positive feedback, and faith in my talent, were a stronghold of encouragement that lifted my spirits during discouraging moments. And his affirmation frequently set my feet back on solid ground allowing me to continue forward.

An enormous bucket of thanks also goes to my agent and primary editor, Jessica Suggs. Without her excellent expertise, diligent work, and faith in the story, it is doubtful *The Buzz @ Chicky-Pie's Café* would've made it into print. Her invaluable experience in the publishing industry, cheerful spirit, support, and friendship made this otherwise overwhelming endeavor possible and joyfully rewarding. I am also gratefully indebted to Denise Harmer and her professional copy-editing eyes for a final look on the manuscript. The important finishing touches on my cover design were joyfully and patiently led by Jessica Appel to whom I am very grateful too. All have given this book their professionalism and expertise for its' presentation, readability, and final polish. More importantly, our working relationships have also resulted in friendship.

Not wanting to go a step further before acknowledging another important person who has been instrumental in my perseverance of this work, is the talented and award-winning author Joanne Bischoff. With a kind and gracious spirit, she willingly gave glowing praise to my rough draft of *The Buzz @ Chicky-Pie's Café* for which I am immensely grateful. Her amazing and exquisite writing talent and her encouraging words of support for my story and writing skills were both timely and immeasurable in value.

For her supportive expertise in legal affairs and knowledge of the justice system as well as her experienced understanding of processes to protect children from abuse and neglect, I am forever grateful to my daughter and Attorney, JD Ivy D. Gentry.

And most importantly, I am eternally grateful to my friends, all the staff, and volunteers at Gabriel's House in Oxnard, CA. Their devotion to Christ and their faithful work at this transitional home for women and children at risk continues to bring them hope, help, faith, and encouragement year-round. We are all indebted to the faithful who work with Forever Found in Simi Valley, CA as well. Their work to rescue and restore children who have been trafficked in California and India is another wonderful testimony to the love of Christ being given to the hurting and abused.

Big hugs of thanksgiving also go to my friends, Sandy, Stacy, and Josie, who graciously read the first few pages of my manuscript and encouraged me to continue with the story. Their frequent and anxious requests to read the whole book were an ever-present impelling voice in my head.

It's my hope and prayer that *The Buzz @ Chicky-Pie's Café* will inspire readers to engage in their communities through mentoring, volunteering, and other forms of helps to the hurting. And with that in mind, it is also my prayer that this book will give impetus to others towards God's purposes in their life.

AUTHOR'S NOTES

People often ask me what inspired *The Buzz @ Chicky-Pie's Café*, and I am always thrilled for the opportunity to tell them the backstory. Although writing a complete novel never entered my mind as something I could ever do, interestingly, God led me into it through a vivid bad dream. So, much like my heroine Elise, a nightmare gave me impetus.

On the morning when I awoke with the remnants of that nightmare still roaming my thoughts, I used my well-honed skills of dream interpretation in an attempt to decipher its' meaning. Ask anyone who's known me more than a few years, and you'll learn that I've always been a very vivid dreamer. So, it was only natural that I learned to interpret my dreams long ago to solve the nocturnal mysteries that played across my mind. After all, these images would sometimes remain with sharp recall for days and even years. So, on that fateful morning, I tried to figure out what my dream meant.

The nightmare I had was much the same as the one Elise has at the beginning of *The Buzz @ Chicky-Pie's Cafe*. So, knowing that most dreams are merely pictorial reflections of the events and emotions a person is experiencing, it baffled me. Why had *I* dreamt that? I wondered. Yet try as I may, nothing about the dream lined-up with my own past or current emotions and life challenges. As the day progressed, my resolve to solve its' mystery evolved into the imagining development of a character whose life and circumstances *did* fit the dream. It wasn't long before I realized a whole story was developing and I was narrating it.

As mentioned, writing a complete novel was never something I felt I could do. No, the tenacity it would take me to persevere through the lengthy task of writing a novel hadn't even been a pipe dream. Yet, as the story progressed, it became an exciting new adventure in creativity. One that I'd only snacked on through short stories here and there. Of course, there were many moments of doubt that wriggled their way into my resolve with threatening challenge. But each time they came, God gave me His encouraging confirmation to go forward. My acknowledgment page also mentions one of those times with the clear reminder that came "smack-dab-middle of a dream" (as the sheriff in my story would say). It was when I was awakened with the voice-like thought of **Philippians 1:6; "...being confident of this, that he who began a good work in you will carry it on to completion ..."** Rising up the next morning, I lifted my grateful prayers of thanksgiving to the Lord for His encouraging word that came in the night.

Then, after nearly nine solid months of imagining and writing *The Buzz @ Chicky-Pie's Café*, another mysterious event brought astounding confirmation to this story's purpose and necessity. Our neighborhood welcomed a few new neighbors, and a block party was held to afford the opportunity to meet and greet them. I quickly learned that one of the latest neighbors had written her memoirs, and I mentioned to her that I, too, was a writer. She began telling me the gist of her life's story, and my mouth dropped in surprise as she described her early beginnings.

"Sonia," (not her real name), "you're not going to believe this, but I'm writing a story that sounds a lot like yours," I told her.

I gave Sonia a brief description of Elise's character and her story that, by that time, was more than twenty chapters long and well on its way to completion as a novel. To my surprise, tears began to well in Sonia's eyes. "That's my story," she said. "You are writing what happened to me."

It was one of the most astonishing experiences I've ever had, yet full with confirmation that I was supposed to write this book. I'd never met Sonia until that day, yet her own personal story was a near-perfect match to the story I'd been writing for nine months prior.

To this day, with the full completion of *The Buzz @ Chicky-Pie's Café* and up to the brink of publishing it, neither my neighbor Sonia nor I have read each other's books. Not out of disinterest but entirely from lack of opportunity. Her book, to my knowledge, has yet to be formally published, and we just don't see each other often. Yet every time I recount this extraordinary revelation, chills run up my arms for its' timely and uncanny coincidence of a mirrored story.

Not long after that amazing revelation, I was invited to serve on the board of Gabriel's House, a home for women who face addictions, abuse, and homelessness. Two months before being asked to be on the board, God had highlighted a simple phrase that had me wondering. It's one that's embedded in chapter seven. *"Some childhood memories never go away. They're like a waxy crayon colored into our hearts, nearly impossible to erase or cover-up."* I'd heard a similar comment somewhere, and it had stuck with me with nagging curiosity. I knew it meant that many of the harmful and hurtful things that happen to us as children remain with us for a lifetime. So naturally, I included it in the story.

The blessing of serving in that ministry and getting to know many of these dear women's stories, continues to affirm my

Lord's leading to write this book. It's my prayer that *The Buzz @ Chicky-Pie's Café* will bring hope and help to many hurting women who have faced abuse, trafficking, and molestation, by encouraging them. It's my hope that it will also inspire many mature women to mentor and minister to those who have suffered in that way.

Children are being sold today like they are commodities, in every state in American and around the world, even in your own community.

Today, an estimated 1.2 million children are victims of modern-day slavery, and 152 million children are subjected to child labor or commercial sexual exploitation worldwide. Human trafficking is the second largest criminal industry in the world—with traffickers profiting over $150 Billion per year. Out of those people who are trafficked worldwide, both adults and children, 4.5 million are sexually exploited.

Forever Found's heart beats to prevent the exploitation of our children, to support the rescue of those enslaved, and to give each child that has been told they are only worth as much as their bodies can make, the opportunity to find restoration—to be free!

To learn more and get involved in this fight, visit www.foreverfound.org.

Gabriel's House is a program of The Kingdom Center, which originally began at a motel in March 2010. Under the leadership of Pastor Sam Gallucci, a group of compassionate citizens came together to house homeless families in a motel in Ventura, California. What once had been a place of hopelessness was redeemed for the glory of God.

Witnessing the positive impact of this ministry effort, the City of Oxnard invited The Kingdom Center to partner with them at a property that had previously served as a drug rehabilitation facility. So, in the fall of 2011, **Gabriel's House** was launched in a large ranch house on a beautiful 2.5-acre farm once owned by a prominent Ventura County agricultural family.

Since then, hundreds of women and children have been served at Gabriel's House. Dozens of families have been reunited. Many of their residents have successfully begun, returned to, or finished their education and professional training. Virtually all the women at Gabriel's House have successfully found employment. A great majority have transitioned out of Gabriel's House, having successfully re-entered society with gainful employment and housing for both themselves and their children.

This is why Gabriel's House is known as a place of Hope.

To learn more or to get involved, go to www.gabriels-house.org

1450 S. Rose Avenue, Oxnard, CA 93032

P.O. Box 654, Oxnard, CA 93032

(805) 487-3400

DEVOTIONAL THOUGHTS FOR READERS

Day One: *Seeking Freedom—Part One*

Soon after Elise escapes her abusive home, she finds a flyer with these words written at the bottom of it: **"'For I know the plans I have for you,' declares the Lord, 'plans to prosper you and not to harm you, plans to give you hope and a future'" (Jeremiah 29:11).**

You may have read or heard that verse many times before, and perhaps it's been one that has given you hope and comfort. Can you imagine how Elise might have felt to read those words for the first time? Anyone coming out of a situation like the one she escapes from would likely read it with a mixture of hope and apprehension. The fear and pain that drove her to leave made her hesitant to accept God in faith. Yet, faith in God is what ultimately empowers Elise to set aside her fears and courageously face her abusers for a godly purpose.

If you feel held captive by circumstances beyond your control, have been harmed in any way, or feel uncertain of your future, Jeremiah's words can be a good place to start.

Meditate on this: Jeremiah gives us comfort by letting us know that God loves us and <u>doesn't want us to be harmed</u>. He gives us <u>hope</u> by saying He wants us to <u>prosper</u>. And God sets our hearts towards a good <u>future</u> to keep us encouraged.

If you are in an abusive and/or dangerous situation, here are some helpful things you can do:

1. Seek wise counsel.
2. Pray for God's protection.
3. Pray for God's leading to find a safe way out.

Day Two: *Seeking Freedom—Part Two*

Looking deeper into **Jeremiah 29:11** by examining it in context to the verses before and after verse 11, we see an amazing analogy to the situation Elise found herself in. In **Jeremiah 29, verses 1-7,** we see that the prophet Jeremiah was speaking to Israelites who had been exiled out of Jerusalem into Babylon. They were forced to go to a land filled with people who were hostile to them. Elise was also forced to live in a different place with people who were abusive to her. Yet, in **verses 4–7,** God tells the exiled Israelites to make the best of it. His instruction to them is to "build houses… settle down…plant gardens…marry…have children…and seek peace…" Genesis 2:28 (author paraphrase). In today's vernacular, a plaque on the wall would put it this way: *Bloom where you're planted.*

At the beginning of *The Buzz @ Chicky-Pie's Café,* when Elise is living with the Burrows, things are very difficult, even dangerous for her. Yet she found ways to have some happiness through cooking, hobbies, and pouring her love into the children that she nannied.

In verse 10 of Jeremiah 29, God promises to bring the Israelites back to their homeland after a period of time. **Verses 12-13 say: "'Then you will call on me and come and pray to me, and I will listen to you. You will seek me and find me when you seek me with all your heart. You will find me,' declares the Lord, 'and will bring you back from captivity.'"** Likewise, in the story, after Elise comes to faith in Christ, she returns to her original home, her real mother, and the loved ones she was forced to leave behind.

There are many types of captivity: emotional, physical, geographical, and spiritual. All can foster fear and a sense of being trapped. If you find yourself in a place of fear or captivity, come to God with faith in Jesus Christ and trust in His promises. The freedom He will give you will set you free within, no matter what kind of physical or emotional shackles have a hold on you now.

Whatever kind of fearful situation you may be facing, until you can get help, here are some things you can do in the meantime:

1. **Pray & Trust:** Let your heart and emotions relax into His Spirit.
2. **Meditate on this scripture.** "'For I know the plans I have for you…plans to prosper you and not to harm you, plans to give you hope and a future'" Jeremiah 29:11.
3. **Bloom where you are.** Find fun, creative, loving, and purposeful things you CAN do.

Day Three: *Discernment and Dreams—Part One*

Have you ever had a strange dream that had you wondering what it meant? Do you sometimes have trouble knowing what to do in difficult situations? **James 1:5 says, "If any of you lacks wisdom, let him ask of God, who gives to all liberally and without reproach, and it will be given to him" (NKJV).** This verse tells us that we can pray and ask our great creator for wisdom <u>in all things</u>.

Elise has two important dreams in the story; one happens in the beginning of the first chapter, and the other is in chapter twelve. In both dreams, Elise sensed danger, but one was directed toward her and the other toward the danger of someone else. When she confides in Lily about her second dream, Lily tells her to be careful, "Dreams can be tricky." Lily advises Elise to ensure any dream interpretations don't conflict with God's Word. Elise states that she doesn't think God would want children to be abused, and Lily agrees, backing her agreement with Scripture.

The idea of wanting to set someone free from danger is not in conflict with God's Word. However, if Elise had examined either one of those dreams and determined she needed to harm someone else or do something God forbids in His Word, it would not be a true interpretation or wise response to the dream.

From the time I was a very young girl, I have been a vivid dreamer. Sometimes, I'd have a dream so clear and meaningful that I could remember it for months or years. This led me to learn how to interpret my dreams. Through my studies, I quickly ascertained that <u>dreams are not usually prophetic or predictive of something to come.</u> Nor are they usually directives from God for some kind of action. Instead, **they are mostly symbolic reflections of the emotions you're feeling** about something currently happening in your life. Over the years, further research I've done on this subject has confirmed my methods, theories, and techniques for dream interpretation as valid.

One important factor I've learned is that pictures in a dream symbolize things. The feelings or emotions you feel in your dreams are key to the meaning of it. Elise was living a nightmare of abuse, and her terrifying dream reflected her feelings of <u>fear, worry, and danger</u>. The <u>cars with open doors</u> represented ways (doors) of escape, but her concern, or <u>feelings</u>, about them being <u>safe</u> (in the dream) reflected her <u>worry</u> about how she could <u>safely escape</u> her current environment. So, although the dream may or may not have been a directive given by God, applying her emotions of fear and danger to the reality of her situation gave her the impetus to form a good plan. And praying for God's help was the most important application she made after each dream.

As a well-seasoned Christian, I've learned that we should always be careful not to let our emotions and perspectives guide our actions or beliefs.

1. When you consider James 1:5 alongside the advice of Lily regarding dreams and their interpretation, do you see some wisdom there?

2. In this story, do you think Elise has dreams that were directives from God?

3. After each dream, Elise prayed for God's help. How important were those prayers as a response?

4. The effect both nightmares had on Elise was fear of something. Do you think she applied good solutions to those fears?

Day Four: *Discernment and Dreams—Part Two*

Hebrews 4:12 says: "For the word of God is living and power-ful, and sharper than any two-edged sword, piercing even to the division of soul and spirit, and of joints and marrow, and is a <u>discerner of the thoughts and intents of the heart</u>." Here, we see a few key things about God's Word. One is that the Bible is a powerful tool that can help us divide truth from lies. Whether we are trying to determine if our interpretations of God are true or someone else's are, laying God's Word next to them will reveal the truth.

God's Word is also helpful for discernment because it gives us **insights into our hearts and intents**. So often, we let our feel-ings drive our actions rather than letting God's Spirit and Word guide us.

Elise's husband, Pete, expresses concern about her plans to return to the Burrows' house to rescue Bea and Bobby. He worries that she might do something illegal or dangerous, putting her life at risk and jeopardizing her relationship with him and Bella.

1. **Was Pete wise and loving by cautioning her not to break the law? (Answer: Yes)**
2. **Do you think he also may have let his emotions stand in the way of what God wanted Elise to do?**
3. **Did you notice that many of the emotions Elise admitted having—feeling like she's trapped, needing to escape, fearful of relationships, and being distant from those who love her, were also some of the emotions she was feeling previously and during her second dream?**
4. **Is it possible that her second dream was only about what she was feeling at that time and not God's directive to rescue Bea and Bobby?**

While it's possible the second dream wasn't a directive from God, it did remind her of a promise she'd made. It also propelled her to accept Christ, which led to a sense of godly purpose. Her new faith gave her the courage to return and rescue two vulnerable children in danger of the same abuse she'd endured. So even though she wasn't sure the dream was given to her as a directive from God, she found strength and proper ways to do what was right for those children.

Final thoughts: The next time you have a vivid dream that has you wondering about its' meaning, immediately write down everything you saw and <u>describe the emotions you felt</u> during the dream. Then, ask yourself if any of the feelings you had during the dream may indicate what its' meaning is. If you think the dream may be God telling you to *do* something, pray and ask the Lord to reveal His intentions. Then, look in the Bible to see if that action would align with His commands and directives. If you don't know much about God's Word, ask someone who does, like a pastor or Bible teacher.

Day Five: *GIFTS*

Ephesians 2:8-9 says, "For by grace you have been saved through faith, and that not of yourselves; it is the gift of God, not of works, lest anyone should boast" (NKJV).

In chapter three, Elise helps Betty with a sewing project, and she learns a little about God as a loving father who likes to give His children gifts. Betty tells Elise that God doesn't give gifts because we deserve or earn them but because He loves us. Then, several years later (chapter twenty-six), Elise is at an Easter church service and hears a similar statement by the pastor that brings that jewel of memory back to her mind. "All we need to do is accept <u>His gift</u> by believing Jesus died for us…" the pastor says.

This is a mirror of Ephesians 2:8-9. As this Scripture settles further into her heart, Elise is drawn by God's Spirit to receive the gift of salvation. It is the moment when the seed of God's Word, planted by Betty and watered by many, comes to fruition. It's a perfect picture of grace realized because grace is undeserved favor.

In our culture we often hear the saying: "I have arrived!" It means someone has reached a goal or stature of importance in life. But God's Word promises a different kind of position we can acquire. One that puts us in the position of righteousness before God's eyes, one we can't do anything to deserve. You may be struggling to find purpose and joy in your life. If you are trying to be a better person because you think that's what it takes to get God's love, you have it all backwards. You are in essence trying to earn your salvation by works rather than accept God's gift. If being good could keep anyone from Hell, why would Jesus willingly die on the cross? His death is what paid the price for the gift of our salvation. As Betty said, "It wouldn't be a gift if we paid for it," or if it was something we could earn.

As you consider this important principle in Elise's story, look at the difference it made for Elise:

1. **Do you see how grace made a difference for Elise?**
2. **In chapter three, Betty gives Elise two gifts. What were they?**
3. **How important did those gifts become for her?**
4. **The first gift Betty gave Elise provided help toward her physical freedom. How is that first gift similar to the message within the second gift that she gave Elise? How is it different?**

Our society and culture condition us to believe we must

strive to be good enough for God. From the time we are children and throughout life we can earn rewards for our hard work at things, but God's Word says in **Romans 3:10: "There is none righteous, no, not one" (NKJV). In Romans 3:23, the Apostle Paul continues, "...for all have sinned and fall short of the glory of God" (NKJV).** The word "grace" means something given that is undeserved. <u>If you have never accepted God's gift of salvation, don't wait until you think you're good enough. If you do, you'll never *arrive*.</u>

ABOUT THE AUTHOR

Iris Carignan is a published author, award-winning artist, poet, an inspirational speaker, and an advocate for women.

In 2016, Iris published a collection of stories and poetry in her book, *Fresh Eyes: Seeing God in the Unexpected*. In 2019, Iris wrote and illustrated a children's book, *Moriah's Wings*. Iris's one-of-a-kind paintings illustrate this beautiful children's story, creatively connecting her gift for art and the written word.

Iris is currently on the board of directors for *Gabriel's House*, a Christian nonprofit providing a home and support to women facing abuse, trafficking, and homelessness. Her empathy and encounters with these women inspired Elise, the heroine of *The Buzz @ Chicky-Pie's Café*.

Her volunteer work continues with her involvement in community-based non-profit organizations including *James Storehouse* and *Forever Found*.

Born in Georgia but raised in Southern California, Iris draws from her Southern roots to infuse life into her Southern characters. When not writing or painting, Iris enjoys spending time with her three children and seven grandchildren. Iris resides in Thousand Oaks, California, with her husband of more than 50 years, Larry, and their sweet multi-poo, Caeser.

www.iriscarignan.com

Facebook: iriscarignanbooks

Instagram: iriscarignanbooks

LinkedIn: iris-carignan

Learn more about the non-profit organizations mentioned above on their websites:

Gabriel's Housewww.gabriels-house.org

Forever Foundwww.foreverfound.org

James Storehousewww.jamesstorehouse.org

Elise, Mell, and Lily return in the compelling sequel to
The Buzz @ Chicky-Pie's Café.

Be the first to receive book release details when you sign up for
Iris Carignan's monthly eNewsletter!

Sign up today at https://mailchi.mp/iriscarignan.com/
buzzemaillist

www.iriscarignan.com

NOTES

[page] 11. I planted, Apollos watered…: 1 Cor. 3:6,9 NKJV

[page] 31. Where two or three…: Matt. 18:20 NKJV

[page] 58. For I know the plans…: Jer. 29:11

[page] 62. Out of the eater came…: Judg. 14:14,18 NKJV

[page] 78. But we have this…: 2 Cor. 4:7-9

[page] 95. Whatever things are true…: Phil. 4:8, author's paraphrase

[page] 117. Taste and see that…: Ps. 34:8

[page] 151. Whoever causes one of these…: Matt. 18:6 NKJV

[page] 158. Making the most of every…: Eph. 5:16

[page] 158. With the Lord, a day…: 2 Peter 3:8

[page] 161. Not willing that any should…: 2 Peter 3:9 NKJV, author's paraphrase

[page] 167. Where two or three…: Matt. 18:20 NKJV

[page] 200. With Christ I can do…: Phil. 4:13 NKJV, author's paraphrase

[page] 204. Marriage is honorable among…: Heb. 13:4-6 NKJV

[page] 259. Curds and honey He shall eat…: Isa. 7:15,18 NKJV

[page] 266. Grieve, mourn, and wail…: James 4:9-11

[page] 344. But you will be fed…: Ps. 81:16